NEW CLONE CITY

The Wild Word

www.thewildword.com

The Wild Word

Published in 2018 by The Wild Word

Paperback ISBN: 978-3-947555-05-5
Ebook ISBN: 978-3-947555-06-2

Cover artwork by Linh Nguyen
Cover design by Kusi Okamura
Print support by Jesse Gordon
Design support by Kultmacher
Printed by Ingramspark

Published by The Wild Word
Berlin, Germany

www.thewildword.com
thewildword.com/newclonecity
facebook.com/newclonecity

For media requests contact editor@thewildword.com

To
Pat Cadigan,
greatest of the cyberpunks,
and
Anna Campbell,
unforgotten and inspirational

CHAPTER ONE
Rednecks

J immy is turning into a redneck.

Jimmy fucking hates rednecks.

He's just back from vacation. Back in dirty New Clone City after four weeks of sitting around on a boat. Zoning out on waves and clouds and winds and seagulls. Commiserating, conniving, communing with jellyfish. Appreciating the beauty of invasive fauna and putrescent ecosystems in decline. Thus ritually purified, he's just turning the corner of Danube and the B Village when he sees two white guys lounging around on the street, up against a wall, each side of a window, drinking beer. Maybe more lurking than lounging. Difficult to tell.

Ring-a-ding goes Jimmy's little head-bell.

The guys are acting kind of nonchalant. As nonchalant as you can be when you're just wearing a towel on a city street. The skinny guy with the long greasy brown hair has a burgundy red towel wrapped around his waist. The other guy is blond, straggly beard, brown towel. They eye Jimmy coming up the street, sizing him up for something.

Jimmy might be fresh from his boat but he's not like, fresh off the boat.

Something is going down.

Going to go down.

But these guys are carrying nothing more serious than beer bottles, so it's not set to be a life-threatening incident.

Not that beer bottles can't be life-threatening.

Swift sideways hand swipe to the neck then grasp and smash on the way down with just the right angle to the edge of the bar to reveal that ragged sharpness and stiletto glinting points still wet with foam…

Not those kind of bottles. Not in the hands of these guys.

As Jimmy draws level with the window a big black woman suddenly appears in the window frame, like she's been hiding off to one side. She's maybe in her late twenties, same as the guys outside. She looks good. Tall, big-built. And wearing a towel. A big yellow bath towel.

Then, at some pre-arranged signal, they all suddenly get naked. The skinny guys simply drop their towels, but the woman just opens hers, *grande-dame* style, using both hands. Like the curtains parting for a theatre performance.

They shout, "Free love," in chorus.

The blond guy goes, "Naked is good". And the other one shouts, "Winter is over".

Something about this last statement moves Jimmy to respond. The street is baking hot, almost 40 degrees C. There's no wind. There's a stink of garbage and pissed-in doorways. The light is so bright it hurts your eyes.

He turns to the winter-is-over guy and says: "Yes. Of course winter is over. It's fucking August."

The trio seem to find this highly amusing and clink their bottles and burst into shrieks of laughter. A couple of teenage girls wearing hijabs are following the proceedings from the other side of the road, and run off, giggling.

Mr. Red Towel says, "No need to be so uptight," and blondie chimes in, "Yeah, take a chill pill dude."

Miss Yellow Towel tilts her head and bats her eyelashes and closes the curtains on her performance with a flourish.

It's a momentary stand-off. There's no danger. Nobody is going to do anything bad to anyone else.

Jimmy homes in on the eyes of Mr Red Towel. Flits to blondie. Lingers a little with the *grande dame*.

"Acid heads," he says, to no-one in particular.

"So?" says blondie.

"Rich kids."

"So?"

"Just fuck off home, why don't ya?"

"I don't understand why you were so nasty to those hippies."

Julia pours him a drink. A drop of Suntory's finest. *Glen Akaishi Single Malt* from the Isle of Skye. She drops some ice in. He looks over, one eyebrow raised.

"Don't look like that. They're only ice cubes. It's hot. Think of it as a cocktail."

He takes the glass, swirls the whisky around. Then takes a slug, savouring it.

They're in their apartment. Down the road from peace and love and four floors up.

"Besides," she continues. "You were a hippy once."

Jimmy nearly chokes on his ice cube.

"No way. The fuck you get that from?"

"An acid head then. You were a friggin' acid head when I met you."

He wags a finger in denial.

"Shrooms, man, only shrooms. No chemical drugs."

"Except speed. And coke if you can get it. And ecstasy."

"No, no ecstasy. No psychotropic chemical drugs. Unless they're really really good."

Julia smooths out an imaginary crease in her jeans.

"So?"

"So what?"

"So when did that bug crawl up your ass? You were a love child once."

Jimmy puts his drink down and reaches for the coffin nails.

"That," he says, taking one out, lighting it, and drawing a deep drag, "is the meanest thing you've ever said to me."

On any given day Jimmy is liable to be found wandering the streets of New Clone City. Like as not he'll make a stop at Samson's Oz Eatery, just off Carlos Marx, corner of Danube and Erk, purveyors of finest recycled kangaroo donna, fake ostrich burgers our speciality. The tables spill out of the restaurant onto the street. The benches are high-backed, pew-like affairs, in a fetching dark brown. The result is that pedestrian folk and those that pass as such have to navigate their way around the excrescences of Samson's establishment.

Being of a nautical bent, one of many, Jimmy thinks that when seated he should be decked out in yellow and black stripes and entered into maritime charts as a navigational hazard. Passing ships would approach at their peril. In times of fog or reduced visibility, a bell could be sounded. At night he would flash, a quick flashing group of six followed by a long flash, to mark the southernmost extent of the danger area.

As it is, Jimmy juts out into the disconsolate consciousness of the streaming street and takes in the varied tribes of the New Clone vibe.

Contrary to its rap—unjustly earned, in Jimmy's view—as a seething den of fecklessness, inebriety and the myriad sins of the impoverished, the NC is a place of work. People queue for stuff. Meat is cut, veg is sorted, faces are lined, hands are calloused. Nobody's lounging, except maybe Jimmy. But plenty are hustling. Mommas are chiding and chaperoning, hunting and gathering. Poppas are blustering and doing their manly thing, expanding waistlines and clipping ears. Teenagers are preening and strutting their stuff. Romanian Jehova's Witnesses are trundling little shopping trolleys of potted biblical hermeneutics, on the off-chance of would-be Romanian converts. Panhandlers work the steps of the town hall. A teenage girl in a headscarf and full-length black dress sits wearily down on the top step of the underground station with a little cardboard sign when a middle-aged blond harridan forces her to get up to clear her way down the otherwise empty staircase. Nobody trips the blond woman up or spits in her face—two perfectly legitimate options in Jimmy's view. No time for that in the NC. Places to go, people to see.

Jimmy sees stuff but doesn't intervene. He is a rock. He is an island. He is Simon and fucking Garfunkel.

Not all the gods in the NC speak Romanian. Although given their reputation for big-time polyglotism, you'd think there would be more of a babbling Babel than there already is. As it is the Romanians hang out with the other JWs, looking wet and faintly lost, waiting to be spoken to. The Salafis on the other hand, are out there and down on it. They are speaking to the brothers and wearing serious beards. They are exhorting and admonishing the sisters and are recruiting to the cause. Their more homegrown counterparts wear Odin not Jesus t-shirts and skulk around the NC, because it's not their turf. They too are busy recruiters. Buddhist monks occasionally flit down to the Arcade for new batteries or to the newsagents for lottery tickets. They do their recruiting over zen and lentils.

Mrs Samson, Deli to her friends, brings Jimmy his fake ostrich on a bed of horseradish in an onion bagel and a side order of beetroot fries. Sets down a glass of ayran. Says, "Jimmy-san, what's eating you?" Deli is Japanese-Australian, tired eyes, friendly face. Immigrated in the Eighties, swept off her feet by the charm of Samson "Sam" Özgur, one-time Turkish revolutionary and member of Dev-Yol's central committee in exile.

Jimmy tells her the story of the hippies. Of Julia's disapproval. His fears for the NC.

Deli takes Jimmy's hand and turns it over, like she's going to read his fortune.

"Jimmy, you're such a romantic. You think New Clone is some kind of mongrel's paradise, a little melting pot ghetto. You want to be king of the Heinz 57. You only see what you want to believe and everything else gets your goat."

Jimmy takes a swig of his ayran with his free hand and gets a little milky white 'tache for his trouble.

Deli looks him in the eyes.

"The NC is all you think it is, but it's a rich kid's playground too. There's no way you or me are going to stop that."

"It worries me."

"Can't you worry about something else?"

"Like the firebombings?"

"There you are!" Deli gives his hand a squeeze and jumps up excitedly, heading over towards the samovar. "Firebombings! Good! Good thing to worry about!"

She brings back the tea and sets the two little glasses down on the table, each with its own dinky spoon, each with two lumps, each in its own sharply upturned tinny saucer. Then she sits back down and leans across conspiratorially.

"Can't you maybe off a few firebombers? Sam has been thinking about it."

She looks around to make sure nobody is listening.

"Deli," Jimmy says. "Everyone's been thinking about it. But I guess the answer is no. They don't exactly advertise."

"Aw Jimmy," Deli says. "Just you and Sam. We'd be rooting for ya."

"Great bagel Mrs O."

Jimmy wipes the crumbs off of his shirt.

"But that shit is out of the question."

So here's the mugshot: Jimmy Lee Chang, of the Singapore Irish Changs, first generation immigrant to the NC via a sojourn in Belfast, abides at 12, the B Village. Stated age, 49. Confirmed by the documents, doubted by his intimates. Profession given variously as "artist" or "freelancer". Known forms of artistry include piss artistry and con artistry, barely suppressed kleptomania and a knack for fencing stolen goods, with nothing more than a suspended sentence ensuing. Minor criminal activities aside, Jimmy turns his hands to many things to earn a proverbial buck, including: journalism, photography, coding, amateur sleuthing and occasional musicianship. Anything, basically, to get by, and which does not involve keeping regular hours or being a contractually obligated wage slave ensconced in a commercial chain of command. Has been known to live for years at a time off his "wife" Julia "Chippie" Grzyb, of the Lithuanian Grzybs, until she throws him out and he gets his shit together enough for her to let him back into their mutual home.

Jimmy's main aim in life is not to be ashamed of anything he does. Jimmy feels that when judgement day comes, and he faces that great revolutionary workers' tribunal in the sky, it's not going to be like: "Jimmy you piece of shit, what the *fuck* were you thinking?"

Comrade Goldmann has the chair.

"I call on comrade Durutti for the prosecution."

Comrade Durutti gets up, adjusts his bandoleros, pushes back his kepi.

"Jimmy, call yourself a syndicalist? I heard you had shares in some fucking *startup*, you sycophantic running dog of imperialism. Did you even *try* to eat the rich?"

Jimmy looks at his shoes and sees little bands of stock market ticker-tape running over his toes.

"I'm a vegetarian."

"But are you a vegan?" they all chorus.

Comrade Durutti says, "My case rests," and sits down.

Next up is Comrade Feinberg.

"Jimmy, I heard you wimped out of transformative surgery. And what's that on your face? A fucking beard? Classic capitulation to heteronormative conditioning. You should be out there on the streets fighting patriarchy. What do have to say in your defence?"

Jimmy: "I, uh, I'm like, already dead?"

The tribunal cries: "No excuse, loser…"

Jimmy wakes up in a sweat.

There's a blood moon rising over the NC that night and it sends a noxious pulse through the city, like the too-loud bass of a passing car or the rumble of a subway. Over in the Calvary district, nationalist Turks and secessionist Kurds launch at each other with baseball bats and knives until the police intervene. Heads thunk into curbstones, gutters run with gore. Miraculously no-one is killed, though not for want of trying. Fist-fights break out in subways. Rentboys get set upon, tricking street-walkers find their johns to be even more disgusting and sicko than usual. A junkie sits in the public lavatory on Sun Boulevard and lines himself up for a golden shot. Out in the suburbs, a bunch of Nazi bikers are drinking Jimmy Deans and decanting petrol for Molotov cocktails. And down by the tracks in the NC, an old man feels the pulse and, finding it indistinguishable from the noise of the speakeasy downstairs, picks up the rifle he's been saving for this one special occasion.

It's morning, and Jimmy's out on his constitutional.

His constitutional consists of a 400 metre trek to the newsagent's for 20 Green Lungs and a box of matches. Pausing outside of Erdogan's News Emporium he takes in the window display and browses through the necessities of NC life: rolling papers, regular, large and extra-large. Bongs. Vials of flavoured e-liquids. Machetes. Ghurka knives. Pocket knives large and extra-large. Flickknives. Tasers. Pepper Spray. A handy pocket-sized crossbow. A double-edged axe small enough to fit into a rucksack or under a car seat. *Katana*-style samurai swords. Extensible steel batons. Not a newspaper in sight. But a screaming billboard headline tells him "Bonobo shooting shakes the NC!"

Jimmy raises an eyebrow.

Not that death as an outcome to nocturnal ructions is any big news these days. But shootings are rare. And shootings of bonobos—the hipsterish *bohemian nouveau bourgeoisie*—almost unknown. Federal policy forbids possession of firearms to all but bona fide gun nuts, making them difficult to come by for your average Joe. Bladed weapons are therefore *de rigeur* on the sweaty streets of the NC. And the bonobos usually clump together, to avoid the riffraff.

Jimmy enters and sees the proprietor, Olaf Erdogan, big, thick-set, grizzled chops, behind the counter.

"*Hej* big man."

"*Günaydin* Jimmy. The usual? Twenty lungs and a box o' strikes?"

"Better throw in a *Spleen*, Mr E."

"Jimmy, whatcha want with that rag? You'll be lowering the tone of the place."

"Bonobo killing Mr E. Gotta catch up. Stay abreast an' that."

"Ah that one. Tragic I'm sure. Poor bugger."

Olaf crosses his arms and looks around surreptitiously.

"Mind you, they're so fucking loud, those bonobos. Had to chase a bunch off me doorstep last night. They don't listen y'know. Wouldn't budge. Had to get, like, *massive*, before they'd shift."

Jimmy conjures up an image of a seething mass of Turkish-Swedish ire.

"That'd be enough for anyone Mr E. But at least you didn't shoot 'em."

"Ah no. That'd be a bit harsh now, don't you think?"

Jimmy takes a little detour into a breakfast café on Carlos Marx on the way home. Julia won't miss him. He'll be back by the time she finishes her yoga routine and her cracked oats have done soaking. Jimmy orders eggs and coffee at the counter, then takes a seat at a table outside. Spreads his *Spleen* out across the table. Unwraps the cellophane from his *Lungs*. Strikes, lights and inhales. The street scene shimmers a little as the nicotine and certified organic additives hits his morning brain. Someone turns the sound down and hits the half-speed button on the traffic streaming by, the bikers, the pedestrians. They slow to crawling as he takes in every detail, the sun glinting off the chrome of the passing cars, the red plastic hard hat of the guy operating the jackhammer in the roadworks down the street, the syringes in the gutter, the hooded crows sat malevolently on the traffic lights. Then whoosh back to full speed with a vengeance as a crashing wave of sound breaks over him.

Jimmy pulls an earlobe, takes a sip of his cappuccino. Peruses his *Spleen*.

Seems the shooting was down by the overground station, on the corner of Railroad and Walter. Cheap tenements backing onto a rundown goods yard. Perfect place for a cellar club. Cobblestone streets and the rumble of trains day and night. Add in a thundering bass, 48 hours solid. Perfect place for some nut to lose his rag. Grab that ancient piece he's had stashed all these years and let rip at some poor kid emerging blinking into the light of a queasy Sunday morning. Just random. Could have been you, could have been me. Snuffed out by some fucking redneck gun nut.

Jimmy stubs his cigarette out and looks down the street.

The radio from the caff plays *Aldırma Gönül*, pours out a lament of wild waves, appointed bullets, appointed ends, served up along with the eggs and the orange juice.

Jimmy gets up, folds the paper up, throws it in the trash.

CHAPTER TWO
Claire

Claire is sat in the U, flanked by two black panthers.

We're not talking Huey Newton or Bobby Seale here, although that might also be appropriate.

More in the line of *panthera pardus*, or possibly *panthera onca*.

Big mean mothers. Long sharp teeth. Twitchy tails. Glinting green eyes. A lustrous sheen in their satin coats.

Claire herself is also possessed of a green-eyed glint. She stares straight ahead, seemingly oblivious, but obviously fully aware, of her companions. She has fluorescent green buds in her ears, a shock of red hair, shaven on the left side of her head to reveal tattooed flames streaming backwards. She's wearing a tee saying "Kill All Cars", black jeans and thick-soled shitkickers with a bunch of buckles on them.

The panthers are just overlay.

The carriage rocks to and fro, screeches in the curve, stops at Han Plaza. People move, get in and out, sweat, sniff, scratch. Stare at their devices. Mind the fucking gap. And mostly, just try to limit sensory input.

The U is a riot of input, a jungle of overlay and invasive personalized advertising.

Even if you just do it old school—no overlay, no augmentation—it's hard to ignore the screens everywhere, vying for your attention. There's an old guy in the corner reading a *newspaper*, for god's sake. Totally analogue. He's got his head buried in it and rustles the pages every now and again. It's quaint, in a freaky, throwback kind of way. Claire figures it's really just shielding. Cladding. Input reduction.

The guy keeps his head down, rustles, avoids eye contact.

Everyone avoids eye contact.

Most just fiddle with their phones. Worry their implants. Surreptitiously wipe the pus from seeping wetware. Noodle the weeb. Perform the spastic eye movements required to check their incoming on their spex.

But see you and raise you that most have their overlay muted or offed, just to minimize the danger of a *pewomt*.

That's a Psychotic Episode While on Mass Transit, to you and me.

Claire is not most.

Claire is inured to that shit.

Claire is a full-on overlay junkie.

Although she gives no sign of registering zip, she has maxed the range on her expensive—stolen—state-of-the-art device and is taking it all in.

She takes in the Jehova's Witness with Moses coming back down the mountain with the tablets, floating over his shoulder.

Like: "Where ya bin Mo?"

"Ah, just popped out to get me tablets."

She sees two Salafis sat opposite each other, each projecting a mighty black-turbaned warrior with a long curving scimitar held aloft. The scimitars cross just over the rear carriage window, and below them hangs the holy book, hyperreal and blinding.

She sees an uncomfortable Nazi, with flickering subliminal images of torchlight processions, rats and Riefenstahl.

She sees a pretty guy with a big silver earring and nail varnish, whose overlay makes him appear entirely blue. He's wearing a necklace of skulls and has four extra arms bearing, in turn, a curved blade, a trident, a severed head and a bowl.

And she sees Nerd Boy sitting opposite, who has *nada* overlay, but seems to be giving her the eye, evil or otherwise.

To start with, she has him pegged for a tail.

He's like what, nineteen, twenty? And a black hole. He has lanky dark hair, spex, and some piece of retro blackbox kit with the brand-name filed off that he's actually typing stuff into. He's giving away nothing. But she can tell that he is hyperaware. She can feel him looking away every time her gaze flicks towards him.

She can see the telltale ooze of fresh wetware from behind his ear.

Is he on to her, or just coming on to her?

Either way, he is up to something.

She considers the tail theory, then rejects it as routine paranoia.

He doesn't *look* like a cop.

He doesn't have that nark/spook/cop vibe that we all know and love.

But it's sure as fuck unusual to be rigged up to the eyeballs and just, like, hanging there.

She hooks into the carriage surveillance feed and looks down on him.

He has nice hands, like a musician.

She can see his fingers flickering across some keyboard that he has nestling in the crook of his knee. He's sat with one ankle resting on the other knee, turning his bent leg into an impromptu worktop.

He has a beautiful curve from his collarbone up the side of his neck as he types.

Get a grip, she thinks.

He is probing your defences.

He is calling you out.

She looks at him straight, eyes blazing.

She is about to say something when she realizes the U has reached Carlos Marx.

It's her stop.

She jumps up, with a semi-lunge into the guy's space.

He flinches back in surprise, and she's outta there.

She comes up the steps out of the U and she's just stunned by the sunlight, the traffic, the mess of overlay, the noise.

She stands there for a moment, taking it all in, thinking what the fuck, savouring her anger then letting it subside.

She ignores the little red man saying, "Don't Walk," and slides through a gap in the traffic. West down Carlos Marx, then sharp right into the Passage.

Under the arch of the People's Opera and she's out onto Richard and the Anglo enclave. Then right, into the B Village.

She pauses for a moment, darkens her spex a tad and adjusts the volume on her buds. Does a 360. Spins slowly around.

The beating of wings as a couple of pigeons flutter up to the nearest rooftop.

The harsh glare of the sun muted through orange-tinted lenses.

An old flatbed truck rumbling across the cobblestones.

A bit of white noise in her ears as they start to max out from bud overuse.

She checks her stats.

Damn.

Something is seriously wrong.

She's been tagged.

That nerdboy fucker has fucking *tagged* her.

Claire backs into the shade of the sloping entrance to an underground garage. She takes a moment to call up a scratch app and punches in a few coordinates.

Then she waits.

Nerd Boy is not long coming.

He's moving cautiously, scoping the street out to find her.

He's got a trace on where she should be, he can see her tag, but he's having trouble locating her in meatspace.

He takes a step out past the brick corner of a sub-T garage and is literally yanked off the street.

There's an arm round his neck, and he can feel something sharp poking up under his jaw.

"The fuck you up to, Nerd Boy?"

He starts to struggle, trying to use his shoulders to wrench himself free.

The blade under his jaw draws a little blood. His nostrils flare as he inhales the scent of summer sweat on her arm.

"Best calm down a little." She presses his wetware patch with her thumb. "Don't want you hurting too much now, do we?"

The fight goes out of him, he eases back into her heady pheromone-fuelled embrace.

"Better. Now tell me just what the fuck you think you were doing back there."

"Nuthin'."

Claire applies the slightest bit of pressure to the handle of the blade.

"Ok, ok. It was a tag."

"No shit, Sherlock. But only the feds and the spooks get to tag people. Are you some kind of spook, kid?"

"Kid yourself, you're not that much older. And no, I'm not a spook."

"So?"

"So, it's just a black tag, is all. Just a hack. Re-engineered police issue."

Claire glances out into the street: no traffic, little old lady pedestrian coming up from Danube.

"What about you?" Nerd Boy says back over his shoulder. "How did you project your GPS like that?"

"Sugar, maybe you're not the only one can do a little hacking."

Jimmy is returning home from his constitutional when he clocks two young people in a clinch in a garage entrance.

That in itself is nothing special. The B Village being a favourite weekend venue for al fresco intimacy of all kinds.

Not so common on a workaday weekday morning though.

Jimmy risks another glance.

Interesting.

She seems to be taking *him* from behind.

Then he sees the glint of a blade.

Jimmy stops short. Adjusts his analogue sunglasses. Scopes out the situation.

There's a tall and mean-looking punk redhead up close with a skinny guy with long black hair. She's got an arm round his neck, pulling him in tight. And in her other hand she's got a stiletto blade pressed up against his carotid artery.

So much more efficient than the jugular vein, thinks Jimmy.

The woman hasn't seen him yet. Skinny guy is signalling wildly with his eyes.

"Do you want me to call the police or start selling tickets?" Jimmy says.

Claire sees an old guy smart-assing on the street and realizes this has turned into a situation.

"Get lost, jerkoff."

The old guy shifts his posture slightly. Turns the back knee slightly inward. Swivels his hips a little and lets his weight down on his back leg. Leading leg comes in with foot slightly raised. Shoulders relaxed, hands ready.

Claire recognizes the set-up routine for the *Bai Jong.*

Basic Jeet Kune Do combat stance.

The situation now seems to be some kind of cluster fuck.

"Call me old-fashioned," the guy on the street says, "but foreplay looked a little different in my day."

Claire knows now that there is going to be no way out of this. Not without a whole lot of nastiness.

"And you know, I'm all in favour of women taking the initiative…"

The old guy is still talking.

"But there seems to be quite a lot of, uh, bleeding going on…"

Claire feels the kid starting to twist in her grasp.

Not breaking away, just turning.

She relaxes the grip on her blade a little, looks out—long shot—at the guy on the street.

He's waiting. It's her move.

She pans back—close-up, refocus—to see Nerd Boy fully turned now, looking straight into her eyes.

Striking blue irises, pupils fully dilated.
Claire pulls her head back slightly, just to check the rest of his face.
They both blink for a second.
Lean in.
Connect.
Kiss.

The old guy goes, "Yew, do you mind? I've just had breakfast."

CHAPTER THREE
Doc Mucus

Jimmy's down on the street, watching Claire and Nerd Boy's feeble attempts at restraining themselves from copulating there and then. "And besides, you need to get that seen to."

Nerd Boy jerks his head loose from Claire's mighty mouth clamp and looks at Jimmy. Looks down at his blood-soaked shirt.

Goes, "Uh-huh," and shrugs, like, what now?

Jimmy does an eye roll and launches in.

"Look kid, it's all good with me. You two want to lie down right here and make out in an ever-spreading pool of blood, that's like, fine, you know. Hunky dory and that. I'm just saying, is all. Like you could do with a stitch or two. But hey, what do I know?"

Nerd Boy keeps one hand around Claire's waist, touches his neck with the other. Looks at the blood on his fingers, takes a look at his blood-stained shirt.

"Stitches. Gotcha. Great idea."

Looks at Claire.

"Ah, there's a problem though."

"Like what?"

"Like, insurance?"

"Well, if it wasn't for your girlfriend there, I'd drive you round to see Doc Mucus."

Nerd Boy looks from Jimmy over to Claire, then down to the "Kill All Cars" motif emblazoned on her chest.

Claire cups his bleeding chin in her right hand, pulls his gaze back upwards. Turns to Jimmy.

"I think we can leave ideology out of it, just this once."

Jimmy walks them down to his car, feels in his pockets for his keys, realizes he's left them upstairs. Tells the two of them to wait, he'll be right back.

Claire grabs his arm as he's going. Looks him in the eye.

"Mister? How come you're doing this? You don't know either of us. Why should you want to get involved?"

Jimmy looks back at her, at the two of them. Takes in the morning sun and the leaves on the sycamore trees. Checks out the rumbling orange garbage truck coming up the road. Catches a waft of ripe garbage in the heat of the morning. Sees a few interested crows in attendance.

"Ah shoot," says Jimmy. "Maybe I'm just a sucker for a happy couple."

He walks across the street to the tenement block and goes up the four flights of stairs to the apartment he shares with Julia. The view down the hallway is blocked by the open bathroom door. Jimmy can hear the sound of a hair dryer.

"Jimmy, that you? Where've you bin?"

He grabs the car keys from the row of little key hanger hooks in the hallway, steps around the bathroom door to see Julia, fresh out of the shower, drying her hair in front of the mirror.

"Nothing honey. Just a couple of crazy kids caught up in ruckus."

He moves in behind her, caresses an ass cheek appreciatively, plants a kiss on her neck.

"Gonna drive 'em round to see the Doc."

She tips her head to one side to give him a bit more neck to work on, musses his hair with the hair dryer.

"Jimmy Chang," she says. "There's no figuring you. One day you're making like redneck of the month, next day you're the friggin' good Samaritan."

"That's me," says Jimmy. "Man of many parts." Arm around her ribcage, up underneath her breasts.

They look at each other in the bathroom mirror. Julia turns off the hair dryer, lays it down by the wash basin.

"There's one part," she says, leaning back into his arms. "There's one part I ain't seen so much of lately."

Jimmy lets his hand slide down over her belly, feels the beautiful curve of it.

"Sorry babe, bad timing. Gotta run, before this dumb kid loses any more blood."

"You could just call an ambulance."

"No insurance. I'll just drive him round."

She turns to face him.

"My man, you just don't know what you're missing."

"Sugar," he says. "I do. Believe me I do."

A quick kiss and he pulls himself away, back out into the hall.

Julia sighs and turns the hair dryer back on.

"And Jimmy?"

Jimmy is halfway out the door. "Jay?"

"Take some kitchen roll. Don't want 'em bleeding on the seats now, y'hear?"

Jimmy chugs his bleeding and strangely solicitous cargo round to see the Doc.

It's not far, just a few blocks. They could have walked it. Don't ask me. Jimmy's like that sometimes.

They wind their way down Danube, past the swimming baths with its Art Deco murals, past the health place where they check kids' hair for nits, past the Russian supermarket that's now pan-Asian halal. Then up behind the town hall—Rat House, as it's known by the locals. He double parks on the corner of Danube and Anzac, outside the Turkish bar that used to be Greek, opposite the Tandoori Palace that used to be a corner dive.

Jimmy's gets out of the car and looks around. He's feeling old.

The city's changing around him, morphing as he stands there into something else entirely. He's always thought of the NC as having a reassuring solidity, but now he's not so sure.

There's a long queue of people up behind Rat House and the sun is starting to beat down.

Jimmy leans briefly against the car while the other two get out.

Nerd Boy's got a thick wad of kitchen roll pressed up against his neck.

Claire gets out the other side and pops a stick of gum in her mouth, adjusts her spex. Says, "There's a doctor's here? He's not tagged or nothing."

Jimmy: "Tagged?"

"Tagged, you know? Like, geopositioned. Weebed up. Hello?"

Jimmy scratches the back of his head.

"Tagged. Gotcha. No, that shit don't apply here. Doc Mucus is strictly old school."

He presses the button on the car key and the vehicle beeps and flashes its approval and hunkers down to await the arrival of the inevitable parking Nazis.

Doc Mucus has his practice at 64, Anzac. You ring the bell marked "Clemence Mucus MD" and get buzzed through. A sign in the hallway says 3rd floor, so you either take the clapped-out elevator or wheeze your way up the winding stairway.

They decide on the elevator so they all squeeze in and manage to close the stiff brass scissor doors behind them. Another door slides shut and the contraption creaks up to its destination. Nerd Boy and Claire are oblivious to the proximity enforced upon them by the lift, but it's a little too close for comfort for Jimmy.

With a final gasp and shudder the elevator attains the dizzy heights of the third floor and ejects them onto a dank landing.

The practice is over on the other side, behind a big dark wooden door. They ring and enter, and find themselves standing in front of a reception counter.

The woman behind the counter is wearing white jeans and a white denim waistcoat with a tastefully frayed trailer-trash fringe around the shoulders. She has tattoos down her arms depicting racing cars and playing cards and laughing skulls and checkered flags and girls in cocktail glasses. Her long black hair is teased up in a bun. She has leopard skin cat-eye reading glasses and red lipstick.

She holds up an index finger and says, "Don't tell me, let me guess."

The three of them stop dead, like they're caught in the act.

"Swiss family Robinson? The Munsters? The Addams family?"

"Uh, look Miss…"

Jimmy looks down at her name tag.

"…Shirley…"

"The Von Trapps? The Waltons?"

Claire meanwhile is getting a little impatient "The fuck?"

Nerd Boy takes his wad of kitchen roll from his neck to demonstrate the nature of his predicament.

Jimmy sighs, exasperated.

"It's the three fucking musketeers, so maybe you'd be kind enough to tell Clem that Jimmy's here for a bit of stitching."

They hang out for a while in the waiting room. Nerd Boy sits in a corner, looking forlorn. Claire stands staring out of the window through the flickering virtuality of her spex. Jimmy thumbs through some old copies of *Bridal Shower* and *Proctology Digest*. There's an old guy in a duffel coat who looks like he's gone to sleep and a mother with a wall-eyed kid with a finger up his nose.

Finally the door opens and Shirley shoos them through.

"Jimmy, my boy! Good to see you!" Clem is up and round his desk in a geriatric flash, gives Jimmy a decrepit bear hug that smells of nicotine and embalming fluid.

"Doc, how's it hanging? Looking good…"

Jimmy's lying, and he knows it. The Doc has the air of a wizened pumpkin, all liver spots and spidery red veins. If it weren't for the teeth, he could be a stand-in for Nosferatu.

"And whose are these delightful children that you've brought with you? Not yours, surely? Or have you been keeping something from me?"

"Na Doc, no procreating. These're just some waifs and strays I picked up on the street. This one is…"

"Claire."

"And the other one is…"

He waves a hand towards Nerd Boy.

"Ilya."

"That's it, Ilya. Right."

The Doc stretches out a wizened hand to Claire, who takes it with disdain, like it was something she'd fished out of the garbage. The Doc hangs on to her hand and peers up at her through bottle-bottom glasses, coming alarmingly near in the process. Claire flinches.

"Don't worry dear, I don't bite."

"No, but I might."

He turns to Nerd Boy.

"And the young man? Ah, now I see it. A little loss of blood, is it?"

He licks his lips with the purple reptilian appendage living in his mouth.

"Nothing a little needlework won't cure. I'll get Shirl to bring in my sewing kit. Take a seat."

Apart from Doc's expensive office chair there is only one cheap plastic seat, which is graciously offered to Ilya.

After a while Shirl sashays into the room bearing a metal tray with a large bottle marked "Surgical Spirit" and six shot glasses. She sets the tray down on the desk, fills the glasses and passes them round. They clink glasses, the Doc says, "Chin chin," and Shirley says, "L'chaim". She shoots and leaves.

The Doc adjusts his glasses and moves in on Ilya.

"Terrible thing, knife wounds."

He pours some alcohol onto a swab, takes a swig from the bottle to steady his hands, launches in.

"I remember back in '63…"

Finally they're done, and on their way out when Doc Mucus calls Jimmy back into the office.

"Jimmy, a word in your shell-like ear."

Jimmy tells the others he'll be down in a minute, then goes back in and closes the door.

"What's up Doc, something the matter?"

"No Jimmy, nothing serious, it's just… Well you're looking a little grey around the gills. Why don't you pop in and see me yourself one of these days?"

"Na Doc, I'm good. Bearin' up and that."

"Of course, of course. It's probably nothing. Just an old man's intuition perhaps. Maybe you just do it for me, huh compadre? Why don't you get Shirl to give you an appointment on the way out?"

CHAPTER FOUR
The Junction

Claire and Ilya are down on the street waiting for Jimmy to emerge from the Doc's.

They are not saying much. Now that they have engaged in various short bouts of fierce physicality, small talk is about the last thing on their minds.

You can feel the air, like, crackle between them.

They are *loaded*.

Like one of those ancient Frankenstein movies where the crazy doctor is cranking up his gear and there is all this retro geeky Tesla tube and Van de Graaf generator shit giving off huge arcs of static electricity and there's a storm outside and the doc's lunatic henchman is hyperventilating like a frigging orangutan.

Fuck, they are *overloaded*.

Ilya is standing there chewing a fingernail and occasionally looking up and down the street but mostly just looking at the floor. Every now and again he risks a glance at Claire and his pale cheeks flush crimson till he looks away again.

Claire decides some displacement activity is in order. She calls in to work to tell them she'll be late. She already is late. Medical emergency. Accident, that kind of thing. It's ok, they're cool. They're not short-staffed. She'll be along soon.

She looks at Ilya.

Soonish. Yeah. Could be a while yet. This, uh, friend of hers needs, like, attending to.

But she'll be there.

For the meeting? Sure, of course. No way would she forget.

Yeah take it easy. Yeah catch you later.

The old guy Jimmy finally comes out from the doctor's.

She feels a rush of relief that takes her by surprise.

She doesn't know him from Adam but he feels so familiar. The way he took that situation in hand. It could have become totally fucked up, but as it was it just eased into something different, something ok.

Not much random generosity in the NC.

The guy Jimmy says, "Ok kids it's been a learning experience and all."

He extends his hand towards her.

"Have a great life."

She takes it, a little disoriented by the sudden change of tempo.

"Mister…"

"Jimmy."

"Jimmy. I, uh. Yeah. Thanks. Same to you."

"Nice knife work. Maybe a bit more control around those pressure points. Save yourself some trouble. But commendable stuff."

He turns to Ilya, reaches out a hand.

"You too kid. Watch out for yourself. Try not to antagonize your new girlfriend."

Ilya flushes red again. The guy Jimmy says a generic, "See ya," to the both of them and walks back to his car.

She watches him retrieve the parking ticket from under the windscreen wiper, scrunch it up and flick it into the gutter. Then he gets into the car and backs it around the corner into Anzac, almost down to where they are standing.

She doesn't move. Ilya doesn't move.

The car doesn't move.

She can see Jimmy looking at them in his rear view mirror, the line of people outside Rat House, the bustle in the distance up on Carlos Marx where it crosses Anzac.

She can see Ilya, and she knows she is going to have to fuck him as soon as possible or she's going to explode.

She knows what she wants, but she doesn't have a clue what to do. If they go back to her place she can forget work for the rest of the day. And if she skips work and just turns up for the meeting someone's going to be pissed off for sure.

She hears the whine of the car in reverse and sees it pull up next to them. The window on the driver's side slides down and Jimmy's looking across at her.

He's got an eyebrow raised and a strange smile on his face.

"What?" she says, as defiantly as she can muster.

But she already knows what.

"I don't know what it is with you guys."

They are back in Jimmy's car, looking relieved.

"Are you wearing some kind of special lost puppy deodorant, or what?"

Jimmy looks at the two of them in the rear view mirror. They are sitting there grinning, holding hands.

"So?" says Jimmy, one hand resting on the steering wheel.

"So what?" says Claire, with a lascivious glance at Ilya.

"So where to now? Want me to drop you at your place?" says Jimmy.

"Nah, too far, too complicated," says Claire.

"And you, lover boy? Live round here?"

Ilya looks over to Jimmy from under a lank black skein of hair covering half his face.

"Yeah, but I've got my little sister staying for a couple of days. That would be like, totally out of order."

Jimmy drums his fingers on the steering wheel, blinks out at the midday sun and takes a moment to think.

"Well, by the look of you you'll be wanting to spend a bit of quality time together sometime soon. How about, I take you round to the Junction? There should be someone there by now. They have a back room you could maybe use. Gary won't mind. He's a pretty liberal kind of guy. For a Viking berserker, that is."

They drive back down Danube, up into the B Village and left into Richard. The sun is beating down, they have the car windows open. Jimmy cranks up a little Serbian gypsy bhangra crossover on the ancient car stereo to go with the moment. They turn right into Heisenberg and draw up on the corner of Schroedinger in front of an improbable and unsavoury looking dive.

"This is it kids."

He grabs the remains of the kitchen roll from the floor of the car and thrusts it at Ilya.

"You might be needing this later on."

Then he jumps out of the car, followed somewhat reluctantly by Claire and Ilya. He zaps the car with his key and pushes open the front door of the bar, to be greeted by an automatic "We're closed!" a split second later.

"It's a social call."

"Jimmy, dude, how the fuck are ya?"

Claire and Ilya enter just in time to see a giant in a floral apron putting down his mop and bucket and embracing Jimmy in a bear hug.

"Mind the ribs G, you know what happened last time."

"Ah come on Jimmy, a bit of amateur chiropractic never hurt nobody. And who are your friends?"

Gary stretches out a giant hand to Claire and Ilya, who stand there looking dazed.

"Guys, take a pew. What can I get ya?"

While Jimmy and Gary chitchat about old times and Gary fixes the coffee, Claire takes in the Junction, the defining feature of which is its overpowering stench of nicotine. The walls are brown and adorned with scenes of longships with striped sails advancing on hostile shores, details of Norse figureheads and heavy metal guitar players in various poses. There is a dart machine and a huge TV screen. A couple of high freestanding tables with bar stools around them and a bunch of low tables. Also stools at the bar, where they are now sitting.

Claire sniffs at her t-shirt. It already reeks of stale nicotine.

She whispers to Jimmy while Gary is out back: "Is this place kosher? It looks like a fucking redneck palace."

"Don't worry. I thought that too, first time. G is a bit of a head-banger. But his heart's in the right place. And his missus reels him in when he gets too over the top."

Claire leans further in: "But doesn't he know there weren't any black Vikings?"

"Ah shit, you've got to watch yourself there. Whole can of worms. Gary's channelling Leif Erikson…"

"Leaf who?"

"… or possibly Eric the Red or maybe just Njorl's Saga. Big Viking schtick. I would go along with it if you know what's good for you."

Gary comes back with a tray of dubious-looking coffee, which he puts down in front of them. He pours four glasses of a thick and vaguely medicinal-smelling liquid and picks one up.

"Put hairs on your chest. Skol."

They down their second shot of the day with various degrees of sput-tering, hacking and back-slapping. Gary looks at the three of them and says: "So guys, to what do I owe the pleasure? I mean, assuming there is some kind of ulterior motive to this social call."

Jimmy claps his hand down on the table and says, "G, I'll be straight with you. These kids have been through a mightily traumatic experience this morning and need a bit of privacy to work a few things out of their system."

"Ah. I wondered about the kitchen roll. But this is a respectable place you know. Not some fucking knocking shop."

He gives them a hard stare, then bursts into huge, guffawing laughter.

"Come on, I'll show you the boudoir…"

Gary leads them through to the back room. There are a couple of old sofas, some low tables and some upturned crates. A faded print of Ice-landic mountains on the wall. A grimy window with orange curtains and white metal bars. He turns to Claire and gives her a large old-fash-ioned key.

"Half an hour. Forty-five minutes max. Don't stain the furniture. Not that anyone would notice."

He looks at Ilya, still clutching his kitchen roll, and pats him on the shoulder on the way out. He pulls the door to behind him and is gone.

There is a moment of silence after the door has closed and the world rearranges itself around them. Claire locks the door and looks over to Ilya, stretches out a hand to him and is almost overwhelmed by the sensation of skin and flesh and bone, the sudden pounding in her ribcage, the sound of racing blood in her ears and the fire deep down.

She leans back on the wall behind her, reeling him in. Their kiss is a ripe peach explosion: parting skin, sweet flesh, juice, sensory overload. She feels his lips with her teeth, explores his mouth, wonders how far her tongue will reach down his throat, whether she can reach all the way to the depths of him, lap up the sweet bitter animal taste of him, instantly addictive.

There is an arm tight around her waist, a hand next to her head against the wall, a face up against her face. Her fingers play around the edges of the dressing on his neck. Mixed in with the sweat and the pheromones is the iron antiseptic smell of a freshly stitched wound. The skin of his neck is stained with iodine disinfectant.

She feels simultaneously lustful and tender and protective towards him and would really like to hurt him again.

She says, "Sorry about the neck," and feels his hand on her ass.

He clears his throat and says, "You know I can't really believe that." His voice sounds hoarse and from somewhere deep within him. She twists his long black hair in her fingers and pulls his head slowly back to expose more of his throat.

She bites into the side of his neck away from the wound, just enough to feel the subcutaneous nerves firing underneath her teeth. She tastes him, the salt of his neck, her tongue looking for some hidden sweet spot in the smoothness of his neck.

"Maybe you're right. It's what you get for sneaking up on people."

It occurs to her that there is something feminine about him that totally turns her on.

"I guess so. It was worth it though."

She licks the depression made by a collar bone.

"How come?"

"The hottest fight I've ever had."

His hands are everywhere, his long musician's fingers. She feels a thumb over a nipple and a hand opening her jeans while his mouth searches for hers again. Multitasking. She likes that in a guy. Maybe he even is a musician. Maybe a pianist. Could even be an organist. Don't they do things with their feet at the same time? Maybe even a singing organist.

She feels her jeans slip, a hand sliding down into her pants.

Good, but way too fast, too out of control.

She reaches down and unbuckles his belt, quickly pulls the belt free.

"Stop. Turn around. Give me your hands".

He gives her a long wide-eyed look then extracts his hands from shirt and pants and turns around in front of her, stretching his hands out behind him.

She pulls his belt tight around one wrist then wraps it around both arms and ties it off.

She fishes a light tube bandana out of a pocket and slips it over his head to cover his eyes.

She turns him round and unzips his jeans, extracts his dick and puts a finger to his lips.

"Shhh."

She has him. By the handle.

She runs her hand around the shaft of it, like a prospective customer in a bicycle shop.

Such strange appendages, dicks. Unpredictable. Unnecessary. Ugly even, sometimes. Though this one thankfully not. So full of themselves. So desperate to run the show.

She feels a surge of energy then a relaxation, like a gear shift. Feels something in him flutter, then the wet of his tongue around her finger and the smooth skin of the dick in her hand. She quickly checks out her surroundings. A sofa handily positioned next to where they are standing. No faces at the window. It's all good.

She wonders what it would be like to take the dick she has in her hand and lay him down and fuck him with it. A detachable penis. Now that would be a practical bit of bio tech kit. You could keep it by the bedside until you needed it. Make sure it didn't go off till the right moment. Could open up a whole new world of possibilities.

She becomes aware of Ilya grinding his hips rhythmically into her hand.

"Now now," she says, stroking his cheek with her thumb. "Ladies first. If you would like to get down on your knees, I have a little something that requires your attention…"

CHAPTER FIVE
Fuji City

Fuji City.

Aspirational slop-bucket of the western world.

Cage-haven end station to the migratory masses.

Transformer of dreams, it feeds on hope and humanity, which it distils ineffably down to pure bile and bitterness.

It's a tar pool of waiting and redundancy.

Fuji City sits like a malevolent bird of prey atop the old Temple Hill, occupying the site of the disused airport. Its wings are spread forwards liked the curved wings of Horus, its body sandstone, unornamented, forbidding. The runways of the old airstrip and the grass around them are now recreational spaces for the citizens of the NC, but Fuji City rests gaunt and guarded, a separate world.

Admittance is granted to genuine wristband-wearing fujis and their various guards, overseers and attending wardens. To the rest of the population, not. This makes it a secret enclave within a city, akin to Beijing's Forbidden City or San Francisco's Alcatraz.

For Fuji City too is an island. An impenetrable bastion awash in a sea of dark rumour, invigorated by the frequent visits of the riot squad, paramedic units, the fire brigade, and those hearse-like vans with whited-out windows.

Undercover reports in the Daily Spleen, colour supplements in the Spleen on Sunday, tell of shock, horror, overcrowding, filth, lice, vermin, foreigners, insanitary habits, strange religions, indecipherable scrawlings, unspeakable utterances, unintelligible languages, insalubrious conditions, insufferable proximity, gender segregation, flashing of tempers, flashing of illicit hidden blades, blood feuds, slopping out of bloodied aftermath, the stench of vomit, diarrhoea, dysentery, the fear of ebola, zika, infections unbounded and magnified by the otherness of their vectors, the aura of despondency, frustration and despair transmogrified into one of boundless threat by the subtle race-hate prism of the gutter.

Fuji City is the Ellis Island of purgatory, Lady Liberty with fangs and the stench of death.

There were shit jobs, there were fucking awful shit jobs, and there was this.

It wasn't the work in general.

Alain Firengi was a black ops man through and through.

He had studied psychology and had majored in the parapsychological aspects of counterinsurgency theory and practice.

He didn't mind the hours and the pay was ok.

But trying to make an effective unit out of this rag-bag bunch of sicko fuji cholos was going to be like teaching fleas to sing.

There was no way it could happen.

He twisted on his bar stool and swore quietly to himself.

The bartender looked over with a raised eyebrow.

Al tipped his empty glass and the bartender brought over the bottle of Jimmy Dean and poured him a large one, no ice.

Over in the back of the room an athletic and silicon-enhanced dancer wearing only a sequined thong was gyrating energetically around a chrome pole. Her painted mouth wore an alternating smile and pout, but her eyes were glazed and corpse-like.

Al swigged a mouthful of his drink and lit a cigarette.

This project was fucking dead in the water. It was underfunded, understaffed, and the timeline was frankly ridiculous. They wanted it up and running by the new year. How the fuck was that supposed to happen? They didn't even have a proper vetting procedure in place and if news of it got out it would blow the whole Agency out of the water.

It was a total snafu. A cluster fuck of such mindblowing proportions that it hurt his brain just to think about it.

Strategy of tension my arse.

If he was going to run this fucking false flag fuji contra smokescreen, he was going to need backup.

But even in the Agency there was no-one he could trust with it.

He raised the glass to his forehead and closed his eyes.

Almost no-one. Maybe one exception.

The picture that came into his mind was of a dark-haired, dark-eyed woman. High cheekbones, thick eyebrows, long lashes. Piercingly intelligent.

Laila.

Why hadn't he thought of her before? They would make the perfect team. She was a natural organizer, she'd be perfect for the recruiting stage and when things really started moving she'd know where to plant the stories and rumours they'd be needing.

Plus she was hot as hell.

Like him she was second generation. An over-assimilator. He smiled at that. Her family had been Turkish Kurds who had fallen out with the guerrillas and headed west.

She reminded him somehow of his mother, back in Iran.

His mother had been an actress, before the so-called revolution. A francophile, she taught him to drink wine, speak French and to hate the Mullahs. His father had been Tudeh Party, communist man of the people and wife beater.

Al hated the Mullahs for killing his father.

Al hated the communists for their hypocrisy.

But above all else, he hated his father.

He finished his drink. Put some money down on the bar and a fifty with his phone number on it into the pole dancer's string tanga on the way out.

Suleika rocks gently to and fro and looks at the ground.

She's on her knees at the entrance to the U, where it comes up in front of the Arcades. The U spews out its inventory of busy busy denizens of the NC, who flood up the stairs towards the palace of consumption. They come up onto the traffic island between four lanes of cars and wait for the red man to stop holding out his arms and for the green man to start walking.

They see a black-clad figure, hunched and hooded at the top of the steps and avert their eyes. Only the very young linger and stare wide-eyed, until the tug at the end of their upstretched arms tells them to catch up with the adult world.

Only maybe one in a hundred, one in a thousand will fish in purse or pocket for a coin to be dropped into the wooden bowl down on the paving stones. Next to the bowl there is a picture sheathed in cellophane. It's a faded picture of a young man, bright-eyed, beardless, smiling. Beneath it is a card with a detailed hand-written explanation in a language hardly anyone here understands.

No-one picks up the card.

No-one bends down to read it.

Suleika kneels and rocks, and fingers her prayer beads.

After all, she is just a feature of the landscape.

The world washes around her. There are endless pulsing waves of feet and legs, shoes, buggy wheels and zimmer frame struts, the occasional wheelchair. The rumble of the passing trains beneath her. The stench of internal combustion engines. The shrill peep peep peep of the green man's exhortations to walk, goddamit. The braking and starting of cars and trucks at the crossing.

All this is the world. And the world is just a backdrop to the pain of her existence. Her legs are stiff and swollen from the endless kneeling on the cold hard ground. Her back and shoulders are hunched from habitually keeping the world at bay. Her heart aches for the life and the loved ones she has lost and left behind. Her head is full of memories that are too painful to behold but which are nonetheless all she has to hold on to.

Her soul too used to be a beaten, broken, fluttering thing that called out to death for relief.

Until everything changed.

There is a moment, as the ex-passengers of the U come up the steps, when each one is at head-height with Suleika. A moment when, theoretically at least, she could catch their gaze, were she to raise her head.

She never does.

She spares them the cold incineration of her stare.

This world is full of men. And how could she ever look one of these men in the eyes without wanting to kill him?

And how could she, an old and broken woman, ever take revenge on the world of men and their god?

She fingers her prayer beads.

She remembers the day that God became a woman.

It was a magical transformation. A revelation. The only reason for her continued existence.

If God were still a man she would have to kill herself.

Even hell would be preferable to so much injustice.

At night, after the Arcade has shut down, she returns to her cubicle, her honeycomb tube-bed in the hive at Fuji City.

At night she is alone with her thoughts, along with the thousands of others in the hive.

During the day she is flanked by drunken angels.

Her angels sit on the low wall behind her, drinking cheap alcohol and smoking and engaging in raucous arguments in the guttural language that belligerent angels speak.

She has never seen her angels. She has never risked turning around to look at them. At first she was terrified of them, until she learnt that their mission was to protect her. Should there ever be any threat to her person, she knows they will fly up like a murder of ragged and cancerous crows to harass any evil-doers.

Thus protected, she can continue her mission.

Her revelation went like this:

She was sat, like every day, at her place at the top of the steps, when there was a sudden illumination. It was a rainy day, but at that point the clouds above her parted, to reveal the sun, which cast a sudden ray of light down to where she was. The ground lit up, and she saw a hand reaching down to drop a fifty into her bowl, a sum so outlandish that it took her a moment to process it. At last she stretched out her hand to clasp the note, and in spite of herself, looked up to see who her benefactor was. With the sun shining down she had trouble making out the face of the lithe figure in front of her, who seemed somehow to be shrouded in an aura of blue light. At last she could make out the face of a beautiful young man. In disappointment, she dropped her gaze back to her bowl.

At that moment she saw henna'd hands dropping a card into her bowl and heard a mellifluous voice calling her "sister" in her own language.

She looked up, and saw that the young man had turned into a woman before her eyes. The woman smiled, and their eyes met, and Suleika felt the warmth of her gaze illuminate her soul and pierce her heart.

Suleika could no longer see the stranger, for her eyes were blinded by tears. She held her hands up in thanks and could feel the warmth of strange hands around hers, could hear the words of love and kindness in the susurration of the stranger's whispering, and the awkward and unaccustomed silence of the angels behind her.

And then the stranger was gone, and left behind was the fifty in her hand, and the feeling in her heart, and the card in her bowl.

And on the card it said: "Church of Kali, Mistress of the Heavens. God is a Woman. Believers, Come!"

Chapter Six
The Church of Kali

It takes a lot of dedication to be a thug.

The rituals, the scriptures. The praying.

The combat training. The mystical gesticulations. The mixing of poisons. The incessant sexual indulgence.

Not for the faint-hearted, thuggery.

Gene—Jeanie to the initiated—is many things, but faint-hearted isn't one of them.

Fuck no.

Gene is a man of wealth and taste. Taste mostly. Wealth, actually, none.

Gene paints her nails and keeps her body taut. Like a wound-up spring. Like a landmine waiting to explode.

But just a sec, you're probably thinking: "Thuggery? WTF?" or "Not like any thugs I know".

And there, you'd be right.

Not like any thugs you know, and you may think you know a few.

Gene is an elected, specially selected, devotee of the goddess Kali, the great and good, destroyer of worlds, *Durga* be her name, death to the non-believer. Ah, scratch good. Great and bad. As in, bad father-fucker. Shiva-fucker. Rampaging beatific head-fuck calamitous cosmic shit-storm. Sucking up all the deep down badness of the universe till it burns her to a crisp and keeps her coming back for more. Chopper of limbs and lopper-off of heads. Stitch a karmic necklace of decapitated dead-beats. Dig it, believe it!

Turn the other cheek on that, honey lamb.

Gene sits in her kitchen, drinking coffee. She skits through her in-coming, texts a few. Gets up and feeds the cat. Today she is meat-space modest, demure even. Silver earrings, black nails. Dressed for a job interview with some sleazebag restaurant owner known for outward hipness and an abusive attitude to staff. Known for hiring and blackmailing rent boys. Giving them straight jobs then working them for information. Finding leverage, till he has them over a barrel. Or table top, sofa back. Devious, insidious, slimy fucker.

Right up Gene's street.

The Church of Kali Mistress of the Universe is an unassuming four-storey affair up on the corner of Airport and Henry, casually fronted by Tarik's Society Coiffeur and Massage. Tarik will give you the full treat-ment, hot towels and shave perhaps, or a permanent wave, and maybe pass you on through to the back rooms should you be lucky enough to be one of his *preferred* customers.

The back rooms, needless to say, are the stuff of local legend. As the shop floor turns from scuffed linoleum to deepest crimson shagpile, as the smells turn from Brylcreem and Elnett to opium, musk and hash oil, so the stuff of work turns from hair and skin to deepest desires and the longings of the heart.

Tarik's is no mere knocking shop.

Here the work is organized along strictly hierarchical lines, a clean di-vision of labour. Most of the wetwork is carried out by the latest recruits. Kothi boys for the men. Polony remoulds or zhoosh backstabbers for the women. The recruits are organised into shifts, overseen by an elder Hijra or Ken. Elder being anything above twenty-four.

Dress codes are strictly western. As is the clientele, usually referred to as "The Johns", "The Joans" or collectively: "Charlie".

It was here that Gene started turning tricks.

His life before the church had been one of freelance promiscuity, get-ting mightily out of it, and generally recovering from the trauma of small-town deviant adolescence.

And if, whilst giving head in a darkroom, the backpocket contents of those unbuckled jeans were to wander surreptitiously, magickally even, into Gene's possession, why, then that was all to the good.

But after a year or two of existence in the NC, things started to turn a little stale. There was something missing in Gene's life. Something he found difficult to define. Purpose, perhaps. Revenge. Empowerment. The overthrow of dominant social relations. Economic justice and the right to laziness. Let's call it by its name: Total Revolution.

It was then that Gene met Miss Whiplash.

It was three-thirty a.m. down on Alberta and O. Gene was sitting in 69 Roses drinking whiskey sours when a six-foot svelte apparition in black latex and thigh-high stiletto boots walked in and sat on the next free bar stool. The fug-that-passed-for-air experienced a slight ripple. A twinkle sprang from eye to eye in the array of red-hatted gnomes perched high over the bar around the blind TV screen. Speakers and talkers found that their sentences had developed a minimal hiatus as they checked out the legs on that. What a dish and bucket! Yet the tremors and interruptions were but fleeting, seismic, subliminal lapses. Conversations resumed. Drinks were drunk. Miss Whiplash ordered a Vera Lynne and a tonic for the troops.

Mandy, behind the bar, part Polish, polishing the glasses.

"A stiff one Mister?"

Mister Whippy to her friends.

"Girl's best friend." And a wink.

Three fingers of gin and a splash. Ice, lemon. Black straw. Miss W drinks deep and relaxes. Her stubble is starting to show.

Gene is impressed.

They start to talk. This and that. Pleasantries.

"Dilly boy."

"Ma'am."

"Busy night?"

"Doing my bit."

"Keeping your end up?"

"It's hell out there."

They clink glasses. Gene skins up.

"And you?"

"Meal break. Working girl. All go."

"Johns lined up then?"

"Queueing down the hall. Going to have to start taking 'em in batches."

Gene shifts uneasily on his red leatherette barstool.

"Can they touch you?"

A wry look.

"As if."

"You plunge them?"

"Plunging's extra. My terms only."

"And?"

"In this drag? What do you think?"

Gene leans back, once-over asset check.

"I'd say top femme, dominatrix schtick. Niche market."

"On the up and up, sweetness. The in thing. It's a domination bubble."

Gene blows smoke across his whiskey sour, passes the spliff, finest Afghan, across to Miss W. Feels that first full-body tremor of arousal.

Miss W scratches her switch—long red fake henna locks—with her straw. Extends a lacquered finger underneath Gene's chin.

"Know what, baby girl?"

Gene dry-mouth swallows: "What's that?"

"Maybe it's time I took an apprentice".

"You mean?"

"Yup. Ever thought about a career in discipline?"

And so it was that Gene was initiated into the rites and practices of the domination trade. And that in turn gave rise to Jeanie. Not so much gave rise to perhaps, as formalized. For Jeanie was certainly always there with Gene, but she was without form in the world.

It was Miss Whiplash who taught Jeanie how to ride the wave of her Johns' desires. How to become a multi-faceted plane of projection. How to incorporate the archetype. How the key was not in working, but in *letting them work for it*.

Jeanie was a natural. It was as if she had merely been waiting all this time for someone to come along with the keys to her pen. Released into the wild, she learned quickly. She relished her status as apprentice. She found the discipline of her mistress to be a fitting counterpart to her own instinctive rebelliousness. And in time, when her mistress deemed she was ready, she was introduced to the Church, and Madame George, and the sisterhoood, and Kali Ma, *Durga* be her name.

Actually, the Church of Kali is more than just a knocking shop.

The Church's main hub in the NC is carefully stashed at a secret location, known only to the initiated.

I'd tell you how to get there, but they'd kill me if I did. Before that, I'd have to kill you. And probably your extended family, social media network and fleshmeet friends.

Better leave these things unsaid, eh?

No, actually I'm just pulling your leg.

You could look them up in the phone book, if you could find anyone with a phone book these days.

Or just like, noodle the weeb.

Check out their online temple, hearth palimpsest, scrolling virtual scrollset, their 127.0.0.1 congregation.

It will give you some phoney baloney, some leave-a-message hootenanny with a we'll-get-back-to-you on the side, whilst all the time garnering your IP, probing your online flaws and orifices, insinuating, extrapolating, inferencing, just to see where it is you is at. Where it is you're coming from. Dig?

But be that as it may, here's how you get there.

You get off the U at the Arcades (assuming you use the U, and not some other means of personal transport, such as solar driven skateboard) and head on down Carlos Marx in the direction of Han Plaza. Down past the slot machine palaces and Hirohito's pan-Asian sushi hubble bubble joint and the wig shop full of long-necked disembodied female mannequin heads next to the halal dress shop full of headless buttoned up female mannequin bodies modelling the latest in demure styles for the otherwise devoted and devout.

Your quest, being other-natured, other-nurtured, leads you further on, further out, further in, down past the kiosk selling tickets to the parking lot and left into the parking lot itself. Over to the far left hand corner where you run up against the back end of an office building. (Why are you running? Slow down a bit.) There are three unmarked stairways leading down to separate cellar doors. You choose wisely grasshopper and take the left-hand stairway downwards, only to pause in front of the brown metal firedoor.

Remember, you are the supplicant.

Kalipedia, fountain of knowledge eternal, and ultimate reference for the Kali OS in its present iteration, defines supplicant in the following terms:

In the greater network of being that is the dimension of the universe which we, the earth-bound, inhabit, a supplicant is an entity at one end of a point-to-point interdimensional segment that seeks to be authenticated by an authenticator attached to the other end of that link. The supplicant is thus required to submit credentials in order to connect to a sacred network. If the authentication succeeds, the authenticator typically allows the applicant ingress to the network.

Of all the forms of Devi, Kali is the most compassionate because She provides mojo or liberation to Her children. She is the counterpart of Shiva the destroyer. Together, they are the destroyers of unreality, bad faith and karmic neer-do-wells. The ego-as-supplicant sees Mother Kali and trembles with fear because the ego recognizes in Her its own eventual demise and spiritually kacks its kegs. A supplicant who is attached to their ego will not be admitted to the Mother Kali network and She will appear in a fearsome form and basically bite your good for nothing ass. A mature soul who engages in spiritual practice to remove the illusion of the ego sees Mother Kali as very sweet, affectionate, and overflowing biome with incomprehensible love for Her children, and shitloads of other Gaia-like good stuff.

There follows a KaliOS network-diagram example: *Kali Ma wears a garland of skulls and a skirt of dismembered arms because the ego arises out of identification with the body. The attachments of the ego reveal fundamental truths about the supplicant. Therefore choose one or more of the following statements as a personal mantra:*

a) *In truth we are beings of spirit and not flesh. So liberation can only proceed when our attachment to the body ends.*

b) *In truth we are beings of flesh and not spirit. So liberation can only proceed when our attachment to the spirit ends.*

c) *In truth we are beings of leisure not work. So liberation can only proceed when our attachment to alienated labour ends.*

d) *In truth we are beings of freedom not servitude. So liberation can only proceed when our attachment to the rigid gender memes of the oppressor ends.*

e) *In truth we are beings of earth and not money. So liberation can only proceed when our attachment to the baleful vicissitudes of racist ecocidal fossil-fuel capitalist patriarchy ends.*

Having made your choice, continue.
Thus the garland and skirt are trophies worn by Her to symbolize having liberated Her children from attachment to the corporeal, the body limited. She holds a sword and a freshly severed head dripping blood. As the story goes, this represents a great battle in which she destroyed the demon Raktabija, his corporations, excrescences, media outlets, vapid trumperies, militias, fakeries and pollutions. Her black or sometimes dark blue skin represents the womb of the quantum unmanifest from which all of creation arises and into which all of creation will eventually dissolve. She is depicted as standing on Shiva as cosmic surfer who lays beneath Her on his long-board, heavy hung and snow-white tan with a look of well-stoned blissful

detachment. Shiva represents the pure formless awareness of sat-chit-ananda (being-consciousness-bliss) aka chit-chat-ananda (pure MDMA co-consciousness ecstasy) while She represents "form" eternally supported by the substratum of pure awareness.

And when we say "form", as bad-ass demon slayer, She really does have form.

Therefore a supplicant, in some contexts, refers to a user or client in a network environment seeking to access network resources secured by the KaliOS authentication mechanism.

In its most basic form, this means that you have to knock on the door.

If they don't like the look of you, you'll have to give them the password.

What do you mean, you don't have a password?

If they don't like the look of you, it won't matter.

Every password will be the wrong one.

CHAPTER SEVEN
The Clock of the World

Jimmy's back at the Doc's.

Doc Mucus sits impassive behind his desk, peering at some blood test results through his bottle-bottom glasses. He licks his false teeth with his reptilian tongue and makes a clucking noise, perhaps of disapproval, or maybe just uncertainty.

Jimmy realizes that the folds on Doc Mucus's neck remind him of a chicken, and makes an effort to look out of the window.

It's bright outside. A couple of picture-book clouds float innocuously over the orange-tiled roof of the tenement opposite. The early September air has a chill to it though, in spite of the sun. Like it's looking down on the scurrying denizens of the NC and saying: it won't be long.

First fall, then winter.

Doc Mucus clears his throat and Jimmy brings his attention back to the situation at hand.

"Jimmy old son…" the Doc starts up.

"Clark Kent," says Jimmy.

"Say what?"

"Daily Planet."

"Jimmy, you're losing me here."

"Jimmy Olsen, Clark Kent aka Superman's best buddy cub photographer at the Daily Planet newspaper."

The Doc removes his glasses and massages his eyelids. The back of his hand is speckled with liver spots. In the few moments between his hand coming back down and the glasses going back on, Jimmy catches sight of his eyes, normally huge behind thick optical lenses, now red-veined tiny orbs, glistening dully in their skin-fold nests. Little night-creature eyes.

"It's a comic Doc."

The Doc pokes his glasses up along the bridge of his nose with a bony index finger.

"Jimmy, this is no time for comics."

That brings Jimmy up short.

"Doc, what is it?"

"Jimmy, how long have we known each other?"

The Doc looks serious, ancient.

"Jeez Clem, don't ask me. Must be yonks. I think I was just off the boat. Septicemia and no health insurance, you remember? I was desperate. You didn't hesitate. I'll always thank you for that."

"So I hope you know you can trust me?"

Jimmy looks puzzled.

"Sure Doc, no question."

They have a moment of eye contact. The Doc, blinking in his massive hornrims, Jimmy, fully present now, focused.

"Come on Doc, just give it to me straight."

"Jimmy, your blood tests are not good."

"Meaning?"

"Meaning, you have a rare form of pancreatic cancer which seems to have metastasized to other organs."

Jimmy feels the clock of the world grind to a halt around him.

"Fuck."

The Doc pulls a bottle of clear liquid and a couple of glasses from a metal filing cabinet under his desk. He pours out two shots and hands one to Jimmy.

"Here, drink this."

Jimmy's not responding.

Jimmy's flashed, time-travel transported and diving off Sudong Island, poking around in the wreck of HMS Goodwill, tasting the rubber of the air supply mouthpiece, the salt of the water. Up above's a shifting ceiling of glinting sea waves and piercing shafts of sunlight. Down here there's ethereal calm, the pull of the current, the cool of the water, the sailors' graveyard below him.

Jimmy floats suspended, the air tank on his back, his long swim fins curling gracefully with each slow-mo cycle of his legs, a lazy stream of bubbles wobbling relentlessly to the surface. He raises his hand to his facemask. The skin of his fingers is pale, wrinkled by the time he has spent in the water. He checks his air supply. Almost gone.

His time's up, and he kicks for the surface, feels his ears pop as he rises, breaks the surface and out into the bright early morning sun and the sudden, insistent sparkle of its myriad reflections. The lap and laugh of the waves. The heat of the day and the brightness of the surface world. Jimmy slides the mask up onto his forehead, pulls out the mouthpiece and lets out a yell, a cry of sheer exuberance. He's a skinny Singapore beach bum and it's good to be alive.

"C'mon kid. For the shock."

Jimmy shakes his head like there's water in his ear and takes a deep breath.

"Sláinte."

"Şerefe."

They knock back the shots and Jimmy pushes his glass over for another. The Doc pours and they take longer this time, drinking slowly in silence, Jimmy savouring the burn of the spirit on his tongue and in his belly.

In spite of it all, he can't help the feeling that something's not right.

"Doc?"

"Jimmy?"

"I'm not in pain."

"It's the way of things lad. It'll come. Big C'll creep up on ya. Catch you unawares."

"How long have I got?"

"I'll give you three months. Half a year max."

"And what are my chances?"

"Chances?"

Now it's the Doc's turn to look puzzled.

"Ah, you mean survival? Pretty minimal I'm afraid. I'll give you a prescription for some medication to help with the symptoms of course. But apart from that there's basically nothing we can do. Not in this part of the world, at least."

"Huh?"

"There's some guys in East Asia doing some cutting edge research. Gene splicing, recombinant DNA therapy, that kind of stuff. Heard some good things about it. Way out there. Golden shot though, kill or cure. Not even legal over here. And prohibitively expensive, of course."

The Doc sets down his glass, rearranges some papers and starts tapping into a keyboard and gazing into the battered monitor sitting on his desk.

Jimmy's looking at the floor and trying to come to terms with the sudden massive rearrangement of his emotional state. He's got the weight of the world on his shoulders and he's feeling old old old.

"So that's it then?"

"Well…"

The Doc turns the monitor around and shows Jimmy a lurid green website with Mandarin characters. Mega wonderdrug hype. Big, full-on media splurge. Interactive vids and lots of lab coats and face masks, twisting mitochondrial strands and clarions of hope and the general glorious onward upwardness of science in the People's Republic.

"Of course, if we could get some of this stuff into the country, then you might be in with a fighting chance. I could even upfront some of the cash. You'd uh, you'd have to pay me back though."

"Shit Doc, sounds like serious money. There's like, no way I can see me getting hold of that kind of cash in the near future."

Dr Clemens Mucus MD turns the monitor back round, leans back in his chair, clears his throat, gives Jimmy the full benefit of his raptor stare.

"We can worry about that later on down the line. Our main problem would be with the authorities, drug enforcement, customs. Experimental therapies essentially go down as class A. Sentencing is commensurate with that."

Doc's purple tongue darts out to moisten his cracked lips. He removes his glasses again and buries his face in his hands.

"No, but the whole thing is too risky. It would mean smuggling it in. I have my reputation to think of."

He looks up.

"And of course I have no idea who I could possibly ask to do something as risky as that."

Jimmy's hangdog head also rises and when his gaze meets Docs there's a light in his eye where no light had been.

"Doc. You might not know it, but Mule is my middle name."

Chapter Eight
Laila in Fuji City

Laila is standing in a little pokey broom cupboard of an office up in Fuji City looking out of the window and wishing she wasn't there. The autumn sun is weak and watery behind a cloud hijab, the fujis wandering round on the tarmac outside wrap themselves up warm against the wind blowing across the old airfield runway.

She opens the window and lights up a cigarette. She's got five minutes downtime in her processing schedule. That creep Al has got her sorting candidates for that crackpot fuji contra scheme of his. Her cover is some integration, welfare schtick. Aptitude assessment baloney. But the camp authorities bought into it, she came of course highly recommended. And now she's here, sifting the corn.

She blows smoke out of the window, makes a twirling gesture with her free hand, like down, and into the barrel, then closed and up, with a handful of grain. She brings her palm to her mouth and purses her lips to blow away the chaff. Then, with her hand cupped like a funnel, she lets all the imaginary grain fall slowly to the ground.

She smiles at her agrarian fantasies and flicks her cigarette butt out of the window. She checks her purple nail varnish and buffs her nails against the lapels of her jacket.

She's power dressing. Not her normal look, but Al said he wanted her intimidating. Businesslike and sexy, pull out all the stops, is what he said. You know the routine. Modern, western, integrated, atheist, independent, assertive. Laila gets it. She totally gets it. She's all of those things, and a whole bunch more.

But she's not sure about being told what to flaunt and when.

But shit, it pays the rent.

And you don't get anywhere in the Agency by questioning the chain of command.

There's a knock at the door, it's the next guy on the list.

She calls for him to come in, tells him to take a seat and walks round behind her desk. Her chair is a plush piece of comfort office design, but she's got the guy seated on a basic chair of steel and wood, like something out of a classroom.

His name is Ahmet Al-Sabty. He's a fresh-faced engineer from Homs, managed to get out before the siege started in earnest. Kept his nose clean in the civil war. Avoided conscription, pressganging, kidnapping. Skedaddled to Turkey as soon as he could. Crossed the water. Did the long march. Now he's here. Parents dead. Little sister abducted. Dark serious eyes, but somehow unbroken. Like he's still looking for hope. Like he still believes that somewhere down the line there could be a happy end.

Laila has no use for him.

She feels her heart go out to him as she checks out his physique, his trimmed, slightly hipsterish beard, cute ears, winning smile.

But he's not what she's looking for.

She's got Al on an implant behind her ears. He's got a vid feed to the office next door and occasionally expresses an opinion on one candidate or another. But most of the time there's no need. He's given her plenty of leeway, basically trusts her judgement. Anyway, who knows what the fuck he's up to right now? Might even have a couple of hookers in there, for all she knows.

She types some stuff into the keyboard on her desk, her long nails clacking loudly on the keys.

She doesn't want to prolong the agony.

He's a sweet guy, he deserves a break.

Ain't life a bitch.

Next.

Next up is hardly through the door and Laila realizes she's has hit paydirt.

He's clean-shaven but she can tell he's not happy with it.

She seems him flinch, minutely recoil on entering the room and finding himself being interviewed by a woman. There's a flicker of anger in his eyes which he quickly packs away.

Laila feels a surge of adrenalin and a slight rush of goosebumps.

She is a hunter. And this guy is lunch.

She gestures languidly for him to sit, brushes her hair back from her shoulder, leans forwards to show him some cleavage.

Her mark is sweating. She can tell he's a hater.

She asks him some bullshit questions about his background in perfect Arabic.

They both know it's phoney, but they go through the process.

She types some more stuff into her keyboard. None of it's to do with what he says—she has his file after all. Instead, it's all body language clues, inferences, assessments.

The room is decked out with the latest in somatic monitoring gear and she has a bunch of input streams up on her screen. They're giving her his heart rate, body temperature, skin flush, deviation from average voice modulation. But really it's just backup. She doesn't need all of this crap to be able to tell he's lying through his teeth.

His file says Damascus but she can hear an Iraqi twang to his voice. She has him pegged as western provinces, maybe Falluja or Ramadi. There's enough Syrian overlay in his speech patterns to pass cursory inspection. But he has no idea who he's up against.

She bats her heavily mascara'd lashes behind her harpyish, cat-eye glasses.

"So Mr Jamal," she says, her Arabic lightly inflected with a Lebanese accent from her years stationed in Beirut. "Do you have any military training?"

Jamal's monitor feeds light up. She can see his eyes flit momentarily up and to the left before answering.

"No, none at all."

She can see the tightness in his facial muscles, the effort he is making to control his breathing.

"Ah, that's quite an achievement. How did you manage to avoid conscription?"

"Reserved occupation. I worked as a male nurse."

It's bullshit. She's seen enough of combat to recognize the battle-hardened. She's enough of a fighter to instantly recognize an enemy.

"And religion?"

Bingo.

All her feeds light up. This guy's struggling with his answer and he hasn't even said anything yet.

"Not really. My family were never very religious. My father worked for the government. We didn't go to the mosque or anything."

Perfect. A perfect stream of bullshit.

If there's one thing Leila knows it's this: the guy is lying through his teeth. It's clear as day that he is one mean son of a bitch.

And now he's going to be her son of a bitch.

"Mr Jamal," she says. "Welcome to New Clone City. I'm sure we can find something useful for you to do."

Chapter Nine
Happy-Slapped

Ever since Jimmy left the Doc's he's been wandering round like he's happy-slapped. He knows that he's been thrown a lifeline, but it's the death sentence that's got him worried. Too much information. He just can't seem to get a handle on it.

"I just can't seem to get a handle on it."

He's back at Samsun's Oz Eatery, talking to Deli.

"It's just doing my friggin' head in."

Deli, always a sympathetic listener and good for a bit of gossip, has set aside her tea towel and has sat herself down on the red leatherette bench on the other side of Jimmy's table. She pats his hand and leans in.

"Jimmy love, it's only natural. It'd do anyone's head in. How did Julia take it?"

Jimmy drops his gaze sheepishly.

"Haven't told her yet."

He looks up. There's a tear running down his cheek. Deli reaches up and wipes it away with a gentle swipe of her scarlet-lacquered thumb.

"You've gotta tell her J."

Jimmy sniffs.

"Sure. I know I do. But I just can't bring myself to do it. Every time I go home I just think it would destroy her. It'd just cut her up completely."

"Jimmy you dope. This is not about her. This is about you. You can't just keep it bottled up. That's just crazy. And you think she hasn't noticed something's up? The way you're moping around?"

"You're probably right Mrs O."

"You know I'm right Jimmy."

A ring at the door announces the arrival of guests. Deli picks up her tea towel and gets up to greet the two punters who have just walked in.

She shows them to a table, brings them a menu, takes their order, generally bustles around. It's just past noon, the lunchtime trade is starting to pick up. There's an enormous recycled kangaroo donna kebab rotating on a spit in the window, which slides back for easy ordering from the street. Sam, the owner, is standing behind vitrines of green salad, piles of sliced tomatoes, bowls of sauces—chili, garlic, herb—sharpening what seems to be a two-foot sword with a sharpening steel. That, together with his enormous black mustache, embroidered waistcoat and cummerbund-style belly wrap give him the air of some mediaeval Janissary.

Jimmy only becomes aware of the regular swipe of steel on steel when it suddenly stops, and Sam rotates the kebab to reveal a still-bubbling crust of flame-grilled ersatz meat, which he starts to hack into with determination.

Jimmy finds the scene strangely soothing. Sam, sawing into the big round kebab, the ever-increasing pile of meat shavings on the grille below the kebab spit. Deli, swishing round the room, her copious black hair tied back in an unruly bun, emanating warmth and a magical feeling of belonging to all her customers. The old copper samovar steaming gently in the corner. Sam's two gophers, chopping veg and expertly flapping the *dürüm* wraps onto the grill to warm them up. Out on the street, the passers-by are hunched against the cold, leaning into that old East wind and patently wishing they were somewhere else.

But in here, in the steamy warmth of Samson's Oz Eatery, with its cheesy acoustic backdrop of Turkish arabesque, Jimmy knows that everything is as it should be. He's here in the moment. It's enough.

Deli brings Jimmy some tea and his lunch, and makes a palms-up gesture around the room, accompanied by a shrug of the shoulders.

"Filling up. Catch ya later."

She kisses his forehead and leaves him to his own devices.

Claire is just up from the U and heading down Erk. She's looking good and pretty much oblivious to the weather and the people around her. Her mind is on Ilya. In fact, Ilya is more or less all she's been thinking about for the past couple of weeks. She's got him under her skin, and that's something she wasn't expecting to happen. They are an item, and that hasn't gone unnoticed at work either. The collective is starting to talk. There is a lot of eye rolling and smirking when Ilya comes round to pick her up from her shift, and it's starting to bug her quite a bit. They just don't get him. It's like: what's she doing with that nerd guy? He doesn't fit somehow with their worldview. For a bunch of vegan eco-revolutionaries the hacker guy with the lank black hair is something they can't quite pin down, classify, categorise. She'll be sitting in a meeting and some topic will come up, maybe some programming deal, and there will be these snide remarks and she'll be like: what? What the fuck? And they will be all: hey, don't be so uptight. No need to be so aggressive. And she'll be like: if you've got something to say, just come out and say it. Otherwise, you can just stick it up your ass.

So all this is swirling through her head as she heads down past the Rat House towards Danube and the cop shop on the corner of Sun Boulevard and Wildebeest Row. There's been a break-in at the collective and they have assigned her the dubious privilege of going down to the pigpen and dealing with the paperwork. Like, thanks for that one too. No love lost for the cops from any of them. But she pulled the short straw. Most of them have it pegged as some kind of state-sponsored thing anyway. Undercover operatives, political police, narks, proxies, whatever. No real way to tell, these days. But they need the insurance money, and for that, they need the paperwork.

So here she is, barrelling down the street, full of contradictory shit and feeling like she's going to have a go at the first person who crosses her.

She pulls up at the corner of Erk and Danube and waits for the little green man to do his thing. From the corner of her eye she catches sight of the snaking lines of forlorn entrance-seekers behind the town hall. In front of her, a couple of kids are being pulled back off of the street and vigorously admonished by their irate mother in a tongue Claire can't quite recognise.

The lights change to green, the juvenile jaywalkers are released from their mother's solicitous clutches to go spilling noisily across the junction. Claire crosses and smiles at the woman as she passes. She can see the cop shop down on Sun Boulevard clearly now, and shit, there's a queue there too. At least forty people lined up on the street, goddam it.

Ah yeah, well make my day, why don'tcha.

The sight of what awaits her pulls her up short, stops her in her tracks. She looks around, as if for a weapon, some way of dealing with this unexpected turn of fate. Maybe a newspaper? Maybe a coffee? She checks out the street overlay and tags on her spex but this area is like, Deadsville. With a sigh she digs into her coat pockets and pulls out her earphones. At least she won't have to interact with anyone.

Anyone except the cops that is.

And as she fits her earplugs into her ears she turns side-on to the wind and finds herself looking straight in at Jimmy, who's sat in the window of some food joint like a left-over pet shop puppy. It takes her a moment to twig exactly who it is that she's looking at, and a broad smile spreads over her face. Jimmy manages a wan grin, and raises his glass of tea at her.

That's all the invitation she needs. Thankful for the sudden rescue from the cop shop queue she bursts into Samsun's and plonks herself down opposite Jimmy.

"Jimmy, dude! Good to see ya! How the hell are you?"

"All the better for seeing you kid."

Jimmy pats her hand in an avuncular fashion.

"How's the boyfriend? Russian sounding name. No don't tell me. Ivan. Vanja. Vladimir?"

"Ilya."

"Ilya. Told ya. Russki. You two still hanging out?"

Claire is amazed to find herself blushing. She fishes in her shoulder bag for her tobacco pouch.

"Still going strong."

"Good to hear it. But you'll have to go outside with that."

Jimmy points towards a small No Smoking sign hanging discreetly below a faded print of the first suspension bridge over the Bosphorus.

Claire pulls the glue strip on her cigarette paper expertly across her tongue and finishes her rollup.

"Ah, sure. Force of habit." She taps the end lightly on the table surface. "I'll save it for later."

She examines the face of the guy sitting opposite her. He looks drained, weighed down. And maybe ten or twenty years older than the last time she saw him.

"So what's with you? You look kinda washed out."

"Me? Never been better. Fit as a fiddle."

Jimmy takes a sip of his tea.

"You're shitting me, right? Like, something's up? Ah shoot, I know it's none of my business. Jeez, we only met once. My mother's always telling me not to stick my nose in. Like, curiosity killed the cat, an' that? Christ, she ought to know. I friggin' got it from her. And the cat's dead and buried, so you might as well tell me."

Jimmy bursts out laughing. He nearly chokes on his tea he's laughing so hard. Claire has to get up and give him a slap on the back. The other guests look over. Deli gives a little wiggle-fingered wave from the counter.

"I guess there's no saying no to a line like that. Sounds like your ma did a good job with you." Jimmy stops choking and looks her in the eye. "Ok, I'll tell you. Here's the deal."

And Jimmy tells her about his last visit to the Doc, about the cancer diagnosis, about the Chinese wonder drug, about having no money, about not being able to tell Julia, about not having a fucking clue what to do.

Claire listens, and takes it all in.

"Jesus H. Christ Jimmy. That's some fucking heavy shit. That's the heaviest shit I've heard all week."

Jimmy raises an eyebrow. "You reckon?"

"Damn right I reckon. I mean, what are you going to do? When are you going?"

"What do you mean, when am I going?"

"I mean, when are you going, you dope. You're going, right? You can't just sit around and wait to pop your clogs. You said the Doc would give you the airfare up front. So what's your problem?"

Jimmy shifts in his seat and swirls the dregs of his tea around the bottom of his tulip glass. Claire can see that he's moved, conflicted. Struggling. He reaches out a hand and brushes her cheek with the back of his fingers. She doesn't flinch.

"You're a good kid."

"Yeah, I'm a real good Samaritan. And you remember my name, right?"

"Sure it's…no don't tell me, it's on the tip of my tongue…"

She punches him in the biceps.

He laughs.

"Ouch. It's Claire. Karate Kid Claire. She of the violent tendencies. How could I forget?"

"That's alright then. And I need a smoke."

Jimmy fishes in his pocket for his wallet and leaves a ten on the table top.

"Me too," he says, and they get up and go outside.

They stand outside in the street and Claire says "Want to walk down to the cop shop with me?" and Jimmy looks at her like she's crazy and says, "No," and they both laugh and head that way anyway. And Jimmy cadges a cigarette off of her and starts rolling it but the wind's blowing and he's out of practice rolling while walking and holding on to the tobacco pouch at the same time and he keeps losing flakes of tobacco out of his rollup so they have to stop. He says, "Hold on a sec," and gives her back the pouch and turns his back to the wind and finishes the thing no problem.

He sticks it in his mouth and says, "Got a light?" and she gives him a light and he takes a deep drag and they turn and continue on down the street.

The corner of Erk and Sun Boulevard is all that one would expect of the pulsing underbelly of one of the seedier parts of a generally down-at-heel metropolis. There's an Arabian bridal shop on the corner sporting extravagantly outdated gowns like something out of a Ginger Rogers movie. And like most everywhere else, none of the mannequins have heads to avoid the religiously contentious issues of feminine cranial displayability.

On the other corner there's a 24/7 liquor store selling phone packs, disposables, app credits, wetware patches, e-smokes, alcopops, dried noodles and bus passes, fronted by a picture of a guy in a check suit holding a phone with a blue globe for a head. There's a bus stop full of youths doing their best to look disreputable and a couple of teenage mothers pushing prams. There's a multilingual chemist peddling painkillers, suppositories, sanitary items, insanitary preventions and cures, digestive enhancers, dental floss, follicle cream, latex sheaths, gloves and dental dams, morning after pills, unguents and expungents.

And there is the cop shop in all its grimy redbrick splendour, encrusted with the accumulated foul exhalations of innumerable internal combustion engines of both the Otto and Wankel varieties, the noxious particulate mixtures favoured by Mr Diesel and Co. as well as the filthy residues of domestic coal and lignite burning, all rounded off with a generous topping of pigeon shit.

Claire and Jimmy both pull up at the crossing and take a drag on their respective smokes.

"Here we are then," says Jimmy.

"Here we are then," says Claire.

"You're doing what, here, precisely?" says Jimmy.

"Break-in," says Claire. "Vegan wholefood collective where I work. Burglary. I got suckered for the paperwork."

"With friends like that..."

"It's Ilya. They've been down on me from the get-go. Don't dig him at all."

"You could tell them where to get off."

"Already did."

"Ah."

And then, as they cross the road: "You gotta queue?"

"Suppose so."

"Want me to wait with you?"

"Sure, why not?"

So they wait together. Pretty soon the queue fills up behind them, so they're kind of pressed in from front and back. People are wrapped up against the cold, big coats, big scarves and hats, the occasional stamping of feet. There's a continual stench of exhaust fumes as cars stop and start at the crossing. The sky is leaden and overcast, the street is two strips of grey tarmac separated by a central reservation of dirty, stunted, nearly naked vegetation.

Claire is chirpy nonetheless.

"I don't quite get it with you."

"Join the club."

"I mean, I know the cancer thing must be a total pisser. Unimaginably. Absolutely. I mean, no question."

"Right."

"Right. But what I don't get is, how come you're hesitating? Like, here you are, moping around the NC and wondering how to break it to your old lady and shit, but if it was me, you wouldn't see me for dust man, I'd be friggin' out of here."

"You reckon?"

"I reckon and a half. If someone said to me, you're probably going to croak—no, skip that, you're certainly going to croak, but there's this miracle drug out there that might just save your skinny ass, then that would be me, gone. You with me?"

"I'm way ahead of you kid."

"Yet here you are. Mopety-mope. Standing in a queue outside the copshop on a wet and windy Wednesday. *Qué pasa, compadre?*"

"Must be the charm of the present company."

Claire's cheeks flush red and she pulls in close.

"Don't bullshit me. I like you Jimmy, but if you can't be serious, you can friggin' eff off."

Jimmy's a little taken aback. He bites down on a fingernail and worries a sliver loose, all the time keeping his eyes fixed on Claire's. The queue has inched forward maybe a couple of feet since they've been here.

"I appreciate it, kid."

"Appreciate what?"

"Appreciate what you're doing here. You're confronting me with my contradictions. You're forcing me to fess up to stuff I won't even admit to myself."

"Yeah. So?"

"So I'll tell you. There's a simple reason. There's a reason beyond all the self-delusional bullshit and the stuff about not being able to tell my old lady. There's a reason you might not understand and will probably make you think I'm crazy."

"I already think you're crazy." She gives him a smile this time, and a nudge in the ribs with her elbow.

"But I'll tell you anyway. You're right about the drug. I've got to give it my best shot. I'm going to have to go for it. But the reason I'm hesitating, the reason I'm still officially undecided, is that, for the first time in my life, I feel like I'm really free."

"Free?" Claire is incensed. "Are you out of your friggin' mind? What's free about waiting to die?"

The other people in the queue have given up their pretence of not listening and have turned to face the two of them.

"I said you wouldn't get it."

"So explain it to me."

"Yeah, explain it to her," echoes the queue chorus.

"Look. If you know you're going to die. If the date of your death is more or less fixed. Then that gives you all the freedom in the world to do anything you want. I know it's not easy to get your head around. I know I should get on a plane and try to bring the drug in. But that'll just be me scrabbling around trying to survive. But you know, if I just like, accept death, then there is really nothing on earth that could stop me from doing anything I want, as long as I'm fit enough to do it."

"You don't look that fit."

"I know. There's the catch. I feel like death warmed up. And there's another thing."

"Namely?"

"Namely, I haven't got a clue what I want to do with all this freedom."

Claire takes a deep breath.

"Jimmy, dude, with all respect."
"Yeah?"
"That's the biggest crock of shit I've heard in a long time."

There's a noxious wind blowing over the NC as Claire leaves the police station. It's already dark, and the cops kept her waiting for hours—even after the queuing—for a minor formality that would probably have taken her about 5 minutes online. The cold hits her as she steps out onto the street. Ok, it's November. But it's too cold for November. New normal crazy. Unpredictable as the rest of the year, the rest of all the past years that Claire can remember, located as they are on an ever upwardly trending graph of record temperatures, meteorological anomalies, regularly recurring once-in-a-thousand year events, excuses, illusions, self-delusions, and downright wishful thinking. This particular cold front has just swept down from the Arctic, hitching a ride on the back of a jittery jetstream that still doesn't know what has hit it. A cold front still bereft of a name, so why don't we call him Arnold, how come only storm systems get names, call that climate justice? Our newly designated coldfront Arnold sweeps in, front on a mission and all, and scares the shit out of all the remaining flora and fauna in its path. October was warm, like, Indian summer warm, and now this sudden banjaxed hold-up assault-like plunge in temperature. Trees give up their leaves as if surrendering: so take them already, it's just foliage, you want me to empty my pockets? Urban animals—rats, rabbits, foxes—go scurrying off to whatever burrows and hidey-holes they have managed to prepare. The rest of the city's mammalia—anything on two legs or wheels—skedaddle off into centrally heated spaces or at least the comfort of the U.

Up above the police station there's a lot of buffeting going on. Flying debris, wrapping papers, autumn leaves. Far from ideal flying conditions. The birds have given up and gone home. Head-under-the-wing stuff. There's not a soul in the sky. At least, not in the immediate cylinder of sky starting on the cop shop roof and heading up into the stratosphere. Observational satellites flit by at higher altitudes chasing their designated orbital paths. National and international space stations chug leisurely by, pursuing objectives notionally noble and operationally military. Only a plucky drone operator holds his own. Dragonfly-sized remote-controlled airborne monitoring vehicles (aircams to their friends) are not the optimal surveillance vector for these conditions. A strike by a bit of flying junk, say a sheet of newspaper or a plastic bag, can have serious implications for such lightweight platforms. But to be honest, Operator M— let's call him that, since today we are clearly in some kind of liberal (small L) name-dispensing mode—hasn't had this much fun in weeks. Normally he just drones around, hanging in there, doing his skyborne monitoring thing, maybe perching on a rooftop for a bit of landing practice or to save batteries. Like, yawnsville. But today, there is at least a bit of challenge to the job, some payback on those years of console training and reflex-sharpening gaming allnighters. Factoring in all the stabilization enhancement his little unpersoned gyrocopter will allow, he acquires the target, crossmatches with her phone GPS, locks and loads and switches to auto. The resulting stream of nocturnal telemetry now transmits directly to his glasses and all he needs to do is undertake an occasional manual intervention to keep the thing on track.

Of course active drone monitoring is a little overkill just for the purposes of tracking our Claire's whereabouts—a quick review of her phone logs would have been just as effective. But it seems that for some reason unbeknownst to her, Claire has brushed against some little virtual tripwire, turned up maybe on the wrong screen at the wrong time, been in contact with some subversive reprobate that she would have been better off not knowing. Who's to tell? Not me, said the wolf. Not me, said the pig. Not me, said the little dragonfly eye in the sky operator who was after all just doing his job and who had no interest in the whys and wherefores, no stake in it, frankly couldn't give a toss. And of course, not us. We're the last around here to get told the motives for anything.

Claire moves on, oblivious. She's got a meeting of the collective at six and a date with Ilya at eight, assuming the big vegan cheeses manage to keep their egos and verbal diarrhoea in check and finish up on time. She considers walking it but opts for the bus, which, when it comes, is full to its double-decker brim with the NC's particular brand of irate nine-tofivers. The bus lurches off like it's fresh from a pitstop and comes to a precipitous halt about fifty yards down the road. Anyone standing in the bus is immediately catapulted into whoever is standing next to them, causing a human chain reaction to ripple down to the front of the bus. Claire is standing on the platform next to the driver, a woman in her early thirties with arms like a Mexican wrestler and broad range of colourful expletives at her verbal disposal. Which she deploys to skilful effect as a wave of abuse cascades down the bus towards her, echoed by voices from the top deck, casting doubt on her parentage, her driving skills, the efficacy of her leg muscles, her sexual orientation, her humanoid lineage, her immigration status, the preferability of pre-natal termination in her specific case, the unlikelihood of longevity or even of getting off of her shift in one piece. Claire grins at her sheepishly and the driver gives her a lascivious wink in return, opens the intercom and tells everyone to shut the fuck up or get out and fix the brakes if they're such wise guys.

All opprobrium immediately ceases and Claire wonders whether she has just been flirted at, or whether she herself is doing the flirting. For a brief moment she thinks of Ilya and feels confused, and momentarily guilty. Then she looks back at the driver and thinks, "Ah what the fuck," and goes with the flow for the rest of the ride.

She gets off the bus down by the rattle-bag overhead railway bridge with the driver's phone number scrawled down on the back of a ticket in her pocket and heads up the Bohemia Road towards the traffic lights, then left onto Ricksville past the plethora of prayer rooms and meeting halls like some congregational red light district, past the antiquarian smithy and the only horse-drawn undertaker left in town, past Willy's Wiener Schnitzel Palace and up onto Luxemburg Square.

She gets to the door of the collective and the lights are on but the blinds are down so she uses her key to get in.

A couple of her co-workers are still in the shop, bagging up the meagre takings from the till, wiping down the coffee machine and washing up the last of the cups. The rest of the crew are already out back, hanging around until the meeting starts.

Then the clearing up is done and the crew is complete. Phones and spex are turned to camo mode and arranged on chairs in a circle. The apps are linked to a central server that puts them through a routine of virtual calisthenics, keeping them busy while their owners nip downstairs to an alternative meeting room in the cellar. Suitably sound and tech-proofed, they turn their attention to the business at hand.

The business at hand being urban monkeywrenching, carbon sabbing, infrastructure hacks, antipolluter agitprop, direct action and generally taking the struggle to the man. It's not so much that the shop is a front—they're all seriously into it and anyway need to make a living, it's more that there's only so much mileage in a vegan lifestyle when it's total revolution you're after.

Hence the diversionary tactics. Hence the cellar.

Hence Operator M and his eye in the sky.

CHAPTER TEN
Tricks

Gene is out doing a few tricks on the street.

Just to keep his hand in.

It's not like he needs the money. His studio, his regular johns take care of that. Shit, he could make money out of his waiting list if he had a mind to.

No, he's tricking the street because he wants to. Maybe not *likes to*, but *wants to*, sure. There's some deep part of him that needs that particular fix. Needs to know what's going on, needs to breathe in the foetid air of the gutter, the exhalations of the city, the dank humours of the main drag, the exhaust fumes of the cruising johns, the perfumed auras of his sister tricksters and trickstresses.

The trans strip in fair NC is unusual in many respects. It's geographically confined to just a couple of streets, basically the corner of Columbia and Charlie's Garden that back on to Coney Heath, a large park area, which itself provides a ready source of illicit stimulants and undergrowth in which to indulge in the furtive nocturnal manoeuvres that go with the trade. It's also organized as an autonomous self-defence and mutual assistance syndicate, fully affiliated to the NFS, the National Federation of Sexworkers.

Said status due, in no small part, to the efforts of Gene and his friends. And the handy proximity of Tarik's Society Coiffeur and Massage round the corner where Columbia turns to Airport and of the main hub of the C of K down on Carlos Marx. Both of which are handy backup when push comes to shove.

These days, incidents are kept to a minimum. The johns are for the most part polite and on their best behaviour. The new ones are quick to sniff the *mores* of the street. And anyone who steps out of line rapidly finds themselves surrounded by a bunch of incensed and militant trans and drag queen sexworkers who really have zero tolerance for that kind of thing.

The pimps who used to run the place are long gone, terminally displaced after a brief but admittedly bloody struggle which didn't go well for them. A couple of well-tended shrines set into tenement walls keep the memory of the martyred sisters of the pimp wars alive.

There's also minimal spillover from the regular turf conflicts in the park. Control over the NC's distribution networks for Mary J, Special K, Apple Jack and Iced T are regularly re-decided in short but furious spats that usually end up decimating the footsoldiers and leaving the big players unscathed. However, an unspoken but well-patrolled DMZ has been established to delineate the sex trade from the drug trade, and infringements are dealt with swiftly and effectively.

Tonight, the air is clear and the girls are out in force.

Jeanie is wearing thigh-high vegan leather stiletto-heeled boots, fishnets, a black latex mini, a fat big-buckled elasticated belt, a black-and-red corsage, elbow length black satin gloves with a row of heavily encrusted and bejewelled rings over the fingers, a black feather boa, black lipstick, her best eyelashes, and her trademark shoulder length flame red shickel, artfully windswept and unkempt.

She moves through the fair, stops to chat with the girls, strokes an appreciative pensioner over his stubbly and grizzled cheek, takes a jasmine tea at the mobile noodle canteen over by the entrance to the park. Above all, watches. Not so much looking for trade as monitoring the pulse of the vibrant queer biotope, checking out the comings and goings, seeing who is on active shift, who is winding down, or maybe just taking a breather.

It's not that she even needs to do it.

Security is not her main schtick any more.

Nowadays it's more a question of routine. There's always a girl on shift in the little ground-floor shop they've rented out. The Crow's Nest. No-one gets in a car without it being logged and the registration number checked against their own dedicated database. They've even got plate scanners set up at the entrances to the strip that sound an alarm when straightlisted johns try to break their bans.

No, Jeanie likes to watch the place ticking over. She's like some old big-nosed bear that can sniff the wind and tell you there's a new hive about three klicks upwind that's just oozing honey, or some ripe piece of rancid carcass over on the other side of the river that's just about to reach its peak, or maybe some big unfamiliar and dangerous animal moving through the woods towards her brood.

Jeanie drains her tea, lights up and squints down into the rays of the setting sun.

There's a big silver phaeton turning the corner into Charlie's Garden at cruising speed. Ultra-expensive, tinted windows. Sports turbo. Big car, thinks Jean.

Little dick.

Over compensator.

Let's see what he's got for us.

The car idles slowly down the strip, pausing occasionally next to one or other of the girls, who'll go over, a window will come down, she'll lean in. A quick exchange, but no go. Fussy customer. Newbie maybe. Picky, or unsure. No accounting for taste.

Still, if you've made the decision to come *here*, you've already made a pretty major statement in terms of sexual preference. Although for some, it's not something they'd readily admit to. The *transgressive* in trans still being a major element. Forbidden fruit, and all.

The phaeton reaches the corner by the park entrance, pulls up directly opposite the noodle-mobile. A window glides effortlessly down. From the interior of the vehicle, Jean can make out a pair of dark eyes smouldering heavily in her direction. Big guy, slicked-back hair, tan, thin balbo beard outlined along his jaw, muscular frame, expensive-casual clothes.

Jeanie breathes out a mouthful of smoke and lets the seconds tick by.

There something about this guy. Something that spells trouble, casual violence, anger issues, pent-up rage. Money, power, and a habit of being obeyed.

And hatred. Lots of hatred.

Their eyes lock. He beckons her over.

She flicks the ash off of her smoke, purses her full black lips and with the tiniest sideways movement of her head gestures no. Lets her eyes glaze over. Rapidly uncurls the fingers of her right hand for him to move along. Feels a rush of adrenalin as she sees his cheeks flush and the anger rise in him. Hears a slight squeal of tires as he moves off a little too quickly.

Makes a mental note of his number.

Watches as he stops again a hundred yards down the street.

Watches as a long-legged blond-haired sister struts over to his window and leans in.

Notes the bad feeling in her guts as the sister gets into the passenger seat and the car pulls off and out onto Columbia and down in the direction of Fuji City.

Jeanie spits, flicks the stub of her smoke into the gutter and saunters over to the Crow's Nest. Cheek-kisses Sandy, the girl on watch, the requisite number of times and pulls up a chair.

"See the phaeton?"

"The big silver strap-on? Sure thing. What of it?"

"Anything pop up on the plate scanners? Any dirt on the john?"

Sandy's iridescent fingernails clack expertly over her keyboard as she chews loudly on her juicy fruit cherry.

"There's nothing. Clean skin. No previous."

"Who was that got in with him? Blond girl. "

"That'll be Ursula. Ursula Undress. One of the new ones. Why, you worried?"

Jeanie pulls on a long silver earring.

"Just didn't like the look of him, is all."

Sandy swishes her long blond hair around over one shoulder with a practiced roll of the head. She swivels round on her retro pink eggchair and looks up at Jeanie.

"I can do some scratch and sniff if you like. We've got vid feed of his eek. We can do a recognition search and that."

"Ok Sandy, see if you can widen the net a bit. Tap into dipshit DB, narks, vice, whatever. But be discreet. You know the routine."

"Sure sis." A giant silver-eyelashed wink flutters down over green cat irises.

"Mum's the word."

Time moves slowly as the street sinks into darkness. Jeanie stands at the door of the Crow's Nest and feels the cold damp air of the park waft over, laced with traces of cannabis and the dung of the animals in the petting zoo. A gust of wind sends flurries of the park's autumn debris down the strip, the barely distinguishable yellows and reds of sycamore, maple, birch leaves tumbling along the pavement at her feet.

Night is falling. Winter is coming. The dazzling and bejewelled tricksters lining the strip are fading to black, starting to blend in with the encroaching dusk.

And then, inevitably you might say, the street lights fizzle into life, to re-cast the scene in the ghastly familiarity of orange sodium lamps.

But before that, in that split second before maximum twilight and re-illumination, there was a brief moment of uncertainty.

A moment, Jeanie felt sure, that anything was possible.

CHAPTER ELEVEN
Blue-Arsed Flies

Claire's meeting is dragging on. The air down in the cellar is stale at the best of times, but with six people in it in varying degrees of agitation there seems to be no oxygen left at all.

"Ok, we've dealt with all the usual stuff, anybody have any ideas for something new?"

It's Josh who's talking. Tall and lean, with a rather Jesus-like mane of straggly curls, he's one of the main movers and shakers in their little collective.

People stare at their feet, or intently at their fingernails. The place is not only devoid of air, ideas are also in short supply.

"How about we block a motorway?"

It's Suki this time, a short butch powerhouse of a woman with a denim waistcoat and exquisite Yakuza-style tattoos running up both arms. Always up for a ruck.

"That would be like, really taking it to the auto industry. That would really hit the petrol-heads where it hurts."

Josh: "Nice idea Suki, do you think we could do it without getting arrested?"

"Or run over, or lynched?" The voice is Ramon's, the self-professed group "realist", always up for a downer.

"Ok, point taken." Josh is in full-on mediator role. "Even given the urgency of the situation, we don't want to get into anything that would take us out of action for longer periods."

"Yeah, bit Kamikaze, that one."

Charlie, tall, short dark hair, a profusion of piercings. Black eyeliner, purple lipstick. Knuckleduster rings.

"Although, you know, maybe that's what we need."

All eyes on Charlie now.

"A good bit of Kamikaze. Up the ante a bit. It's all the rage you know."

"Charlie…"

"Everyone's doing it."

Silence is the sound of several jaws dropping. Simultaneously. Even Josh is apparently lost for words.

Claire butts in.

"Guys. She's just shitting you. It's just a wind-up."

Audible sighs of relief.

"Or? Charlie?"

"Claire, trust you to rain on a girl's parade."

Charlie folds her arms with a self-satisfied grin.

"Mind you, I had you going there for a while."

Charlie turns and high-fives with Jared, the short, bearded guy seated to her left.

Josh leans forwards in his seat, pushes his analog glasses up the bridge of his nose.

"Yeah, nice one Charlie. But to tell you the truth, if we can't come up with anything serious then I'm outta here. Got other stuff lined up for tonight, if you know what I mean."

Suki makes the universal finger-on-nostril gesture of the coke snorter, while Ramon says "Oh yeah, what's his name?"

Josh's cheeks flare red and you can tell that the ragging is getting to him.

"Josh has a point," says Claire.

"Yeah, Claire's in a rush too. Can't keep lover-boy waiting."

"Fuck you, Suki. Just fucking shut it."

The temperature in the room drops 20 degrees. But Claire is just warming up.

"What is it with you guys? There's a fucking ongoing ecological catastrophe happening right now and the best thing we can come up with is to sit around backbiting and bickering? That's just so fucked up."

"Claire…" Josh makes to interrupt.

"No Josh, it's true. There are people out there on the front lines stopping pipelines or fighting whalers or confronting loggers and we're just stuck in the middle of this fucking moloch of a city and don't even know where to start."

"You mean, apart from the demos?"

"And the leaflets?"

"And the posters?"

"And the graffiti?"

"And the carbon sabbing stuff?"

Claire takes a deep breath.

"Yeah, that's all good stuff. It's probably even totally necessary stuff, and I'm not knocking it…"

"You are fucking knocking it. That's just what you've been doing."

"Ok Ramon, you're right. But I don't mean it like that. What I mean is: it totally pisses me off that we're running around like blue-arsed flies and it's getting us nowhere. And what pisses me off even more is that you guys have got nothing better to do—during a fucking meeting for god's sake—than wind me up about my new boyfriend. What the fuck has it got to do with you anyway?"

"Easy Claire."

"Yeah no offence Claire."

"Anyway, those are two separate issues," says Josh, doing his best to clear the air.

"Of course they're separate. But they're related."

"Oh yeah? Meaning what?"

"Meaning if things were really happening, if what we were doing here was really making a difference, then we wouldn't have time just to sit around carping. We'd be…"

"Out on the streets?"

"In the vanguard of the revolution?"

"Swamped by police spies?"

"In jail?"

"Dead?"

"Yeah, well maybe one or all of those things. How the hell do I know? I just know that it's not enough. And too much at the same time. And it's pissing me off."

"Claire, that's starting to sound like a resignation letter."

"Yeah, well maybe it is."

Claire, voice breaking now.

"Maybe it fucking is."

And she gets up and walks out.

Chapter Twelve
Ursula

It's just after half past seven on a cold and windy night in the NC. A car pulls up on Columbia and backs into a little side road that leads into the park. Further down the lane there are a couple of lights from dormobiles and converted trucks, suggesting some semblance of habitation, but up this end there's nothing, just the detritus you'd expect from a bunch of people making out in their cars. A door opens and a long-legged figure is roughly ejected and collapses onto the verge, bleeding and torn. The door is pulled to and the vehicle speeds off in a cloud of dust, turns down Columbia and heads off past the police motorcycle barracks in the general direction of Fuji City.

Ursula needs time before she can even attempt to move. She lays a while breathing heavily, smelling the musty earth below the grass and nettles her upper body is lying in, feeling the abrasive scratch of the gravelly dirt rubbing its way into the lesions on her knees.

Finally she finds the energy to make it onto all fours. She hangs there panting like a dog, her long hair hanging down around her face and forearms, feeling the pains in her ribs, her jaw, nose, stomach, ass. She grits her remaining teeth and struggles to her feet. She has hardly attained her full height when she doubles up again as a stream of bile forces its way up her digestive tract and she heaves the vile-tasting liquid up and out into the night.

She wipes her mouth with the back of her hand and sees a smear of blood along with the spew, snot and mascara stains that have accumulated on her face.

Giddily, unsteadily, she puts one foot before the other and heads towards the street lights down on Columbia.

A bunch of guys hanging out in front of the new mosque on the corner of Columbia and the unnamed track leading up to the baseball diamond see a lanky figure in fishnets and miniskirt staggering drunkenly towards them. They're all big-city guys, so the sight itself doesn't elicit much of a response from them. Only when she is finally level with them do they realize something is seriously wrong. She raises a hand as if to hail a cab, and in doing so, twists and folds in on herself and collapses onto the pavement.

The guys do the honourable thing and pick her up, carry her into the courtyard and lay her down on a divan in one of the small rooms in the outbuildings adjacent to the mosque proper. They're debating what to do, whether to call the ambulance or the cops or both when a voice from the divan says, "No cops."

That raises a few eyebrows and gives cause for a few knowing looks, but these guys are also used to taking care of their own so they acquiesce and say, "Ambulance?", but their unexpected guest just shakes her rather lopsided tresses and with considerable effort finally produces a card from a gold lamé clutch bag she has somehow managed to hang on to.

The card says simply "The Crow's Nest" with a number printed underneath it.

Jeanie is still sat in the Crow's Nest nursing a coffee when the call comes in. She hasn't been much further than the end of the street ever since Ursula got in the car, and certainly hasn't been in a mood to turn any tricks so far this evening. This is the third time she has been back into the Crow's Nest, each time on a pretext, with a brief question —"Any news of Ursula?"—thrown in.

Now there is news. Sandy has taken the call, and Jeanie can immediately tell that something is up. By the time Sandy has written down the address she's shaking and the tears are streaming down her face, so Jeanie just takes the pad from her hands and kicks things into motion. The first call is for a car, which arrives within two minutes. The second is to the Church of Kali, medical emergency coming in. Then she turns to Sandy, who is blowing her nose into a Kleenex.

"You gonna be ok?"

She reaches out and wipes a smear of mascara away with her thumb.

"Sure, I'm fine. It was just the shock."

"Then I want you to put the word out as quickly as possible. I want that phaeton straightlisted now. I want the name of that john as soon as we can, and I want that bastard delivered up on a platter. I want every queer sexworker in the entire fucking NC on the lookout for this guy. And we need to make sure that we've got enough security on the strip and that everyone knows what has happened. Think you can handle that?"

Sandy looks up at her with her big green eyes.

"Sure Jeanie, I'm on it." She turns back to her console. Then, as an afterthought: "How about you?"

Jeanie throws back the rest of her coffee as a large red car pulls up outside.

"I'm going for Ursula."

It's not often you'll see a congregation of the Muslim faithful handing over a six-foot semi-conscious transvestite to a carload of militant queer prostitutes wielding baseball bats. But the NC is always good for a few surprises and tonight would seem to be one of those nights. Jeanie and her pals roll up in a big 6-wheeler requisitioned on the spur of the moment and come to a screeching halt in front of the mosque. They've got their warning lights flashing and one of the girls stays with the car and opens up the tailgate whilst the others march over towards the main entrance to the mosque, their movements carefully monitored by an array of state-of-the-art security equipment angled down towards them from the top of high concrete walls. They are met at the gate by a besuited delegation of guys from the mosque, who don't exactly bar their way into the grounds, but simply fill the space in the doorway. Jeanie is in no mood for messing around but one of the suits simply opens his palm in a gesture for them to stop and says: "Please wait, we'll bring her".

And so there's this little standoff while they go to get Ursula. But in spite of the situation being fraught and all, there is not much in the way of aggression going on. Jeanie's girls are riled up, and would be more than up for cracking the skull of any straight dick that came their way, but they can appreciate that these guys are actually helping them out here.

For the mosque security detail, this is certainly the first time that they've had a bunch of sexy genderbending mommas come up to the gates of their prayer house wielding billy clubs, but they are more intrigued than anything else, and are keeping a remarkably worldly cool about the whole thing. Jeanie even recognizes a couple of guys as regular cruisers of the strip, which after all is just down the road, past the overnight layby for transcontinental muslim truck drivers. But if those guys recognize her, or any of the girls, they are certainly not admitting it and keeping well to the back of the security group.

After what seems like an age, Ursula is carried out, ceremonially, in a kind of role-reversal Pietà scene. One of their guys has simply picked her up in his arms and she has her arm around his neck and her head on his chest, but is otherwise too weak to do much anything else. The throng of suits and other members of the congregation part as they come down the steps towards the gate, where she is carefully delivered over to two of the girls, who, between them, carry her back to the car and lay her on some blankets spread out in the back.

Jeanie, in parting, doesn't say anything, but instead raises her hand to her heart, lowers her eyelids and bows her head slightly in thanks.

And with that, they're gone.

CHAPTER THIRTEEN
Function of Unpredictability

Nights in the NC are a mixed bag.

Some nights are joyous, even riotous affairs.

Riotous in the sense that there is a riot going on.

Then the police come storming in, crack a few heads, spray some pepper and maybe even fire some baton rounds, rubber bullets, non-lethal pellets, just to keep their hand in. They'll do a bit of kettling, which is good for the overtime, and send in a few drones for facial recognition and permanent-dye colour tagging before sending the snatch squads after the ringleaders.

Operator M in particular is a great fan of such days. There is real action going on, and he gets to fly the bigger, tooled-up models with all the software options enabled. What fun! On nights like that he'll go home as dawn is breaking, weary, but contented.

Nights like that make it all seem worthwhile.

There are other nights in the NC, however.

Nights in which the world seems poised between two states, literally on a knife's edge. Nights in which Schrödinger's cat is still making up its mind which way it's going to jump, still bearing the possibility of extended life and sudden death within itself.

On those nights, there have been reports, which perhaps should be just discounted as rumours, of the world slipping sideways when one least expects it. Everything will be hunky dory until you turn a corner and discover someone bleeding to death on the pavement. And if you're lucky this person won't be you.

Perhaps some future scientist of psychosocial phenomena will be able to unravel the mysteries of random violence (Vr) in the urban context. He or she will come up with a formula, a scientific law suggesting that the pseudo-Brownian motion induced in a given social body X will have n degree of chemically induced agitation, modified by a three-dimensional array of socially aggravating factors *aggr*, multiplied by a globally mitigated media-induced rage factor R, with a tangential impact of genetic disposition and psychotic modifiers Q, processed of course through an overarching function of unpredictability *ran()*:

$$Vr = ran(X^{n/}aggr[i]*R \rightarrow tan(\theta))$$

Q

Having scrawled this down, perhaps quaintly, archaically, on a large green chalkboard, he or she may then cry, "Eureka!" and rush out to receive the Nobel peace prize or attack their spouse with a carving knife.

But this is all mere speculation.

For tonight is not one of those nights. Neither the former nor the latter.

Tonight is a night for retreat, withdrawal, wound-licking. A night for battening down the hatches, for weathering the storm, for waiting for dawn. A night to be with your loved ones. Or, if you can't be with them, then to love the one you're with.

It's ten o'clock. Let's take stock.

Jeanie is sitting by Ursula's bed down in the medical bay at the Church of Kali. Ursula has been examined, and stitched up, and given something to make her sleep. She's lost two teeth, has a broken jaw, three cracked ribs, a ruptured sphincter, multiple lesions and abrasions. Fortunately no major internal bleeding. She's young, and she'll be ok, but the trauma will keep her off the streets for a while, if not permanently.

Jean holds her hand and broods darkly. Every now and then a medical sister will come quietly in to check up on Ursula or ask Jeanie if she needs anything.

Jeanie doesn't need anything. She's in a deep, dark, secluded space where anger is distilled into action. She's in the calm before her storm.

Claire is in bed with Ilya, who has his arms around her. They had a few drinks in the pub after Claire's meeting, but more or less gave up on the rest of the evening and headed back to his place. Unusually for her, Claire is not up for sex. She's feeling shaken and confused, and just needs someone to hold onto her, and Ilya will do for that. It's not a role he's used to, but he seems to be good at it, and for the moment at least he's managing to ignore his erection and just give her some comfort. Claire's no dope, and she knows herself well enough to realize there will be a little more action later on this evening, but right now she just needs to let it settle and to work through the turmoil swilling around in her mind and her emotions. So she lies there in his arms, and lets herself feel safe, for the moment, and is grateful to him for that.

Jimmy is on his way home after standing in line at the cop shop with Claire. It's actually not very far, as the drone flies, from there to the B Village. But Jimmy has to negotiate a veritable minefield of temptation, has to run the gauntlet of gin-joints and speakeasies aplenty. He's a man on a mission, and the mission is: Gotta tell Julia. She has a right to know goddammit and stop being such a fucking juvenile about it. And yet, and yet. There's that little Jimmy leprechaun that's sitting on his shoulder saying just a wee dram won't hurt ye. Jimmy's leprechaun is a Tam O'Shanter lookalike with a broad Scots accent, but the Singapore Irish Changs are known for their pan-Gaelic affiliations so it's really nothing to worry about.

Jimmy's beeline for home took him via Cranky Franky's on Inn Street, Be My Valentine on Danube and Patty's Poison Palace on the corner of Danube and Finkelstien. All of which is such a roundabout path it might better be considered as a diversionary tactic. Jimmy's final pass at the B Village takes him down Richard and up Heisenberg to Gary's Viking juke joint, which is where he is now, propping up the bar in a thoroughly maudlin manner. Not that that is any worry to Gary, who is used to having his clientele falling asleep on their bar stools or gracelessly sliding off of their chairs onto the floor. The air in this place is such a nicotine fug that it's surprising that the guests are even aware of each other through the zero-visibility conditions.

Jimmy clutches his whiskey and slurs his cares across the counter in the general direction of Gary, who is polishing glasses with a rancid tea towel.

"Doc says I'm dying man."

"We're all dying, man," says Gary. Being of a Viking ethos, he is unperturbed by the inevitability, nay, proximity, of death.

"It's not the when, it's the how." Gary warms to the topic.

"Come again?"

"Death'll get you, any which ways you care to look at it. That's about the only damn thing you can be sure of in this life."

"Yeah, so?"

"So if you're going to have a death—sooner, later, whatever—better make sure it's a good one, if you want to get to Valhalla."

"Dude, I don't want to get to Valhalla."

Jimmy takes another swig.

"No offence man, but I don't dig Val-bleeding-Halla. No janna, no heaven, no afterlife, no Shangri-fucking-La. I'm a fucking atheist, for god's sake."

The NC's only known black Viking puts down his tea towel and leans in close.

"So if you don't want a good death, what is it that you want?"

Jimmy sniffs and a tear runs down his face.

"I just want to go home to Julia, man."

Gary's giant paw slaps Jimmy tenderly on the cheek.

"Just aim for the door dude, and keep on walking. I'll put the drinks on your tab."

Our man Al Firengi is feeling sated. He's finishing up a fine bottle of East Coast Chablis and is picking the remains of his impeccable dinner out of his impeccable teeth. It's not often he spends a night at home in his bachelor pad, but here he is, slightly flushed with drink and half way through *Apocalypse Now Redux*, a film he has seen so often he can quote Colonel Kurtz by heart. He could quote the rest of the film's characters if he wanted to, but none of the other characters quite do it for him the way Kurtz does.

Al was thirteen the first time he saw the film. He spent the summer after that collecting snails and encouraging them to crawl along the edge of a razor blade, just to see if it was really true. He repeated the experiment often and enthusiastically, but the results were disappointing. He put it down to poor methodology and inadequate emulation of his idol.

Al vowed to do better.

Right now, Al's enjoying his down time. He has had a little R&R—all in all a fine, enjoyable evening. Tomorrow will be back to the grind. Now that the selection process is over—thanks to the assiduous efforts of that ball-breaker Laila—it's time to start knocking his lowlife elite into shape. Got to move things along, keep the momentum going. Places to go, people to fuck up.

Al uncorks another bottle and rolls himself a smoke.

Settles into the second half of the film.

A few hundred metres away—though to tell the truth it could be on another planet—Suleika nurses a battered cooking pot and its meagre contents as if someone were about to steal it from her. Understandable, since this is something that has happened to her more than once. She's in a bare communal kitchen in one of the deeper recesses of Fuji City. It's late to be cooking, but it means she has the place more or less to herself.

She's spent the day on her patch outside the Arcades, keeping her head down but her eyes open. One of the girls at the Church gave her some garlic and a tin of fava beans, and as she headed back up to Fuji City she even found some nettles and dandelion, which she stuffed into the folds of her clothes even though it left weals on her hands. She knows it's late in the year, and the nettles will be stringy and tough, so she chops them as finely as she can and hopes for the best.

She is sitting at the little table by the window, spooning her soup, when the sound of the door makes her look up in momentary panic. But it's only the Asmadi girl from a couple of cubicles down the line. The girl is about eight or nine with bright brown eyes in an angelic face framed with dark curls. For a moment she stands hesitantly in the doorway, until Suleika gestures to her to come over.

She comes, shy as a fawn, and holds out a hand, clenched around something silver.

"*Nenek, untuk anda.*"

Suleika can only nod her encouragement, for want of a common tongue. Still, they share the common language of the castaway, the dispossessed, and something beyond words passes between them. And Suleika unfurls a bony hand and into it is pressed a little silver package and the girl turns and is gone.

And Suleika places the little gift on the table and ceremoniously unwraps it, to find a little square of chocolate.

Suleika weeps, then finishes her soup, then weeps some more.

Then she takes a knife, and cuts the square into eight, even smaller pieces.

And each little piece she pops into her mouth, where it ignites the smallest of smiles upon her face.

Chapter Fourteen
The a.m.

When Ilya is not to be found in Claire's bed, or otherwise erotically involved in the passionate vagaries of their relationship, he is, inevitably, located at some interface to the virtual. Although admittedly old-fashioned, with the recherché love of the antiquated that only the young can affect with any style, he is, in reality, quite agnostic about the appliances he works with. Sure, his weapon of choice will almost invariably be his old blackbox no-logo machine with its quaint keyboard input. But he has his spex, and his wetware, and any number of intelligent devices that he has modified to suit his own particular purposes.

There is something languid, pre-Raphaelite about his movements as his long fingers flit and his head makes those small, jerky movements that betray ocular cursor inputs.

When Claire wakes up she finds him sitting over by the window, filtering data from his spex and typing at the same time. He's wearing a pair of black jeans and a raggedy black vest, and there's a cup of coffee in front of him on the table. She slinks up to him from behind, puts an arm around his torso and kisses his neck down to his shoulder, her long red hair falling down around his face.

He cranes his neck around till his mouth finds hers and she comes awake to his sweet coffee kiss.

Her palm passes across the flatness of his stomach, and before she can think any further she is undoing his belt buckle and the buttons of his jeans.

Ilya shifts in his seat as her hand encloses his dick and hooks it free of his pants and he's caught between kissing her and saying, "Claire, lover, just let me, uh, just let me finish this…"

But finishing this doesn't really figure in Claire's plans right now and she gently takes the laptop and places it on the table.

She grabs him by the nipples—first one, then the other, as he pushes back from the table and she swings round in front of him. Then she's down in a crouch and taking the head of his dick in her mouth and savouring the dark taste of it. She twists a nipple and bites gently into his glans with her teeth and she can feel him arch back, hear him moan. There's a sheen of sweat on the muscles of his belly and she can feel a surge of blood to her clit and a shudder of energy passes through her cunt.

She sucks hard on his dick and pulls away with a rush of saliva into her mouth, which she spits out onto the palm of her hand and pulls across her labia. Then she's on him, takes him in, encompasses him, and grinding her clit into him as she sweeps him along.

They're both gasping for breath now as they're rocking and rolling but Ilya manages a brief flash of practicality with "What about a condom?", which is sweet, but Claire's like: "Don't stop, it's ok," so now there's no holding them back as the chair starts to creak and protest beneath them until Ilya manages to get up with Claire's legs wrapped firmly around him and walk over to the bed, and he's just about to drop the two of them down with her underneath when she twists him around like a horse and she's got her two knees on the mattress and it's him she's riding, and the old bed is not really making any less noise than the chair but at least the chances of it breaking beneath them aren't as great, and if it breaks who cares, there's a mattress between them and the floor.

And as Claire rides and the two of them sweat and groan and scratch and seek each other with tongues and mouths and fingers, part of Claire is still wrapped up in last night's arms and is surprised to find herself lingering in the warmth of that space. And that space is infusing this space, which is a different place entirely, and maybe there is a part of her that wants to keep those places separate for all time but another mad woman inside her is busy tearing down the walls to something that feels like a flood of light and heat that's illuminating every part of her being and they are both coming together in a long spiraling orgasm that leaves them exhausted and spent and feeling like something between them has just irreparably shifted.

And for a moment they linger in that shared space between waking and sleep and then they're gone, sliding into brief darkness before starting the day anew.

There's a bleary sun rising over the NC and Jimmy thinks he's going to be sick. He has staggered out of bed to take a leak and has gone out onto the balcony in the hope that the cold might shock him into some semblance of humanity. Down on the street, a cacophony of kids passes by on their way to school. The wind is blowing in from the south-east, so the air is tinged with the sweet stench of the biscuit factory, and, further out, the big coffee factory on the edge of town. Jimmy is standing there in a t-shirt, pyjama bottoms, bare feet. His skin and hair still stink of nicotine. His eyes are watering. He feels his stomach churning and goes back inside, quickly closing the door to the balcony and heading over to the bathroom, where he goes down on his knees, opens the lid with one hand and sticks the fingers of the other down his throat in the familiar three-part ritual of supplication-regurgitation-atonement.

Supplication. The subject kneels at the altar of the deity of choice and asks for forgiveness for sins committed. See also: prostration.

The liturgy of regurgitation: The speaking of the sacred words "Ah-huh-ah, hak, hak." Expungement.

Atonement: The wiping of the mouth with the back of one's hand. Ablutions performed with water from the tap of life applied generously to the face. The ritual oath of non-repetition.

Jimmy steps out of the bathroom.

Oblivion.

Jimmy wakes to see the sun streaming in, reflected from a million crystal glints from the surface of the sea. They are on a boat, and the light is dancing around the cabin, forming patterns on the walls and ceiling. His mother has brought him a glass of juice and says, "Get up Jimmy, you'll be late for school". Jimmy is surprised to find that he is eight or nine years old. He is also surprised to see his mother, because she's been dead for ten years now. He says, "Ma, I thought you were dead," and his ma says, "Yes dear, I know, but none of that matters now." She strokes his hair and her eyes are warm but her hands are cold. Jimmy says, "And Pa, is he dead too?"

"Yes dear, quite dead. Now drink your juice and hurry up and get dressed. Mrs Lee will be cross if you're late again."

Jimmy sits up and goes to drink his juice but finds that he can't swallow it. There is something moving around in his mouth and he doesn't know what to do with it. His mother is sitting there on the edge of the bed with her hands folded in her lap, waiting for something. Jimmy looks down into the glass and can see white things surfacing and wriggling in the orange juice. Some kind of larvae, or maybe maggots.

Jimmy looks at his mother, who sighs impatiently and says, "Come along dear, we haven't got all day."

Jimmy's mother fishes a maggot from her ear and pops it in her mouth.

Jimmy spits the contents of his own mouth back into the glass but there is somehow more in there than was ever in the glass. He emits an incessant stream of maggot juice back into the glass, which boils over with a sudden proliferation of maggots, as if they have all along just been waiting for such a signal, and now there is an eruption of maggots that spill out of the glass and onto the bed and Jimmy's Ma is leaking maggots too and the door opens and it's Jimmy's Pa in a state of advanced decomposition and Jimmy screams and screams but the bed just swallows him up and he sinks down through the bottom of the bed and down through the boat into the cold dark water below. In a way it's a relief to be in the water because all of the maggots float up and away from him, to be gobbled up by swarms of scaly fish with big eyes and sharp, jagged teeth. Jimmy sinks down to the bottom of the sea and comes to rest on a reef. A dolphin swims up and says, "You're Jimmy, the dead guy?" and Jimmy says, "Yeah that's me," but it comes out as a big gloop bubble of air. The dolphin sticks its snout in his face and says, "What ya doing down here? You'll be late for school," and Jimmy thinks that's funny, like, school of dolphins or what, but the dolphin is in no mood for malingering and is slapping his face with its fins. Jimmy is like, "Hey, cut that out," but the dolphin keeps on slapping and saying, "Get up Jimmy, get up".

Jimmy wakes to find Julia kneeling over him. She's slapping his face and shaking him and when he opens his eyes she bursts into tears and hugs him. He strokes her hair and wonders what he's doing on his back in the hallway. There's a huge pain in his head and his throat hurts and his back hurts and he generally feels like shit.

Julia says, "Jimmy, you alright?" and Jimmy says, "Yeah".

"You want me to call a doctor?"

"No, no doctor. I'm good."

"Good, my arse."

And Jimmy pats her ass and feels her relaxing, and he takes a deep breath and there they are, just lying uncomfortably on the floor in the hallway.

After a while Julia pulls back and says, "Jimmy, what the fuck is going on? Tell me this is just the drink. Look at the state of you. And Jesus, you stink like a polecat."

Jimmy reaches up a hand to stroke her face and she grasps it and holds it to her cheek and kisses the back of his hand. Her eyes are red from crying and she looks drawn and haggard.

He says, "Julia, babe, it's not just the drink. It's nowhere near just the drink," and her eyes widen and before she can say anything he says, "But maybe we can talk about it on the sofa, yeah?"

So they shift over to the sofa and Jimmy gives her the rundown of the story so far, the cancer, the Doc, the drug somewhere over in Southeast Asia, but he leaves out the bit about feeling free in the face of death because he's certainly not feeling anywhere near free at the moment, just old and decrepit and ill and in pain.

Julia takes it well. She cries some more and hugs him and says, "How long have you known?" and "Why didn't you tell me earlier you dope?"

but apart from that she's ok. She goes to the kitchen to make some coffee while Jimmy stretches out on the sofa.

When she comes back she says, "When are you going?"

And he says, "I don't even have the money yet."

And she says, "Fuck the money. I'll give you the money. I've got some savings stashed away."

Jimmy raises an eyebrow.

"Some that you don't know about," and they both manage a smile.

She's sitting next to him, perched on the edge of their L-shaped sofa, with both hands clasping her mug of coffee.

She looks at him and Jimmy is struck by how beautiful she is.

She says, "This doc. Do you trust him?"

"Doc Mucus? Sure, trust him with my life."

"Do you need a second opinion?"

Jimmy props himself up on one elbow, reaches over to the coffee table for his mug.

"Never thought of that."

He takes a swig.

"No. Can't see the point. Me and the Doc go a long way back. He knows his stuff. Wouldn't bullshit me, that's for sure."

"Sure you're sure?"

"Hell yes. He's always given it to me straight."

Julia takes a look out of the window. A few remaining red leaves from a Virginia creeper wave at her from beyond the pane.

"Then this is your best shot. It's your only chance. Jimmy, honey. I don't want you sitting around here just waiting to die. If this is what it takes, then we have to do this."

Jimmy looks at her, wide-eyed.

"We?"

"Sure honey. I'm coming with you."

"Julia, love. Something tells me that is a really bad idea."

Gene is back at the Crow's Nest, sitting opposite Sandy, who has come in specially. Normally there wouldn't be anybody here this early in the day. Gene is nursing a mug of coffee and looking drawn, like he's been on an all-nighter that didn't go so well. He's in straight drag, no make-up. Sandy has her hair up in some kind of elaborate chignon.

There's a grey, sober world on the other side of the window, and Gene is glad he's not in it. Not that he's anything but sober. The sun has tried and failed to cut through the clouds that lie low and heavy on the NC and sweep in on a chill east wind.

Gene takes another swig of his coffee.

"Ok Sandy, so how did it go? Did you come up with anything?"

Sandy turns from her screen, leans back in her chair and crosses her long legs, smoothing down imaginary creases in her jeans.

"Nothing. A total blank."

"Huh."

Gene doesn't need to say anything. Sandy can tell that he's not happy.

"Jeanie, I don't think you understand. When I say a total blank, I mean total. There's nothing. This guy doesn't even exist."

"Meaning what, exactly?"

"Meaning he doesn't show up on any of the normal sources that we tap into. I tried to access his vehicle registration details and got bounced out of there before I could even breathe. So I figured out maybe we need a more subtle approach. I have a few botnet routines lined up as backup. They'll usually get us what we need if we don't want to go through the front door. But they just kinda got swatted away. What can I say? It's like the mere fact of asking set off some kind of tripwire, and they just clamped down on everything. I gave it everything I got, and I hate to say it Jeanie, but we're fucked."

"So there's nothing?"

"Nothing except what we started with. We've got his plates, we've got a fuzzy mugshot from one of the street cameras..."

"And we've got Ursula."

Sandy adjusts her hairdo with the blunt end of a pencil.

"Well sure. Did you talk to her? She give you a description?"

Gene looks down into his coffee.

"No. She was still out when I left. They gave her something to make her sleep, and she was pretty shook up anyway. I'll look round later today to see if she has anything for us."

"Yeah, well good luck with that. Give her our love. Oh, and the girls chipped in for some flowers. They're over on the desk. You wanna take them in with you?"

Claire comes awake to the sound of a coffee cup being placed on the bedside table and the flesh-on-flesh warmth of Ilya sliding back into bed.

She props herself up on a pillow and takes a swig of the coffee, feeling it warm up her guts and bring the day into a kind of focus. She's in a warm space with Ilya, but it's the collective that comes to mind first. She lets out a groan.

"You ok?"

"Yeah, I'm good."

"You always groan when you're good?"

"Um, more of a moan I guess."

"I don't mean like that."

There's a pause while Ilya pulls back a little to look at her, runs his fingers along her cheek, lightly caresses her ear.

"I mean, seriously. You can *talk* to me you know. Whatever it is."

She looks at him then. Leans over and kisses him.

"I know. Thanks."

"But everything good with us?"

"Sure, you dummy." She takes another swig of coffee. "This has nothing to do with you. It's more like, life, the universe, and everything else."

Ilya's face breaks into a broad grin.

"Ah, well, that's ok then, if that's all it is. Better have some breakfast before you start dealing with that."

Ten minutes later they're showered and sat by the window at Ilya's table. There are slices of cheese and blackberry jam and Ilya has even managed to clear away his computer gear and produce a little chequered tablecloth from one of his kitchen drawers.

"So what's the deal, Claire? Do you want to offload some of those worldly cares onto me?"

She turns her gaze from the window to look at him, feels the pull of his warm, dark eyes and the openness of his expression. She washes her toast down with more coffee and wipes the blackberry jam from her mouth with the back of her hand.

"Ilya, does it ever get you down? The way things are so fucked up?"

"Fucked up? Hmmm, maybe. Like in what way? You mean politically?"

"No. Well maybe that too. But I'm thinking more globally. Environmentally. Like, where are we going with all this shit? Like, we're living some kind of slow-motion train crash and I get the feeling there's nothing we can do about it. And it's not even that nobody cares. Everybody cares."

"Everybody?" he raises an eyebrow.

"Well, everybody except the government and the oil industry, obviously. And the rednecks. And the fundamentalists. But it's all so enormous that we just feel overwhelmed by it. Kind of crushed. We're trashing the planet and fucking it up for future generations forever and here we are drinking coffee and outside people are just walking around and going to work as if nothing is happening. As if nothing is wrong. And that's the trouble. For them, nothing is wrong. But for me, everything is wrong. Do you get me?"

Ilya's face is serious.

"This is about the collective, right? You in some kind of clinch with them?"

Claire does a kind of open-mouthed palms-up WTF expression.

"Do I talk in my sleep or something? How the fuck can you know that?"

"It's no big deal. Maybe I don't know so much about you. But I know that the collective is where you do all that serious let's-get-out-and-change-the-world stuff. And if it's the weight of the world getting you down, I figure it must also be the collective that's not doing its bit to keep it from you."

"Jesus Ilya, you some kind of shrink in your spare time? Where did you get all of that stuff from?"

"So am I right?"

"You're totally right."

"So is there anything I can do to help?"

She smiles and strokes his cheek with the back of her fingers.

"I guess not."

They are quiet for a while then. Ilya gets up to make some more toast. Claire goes back to looking out of the window.

The toast pops up out of the toaster and Ilya catches it and whisks it across to the table in one fell swoop.

"Claire, here's the deal," says Ilya, sitting himself back down on his chair.

"That big burden you've got on your shoulders? Why don't you just leave that here for the day? Maybe take the day off? Call in sick. Do something trivial, touristy, whatever. Maybe go to the little zoo over on Coney Heath?"

"No. No zoos."

"Well a museum then. Or a gallery. Or ice cream. Or pancakes. Or a bookstore…"

He takes her hand. She smiles a wan smile back at him.

"Ok. If you think it will do any good."

"It'll do you good. Believe me."

"But what about you? Aren't you coming with me?"

"I've got a lot of stuff I need to take care of today. But I'll take some time off work this afternoon. I can catch up with you sometime after lunch."

"Promise?"

"Promise."

He leans in close.

"Claire, you know that you're the best thing ever happened to me?"

"Ever?"

She kisses him.

"You better believe it."

For Laila, the day started well but has been sliding steadily downhill ever since. She had an unexpected one-nighter with a woman she picked up in a bar—a vigorous long-haired Canadian by the name of Tanita, with an easy laugh and a facility for coming straight to the point. They were very drunk by the time they got back to Laila's apartment, but not too drunk to fuck in an admirably athletic fashion for the best part of an hour. On waking, Laila feels a tinge of trepidation. She's worried that she'll open her eyes and regret her choice, that the alcohol-fuelled glow will have worn off, that she'll want to usher her amorous guest out of her bed and her flat as quickly as possible. Her head hurts, she feels sore, she has scratch marks on her back and bruises on her butt. With eyes closed she can sense the sunlight filtering into the room, feel the room warming up as the central heating kicks in. She decides to risk it. She opens her eyes, and the first thing she sees are the smile, twinkling eyes and tousled hair of Tanita, who greets her with a "Morning gorgeous" and a kiss on the lips. Tanita tastes of whiskey, and sex, and some other indefinable ingredient that gives Laila the urge to explore the deeper recesses of her throat with her tongue, if it would reach that far. Her fingers touch on a velvety cheek and the fine line of her jawbone as they kiss, then wander down to collarbone, shoulder, breast, with a nipple already hard and alert. Her mouth disconnects from Tanita's, re-connects with her breast.

Tanita laughs, throaty and vibrant.

"You don't waste any time."

"Who has time to waste?" says Laila, as her hand slides down between Tanita's legs.

Cue alarm on bedside table.

Laila groans, and Tanita can feel the energy draining out of her as activities of both hand and mouth come to a grinding halt.

"Shit, gotta be at work in an hour," says Laila, and rolls over onto her back, silencing the vile electronic chirp of the alarm with a slap of the hand.

Tanita is not deterred.

"Maybe still time for a quickie, eh?"

But Laila is already rolling over, out of bed and onto her feet.

"No, no quickies. I'm on a tight schedule. Shower, dress, breakfast, out. That kind of schedule. My boss doesn't like it when I'm late. Sorry."

"Fuck your boss," Tanita calls to Laila's back as she heads into the bathroom.

Laila turns on the shower taps and sits down on the can.

"No," she laughs, "that's just about the last thing I can see myself doing."

By the time Laila gets out of the shower, Tanita is sitting on the edge of the bed. Laila walks over, drying herself with a large bath towel.

"If you get a move on, you can have some breakfast before you go."

Tanita looks up at Laila, who has cast her towel away on to the back of a chair, and is standing there before her, muscled, naked, magnificent.

Tanita slides out of bed and onto her knees.

"Hmm, breakfast," she says, burying her face in the mound before her. "That sounds grand."

The sex was great. Brief, intense, overpowering. Laila comes a couple of times just standing there. Tanita brings her off with her tongue, and herself with her fingers. It's all good. But it leaves Laila with a sour taste in her mouth. Her schedule. She'll be late. Al won't like it.

She heads back into the bathroom as Tanita collapses back onto the bed.

She emerges almost immediately and starts plucking clothing out of a wardrobe. A couple of minutes later she is fully clothed. She turns to Tanita.

"You'd better get dressed."

She can tell that Tanita is more than a little irritated by her change in appearance. Last night in the bar she wore jeans, a t-shirt, a sweatshirt. And up till now they have both been naked. But now Laila is standing there in her power-dressing pants suit and it makes them both feel un-comfortable. Tanita is still stretched out on the bed. She rolls over lan-guidly onto one side.

"Smart duds."

"Yep."

"What is it you said you do?"

"Tanita," she snaps. "It doesn't fucking matter what I do. I need you to get your ass into gear, get dressed, and get the fuck out of here."

She looks over at the clock.

"I'm running late, and that's something I really hate."

Tanita is up now, and pulling on her stuff.

"There's no need to be such a fascist about it. You didn't mind run-ning late with my tongue stuck up your cunt."

"You don't understand. It's not me who's the fascist…"

"You mean it's your boss?"

Tanita pulls her t-shirt over her head, turns to face Laila, eyes blazing.

"So what does that make you? A fucking underling for some corpo-rate fascist asshole? Or what is it you're telling me? There's absolutely no fucking need for this."

"Look, Tanita, I'm sorry it's turned out like this…"

Tanita has sat herself down in a chair, and is pulling on her socks and boots.

"Sorry? The fuck you're sorry. Jeez, what a waste. I wouldn't have bothered if I'd a known you had such a bug up your ass."

Tanita is fully dressed now. She's wearing jeans, hiking boots, a t-shirt and a thick red and black plaid shirt over the top. She draws herself up in front of Laila and is taller than her by a couple of inches easy.

"I think you'd better leave."

"Damn right. There's a bad taste that I gotta get rid of."

And with that she's out into the hallway, picks up her rucksack and jacket from the coat stand, opens the door and slams it behind her.

That was the opener. What a pisser. Now, she's racing across town on her street machine, her smart suit hidden beneath her leather jumpsuit, her face masked by the dark visor of her jet helmet, and she knows there's no way she can make it on time.

She swears violently into her facemask as some dumb-ass car driver pulls out unexpectedly, causing her to swerve out into the road. She struggles to keep the machine from sliding out from under her and turns to give the driver the finger as she opens the throttle to race on down the street.

Her way into Fuji City takes her up by the park, up the cobblestones of Kittyhawk Street, past the ornate French style graveyard with its elaborate mausoleums and family tombs and up towards the police motorcycle barracks. She turns right along Columbia and pulls into Fuji City through one of the rear gates.

She leaves her bike on its kickstand and races up the stairs towards the office she shares with Al. But the door is locked. Sure, she has a key. But it shouldn't be locked, not at this time of day. She looks around desperately, sweating now, in her leathers, in this overheated building. Down at the end of the hallway, she can see light coming through the frosted glass in the doors to the assembly room. Makes sense. Al said something yesterday about wanting to "Address the troops".

She heads down the corridor as quickly as she can without breaking into a jog. When she reaches the door she transfers her helmet to her other hand, runs her fingers through her hair, takes a deep breath, and pushes the double doors open.

Al is in there, standing in front of 25-30 men of various ages, who are seated in a semicircle, as if they are at some kind of seminar. He's been addressing them in Arabic, and doesn't even bother to switch as he turns to face Laila.

"Ah, Miss Lahijani. So kind of you to grace us with the pleasure of your presence."

Laila feels the blood rising to her face, and all eyes upon her.

"Sir, I'm sorry. The traffic."

"The traffic, of course. A bane in the life of this great city of ours."

Al rolls his eyes for the benefit of his all-male audience and makes a gesture of welcome to Laila, as if inviting her onto a catwalk.

"Miss Lahijani is a passionate rider of motorcycles. Not so, Miss Lahijani? She has her own, powerful machine parked outside as we speak. Miss Lahijani, why don't you come forward, and show the gentlemen your protective clothing?"

Laila's heart is in her mouth. She can't believe Al is doing this to her. Making her walk out in front of these guys. Effectively destroying the status she had during the interviews with these men, the power over their lives. She realizes suddenly that all of that was just something that Al had temporarily endowed her with, and was now very publicly taking away.

But what to do? Turn on her heels and walk away? It's certainly what she feels like doing. But something inside her stops her. Maybe it's the situation, or the power of Al's presence. Or maybe it's just the money, or her innate sense of discipline. Whatever it is, Laila doesn't feel she has much of a choice as she steps forward into the centre of the room.

She stares at Al, as if the intensity of her gaze could transmit her thoughts, could tell him to stop this charade, this punishment. But if Al is capable of receiving her telepathic transmissions, he's either not showing it, or ignoring it. His eyes are cold and hard as she walks towards him. He takes her hand and lifts it ostentatiously to shoulder height, as if in a dance. Laila's eyes widen with surprise. This is the first time Al has ever touched her, apart from a single handshake once, when he recruited her to the project. If she has anything to do with it, this will certainly be the last time.

Now that their hands appear to have reached the zenith of their trajectory, Laila makes to withdraw her hand from his grasp. But Al just holds on tight and leads her hand further up. He's a big, powerful guy, and Laila needs a moment to realize exactly what his intentions are. Then suddenly it becomes clear to her. He's expecting her to twirl around, just as if they were dancing salsa together. She pulls back, but it's too late. Her arm is outstretched and he's leading her round. He switches from Arabic as her face comes close to his.

"I think a smile would be in order, don't you?"

"Fuck you, Al," she hisses, loud enough for some of the others to hear.

"That can be arranged, I'm sure."

Al smiles his cold, snake's smile as he leads her out of the turn and forwards, towards their audience.

"Gentlemen!" Al's voice is commanding, authoritative. "Applause for the beautiful Miss Lahijani."

The audience claps loudly. There are jeers, catcalls, whistles.

In the space of five minutes, Al has reduced Laila to the status of a slave girl, a belly dancer for this disgusting band of men.

Laila is seething with rage, squirming with embarrassment.

"Miss Lahijani, but how rude of me, why don't you take a moment to freshen up, remove your things?"

More whistles, which Al silences with a wave of his hand.

"And next time," he says to her as she passes, red-faced and flustered, "don't be late."

After Claire has left his pad, Ilya gets back to the business at hand. He has a couple of coding deals to finish. Well, not so much coding exactly. More like re-coding, if the truth be told. He has a quite specific skill, one that people are prepared to pay significant amounts for. If he wanted to, he could be living in one of the new penthouses overlooking the river. But that's not the way he works. Life was tough when he was growing up, and the way he figures it, life could be tough again anytime soon. So he squirrels his money away, buys into a little blockchain currency here, a little equity crowdfunding there, some credit union deposits there. He shies away from ostentatious displays of wealth. On the one hand, he has everything he needs—his little flat, his equipment, Claire. On the other hand, not much of his money would be readily available, even if he wanted to squander it.

Also, he doesn't consider himself to be much of a do-gooder. Sure, he doesn't mind contributing to a cause if he thinks it's worthwhile, maybe some program for South American street kids or a women's cooperative network in India. He even has a little secret college fund for his kid sister, should she need it. But in a way it's all just chickenshit, just a sop to his vaguely guilty conscience.

He knows he's not like Claire—will never have her level of commitment, that total, passionate immersion in a cause that impresses him so much and that he loves about her. He sees himself more as a loner, an outsider, a *rōnin*. He'll sell to the highest bidder, and once he's decided to take on a job, he'll follow it through without worrying too much about the consequences.

He's a sucker for all those old movies about suave cat-burglars or hyper-specialized criminal gangs that everybody roots for not only because they are much smarter and better-looking than their opponents, who are inevitably just evil dorks, but because they always end up getting the girl at the end.

Ilya's been feeling a lot like that recently. Like he's living a charmed life. Like he can't believe his luck. It's as if his life before Claire was just shit, just some boring dream he was having without really living it.

Now it's his work which is fading a little, losing its allure. It has been the centre of his attention for so many years—more or less the whole of his teens—that now he feels justified in easing off a bit. He can feel himself changing, but even that doesn't really do justice to the meteor-strike impact Claire has had on his life. Scary stuff. Too much to think about sometimes.

Today's first job is playing to his strengths. He has an encrypted site to crack into and perform a little minor surgery on. He has a talent for recombinant engineering. To mere hacking as a mud hut to a cathedral. He'll first do a perimeter search of a target site to check out the monitoring and alarm systems. Then he'll figure out who programmed it, where they work, and what equipment they used. Then he'll spend as long as it takes to crack into the site, which, given the military grade weaponware at his disposal is usually not long at all. Then he'll perform his recoding in such a way that even the original programmers won't notice the difference. Then he'll break into the programmers' machines and forge their records. Then he'll withdraw, and won't need to cover his tracks because he won't have left any, but he'll do it anyway. And then he'll watch the cash flowing into whatever receptacle he has nominated to his client.

All of which requires, no, demands, a considerable amount of energy and concentration.

By way of R&R, Ilya likes to drift through the virtual world, to let himself be caught up in the eddies and whorls of the cybervortex, to ride the ion winds of interstitial netspace. In this world, he is a predator. Not one of the big beasts, but a dark, imperceptible presence, a gaping maw that some unsuspecting lanternfish will swim into and won't recognize till he bumps up against a row of sharp teeth. He carries within himself a kind of negative buoyancy that allows him to float effortlessly down to the deepest recesses of his chosen environment, down through the gaudy, vaudeville stages of the actors and the guileless, through the trap-doors and false floors of the more reclusive denizens, down even beyond the lightless, sightless realms of the bottom-feeders and outcasts to the very foundations of this reality, the numinous realm of the where-no-where, in which the matter and antimatter of the virtual universe fuse and clash and open up cavernous spaces where titanic beings shift and slumber and miss nothing. And yet Ilya, in his virtual incarnation, has discovered a way of being so light, so intangible, that not an electron is disturbed by the weight of his presence. Clearly, he is of this world, as are all beings of the virtuality. But at the same time he, if it is still true to speak of disembodied intelligences in such gendered terms, is somehow between the world and its opposite, and has found a way to superimpose himself onto the fundamental fabric of this universe and so become pure presence, pure unpresence, invisible, amen.

Not something you can easily explain to your mates down the pub.

Not that Ilya has any.

Down there, down among the naked foundations of the weeb, time slows to a thick, treacly soup. For what seems like days on end, nothing will happen. The big beasts will shift and wheeze, with only a crackle of energy around them to betray the level of activity within. But then, when something does happen, it is inevitably information-rich. A sudden shift, a lunge, a rapacious realignment will be accompanied by arcing explosions of virtual light, energy pulses of such intensity that the very fabric of the virtual world will be stretched to breaking point by the forces at work.

Today's event is not of that order of magnitude, not by a long shot.

But nevertheless, something is happening.

Ilya can sense a change in pressure, perhaps like high feathery clouds announcing the coming of a storm front.

It starts with a classic distributed recon maneuver. One of the big beasts is experiencing a bunch of synchronized probes around a peripheral cluster, akin maybe to mosquitos landing on the paws of a sleeping cat. The cat will twitch perhaps in its sleep, and maybe one of the mosquitos will get lucky and find a way through the fur to actually draw some blood.

And maybe the cat will continue to sleep and maybe it won't.

But whatever blood has been drawn has failed to satisfy. There is a surge in intensity, more nodes are affected, there is fluttering rush of intention, like birds or bats, slamming up against a thick plate glass of indifference, and easily swatted away.

The big beast is awake now, and angry, and the fluttering, pecking presences keep coming, only to be crushed as soon as any new appearance manifests itself.

And then, after a while, after the desperate swarm has spent itself, there is a stillness, and wreckage and debris, and Ilya is left wondering what the fuck just went down.

Chapter Fifteen
Gentlemen

After Laila has left, Al turns his attention to the group.

"Gentlemen. Thank you for your patience."

He looks appreciatively around the room.

"Many of you will be wondering why it is that I have gathered you here together this morning. In effect, why it is that you have been chosen."

Al stands with his feet apart, his hands clasped behind his back, chest out.

"You have been selected for a very special task. A task which, should you decide to accept it, will ensure not only very generous remuneration for your services, but also, and this is perhaps uppermost in your minds at the moment, guarantee your future right of residency in this great country of ours."

A murmur of interest passes through the audience. Al relaxes his stance and starts to pace slowly along the front row of listeners.

"You have been chosen because you are all military men."

A sudden surge of protest. Al raises his hand.

"Please, gentlemen. There is no need for pretence. This may be the land of the kuffar, but I assure you, you are among friends here. When I say military, I know that this may not apply in the formal sense to many of you. But in spite of what you may have written on the various forms, applications and documents that you have been obliged to sign to get this far, and in spite of the claims you may have made to my charming colleague Miss Lahijani, we—I—know the true nature of your background."

Al pauses and inspects his audience. He knows he has them now.

"My friends, you are all fighters. This is all to the good. This is the reason you are here in this room. This is the quality that we require from you."

"And what is it that you want us to do?"

A voice from the back of the room, from a hard-eyed man in his late twenties. Al stretches out an open hand towards him, like a showmaster from some TV quiz.

"This, of course, is the question. What we want you to do, is simply to move through the city. We want you to go wherever there are large groups of people. We want you to be yourselves, in the knowledge that we have granted you a kind of immunity. Short of actually killing, or seriously wounding anybody, there is almost nothing you can do that will get you arrested. Or, to be more accurate, if you do find that the police have arrested you, then you can be sure that you will be out within an hour."

From the front row, a wiry man with a pockmarked face raises his hand. Al nods towards him.

"Sir. You say you want us to move through the population of this city, as what we are, as fighters. Will we have weapons?"

"No weapons. We are already treading a fine line here. With weapons, the situation will escalate far too quickly, and other forces will quickly become involved. I have no interest in you coming to the attention of our counter-terrorist cadres. If I did, I wouldn't be standing here talking to you now. No, there are enough of your brothers already engaged in such activities to keep our security forces occupied. Our focus —your activities—have more to do with a, how shall I put it, a hearts-and-minds operation."

"You want us to be aggressive, without killing anybody?"

"Correct, my friend, correct. This, I think, sums up the essence of the plan. Very good. Next question. Yes, the gentleman at the back."

"Sir, we are starting to understand what it is you want us to do. I think that every one of us here will be happy to perform this task for you. You give us the freedom of the city..."

"And money."

"...and money, and a degree of immunity. This is all very good, and more than we could have hoped for. And we are grateful, believe me. But what we do not understand is why? You say hearts and minds. This is something that we are familiar with. But why is it that you wish us to instil fear into your countrymen? This is surely the opposite of hearts and minds, no?"

"Excellent. Excellent question."

A broad smile spreads across Al's face.

"This is indeed the nub of the matter."

Al starts to pace along the central aisle separating the two halves of his audience.

"But before I answer this, let us take a short break. For now is the time for anyone who does not which to participate to withdraw. Let me repeat. If you want out, now is the time. There is the door. No-one will stop you."

He pauses, looks around the room. Nobody moves.

"But if you want in, if you stay, you are in. And you won't regret it. But there is no going back. Trust me on this, and you will find that your future here becomes a great deal easier. And a great deal more interesting. Gentlemen, you have five minutes to decide."

Jimmy is lying in bed and he feels like death. His head is throbbing and his vision is blurred, and his skin has developed strange itchy blotches. Julia brings him a coffee and he manages to resist the urge to throw up. He sits up in bed and stares out of the window into the watery morning light.

Julia sits on the edge of the bed and strokes his hair.

"Honey, you have to call the doctor."

"What for? He already gave me the diagnosis."

"Yeah, I know. I don't mean that. I mean to find out where we are supposed to be going."

"I don't think the Doc would appreciate me talking about drug smuggling over the telephone. Even if it is purely medicinal."

"You don't need to mention that. You'll have to think of something else. But look at you. You're in no state to go round in person."

Jimmy nods and finishes his coffee. He struggles into the bathroom and looks at himself in the bathroom mirror, leaning heavily on the edge of the wash basin with both hands. He's always thought of himself as kind of ageless. He has a lean, wiry figure without much in the way of paunch or wrinkles. Sure, he wouldn't pass for thirty any more, but most people if pushed, would normally place him in his early to mid forties. But today, Jimmy looks in the mirror and sees the face of his father, just before he died. His eyes are sunken, dull orbs surrounded by dark rings. His skin is sallow and grey, accentuated by the silvery stubble of five days' worth of beard. His lips have a blueish tinge and when he opens his mouth and bares his teeth at himself, his gums are grey and his teeth are yellow and he has a metallic taste in his mouth. He sucks at an incisor and can feel a flow of liquid from around the root. He spits into the basin and watches as the blood dribbles down the plug hole.

"You ok Jimmy?" calls Julia from the kitchen.

"Fine and dandy," he answers and turns on the cold tap to wash the blood away.

A quarter of an hour later he is sitting on the sofa, freshly showered and dressed in a sweatshirt and black tracksuit bottoms and kung fu slippers. Julia brings him the phone and he dials the Doc's number.

A woman's voice answers in a lazy drawl.

"Doc Mucus's place. What can I do for you?"

"Shirl, it's Jimmy, how you doing? Can you put me through to the Doc?"

"Jimmy sugar, all good, all good. Let me just see what the old guy is up to."

Jimmy gets shunted into a waiting loop playing Ka's Theme from the Jungle Book. Twenty seconds later he hears a familiar rasp on the other end of the line.

"Ah, Jimmy, young lad. So good to hear from you. How's the old pancreas coming along?"

"Not so good Doc. Feeling a bit rough this morning. That's why I'm phoning. Thought a bit of sun would do me good. Thought you might have a few holiday tips for me. You know, therapeutic destinations an' all."

"Therapeutic destinations? Ah, therapeutic destinations! Of course, of course. Anything I can do to help. So, let me think…"

Jimmy can hear the sound of a computer keyboard.

"Jimmy, I have just the place for you. They say the Philippines are admirable at this time of year. Excellent conditions. Just the right temperature and humidity for a man in your condition."

"The Philippines huh? Ok Doc, sounds good. Anywhere in particular you'd like to recommend?"

"Manila my boy, Manila. Subic Bay is an absolutely splendid destination at this time of year."

"Ok Doc, gotcha. Subic Bay. Maybe I'll pop round for a pick-me-up before I go."

Jimmy can hear the sound of the Doc licking his lips with that reptilian tongue of his.

"Yes indeed, Jimmy my boy. I can certainly help you out with a pick-me-up. In fact, I've got a whole boxload of pills that I think you ought to be taking. Shall we say this afternoon? I'll pass you back to Shirley to arrange the appointment."

"Cheers Doc, that's big of you. I owe you one."

"Mmm, of course, of course. Don't worry about that young Jimmy. We can settle up when you get back from your vacation."

Back up at Fuji City, nobody has left the room. Al walks back in and checks the numbers. They are all there. Good for them, he thinks. Maybe they're not as stupid as they look. Nobody with any sense is going to pass up on a deal like this, and they can bet their bottom dollar that anyone refusing his more than generous offer would be out on his ear at a second's notice, back in whatever hellhole they spent so many months crawling out of.

But here they all are, waiting for him, and his explanation. Al puts his coffee cup down on the desk at the back of the room and turns to face them.

"So, gentlemen. Does anyone wish to leave? No, I thought not. Let us then return to the matter at hand. There was a question before the break regarding the why, the reason behind our operation. A very astute question.

The answer is very simple. So-called liberal democracies have had their day. Even here, in the relatively repressive confines of New Clone City, we still manage to practice, how can I put it, a certain tolerance."

Al's audience hangs rapt on his every word, like a class of overgrown schoolchildren. The sun has emerged from behind its veil of clouds and is streaming into the room through the large windows facing out onto the old airstrip.

"Walk around the NC, and you will see what I mean. Ethnicities from all over the planet rub along together, women can walk the streets at night unmolested, dykes and faggots can be found sharing the same streets with fundamentalists of all persuasions. Such is the reputation of the NC, such are its forms of social interaction. And it is this cultural ballast which forms a heavy counterweight to our society's need for fundamental change."

Al opens his arms wide, like a market stall-holder addressing the punters.

"Gentlemen, you have been selected not merely for your military prowess, but because of your principled disdain for such things. It is a disdain many of us here in this country also share, and it is this disdain which is your passport to a safer future. For, present company excepted of course, we see ourselves faced with a challenge. It is precisely the liberal precepts at the bedrock of our society which will ensure its ultimate demise. I'm sure you understand what I mean. We have become too tolerant. Our various military excursions into your own countries of origin have led us to the erroneous belief that we must let large numbers of your countrymen into our own heartland, presumably as some kind of atonement. This, at least, seems to be what our governing politicians believe. Let me assure you my friends, this is not only wrong, it is dangerous, and will ultimately prove the ruin of our entire society. I think you will agree that society needs a firm hand if it is to survive."

He looks around the room. There is a vehemence in his voice that has not gone unnoticed by his audience, who nod their approval.

"I have been given the task of creating an effective counterweight to our onerous burden of tolerance. This is what I mean by hearts and minds. If we wish to move society in a specific direction, we are going to have to help it along. We are going to have to apply a certain force at specific neuralgic points. You, gentlemen, are going to be that force."

Al looks over the heads of his audience into the light coming in through the window, enjoying its warmth momentarily like a spotlight.

"Your job will be to apply pressure to the weaker links in the chain. To make sure that 'rubbing along' no longer functions. To ensure for instance, that the residents of the NC start to perceive their streets as more dangerous, that women become afraid to walk the streets alone, that queers find themselves hunted, and their lives confined. Any questions? Yes, you sir."

A weather-beaten man in his late thirties stands up to address Al and the rest of the audience.

"The main thrust of your strategy seems clear to me, I think to all of us. And let me assure you it is a role that we will be happy to fulfil. But what remains unclear is why you wish us to approach this so gently. Why are we to be so soft about it? Surely, something more spectacular would be more effective? More in line with a classic strategy of tension perhaps?"

Al beams at his interrogator.

"Strategy of tension? Yes, splendid, splendid question! Sir, you are clearly a gentleman and a scholar, and a man after my own heart. This is an important point, one which it is essential you understand. If we had wanted you simply to perform some attack, some atrocity, there would have been no need to recruit you in this manner. We would simply have given you early clearance and left you to your own devices. I am sure that enough of you would then have been resourceful enough to come up with your own plans. However, you would be mistaken to underestimate our regular anti-terrorist security services, who would be onto your sorry asses in seconds. There are four or five competing services that are primed and thirsting for targets. I doubt if you would last more than a month out there, in the wild. In addition, the classic response to a strategy-of-tension-style bombing or attack is for the populace to call for more security. It is a strategy designed to strengthen the state. This is a fine short-term goal, but a short-sighted one. Too much security ultimately produces resentment among the masses. It is a blunt political instrument. Our aim therefore, is a subtler one. It is to win the hearts and minds of the masses themselves. To give them the feeling that their tolerance has been abused. To lead them back to their natural state of intolerance—towards each other, but also towards the other, the alien, the foreign. In a word, we want them not to call for more security as such, but to call to be rid of…"

Al looks around the room and smiles.

"…to be rid of *you*."

"Does that answer your question?"

"Of course. We are to be your fifth column."

The man sits down.

"Your agent provocateurs?"

"Yes, but in a social, rather than political sense. Just be yourselves. Your belligerent, malevolent selves, in the knowledge that short of murder, you are more or less immune. Any other questions?"

"When do we start?"

A smile spreads across Al's face.

"You start now."

When Claire leaves Ilya's place she figures it's time to fire up her panthers.

There's so much stuff swirling round inside her—troubling her mind, whisking up her emotions, stirring her guts—that she needs some earthing. And there's nothing like a couple of hundredweight of virtual badass feline to fix that.

She adjusts her spex and blinks in the appropriate initiation sequence. Her overlay familiars fizzle into life as she traverses the corner of Silversmith and Cornell.

She has them fanned out in front of her. Loping, long and sinuous. A seething black guard of honour. But it's an unseen seething, scoped only by the bespexed. Who are few and far between at this time of the morning, in this neck of the woods.

She turns out onto Carlos Marx and can see a few bods further down the street clocking her presence.

But it's not other people's reactions she's interested in.

When her panthers are out, she likes to give them a free run. Doesn't appreciate them being walked through by some analogue jerkoff.

She needs that feeling of just being with those animals, out on the street. It centers her, puts her in touch with her warrior self. It makes those flame tattoos on the side of her skull itch like they're newly inked.

She prowls along Carlos Marx, bringing up the rear of her feral trinity, and sinks effortlessly into meditative alphawave space. Lets what's on her mind be *in* her mind.

Feels the post-coital glow of her time with Ilya. That unexpected sweetness. There's a budding there, a promise, something moving her in some totally left-field way. Something she has to follow.

Feels the anger of the whole scene with the collective. Frustration, disappointment, disillusionment. Something she has to leave behind if she wants to make herself whole again.

Feels the momentary weightlessness of her own insignificance in the global scheme of things, then pulls herself back down to earth with a bump.

Fuck that. No, really. *Fuck* that.

She's walking down a dirty, stinking street in the middle of the NC with nothing but two overlay projections for company.

But she could be anywhere.

She could be in the Amazon fucking jungle, or whatever's left of it.

Something in her is pulsing and racing. She feels the air in her lungs, the blood in her veins, the muscles of her legs as they pound along the street.

She is *alive*.

She whistles to her panthers and they respond as programmed, by turning their heads towards her, then sitting, and waiting.

She has reached the beginning of the roadworks on Carlos Marx. People are bunched together on the pavement. There are jackhammers, and a queue of traffic, and knots of unemployed and homeless in earnest nicotine congregations. There are late breakfasters and early shoppers, and panhandlers and guys standing out in front of their fruit and veg shops, guarding their wares, waiting for unsuspecting customers to come along and want something.

The sun is a yellow smear in a grey sky and Claire lingers with her animals.

An androgynous blue angel walks up the steps from the U and heads down the street in the direction of the Arcades.

Claire picks up a coffee from a tiny deli called the Dream of Reason and stands out on the street, leaning on a tall aluminium table with an overflowing ashtray and gradually brings her thoughts back to practicalities.

She has a shift at the shop lined up for later today, so she pens a mail to tell them she's ill.

Wonders when it was that her collective became *their* collective.

Takes a swig of coffee.

Deletes the mail. Nobody will believe it.

Her panthers' tails twitch idly, languidly, on incongruous paving stones.

She writes the mail again.

Sends it this time.

Who cares.

Laila is standing with her back to the door when Al enters the room. She's doing her best to recover some calm and self-control, but it's no use. She is seething. The window is open and there's a cigarette in her hand, and she's shaking, although it's difficult to tell whether it's the cold, or the nicotine rush, or the anger, or all three.

She turns when she hears the door open and throws her cigarette out of the window.

"Al, you asshole, do you want to fucking tell me what that was all about?"

Al pauses for a moment, as if taken by surprise, then walks over towards her. There's a smile on his lips but his eyes are hard and impassive.

"Miss Lahijani, I'm not sure that that is the appropriate manner to address a superior officer."

"Al, don't 'Miss Lahijani' me. And superior or not, I'm not going to be treated that way. Not by you, not by anybody. I'm not one of your fucking hired bimbos."

"Bimbos? That's a little unsisterly, don't you think? Discriminatory, even."

Laila emits a stifled laugh of indignation.

"I can't believe it Al. I really have trouble believing that not only did you insult me in front of all those men, but now you have the gall to fucking lecture me on my language. You must be fucking losing it."

Al takes one of her cigarettes from the pack on the desk and lights it. He exhales smoke in her direction and slowly walks around her to the window.

"No Laila. I think the only one who's losing it is you. One, you'd better watch your language. Two, if you're going to work here, we're going to have to get along. And that basically means that you do it my way. This is not some university debating club. There is a clear chain of command. So you'd better quit whinging and shape up."

"Whinging? Fuck you Al. Just go fuck yourself. I quit."

Al takes a deep drag on his cigarette. There is an expression of triumph on his face.

"Quit? Quit what? The service? This post? Laila, now you are being simply delusional. How exactly do you see that working? Do you think you can just take a step up the ladder and say, 'Al was being nasty to me. Can I go home now?' Get a fucking grip Laila. Nobody just leaves the Agency. There's nowhere for you to go. Or? What are your options? Come on, tell me. I'm curious."

Laila looks at him and says nothing. She knows he's right. There's nothing she can do. It's check mate, and they both know it. But she won't be beaten.

"Al, I have no idea what weird scenarios are playing out in your head, and to be honest, I don't want to know. But I'll tell you one thing. This is not the Taming of the fucking Shrew. This is the twenty-first century. And even if I can't quit, I'm here to do a job, and I demand to be treated with respect. Can you get your head around that?"

"Well! Classical allusions and demands. Laila, you never fail to surprise me. I like a certain feistiness in a woman."

"Al, get this. I don't care what you like."

Al flicks his cigarette out of the window.

"Ah Laila, but you should care. I really think it would be better for you if you did."

Chapter Sixteen

Magical, Mystical

Gene is feeling pretty dejected as he walks down Columbia to check in with Ursula. He's been at the Crow's Nest for the best part of the day, just popping into his studio for a couple of hours in the afternoon to deal with some customers, but straight back after that. The break makes no difference, there's still no news, no more information about the car or the guy. It's bugging him, and it's even starting to affect his work. Even while he was whipping the ass of one of his johns—a sweet guy in his sixties who would come in once a week to have his rear end royally flagellated by a latex-sheathed transvestite domina—he found himself thinking about Ursula and what had happened to her. He thinks his john probably noticed too. He was getting a bit fidgety and kept making remarks until Gene gagged and blindfolded him at no extra cost.

Now there is a cold wind blowing as he crosses the junction of Columbia and Henry, and the air feels like there's snow on the way. Gene's got his head down and his shoulders hunched as he walks down Airport. He looks in and waves at Tarik and the crew as he passes the society coiffeur and knocking shop. Tarik waves gaily back but makes a sad face and blows him a kiss when he sees the mood he's in.

There are times in the NC when the nights seem to close in, when the place to be is indoors, when the only people out on the streets are the loners and the hopeless cases. Gene feels pretty much like a hopeless case now as he trudges down the street. He's wearing a quilted winter jacket with a fake fur hood, and still feels chilled to the bone. But he knows the chill is only partially to do with the temperature. It's the chill of powerlessness, the chill of isolation, the chill that he used to get as a kid when he was out on the streets in the big city feeling penniless, friendless and unprotected. The feeling you get when it's just you against the world, and the world is winning.

Gene knows that a lot of these feelings don't really have much to do with him personally. They're more an effect of the violence Ursula has endured, a repercussion. Gene is no longer penniless, friendless and unprotected. He's very much a part of his community. They're his emotional bedrock, his sustenance, the medium he lives and breathes. Sure, it's a small world, just a village in the conglomerate of villages that go to make up the NC. But it's a thriving, intense, vibrant, passionate village that's also part of a broader global community. Fucked up? Of course it's fucked up, and damaged too. Most everyone in the village is damaged in some way, otherwise they wouldn't be there. But it's being in the village that helps you realize that the damage is not your fault, not your responsibility. That it has been inflicted on you by a fucked-up world, and that now you're in the safest place you can possibly be.

So it's thoughts of comfort and sustenance that maybe cause Gene to stop in front of a little Turkish joint selling *börek* and *gözleme*. There's a curious domed grill, like an inverted wok, in the window, next to a big round wooden board for rolling out the dough. A tag team of two middle-aged women in headscarves have a production line going. One kneads and rolls out the *gözleme* dough on the board with a long thin rolling pin, fills in the cheese and spinach, and folds the whole thing into a fat package. The other takes the package over onto the heated dome and unfolds it into a semicircular calzone-style pancake, shifting it around and flipping it over till it's done. Gene's looking in and finds his mouth watering. One of the ladies catches his eye and gives him a smile. That's all the encouragement he needs. He walks up the couple of steps leading into the place and pushes open the door. He orders a gözleme and a tea and parks himself on a tall bar stool near the door, giving him a view of the street and of the ladies and their production line. The food is great, and there is something about the whole scene that soothes him. There's a big old oven—an arched, pizza-style affair—that's giving off a lot of heat. An old guy with an off-white t-shirt and a pot belly opens up the oven doors and takes out a load of crescent-shaped börek with what seems to be a flat wooden shovel. He slides the steaming pastries down onto a big metal tray next to the gözleme ladies, who joke with him as they carry on working. There's music in the background, a guy playing a saz and singing a keening, flamenco-style song in a language Gene can't understand, but which is clearly about love, longing and loss.

Gene puts two sugar lumps in his tea and feels the weight of his cares lift for the first time that day.

"Manila? You want me to pick up illegal medication in Manila? Are you out of your tiny friggin' mind?"

Jimmy is at the Doc's and he's not a happy bunny.

The Doc sits impassively in his big upholstered chair, looking like some big old Komodo dragon in a white coat.

"You know what they do to drug smugglers in the Philippines? Yeah, I know I'm not actually going to be smuggling drugs, but I think maybe the finer points may get lost in translation, don't you? If you think I'm about to join Dirty Harry's mountain of corpses in Manila Bay then you've got another think coming."

"Ah, so you're familiar with the President's somewhat unorthodox methods?"

"Unorthodox? The guy's a bleeding psychopath. The police are psychopaths. And then there are all the other psychopaths taking advantage of the situation. They'll kill you just for looking at them the wrong way. I think I'd be better off taking my chances with cancer."

The Doc is unperturbed by Jimmy's little outbreak.

"Jimmy my boy. First of all, let me say how admirable I think it is that you've taken the trouble to inform yourself about the local situation over there."

"No trouble at all Doc. Family connections. My granddad was a matelot from the Clyde. Toured the far east. Founded families wherever he went. Singapore, Hong Kong, Philippines. Shit, I've even got cousins in Yokohama."

"Excellent. Local contacts. Jimmy, this is good news indeed."

Jimmy and the Doc stay eye to eye for a moment. Jimmy can feel his anger subsiding into exhaustion, while the Doc's leathery face breaks into an approximation of a smile.

"Secondly, and I feel I can't stress this enough, it's not me who needs this medication Jimmy, it's you. Of course, I'll be happy to hold on to any that's left over once you've finished with it, but I'm not actually asking you to do anything on my behalf. Jimmy, this is purely for your benefit, and I must say that I feel deeply saddened by the suggestion that it might be otherwise."

Jimmy looks down at the floor, then up at the Doc.

"Yeah, sorry Doc. Got a little carried away there. Been feeling a bit emotional all week, tell you the truth. No offence meant."

The Doc slaps his hand on the table.

"And none taken my boy, none taken!"

Then, after a pause: "So what do you think, Jim lad, will you be going to do the pick-up or not?"

"Come again?"

"Manila! Are you going?"

Jimmy takes a deep sigh.

"Do I have a choice?"

The Doc strokes his chin thoughtfully. Jimmy can't help following the liver spots on the back of his hands.

"Jimmy, you always have a choice. You have the choice to stay here and live out your days in the bosom of your family. That's a perfectly valid choice. You can be sure that I will do my utmost to make those days as comfortable for you as possible."

Jimmy sinks back in his seat.

"And how have you been feeling these past few days?"

"Like shit Doc. Never felt so bad in my life. I don't think the pills are helping very much."

The Doc becomes suddenly animated.

"No no! Let me assure you that things would be much worse without the pills. An absolutely essential element in pain management and palliative care. I strongly advise that you carry on taking the pills."

Jimmy feels washed out, beaten.

"Sure Doc, whatever you say. I'll stick with it, no worries."

"That's my boy. Ah, you've always been a fighter, young Jimmy."

"Feels more like the fight's been knocked out of me right now, tell you the truth."

"Hmm, I see."

The Doc pushes his chair back and creaks to his feet. He wheezes around the table and directs Jimmy over to a raised examination recliner in the corner of the room.

"Let's take a look at you."

Jimmy takes off his shirt and the Doc proceeds to poke and prod. He pulls down Jimmy's lower eyelids with a nicotine-stained finger and bangs his knee with a little hammer. He goes to listen to Jimmy's heartbeat when he realizes he's mislaid his stethoscope, and spends ten minutes pulling open all the drawers in his office until he finally calls Shirl on the intercom.

"Shirl! You seen my stethoscope?"

Shirl's voice can be heard in stereo—crackly through the ancient intercom, and muffled through the door separating them.

"You mean the dangly thing with the earplugs? I've been wearing it to parties ever since the last time you examined my chest."

The Doc coughs and flushes a little.

"Your bronchitis. Of course. But do you have it?"

"Have what, Doc?"

"The dangly thing."

"Sure Doc, it's here with the rest of my stuff."

"Well bring it in why don't you. Oh and Shirl?"

"Yes Doc?"

"I think we're in need of a little refreshment."

Jimmy is sat on the examination couch waiting for Shirl to come in. His feet don't reach the ground and when he starts swinging them to and fro he feels a bit like a schoolkid waiting for a medical. The Doc potters around the room looking for his cigarettes and Jimmy looks blearily out of the window. There's a solitary magpie sat on the roof opposite that seems to be watching him back.

Finally Shirl comes in carrying a small oval-shaped tray with three glasses, a small carafe of water, a bottle of dark green liquid and a pile of sugar cubes. Shirl has her hair heaped up even higher than usual and is wearing extravagantly elongated mascara that give her eyes a wild, cat-like appearance. She has a piercing in the corner of her upper lip and a dashing combination wetware/earpiece in one ear. As she sashays across to the Doc's table Jimmy is raised out his torpor by Shirl's perfumed tail-wind and the daringly low cut of her red polka-dot top. Her neck is adorned with a golden anchor on a chain and Jimmy could swear that her tattoos have reconfigured themselves since the last visit, her bare arms now sporting a green and red horseshoe, a lasciviously drawn naked women, a Mexican dia-del-muerte-style laughing skull, and the words "Gloria" and "Mum" in elaborate handwriting, one on each arm. She's also wearing strappy high heels and skinny jeans.

Shirl puts the tray down on the Doc's table and comes over to where Jimmy is sat. She strokes the line of his jaw with a heavily manicured finger and plants a fat kiss on the other cheek. Jimmy is pretty sure that he now has a cartoonish lipstick imprint on the side of his face but thinks it's probably churlish to ask for a tissue.

"Jimmy, chuck," says Shirl. "Doc here says you've been feeling a bit poorly."

Jimmy does a little shrug and manages half a smile.

"Can't be having that. I've brought you a drop of the Doc's special reserve. That'll put hairs on your chest. He only brings it out about once a year."

"Ah, privileged, I'm sure. Is this the stuff you burn the sugar cubes into?"

The Doc, who has been bending over the glasses carefully dripping ice-cold water from the carafe onto sugar lumps on spoons, and from there into the glasses filled with generous shots of vicious-looking fluid, straightens himself as best he can. He's full of indignation.

"Certainly not, my boy. None of that philistine faddishness here, I can assure you. This is a thirty-year old absinthe, and the only way to do it justice is in the style that Baudelaire, Verlaine, Rimbaud and van Gogh drank it. Water as cold as possible. Over the sugar. Slowly into the spirit to let it louche into a pure opalescent white as the essential oils are released from their alcoholic incarceration. Unfortunately I have no specially-crafted spoon for the purpose. But otherwise, we are eminently true to tradition."

The Doc turns and hands the glasses to Shirl and Jimmy, who lifts the swirling cloudy liquid up to the light.

"Doc, not like you to wax lyrical. Seems like there's a whole different side to you that I've yet to discover."

"Aye, Jimmy. Old habits and all. Back in my student days, wine women and song. A love of intoxication and of learning. Long gone, long gone. Water under the bridge."

The Doc's glazed and bloodshot eyes almost seem to moisten a little, as he raises his glass.

"Let us drink! To the spirit of adventure, good health, and may the DTs never darken your doorstep."

"Salut," says Jimmy.

"Here's lookin' at ya kid," says Shirl.

The bittersweet alcohol burns its way down Jimmy's throat and sends him into a spasm of coughing.

"Maybe a drop more water Doc?"

"Nonsense my boy. Just takes a bit of getting used to, is all. Here, let me fix you another."

And so it goes. And so it goes.

It's dark by the time Jimmy leaves the Doc's place and he can feel the tulips brushing against his legs as he walks into the clapped-out elevator. He doesn't know whether to feel disconcerted or pleased. He's sure as hell glad that they've found a place to put all the tulips but perhaps it would be nicer for them to be outside. He stoops to gather an armful but somehow misses. Damn insubstantial, them tulips. Before he can ponder further on the essence of tulipism his mind registers the button for the ground floor, directly before his eyes, and he presses it, with gusto. The jolt of the elevator carriage as it creaks into motion throws him momentarily off balance, and he finds himself in one corner of the lift, holding onto the walls, which seem about to crash in around him. The elevator finally comes to a halt and it takes him the best part of a minute to figure out how to work the archaic scissor doors.

By the time Jimmy gets out onto the street he realizes that he's barely able to stand. The pavement seems to be moving in disconcerting ways and the houses around him are generally conspiring against the perpendicular. He takes a moment to get his bearings, and even in his present state, he is aware that heading home is not an option. Jimmy has some serious sobering-up to do if he wants to avoid crucifixion at the hands of his beloved Julia. So he heads up Anzac in the direction of Carlos Marx and the hope of non-intoxicating stimulants.

He has managed the perilous journey across Danube Street and decides to take a rest on the steps behind Rat House. The magpie that he spotted earlier flaps lazily over and lands next to him.

"You're out of your brain," says the magpie, by way of an opener.

"Are you following me?" says Jimmy, and looks around to see if anyone else is listening.

"I don't need to follow you. I can smell you a mile off," says the magpie.

Jimmy surreptitiously sniffs at his jacket and armpits. He picks up a worn odour of pub ashtray and a faint whiff of vomit.

"Are you some magical, mystical creature sent here to warn me, or help me on my quest?" asks Jimmy, hopefully.

"Nah mate. I'm just a figment of your imagination. You're off of your fucking trolley."

"Well thanks for that."

From his jacket pocket, Jimmy manages to fish a crumpled cigarette that he cadged from the Doc on the way out. He pats his trouser pockets until he finds a book of matches and cups his hand to light the cigarette.

"You want to cut them out. Give ya cancer," the magpie caws. "And cut out the drugs while you're at it."

Jimmy blows smoke in the direction of the magpie, which shuffles off sideways in disgust.

"What are you, the medical magpie? Anyway, if you're so smart, and a figment of my imagination, then you should know it's too late for that."

"Come again?"

"I've already got cancer."

"Could've fooled me," the magpie says, cocking its head to one side.

"And I don't do drugs."

"You're full of it mate," says the magpie. "Why don't you pull the other one?"

And with that it flies off, leaving a tail feather on the step next to Jimmy.

Jimmy finishes his ciggie, puts the feather in his pocket, and heads off towards the bright lights of Carlos Marx.

By the time Gene leaves the little gözleme place it has started to snow. Thick white flakes are swirling down on a mean east wind and Gene pulls his hood up as he heads down Airport. Normally he'd take time to browse the windows of the bookshops on the way down—the Magic Fox, the Trout and Pickle—but today he doesn't give them a second glance. He passes the bleak rear end of the Arcades and turns left onto Carlos Marx. A flurry of winos are having a major altercation in the relative shelter of the porch entrance to the Arcades. Gene doesn't stop to gape, but he gets the gist. There's something about meth-cooked brain cells marinated in the cheapest of liquors that paints the world in bright harsh colours and unbearably sharp outlines. The voices are loud, cracked and slurred. A couple of the guys have dogs—a powerful bulldog on a chain, with a pink snout and a thick collar, and a mangy Alsatian with protruding teeth. The men themselves are weather-worn, creased of face and oily of attire, with a blunted, beaten look that draws Gene's eyes away from their faces as soon as he sees them. A green glass bottle with a dark liquid is pulled out of one hand and into another, dropping and smashing in the process. The volume cranks up, the dogs begin to bark. Maybe there won't be blood. Maybe it's too cold for blood.

Gene rounds the corner and heads down past the entrance to the U. Instinctively he looks over to the right in search of Suleika, and finds her hunched in her usual spot, a few yards back from the steps. But this time, incredibly, she has company. An old guy is sat cross-legged on the ground next to her, and seems to be engaged in conversation with her.

So gobsmacked is Gene by the unlikelihood of the scene that he stops in his tracks. He rests his hand on the metal railings separating the walkway from the road and pauses to take everything in. On closer inspection he can see that there isn't actually a conversation going on. The old guy is gesticulating with his hands and softly ranting, but Suleika isn't responding, at least not verbally. But she is, unbelievably, smiling. She seems to be thoroughly amused by the performance of the guy next to her. Not only is she tolerating his presence, she actually seems to be enjoying it. The two of them are outlined in white—a rime of snow is building up on the east-facing sides of their bodies. The streetlights give the two of them a familiar sodium-orange tinge. But they also seem to be giving off their own light. They appear impervious to the snow, and the temperature, as if they were sitting on a park bench or a river bank, and the traffic rushing by were merely a few mothers with prams, or people in rowboats.

Gene's curiosity gets the better of him and he walks over to where the two of them are sat and goes into a crouch directly in front of Suleika.

"Sister," he says in greeting, "mother, daughter of Kali," and places all the change in his pockets in her bowl.

Suleika bows her head and smiles, taking his hand and pressing the back of it against her forehead. For the first time since he has known her, she speaks to him.

There's not a word of it he can understand, but the mere fact of it, the sound of it, the deep mellifluous rasping whisper of it, touches his heart and fills him with joy. He nods to the guy next to her, who has stopped mid-sentence and is looking at her in jaw-dropped amazement. Turning back to Suleika, he sees that there are tears running down her cheeks. Her eyes are bright though, and the lines of her face are drawn upwards in a smile. Some major transformation has clearly happened here, brought on in some fashion by the guy sitting next to her.

Suleika wipes the tears from her eyes and gestures to her neighbour, who Gene initially has pegged for just another wino.

On closer inspection though there is something strange about him. He's too well-dressed for a wino, for a start. He looks drawn and haggard, maybe somewhere in his fifties, but relatively clean, if not clean-shaven. He has fine east Asian features and—just a guess here—seems to be completely stoned. In front of him is a steaming paper cup half full of what looks like coffee, and, Gene notes, there's a similar one in front of Suleika too. On the ground between them is a large paper bag, which has been ripped open to reveal the donuts inside.

The man turns his face to Gene. There's a glint of benign mania in his eyes. He says: "Dude, you are so blue."

Gene smiles.

"I bet you say that to all the girls."

"No man, it's true. Totally. You're blue and the world is orange, and this stuff…" he gestures at the falling snow, "is like totally psychedelic."

Gene looks around at the snow which remains resolutely monochrome to his perception.

"Here, have a donut."

The guy snatches up the torn paper bag and holds it out to Gene, who takes one, and then to Suleika, who hesitates, but then takes one when the guy insists. He takes one himself and they sit there, the two of them on the ground and Gene in a crouch, eating their donuts in the snow. A throng of people spill out of the U and flow around them, like a rock in a river.

"This is nice," says the guy, wiping sugar from his lips with the back of his hand. "Like the light show."

Gene looks around. There is nothing out of the ordinary. The only lights he can see are the street lights, vehicle lights, and the neon signs on the front of the Arcades. He gestures over towards them.

"You mean, these things?"

"No no man, not those. Well those too. But you and the sister here. I don't know how you do it, but well you, you're so blue, and she is like, just totally out there."

Gene musters the guy from head to toe.

"You're tripping right?"

"Tripping!?" The old guy sits up with a start, spilling his coffee in the process and sputtering donut crumbs onto the pavement.

"Dude, outrageous idea! Inflammable! Blindmending! Uh, not that I know of." Without taking his eyes off of Gene he starts to search through the paper bag with one hand until his fingers come across the last donut, which he holds out before him and scrutinizes intently.

"Have you ever noticed how donuts resemble skulls?" He throws the donut up in the air and, surprisingly, catches it.

"Alas poor donut, your time is up." Taking a bite out of the donut, he eyes the filling intently.

"It's the blood you see. The jam. The bloody jam filling both donut and head. Spill the jam, spill the man. You get my drift?"

Gene raises an eyebrow.

"You are so stoned. Why don't you just head off home?"

"Nope. No home. Home's a big no-no, till I can get my shit together enough to actually get there and walk up the stairs. And besides, when was the last time you had this much fun with a cup of coffee and a donut? Ah, you don't have coffee. Want me to get you one?"

The dude goes to get up but Gene restrains him with a hand on his shoulder.

"No, no coffee. It's all good. Except that it's freezing. And there's a snowstorm. You need to move, you both need to move, otherwise you'll both die of exposure."

The old guy shakes his head slowly to and fro, and winks at Suleika.

"Don't you worry about me. The cold'll do me good. Clear the old head a bit. No good me going home in this state. She'll have me guts for garters. Thanks for the chat 'n' all. You've done your bit."

Gene straightens up and looks around. The snow is coming down thick and fast now, and is settling, turning the world a yellowy white in the light of the street lamps. Cars are driving slower and the road is wet with snowmelt from their exhausts. Street sounds seem muffled from under their new snow blanket. The caucus of winos have stopped arguing and have congregated in the shelter of the doorway to the post office. They have found another bottle to pass around and seem to be observing him talk to the stoner and Suleika. They see him looking and one of them raises the bottle in a toast.

Gene comes to a decision.

"Come on you two, you're coming with me. I've got somewhere dry and warm you can hang out in for a while. It's just down the road."

The stoner acquiesces, and Gene helps him to his feet. Then the both of them help Suleika to her feet and they move off at a ponderous pace through the snow down in the general direction of the Church of Kali.

It's only a couple of hundred yards down the road but it takes them the best part of quarter of an hour to get there. By the time Gene goes down the steps to the main entrance and knocks on the door his fingers have gone numb and his companions are starting to look the worse for wear. A little hatch in the door slides open and a pair of big brown eyes check out who it is that's knocking. They recognize Gene immediately and the door swings open to let them in. The three of them step into a small antechamber hung in dark curtains and rugs, with rows of coat hooks behind a counter like the cloakroom in a theatre. Gene takes his quilted jacket off and hangs it up, but the other two look like they are unable to move. The old guy just stands there shivering, while Suleika remains bunched up beneath her innumerable layers of clothing, blowing on her fingers.

"Hold on," says Gene, darting over to a large samovar on the other side of the room. "Get a drop of this in you first. Then when you're ready you can take your coat off and go and have a sit down."

He brings across two mugs of something hot and steaming which he presses into their hands.

Then, with a smile to Suleika and a wave to Jimmy he says, "I'll leave you to it. The girls here will look after you. There's a friend I need to go and see."

And with that, he's gone.

Ursula is sleeping when Gene opens the door to her room. The lights are dimmed and Gene pulls up a chair to her bedside. Ursula is breathing softly. She's lying on her back with her head to one side. Gene can see heavy bruising around her mouth and her left eye. She's had all her make-up removed as well as the wig she was wearing. Gene sees a young guy in his early twenties with buzz-cut blond hair and fair stubble on his cheeks. He has a row of earrings up one ear and a tattoo starting at his collarbone and running down under the green gown he is wearing. High cheekbones, taught skin. Good-looking guy, thinks Gene.

Ursula shifts in her sleep and Gene picks up the clipboard with medical notes hanging on the end of the bed. Turns out Ursula's straight name is Oren. The rest of the clipboard doesn't make for pretty reading. It lists all the injuries that Gene suspected when he brought her in, plus a whole lot more. Apparently Oren is also on a major cocktail of medication, and is being kept under observation for a couple of days before they release her.

Medical services at the Church of Kali started a few years back as a fairly impromptu affair, but from regular use and force of habit have developed into a small but efficient emergency response unit. There's always a doctor on call within a ten-minute radius, and a roster of nurses who'll attend to anyone who stays overnight. They're not equipped for operations, or anything major, but are quite capable of stitching people up and dosing them with pain-killers, and of looking after patients till they're well enough to walk again. There's a support network of private practices and specialists throughout the NC, and contacts to all the major clinics. Although the unit itself is not strictly legal, it's tolerated, and that's good enough.

Gene hangs the clipboard back up and Oren stirs at the sound of metal on metal. He opens one eye, then the other, and checks out his new visitor.

"Hi," he says. His voice is dark and rasping, accompanied by a kind of bubbling in his throat. "Who are you?"

"I'm Gene. I brought you in. Me and the others. Don't you remember?"

Oren slowly shakes his head—a minute gesture suggesting every movement is painful.

"It was such a blur. But I think I remember you. You look so different." He stretches out the fingers of his hand as if to touch Gene's face. Gene meets his fingers with his own.

"You too. I wouldn't have recognized you without your warpaint on."

Oren manages to crack a smile.

"Warpaint. Yeah. That's what it feels like."

"Like you've been in a war?"

"And lost, yeah." Oren blinks back the tears. "Feels like I lost big time."

He starts to cry now. Softly at first, then stronger, in big, heart-wrenching sobs. There's nothing Gene can do but hold his hand and wait for it to pass. Normally he might put his arm round him and give him a shoulder to cry on, but Oren's too weak for even that, and Gene is afraid the movement would do more harm than good.

They stay like that for a while till the sobbing stops, and Gene hands him a tissue from a box on the bedside table.

"It's ok, it's all ok."

"It doesn't feel ok. It doesn't feel like it will ever be ok again."

They look at each other then, and Gene can feel the weight of sadness and injury and anger in Oren's gaze.

"We have to catch this guy. We have to make sure he never does anything like this again."

Oren nods silently in agreement.

"I know it's difficult to talk. I know it's not something you want to think about. But is there anything you can tell me that will help us to find him? Up to now we have next to nothing."

"You have the car, right?"

"Not even the car. We tried for the registration details, but drew a blank. Could mean he's something official. Maybe diplomatic immunity. We have no idea, really."

"Or military."

"What makes you say that?"

"There was something about him. Something, like, hierarchical, you know? Did you ever go with any army guys? Or police? They vibe the same. Lots of anger."

Gene knows where he's coming from. They get enough of these guys up in Charlie's Garden to be able to recognize them instantly. Violent, brutalized men from all-male or male-dominated institutions. Full of mixed-up longing and self-hate.

"Ok, I'm with you. What else?"

"He had tattoos on his forearms. Under his shirt. Something with a bird, an eagle maybe. And the way he spoke. He didn't talk. He just gave orders. I knew it was a mistake as soon as I got in. But he just drove straight off. It was so quick. I couldn't just jump out. And he was like, 'Do this, do that,' and I was really scared…"

"Do you remember where he took you?"

"He made me put a blindfold on. I couldn't see a thing. But it wasn't far. Maybe ten minutes max. And then we pulled up somewhere. Some kind of garage. Big echoey space. He made me get out. Lean against the car. Then he, then he…"

Oren starts to sob again. Gene squeezes his hand and tries to comfort him. A nurse pokes her head around the door and says, "I think that's enough now. Don't want you upsetting our patient."

Gene nods his head and stands up.

"Sure, sorry."

He lets go of Oren's hand as the nurse comes in to prepare a sedative for her patient.

"You get some rest. I'll come back soon."

He nods to the nurse on the way out.

"Sister."

Chapter Seventeen
Wicked Juju

Jimmy wakes up and his head is throbbing. He's sat in a big old armchair in a large windowless lounge. The room is full of sofas and armchairs and a few coffee tables. A couple of people are sitting around, reading or dozing or listening to stuff on earphones. He seems to be the only man in the room. The walls are decorated with paintings and photos—a few religious motifs, with a blue-skinned multi-armed woman standing on some dude on the floor and sticking her tongue out. And wearing a necklace of shrunken heads, by the look of it. There are a few other scantily-clad figures in the same classical Hindu genre. But they are vastly outnumbered by other depictions of women. Jimmy recognizes a few—Luxemburg, Kollontai, Goldmann, Erhart, Benario, Tereshkova, de Beauvoir, de Jong, Firestone, Miller, Solanas, a squad of Sandinista women, militiawomen from the Spanish FAI/CNT, Rojavan YPG fighters, but there's a whole lot more he has no knowledge of. Where the walls are free of pictures they're lined with books—floor-to-ceiling bookshelves. There's a small kitchen area in one corner and what seems to be a digital media library in the other. The ceiling is low and Jimmy has a flashback of coming down some steps in what was maybe another life. And though it's clean and warm, the air does have a slight cellar vibe to it. The overall impression though is one of quiet concentration. Nobody seems to be speaking, and Jimmy wonders whether it would actually be allowed. But there's no librarian, and no signs, so maybe no hassle, who knows.

Jimmy's eyeing the coffee-making equipment in the little kitchen area and thinks that this might be his next move. He checks his phone for the time but the battery has quit and the thing is quite dead. He has no idea how long he's been here or what time of the day it is. But the people in the room seem fairly attentive, still reading, rather than settling in for the night, so he guesses it can't be too late. He goes to pull himself up out of the armchair but the sudden movement makes him woozy as hell and he sits for a while on the edge of the chair.

The evening's starting to come back to him now. He has outrageous recollections of talking magpies, a multicoloured blizzard, an incredibly radiant old woman sitting on the pavement talking a language both utterly strange and intuitively intelligible. Some weird blue angel crouching down and talking to them both out there on the street. And before that Shirl, and the Doc, and the bottle of absinthe. Jimmy gingerly rubs his temples. He's heard stories of hallucinogenic absinthe but has always discounted them as the stuff of urban legend. Maybe they slipped him a Mickey. But why bother? What would be the point? Maybe it was just an interaction with all the other stuff that the Doc has him on. He's taking a cocktail of at least ten different pills and capsules every morning. There's no reason why something as potent as absinthe shouldn't provoke a reaction with some of his medication. Yes, that was probably it. He'll have to watch out for that in the future.

After five minutes' worth of convoluted cogitation, Jimmy manages to get up and wend his way over to the kitchen area. The meandering nature of his route raises a few eyebrows and causes a few enquiring looks, but everyone is too polite to comment and basically just lets him get on with it. He pours some water into an electric kettle and switches it on. Finds a jar of instant coffee and puts a couple of spoonfuls into a mug. Within a couple of minutes he has navigated his way back to his seat without major mishap or even spilling a drop, and is feeling pretty pleased with himself when a young guy appears and plonks himself down in the seat opposite.

"How you feeling?" he enquires. He seems vaguely familiar to Jimmy, but he can't for the life of him place him.

"Ah, good, good," says Jimmy, uncertainly.

"Oh shit. You're the second person I've brought into here in the space of 24 hours who doesn't recognize me. Maybe I need to start wearing a sign or something."

Jimmy's face breaks into a grin.

"Now I get it. You're the blue angel. You appeared to me in a dream, or something. And guided me here, wherever here is."

"Dream my ass. You were stoned, my friend. More than that. I'd say you were tripping. Psilocybin, if I had to hazard a guess."

"No, I mean yes." Jimmy runs his fingers through his hair and looks over sheepishly at his interlocutor.

"You're right about the trip, but it was purely accidental…"

"No business of mine, I'm not being judgmental about it."

"No, you don't understand. I'm on medication. I had a drink or two, and I think it must have disagreed with me."

"Didn't look like it was disagreeing with you. Looked like you were having a whale of a time."

Jimmy's eyes light up.

"Well, it was good while it lasted. But now I've got a killer headache and feel fucking awful, pardon my French."

"Let me get you something for that."

The young guy springs to his feet and bounces out of the room, greeting a couple of the regulars on his way out. He's back a few seconds later with a glass of water and two large white tablets, which he hands over to Jimmy.

"Thanks dude. Good of you." Jimmy swallows the tablets and washes them down with the water, then sets the glass down on the little table next to him. He stretches out his hand to the young guy.

"Didn't catch your name. I'm Jimmy."

The guy grasps his hand and smiles.

"I'm Gene. Or Jeanie. Depending."

"Depending? On what?"

"Oh, time of the day, time of the month, spur of the moment, whims, urges, wings of desire, that kind of thing."

"Aha."

"You follow?"

"No. Do I need to?"

"No, not at all."

And they both laugh.

"And this place?" Jimmy waves his hand at his surroundings. "Is like what? A shrine to the feminist revolution?"

Gene looks genuinely surprised.

"Hole in one. Man, you're pretty smart, for an old stoner."

Jimmy gives him a wink.

"Wasn't always an old stoner. Used to be a young stoner. Lot of shit went down before we got to this particular developmental dead-end."

"Well in that case Jimmy, welcome to the Church of Kali."

Now it's Jimmy's turn to look surprised. He leans back in his armchair and looks around at the room, as if for the first time.

"Church huh? Doesn't look like much of a church. Didn't have you guys pegged for the religious types."

"We're pretty unorthodox. It's a broad church. Which means you can be as religious or unreligious as you want to be."

Jimmy strokes his chin for a moment and lets that one sink in.

"So that makes you what? Atheist feminist Hindus? I think maybe that's too deep for me."

"Well, we're a bit like the Buddhists. They have a deeply spiritual religion, but don't believe in god. That works for us too. Our spiritual practice encompasses all manifestations of the female principle, in all religions, with a particular focus on the more combative, antipatriarchal manifestations. We're not into dogma, we're just into what works."

"But Kali?" says Jimmy. "That's pretty specific. How come?"

Gene cracks his knuckles.

"Kali is just about the most kick-ass goddess going. She's the mother-destroyer, with a string of men's heads as a necklace. She's a source of solace to just about anyone on the receiving end of male violence. She gets our vote every time."

"Dig that. Like the ultimate angry big sister. Mighty big badda boom. Lots of wicked juju."

Gene smiles. "That's one way of putting it."

"Damn right. Respect man," says Jimmy, getting up, and holding out his hand, palm upwards.

Gene slaps into it, and Jimmy holds on to him to pull himself up. "Jeanie dude, you got yourself one hell of a religion."

There's something crisp and clean about the air when Jimmy leaves the Church of Kali. He walks up the steps and out into the parking lot through a layer of more or less virgin snow and it's almost as if he were out in the countryside. That is, if you discount the sodium streetlights, the big blank side walls of the tenement buildings, the parked cars, the billboards, the traffic and the way the city lights make it almost impossible to see the stars. If you ignore all that, it corresponds almost exactly to Jimmy's vision of what it must like to be out in the country, at night, in the snow. Not that he's ever actually experienced it. They never had snow back home in Singapore when he was a kid, and there never was any on his peripatetic peregrination to the NC either. Since then he has hardly ever left the city. Flew home a few times to see his parents. Went back for his dad's funeral. Went back for his mum's funeral. A few holidays. Summers out on the boat. Not much in the way of winters in the countryside. Firstly, he doesn't know anyone who lives in the countryside. Secondly, the countryside is full of rednecks and nobody he knows wants to go there. All of which makes it a little difficult to commune with nature in the manner befitting. But he thinks it must be nice. All those stars. The darkling sky, shot through with red from the departed sun. The animals in the woods. Are there still animals in woods? Are there still woods? Sure, there must be. And the snow. Deep white snow, coming over the tops of your boots. Jimmy is channeling Peter Breugel the Elder as he trudges across the car park towards the slush of Carlos Marx. He's a peasant in a painting, a mediaeval Gaelic clansman riding with Cúchulainn, a hunter in winter. His feet skid from under him on the metal grille to a ventilation shaft for the U and he almost lands on his ass. He decides to follow the path of the hunter and stick a bit closer to the walls of the buildings lining the pavement for safety. There are not many people about, and those that he meets have a kind of rosy-cheeked shell-shock about them, as if snow were a concept heard about but never experienced, and they're now having some kind of meteorological epiphany. Jimmy grins at the passers-by like a schoolkid and most of them even grin back, although they probably have him pigeonholed as a harmless nutter.

It takes him about twenty minutes to get home and by the time he arrives he has had enough of the great outdoors. He's frozen through and his lungs hurt and he's feeling a little shaky, like maybe his blood sugar is low or he's on the tail end of a relatively soft trip come-down. He fishes the front door key out of his pocket and climbs the four flights of stairs to his flat. He opens the door to the flat and steps into the darkened hallway. All the lights are off. The door to the bedroom is closed. Jimmy takes off his shoes and coat and tippy-toes his way into the kitchen. Turns on the light on the oven extractor hood, which gives the room a kind of submarine, silent running look, with just enough light to operate essential systems by. Jimmy imagines the ping of the enemy sonar and the grim looking captain snapping up the handles on the periscope and issuing terse, whispered commands. He turns to look at the kitchen clock. It's a quarter past one in the morning. Jimmy pads into the bath-room, avoiding the squeaky floorboard in the hall, turns on the bath-room light and even shuts the door before he takes a leak and cleans his teeth. He's wondering whether just to crash out on the couch but the thought of getting into bed with Julia seems like the overwhelmingly more attractive option and besides, it's been at least six hours since he had a drink so that more or less counts as sober.

Jimmy finishes up in the bathroom and steps out into the hall. He turns the bathroom light off and stands there for a moment in the dark-ness before taking a deep breath and pushing open the bedroom door as quietly as he can. The room has that wonderful warm bedroom vibe of a sleeping loved one. Jimmy steps gingerly into the room.

"Jimmy you bastard, what kind of time do you call this?"

Jimmy-the-bastard gives up all attempts at stealth mode and turns to face the voice in the dark.

"Jules, hon, I've been meaning to call you…"

"Yeah well thanks for nothing, asshole. Where the fuck you been? I've been fucking worried sick about you, you runt. What happened to your friggin' mobile?"

"Ah no need to worry babe. No juice on the mobile. Just had a little drink with the Doc…"

"You've been fucking drinking? Jimmy Íomhar Chang…"

"Ah for Pete's sake don't call me Íomhar babe…"

Julia snaps on the bedside light.

"Last time you left this house you were a sick man, a terminal cancer patient going round to see his physician. The doctor's must've shut about six hours ago. I've been trying to get hold of you since eight in the evening. I must have phoned you a dozen times. I phoned the Doc's, I phoned all the bars between here and Han Plaza, I phoned the hospital emergency unit. I even phoned the fucking police to see if they had you in a cell somewhere. And you were just out drinking with the Doc? Why didn't you let me know?"

Jimmy sits down on the end of the bed.

"But that's just it. I wasn't drinking the whole time. I think the booze must've interfered with me medication."

"Meaning what?"

"Meaning I think I must have been tripping for a couple of hours."

"Jesus Christ Jimmy, is that supposed to make it sound better? Where the fuck were you all this time? Like, when you were out there tripping?"

"Out on Carlos Marx mostly. Met some nice people. It was all good. No harm done and all."

Julia is sat up in bed now, holding her head in her hands.

"In the snow? Give me fucking strength. You just do my head in. Won't somebody tell me what I did to deserve this?"

Jimmy sidles a little closer and takes her hand.

"It's in your nature love. You're just a lucky, lucky woman."

"My mother always said you were no good."

"Just goes to show how wrong the old bat could be, god bless her."

"Watch it."

"Best mother-in-law a man could wish for, not a doubt about it."

She punches him in the shoulder.

"Christ Jimmy, you scared me."

He takes her hand and kisses it.

"Sorry love. Didn't mean to. It was a good evening though."

She strokes his face, tenderly now.

"How you feeling?"

"Knackered. Totally shagged out."

She draws back.

"No actual shagging, I hope?"

"Not that I can remember."

She hits him again.

"Can't have been much good then."

"There's not a woman born can hold a candle to you, Julia Grzyb."

"Cut the blarney Jimmy, and get your arse into bed."

Claire's in bed but she's on her own and she can't sleep. Her neighbours next door—two sweet Brazilian girls—seem to be having some kind of party in their kitchen, which is unfortunate, because it's right next to her bedroom. She considers going round and saying something but she doesn't want to be that bad-tempered neighbour who comes round and complains, and anyway, it's usually her having the parties. Besides, even if her neighbours were tucked up soundly in bed, Claire has the sneaking suspicion that she wouldn't be able to sleep anyway. The events of the day are still swirling round in her mind, and still making no sense. They just keep twisting and turning and every time Claire gets the feeling that they're settling into a pattern someone just comes along and shakes her snow globe up again.

She had taken most of the day off, let herself be persuaded by Ilya. He came round in the afternoon and took her out. They went to the park. Went out in a rowing boat for an hour. Came back freezing cold and drank hot chocolate to warm up. Almost like when she was a little kid. It was a side of him she hadn't really seen before. Beguiling, attentive, and somehow nurturing. Like he was sensitive to her moods and her needs, and wanted to take care of her. And the weird thing for her was that she was happy to let him do that. It wasn't really something she had ever really wanted from a guy before. Or at least, never been able to take at face value. They were always too fixated on their dicks. Too hung up on the sexual to ever really get down to any emotional honesty. That wasn't what she was picking up from Ilya. He seemed to be coming on to her from a totally different space.

The only question was whether she wanted that or not.

She throws back the covers and gets up, pads over to the kitchen in the dark and walks over to the fridge. The flat is cold and she's wearing her favourite washed-out old nightshirt. The light from the fridge splashes out into the darkness as she opens the door, illuminating the front of her. She grabs a carton of juice and screws the top off, puts it to her mouth and upends it, then turns and closes the fridge door with her hip. She finds the pedal of her pedal bin with a bare foot and drops the empty carton in the trash without looking. Then she wipes her mouth with the back of her hand and heads back to bed. She snuggles down into the warmth of it and her mind inescapably returns to the collective.

She skipped her shift, sure enough. But she still feels bad about it. It has left a sour taste in her mouth. In spite of her anger, in spite of everything. This was the first time that she'd outright lied to her comrades. Even now, she owes them more than that. They deserve better, and she knows it. It's been her home, political and spiritual, for years now. Ever since she washed up in the NC. All the meetings, the seminars, the demos, the night-time raids, the clandestine stuff, all the busts and the pickets, the leafleting and the zines, the posters, the loudspeaker wagons, the carbon sabbing, the whole thing. And all of the others in the group. They were like family for her. Yes, and a pain in the ass like family too. But always there for her. How could she want to give that up? But there was no escaping it, she had reached an impasse, a dead end. It was like a crisis of faith. All of the stuff they were doing, it was all ok. But it was getting them nowhere. Society kept on drifting to the right. The carbon lobby were as powerful as ever, and getting more powerful by the day, seemed to her. And nothing was getting any better. The Sixth Great Extinction was rolling on, all of the planet's critical system indicators were deepest red and getting redder, they were all collectively presiding over the extinguishing of hope for all future generations to come. It drove her crazy just thinking about it. It made her feel like there had to be something, some quantum leap that would make realization just kick into people's heads, make everyone just wake up one day and say, "We can turn this thing around," and then the process would begin. The cars would stop rolling, the oil would stop flowing, the carbon would stay in the ground, the emissions would cease, the logging would cease, the plastic waste would stop accumulating in the Great Pacific Gyre and everywhere else, the war machine would grind to a halt, the remaining wildlife would be saved, along with their habitats, and the world would wake up at 2 degrees of warming and would say, "Christ, we just made it in time." And all the freak weather would go on for hundreds of years because there would be no way of stopping it, but they would all have stuck their toes in the waters of the Anthropocene and would all have said, "No way man, too darn hot for comfort," and headed back to the Holocene with their tails between their legs.

Yeah great dream, but right now she didn't believe any of it any more. She saw the most powerful nations and corporations and governments and armies on earth ranged against her and her little group and what, maybe a few hundred little groups like them planet-wide and couldn't for the life of her see how that was going to work out. She was twenty-four, and she felt burned out, washed up, and hung out to dry.

She was in crisis, and she cried herself to sleep thinking about it.

Chapter Eighteen
Kittyhawk

Laila's alarm goes off and it fills her with a sinking feeling. She was out late again last night, drowning her sorrows, but after the tribulations of the day—first the scene with Tanita, then the whole thing with Al—she was in no mood to pick anyone up. She groans, and gets up, and mechanically showers and dresses.

She survived the rest of the day at work in stoney silence with Al, who would occasionally lecture her about something insignificant or go off at a tangent on some obscure rant. She always knew this guy was a little strange from the very beginning, but so many Agency guys seem to be warped in one way or the other that it didn't strike her as anything particularly unusual. Now however she has a burning desire in her guts to be rid of him. And she'd be surprised if the feeling wasn't entirely mutual. The thought of sitting in an office with him makes her feel physically sick. But Al was right about one thing. This was the Agency: you didn't just quit. If she pulled back from this one, that would be it. Her career would be over. Al would make sure of it. And she couldn't just report him, go over his head to the next sexist asshole up the line. The Agency hierarchy didn't take lightly to employees complaining about their superiors. So basically, she was fucked.

She pokes around at her breakfast but doesn't feel like eating. She looks out of the window and checks the weather. There's still snow on the ground from last night, but the roads seem to be clear. It will be cold as hell on the bike, even with her leathers, but better than taking the U any day. The weather app on her mobile shows that temperatures will rise to a couple of degrees above, so she decides to risk it. As long as there is no actual ice on the road, she'll be good on the bike. She pulls on her leathers and takes the elevator down to the garage level below the house, swings herself onto her machine and starts it up. Even in her present state, the powerful throb of the engine still fills her with pleasure, brings a smile to her face. In her tightly regimented world, her motorcycle has always meant a little bit of freedom.

She dawdles a little on the way to work. She had set the alarm half an hour early, and still has plenty of time. On top of that, the roads are clear but wet, so she rides with extra care. The sky is a strange mixture of light and dark—big expanses of blue striated with bands of almost black clouds low down on the horizon. The icy blast of the air makes her skin tingle every time she lifts her visor. But still, there is something beautiful about the city, some change in the atmosphere that makes her drive a little slower. As if the frosting of snow had also infected the inhabitants, filled them with a different energy, maybe making them friendlier in some way.

She remembers arriving in the NC, all those years ago, and being horrified by the way the people seemed to ignore each other. The good thing was that her family didn't seem to be afraid all the time, and that her mum could leave the house without a headscarf. The bad thing was the cold, the gulf between people, the way that everyone just seemed to exist as little islands. She couldn't detect any of those bonds of extended family and friendship that had been so important back home. If you didn't have those, you were nothing. They were your only protection against all the shit that society threw at you. The NC was famous for being a brusque, harsh place. People new to the city complained about it constantly. That, and the weather. But Laila has been here long enough now to know that things work a little differently here. Or maybe she has just gotten used to it. Become hardened and calloused like everyone else.

She takes a left at the big church on the corner of Urban and Seuss and opens the throttle up to escape from the vehicles queued up behind her, enjoying the sudden surge of speed and feeling the machine rising up a little on its suspension as the wind pushes her backwards. She's halfway down towards the next set of traffic lights, which are still on red, so she lets go of the throttle and coasts down towards them.

Laila smiles to herself as she thinks back to those first years in the city. She doesn't feel calloused. She feels like she belongs here. She remembers how nervous her parents had been when they pitched up in the NC, uprooted and alone. Even after all these years, they still had that immigrant air about them. Their language skills weren't up to much, and her mother in particular struggled. Their tragedy was that they were cut off from the rest of the highly politicized community of their compatriots. The guerrilla support networks were strong, even here, and that made them outsiders, double outsiders, in their new home. But that was their story, not hers.

She remembers her first day at school as a wide-eyed six-year-old with pigtails. She was on the defensive, she had picked up her parents' outsider vibe and was expecting school to be the same. Her father brought her to the school gates and gave her a kiss and had to give her a little push to send her off on her way across the playground to the school building. She had her head down and was clutching her little satchel as she walked those first few steps. And then she could hear voices, and the sound of running feet, and she looked up to see kids all around her, shouting in their schoolyard voices, and the thing that struck her, overwhelmingly, was that they were just like her. Little immigrant kids speaking a dozen different tongues in a seething swirling mass of arms and legs and dental braces and cheap glasses. A bell rang and a schoolteacher came out onto the steps of the building and called to them in a language she still didn't fully understand yet and herded them all into their respective classrooms. But by the time she was sitting at her desk Laila's apprehension had changed to wonder and she had a broad smile on her face. Her parents might be outsiders, but she was here where she belonged.

She takes a right onto Constantinople Avenue and scoots around the speed bumps, looking into the windows of the cafés and bakeries as she passes by and wondering whether she shouldn't stop and get some breakfast after all. Or maybe something for later. She pulls up in front of a little organic baker's shop with a steamed up window and comes out a few minutes later with a couple of croissants in a paper bag, which she tucks into her shoulder bag as she gets back onto her machine. She draws up to the traffic lights at Southern Cross and checks the time on the big street clock over by the entrance to the U. It's a quarter to. She's good, still has plenty of time. While waiting for the lights to change she takes in the enormous blackened church that dominates the whole Southern Cross junction. It's not derelict, but it strikes her than she's never seen anyone going in or out. The lights change, and she accelerates over the crossing and up onto the cobblestones of Kittyhawk.

She eases off the gas as she starts up the slight incline that leads up behind the park. The cobblestone surface is uneven at the best of times, and can be downright treacherous when wet, or icy, or covered in leaves. So Laila takes it easy as she rides up past the Polish delicatessen, past the big Catholic cathedral and the fancy graveyard next door. She keeps pretty much to the middle of the street as she passes the lines of parked cars on either side of the road and eases into the curve that takes her up towards Columbia. There are a couple of tour buses parked on the right hand side of the road directly in the curve, obscuring her view further up the street and Laila shakes her head slightly as she thinks what a fucking stupid place that is to park a bus.

She's doing about twenty when she pulls up level with the rear of the first bus and experiences a tiny wave of relief as she sees that there's nothing coming towards her on the rest of the street. She's about to open up the throttle again when there's a sickening crunch as the bonnet of a car suddenly slams into her from the side, emerging from the gap between the buses and propelling her and her machine clean across the street. Time slows down as she registers the agonizing pain in her right leg and the shocked realization that she has let go of the handlebars. She feels herself parting company from her machine and drifting up into the air. As her body rises she twists to see what has hit her and looks in through the car windscreen to see a solitary guy wearing dark glasses and a hoodie. Her hand clutches at her leg as she finds herself flying uncontrollably backwards. She can hear the roar of her machine and the screech of metal dragging itself across cobblestones. There's a moment of weightlessness when she's face upwards to the sky and blinking into the sunlight and can see a couple of naked overhanging branches from a horse chestnut in the graveyard and up in the sky the lazy movements of a seagull's wings as it flaps by and Laila remembers having time to think, "Seagulls? In the NC?" before slamming into the vehicle on the other side of the street and everything suddenly switches to black.

For some reason Claire is up early that morning. She's awake before it's light, and she's not particularly rested after a pretty lousy night's sleep. But her thoughts are still febrile and it's not long before she's up and out of bed and making herself a coffee in the kitchen. She sets her little espresso maker on the gas ring and checks her mail while she's warming up some milk. The coffee soon bubbles through and she makes herself a large *latte* in a tall glass which she takes back to bed with her while she waits for the heating system in her apartment to kick in. She checks her mails, her social media feeds and a couple of newspapers but there's nothing that catches her interest. Her mails are just spam, the feeds are just dross and the newspapers are so depressing she can't bear to read beyond the headlines.

She pulls back her curtains and takes a look at the breaking day. There's a rosy tinge to the sky, and through a break in the houses she can see the sun coming up behind the biscuit factory. She drains her coffee and resolves that today will be different. Today will be the day she sorts out the chaos in her head, the day she makes her mind up about something, anything. The day something big will happen.

She pulls off her nightshirt and slips into tracksuit bottoms, trainers, t-shirt and sweatshirt. Puts on her spex and blinks up her current playlist, then inserts her fluorescent green ear-buds and pulls a woolly hat over her head. The whole process hardly takes more than a couple of minutes and then she's grabbing her keys and is out the door and pounding down the steps and out onto the pavement. Her place is on the pedestrian part of Hillman, facing the crematorium on the side where it meets Butcher. She turns up into the graveyard with guitars thrashing in her ears and waves familiarly to the old lady caretaker tending the graves. By the time she emerges behind the police motorcycle barracks at the top of the hill she can feel her heart pounding and the glow in her cheeks. She skirts right around the police barracks and cuts across Columbia and through a little side gate over onto the old airport tarmac. She sticks with that for about quarter of an hour as she falls in with the rhythm of all the other runners and joggers, then hangs a left at the baseball diamond and cuts across Columbia again at the crossing near the new mosque. After that she's in the park, just her and a few moms pushing prams, people on bikes taking shortcuts on their way to work, a few other sporty types like herself. No drug dealers, no drug buyers, no undercover cops, no pushers or tarts or junkies. Could almost be some provincial small-town park out in the sticks, if she didn't know better.

Down by the refreshment stall in the middle of the park she orientates herself towards the northwest to take her in the general direction of home. The rose garden is empty except for a few gardeners raking the pathways, and the children's playground is deserted. She skirts around the little wooded hill on the westernmost side of the park and emerges out onto the dirt track that serves as home to a bunch of travellers in their caravans and a few people in old converted trucks. The place is trash-strewn and somehow spooky even in the daytime so she speeds up a bit as she starts the descent down towards the Catholic cathedral. She hangs a right on Kittyhawk and is heading down towards the Southern Cross when she hears a crash and the sound of metal dragging on stone and sees the shape of a woman in motorcycle leathers flying backwards across the road and slamming into the side of a car. The woman slides down the side of the vehicle and lies motionless on the street, while the car that hit her screeches out from between two buses and speeds off up the street, trailing its front fender along the ground. By the time Claire thinks to look for the number plate it's already out of range so she tries to note the make and type but she's shit with cars so the only thing she can pick up on is the fact that it's red and old-looking. She stands transfixed for a moment till she remembers the woman lying on the other side of the row of cars in front of her and runs out onto the road to find her. The woman is lying quite still and has a nasty wound on her leg and blood running out from under her helmet. Claire can see that she is still breathing but apart from that has no idea what to do. She pulls her earplugs out and punches in the number for emergency services and breathlessly calls for help. By this time a few other people have arrived and they form a little protective ring around them while Claire kneels on the cobblestones and holds the woman's hand and tells her it will be ok, although she really has no idea whether anyone could possibly be ok after something like that.

It takes a while for the ambulance to show up and in the meantime the woman on the ground regains consciousness and starts pawing at her helmet. The consensus in the little group of people standing around is that if she's able to do that, her back probably isn't broken, so they can probably go ahead and take her helmet off. Claire undoes the chinstrap and carefully pulls the helmet up and clear of the woman's head. One of the guys in the group takes off his jacket and folds it up for her to use as a cushion and she lays her head back down on the jacket and there is a think trickle of blood coming out of her mouth. Claire still has hold of her hand and the woman squeezes it now that she is conscious but seems too weak to talk. She has short, dark hair, striking brown eyes with thick lashes and arching eyebrows, and sensuous lips. She looks kind of southern, maybe Latino, thinks Claire, but that's just a wild guess.

Finally a cop car arrives and then an ambulance and it's about time because by now the woman on the ground is shivering with cold, or maybe shock, and Claire is starting to feel the chill through her sweaty clothes. The ambulance pulls up in the middle of the street and the cops block one end of the street with their squad car and go down to the other end to cordon that off too. The paramedics are unpacking the stretcher from the back of the ambulance when it occurs to Claire that maybe they ought to inform someone, so she brings her head close to the woman's face and says, "Do you want me to call anyone?", but the woman just shakes her head. Claire tries again, "No family?" and the woman mouths no, no family. And just to make sure Claire asks, "How about work?" and a tear trickles down the woman's cheek and she manages a whisper, "They know already."

The paramedics come over and check her out and heave her onto the stretcher in what seems like a matter of seconds. They're picking her up but she refuses to let go of Claire's hand and croaks, "Come with me," and Claire looks over to the paramedics but they give her a stern no and lift the stretcher up into the ambulance and pull their hands apart. Claire is over with her and says, "What's your name?" and she says, "Laila," and they are already closing the doors when Claire says, "I'll visit," and Laila nods and one of the paramedics says, "St. Catherine's," and almost as an afterthought Claire says, "I'm Claire," and the doors clunk shut and they are off in a wail of sirens and lights flashing. The police roll up the tape they've used to cordon off the street and stroll back up to their squad car. The little group that had stood around Laila look at each other and shrug and say their goodbyes and Claire just stands there for a while feeling stunned until a passing car honks its horn at her for standing in the middle of the road and she starts to walk slowly down Kittyhawk in the direction of Hillman and home.

Al is having a good day. That bitch Laila hasn't shown up yet but to be honest he wasn't expecting her to. He spent the morning talking to the three squad leaders that he has selected from the men. They have been issued with communications equipment, money, and the address of a safe house that they can use as an operations base. The men will be expected to remain quartered here in Fuji City for as long as it takes for their immigration clearance to come through, but they will more or less be able to come and go as they please. The squad leaders will have to report in at least once a week and keep Al abreast of any developments as they happen. Al made it clear that they will in any case be under constant surveillance, so the reports are more a loyalty test than anything else. City elections are due in the spring, so that only leaves them a few months to make an impact. He's divided the city up into three separate areas, one for each group, with the safe house at the nexus. They have the next seven days to familiarize themselves with their allocated areas and to come up with the outlines of an action plan based on local events and expected congregations of more than a couple of hundred people. Al's three squad leaders seem competent enough but he doesn't trust them further than he can throw them so he's keeping them on a short leash.

Al dismisses the three and leans back in his leather chair, clasping his hands together behind his head and swivelling round to look out of the window. Out on the old airfield the snow has turned to slush where the joggers and cyclists have churned it up, but is still pristine out on the grassy areas. The sun has reached its winter apex in a clear blue sky and the light is glinting off of the powdery surface of the snow. Below his window, in the fenced-off area reserved for the fujis, a couple of young men stand and smoke, staring out through the chain-link fence at the world outside. Al regards them with something approaching pity. It's not as if they are not allowed out into that world beyond the fence. It's more like the fence is a protection for them, discouraging anyone from the outside from getting too close. Anyway, they could be making themselves useful. They could have been working for him. But they must have been just too stupid, and failed the test. What a waste.

The phone rings and Al swings back round to pick up the receiver. He listens carefully to what's being said and replies, "That's awful," in a flat voice, then, "Where did they take her?" He writes down St. Catherine's on a pad on his desk and finished up with, "Yes, yes, I understand," before hanging up. He opens up a drawer in his desk and takes out a small glass and a hip flask of whiskey. He pours himself a slug, lights up a cigarette and puts his feet up on his desk.

Such a good day.

CHAPTER NINETEEN
Madame George

Gene has an audience with Madame George. No, scratch that. Jeanie has an audience with Madame George. Such an unusual event warrants the full dress uniform. Jeanie is sheathed in latex, has her stilettos on, a high-necked black lace bodysuit and a fake fur coat with collar up high against the cold. She's also bearing gifts: expensive Parisian chocolates, a bottle of Drambuie, a box of betel-flavoured beedies, and a couple of rocks of smack.

She takes a cab out to Madame George's place, which is in a converted warehouse overlooking the river. The cab pulls up in front of the building's outside elevator, and Jeanie can see the taxi driver ogling her long fishnet-clad legs as she gets out of the cab so she slips him her card and blows him a pouty kiss over the top of her long silk opera gloves.

Jeanie steps into the elevator and watches the ground fall away as it speeds her up to the fourteenth floor, simultaneously revealing the dark sparkling ribbon of the water and the bridges linking the north and south banks. The air is clear apart from plumes of steam rising from various chimneys and cooling towers, and she can see right out to the airport in the far north of the city, and the first wooded escarpment of the countryside beyond.

The doors behind her slide open and she steps out into a brightly lit corridor with half a dozen doors leading off. She walks down to the end of the corridor and rings the bell. There's a little flicker of light behind the old-fashioned spyglass and the door swings open to reveal a young guy in jeans and a t-shirt who asks her if he can take her coat and tells her to hang on for a second while he disappears into one of the rooms leading off from the hallway. He's back in a second to tell Jeanie she can go in now accompanied by a "That will be all Gary" from around the corner. Gary withdraws and Jeanie pushes the door open and walks into the room.

The first thing that strikes her is the smell, the darkness, and the temperature. The apartment has the musty, fungal, hothouse smell of too much heating behind too much double-glazing, with the walls of the room consisting almost entirely of glass, shaded by a system of external venetian blinds. It takes her a while for her eyes to adjust to the semi-darkness. A voice from one corner of the room calls over to her.

"Jeanie, dearest. So good to see you. Come over and sit down. You must excuse the mess."

Jeanie walks over and parks herself in a large Victorian armchair, but not before affectionately kissing the creased and heavily made up cheeks of the wizened figure of Madame George.

"Madame George. You're looking well. Radiant as ever."

"Ah Jeanie. Lying was never your strong point. I look like an old scarecrow and haven't had a decent fuck in ages. And it's so naughty of you not to come and visit more often. Did you bring any presents?"

Jeanie clears a space amongst the clutter on the little mosaic coffee table between them and spreads out her wares. Madame George's eyes light up like a child's.

"For me?" she cackles, "How marvellous. Jeanie, you always did know how to cheer a girl up."

Madam George rolls one of the little rocks of heroin between thumb and bony forefinger and says, "Shall we?" but Jeanie just shakes her head and says, "Not for me Madam G. Need a clear head these days."

"A spot of smack clears the old head a treat, I always say. But to each her own. What's your poison? And what brings you here?"

Jeanie cracks open the bottle of Drambuie as Madame George hooks a couple of glasses over from the retro cocktail bar behind her. Jeanie fills the glasses and hands one to Madame George.

"Chin chin."

"A tu chingada madre," says Madame George and downs it in one.

Jeanie refills the glass and hands it back to her.

"Madame G. I need your help."

"Jeanie dear, that figures. You wouldn't be here if you didn't."

"We've had some trouble down on the strip."

"Trouble you can't handle?" says Madame George, undoing the ribbon wrapped around her French chocolates.

"One of our girls, got roughed up bad by some john."

"New john?"

"Check. Clean skin. We've nothing on him. And here's the thing. We can't trace him either. Got his plates. But there's nothing. A brick wall. It's like he doesn't exist."

"So you came to me."

It's not a question. Madame George sips her drink between mouthfuls of chocolate, eyes Jeanie intently.

"So I came to you Madame G. What else could I do?"

They sit in silence as Madame George picks her way through her box of chocolates. Finally she's done, and she drains her drink and chooses a fat beedie from the box. For a moment she looks around helplessly.

"A light?" she says, and then, "And some tea? Gary! Where is that boy when you need him? Gary!"

Gary comes padding into the room on bare feet.

"Mrs G?"

"Some tea please Gary. And a light. And my glasses, there's a good lad."

"Mrs G."

"And don't take all day about it."

Madame George turns to Jeanie with a sigh of exasperation.

"That boy. Such sweet buns but really hasn't got a clue. I tell you, geriatric care these days is such a disaster. Just can't get the staff you know."

Time was, there wasn't a queer thing happened on the strip, in the whole of the NC, that didn't escape the notice of Madame George. She predated everything that Jeanie knew about the world, came from a different geological era.

Time was, back before she was even Madame George, she was just little Georgie from the main drag, dilly boy George who'd go with the servicemen off down the backstreets, who carried a little flickknife tucked down her back pocket, who knew how to take care of herself even if she was just skin and bone but good-looking with it. Georgie worked the strip and watched the world go by, became a Maryanne when she was good and ready and flaunted it to all and sundry. And got away with it. There was something about her that struck a chord, that resonated with whoever saw her. She commanded respect, even for those too preoccupied with the sins of their own transgressions to see beyond the warpaint. She thrived in the gutter, and the gutter thrived with her. She opened a speakeasy, still back in the days of sexual prohibition, and it was the underground talk of the town. More than just a bar, it was a home from home for all the castaways washed up in the city, for all the lost souls seeking that one safe harbour. And, crazily for the time, it was mixed. The women dressed in sailor suits or wide-lapelled pinstripes and G-men hats and the men dressed in gaudy outrageous creations modelled after whatever starlet was en vogue at the moment. The police were there of course, vice squad mostly, but old school plain clothes flatfoot. And it was Georgie who seduced them, brought them over, found their preferences, their weaknesses and played on them, turned them one by one till they were beholden to her, could never rat on her, never deliver her up, never launch a raid without tipping her off first. They loved her. They were the vice squad, and she was vice with a capital V. How could they not love her? She was all they dreamed about. She was the dark seductive underbelly of the city, and there weren't enough churchgoers in the force to ever break her hold. She rose through the ranks, so to speak. Became Madame George, became the establishment. Knew the entire hierarchy of the force, gave them freebies and a bottle of champers on their birthdays, knew their kids by name, sent flowers to the hospital and wreaths and condolences to funerals.

Time went on, and her influence grew. She kept lists, kept books, remembered. Used her reach to lever city senators, found herself swaying a vote here, an election there. Taking down a landlord who had overstepped the mark. Taking out a john who had gone too far, or maybe just breaking a kneecap or two as a warning. It was rough gutter justice, to be sure, but that was the way of the world. The world had done

Madame George no favours and she paid it back with tough love. But love was her currency, so there really was no other way. She'd organize street parties and the police chief would come down to have a glass and pay his respects and there'd be Madame George decked out in her finery with a retinue of sharp-eyed ladies in waiting and her squads of sailors cutting a grand figure at the bar or on the dance floor with a gaggle of swooning girls lining up and at the end of the day there'd be a cut for the orphanage and a cut for the police pension fund and the rest for the speakeasy and the rest after that into a secret little coffer that only Madame George knew about and none of your business curiosity killed the cat like but which would come in handy when things got rough.

But the thing with Madame George was that she was a man of her time. It was prohibition that formed her, it was the semi-subterranean nature of her existence that caused her to thrive. And when prohibition faded, she faded with it. She was like some deep-sea creature being brought to the surface, unable to cope with the change in pressure. She was some deep-rooted hothouse rhizome that wilted when transported to the sunlight of a spacious garden. But it was a gradual decline. The speakeasy became a normal bar, a hub for a host of emulators and epigones that sprang up around it.

Things eased up, the world moved on, but Madame George didn't move with it. Her whole life had been poised in delicate counterbalance to the powers that be, and as the powers lost interest, and the struggle relaxed, Madame George found herself somehow superfluous. She let go of the bar and drew back from the world, appearing now and again at a ball or some celebrity event, but increasingly as a relic from some unfathomable era. She stayed true to the faithful, who continued to revere her with a fanatical intensity, and cultivated her old contacts on the other side, who missed her as much as she did them.

Madame George and Jeanie sit opposite each other in their big faded armchairs in the afternoon sunlight. Gary has raised the blinds for them a bit so they can look out across the river. There's a willow-pattern china teapot on the little mosaic-topped table, and a couple of now-empty china cups and matching saucers. There's also a little glass pipe that Madame George has used to take a hit from one of the rocks that Jeanie brought her. The initial rush had Madame G gripping the arm of her chair and rolling her eyes as it knocked her back, but now she's clear and focused.

"Never understand how you do that Madame G," says Jeanie, pouring herself some more tea. "All the junkies I know are just wasted most of the time. It just trashes them."

Madame G feigns outrage, channelling Lady Bracknell.

"A junkie! My dear boy, a junkie is a different kettle of fish altogether."

She twirls her pearl necklace and Jeanie suddenly gets an inkling of what she must have been like in her prime.

"It'll take you, if you let it," continues Madame G, warming to the theme. "And you've got to let it take you, otherwise what's the point? But only on your terms."

She leans forwards in her seat, her eyes hard and sparkling.

"You need discipline. Otherwise you're done for. And purity of course. It's the impurities that most OD on."

"Discipline, I get," says Jeanie. "But it's another kind of smack that does it for me. You're just too hard core for me, Madame G."

Madame George fans herself a little at Jeanie's transparent flattery.

"Ah sweet Jeanie, you always were one of my favourites. Now to the matter at hand."

"Madame G."

"It's not good Jeanie, you know that? If you youngsters are drawing a blank, with all the technical stuff you have at your disposal these days, then really it all points in the same direction. It's either police, or deep state, or political. Diplomatic even. Did your girl say anything about an accent?"

"No accent Madame G. He was home-grown, all accounts. Caucasian, early thirties, dark-haired, maybe southern, difficult to say."

"You saw him?"

"Just briefly. Gave me a bad feeling right then. Should've followed up on it. Feel bad about Ursula too. Partly my fault I guess."

"No Jeanie," Madame G reaches out a gnarled hand and rests it on the back of Jeanie's. "One thing you learn in this business is that you can't be responsible for everything that other people do. You have your instincts, but they're yours and yours alone. And you learn them the hard way."

"If you say so, Madame G."

"I do say so Jeanie. And here's what I'll do. I'll reach out to some of the good old boys. Most are in retirement now, but they still keep their hand in. Still have a few lines into vice and special branch. Give me the licence number. If it's a police vehicle we should have it. And get a picture made up. Find someone who can draw and tell them what you saw. Get that to me. We'll know in a day or two, either way. But if we draw a blank with the police, and it's not a politico, then you know what that means."

Jeanie sets her tea down and looks over.

"State security Madame G?"

"Exactly my dear. State security. Things could get nasty."

Chapter Twenty
Ilya

Ilya's back doing what he's best at, and that's lurking in the under-world. What he saw the other day is still bothering him. Intriguing him more than anything. He's been sifting through the sediment of the whole attack-repulse event and has been piecing it back together, letting the charred and blackened sand of the data explosion run through his virtual fingers, gleaning for wreckage, for pointers, for clues. It's not the battle so much that interests him, as its cause. Once the defence routines were initiated by the beast, then basically it was all over. If there's one thing Ilya knows it's that you can't use brute force when one side has a monopoly of power. It's the mark of an amateur, not the way of the warrior. When the enemy has invincible defences, it can only be stealth that will win the day.

So Ilya sieves and sifts, employs his best routines and his most cunning algorithms to recreate the initial singularity that was the cause of so much sound and fury. He's like a crime scene pathologist, picking out the tiniest of clues, the DNA traces, the scratches and minute indicators that will provide the key to unlocking the event. It takes him the best part of a day but finally he has it. And when he has it, he bursts out laughing. It's so pathetic. A simple vehicle licence ID request. A transaction so common that he has never heard of it being denied, never mind being swatted away so viciously, or followed up by a desperate brute force attack.

As if the beasts would normally give a fuck about that kind of thing. But the weird thing is, they did give a fuck. Their overreaction gave them away, imparted to the signifier a burden of signification that betrayed it. Ilya is intrigued. He takes his little snippet of reclaimed licence plate information and tucks it away for future reference. Because now, his curiosity is fired up, and Ilya is set to go on an expedition. All the way into the cavernous territory of the virtual big beasts.

He checks his schedule and figures he can take the afternoon off for his expedition. He's not intending to fight but he packs a little light digital weaponry just in case. If it comes to a firefight then the best he can expect is to crash and burn, and then he can kiss his digital ass goodbye. No, his only real chance is to go unnoticed, remain invisible, walk up and blow the feather off the tiger's nose. And if he's discovered, then his best chance of survival will be to cause a diversion, keep them confused. Create so many images of himself that with any luck they will pounce on the wrong one and he'll be gone.

That at least is his hope as he sets off.

He's put the outside world on hold, paused or unplugged all incomings, made himself unavailable even though he is very much online. He's voided his bowels and has taken an appetite suppressant, which has the added effect of being an upper. Or was it the other way around? Either way, the last thing he wants to deal with when he's in some life-and-death cyber scenario is having to deal with bodily functions in meatspace. Too gross.

He's also relinquished his beloved retro no-name keyboard and blackbox gear for the exploit. This is going to have to be a purely synaptic event, so Ilya spends some extra care tuning his wetware interface and his glasses, both top-of-the-range military gaming gear. He runs them through a few drills and routines until he's satisfied with the synch, does a final check of his stores and equipment, takes a deep breath, and takes the plunge.

He gets that weird weightless feeling as he drifts down through the levels of world. It's not as if you can just plug in and—bam—you're there. Rather, you have to *feel* your way down. Take each level as it comes and intuit its cracks and crevices, its weakness until you're through, with each level a little tougher than the one before. Until at last you're sinking, like some deep-sea bathysphere, whilst at the same time insinuating yourself through the cracks, squeezing and holding your breath as the passageways become smaller until you're finally there, in the deepest, most alien caverns of the underworld and you are just a wraith with no weight and no substance, leaving no trace.

In the best-case scenario that is.

Ilya takes a moment to regain his bearings and heads over to the scene of the recent flare-up and the site of his surreptitious investigations. He's a stone's throw away from the big beast's perimeter and he can feel the adrenalin surging as he edges nearer. He has no body as such to worry about, but the adrenalin could affect his synaptic interfaces, cause him to over-react and break his cover. So he forces himself to be calm as he drifts closer to the beast's outer defences. He's closer than he has ever been and from here he can see that the beast is in fact a shape-shifter, continually configuring and reconfiguring on its outer perimeter, a constant flux that creates the impression of a living, breathing organism, albeit on a massive scale. The perimeter pulses as Ilya nears it. Irregular waves of energy travel back and forth along its length causing it to expand and contract in great shivering breaths. Ilya is so close now that he could reach out and touch it, but of course he won't, because it would probably be the last online breath he would ever take. At this depth there is no real telling what the repercussions of a virtual wipe-out would be back in meatspace, and he doesn't want to find out. He's heard all the apocryphal stories about the brains of intrepid cybernauts being fried along with their wetware, leaving them mere vegetables plugged into a bunch of expensive equipment. Or about hackers held captive in the lower levels until their outer bodies collapse for lack of support, simply withering away or suffering some kind of seizure. Ilya has never had much time for that kind of talk, and now is not a good time nor place to start thinking about it.

Everything down here is simultaneously slowed down and speeded up in the freakiest of ways, and his weightlessness make self-propulsion difficult, like trying to walk underwater. Ilya's just thinking about the last time he actually was underwater when one of the undulating perimeter waves takes him by surprise and smacks right through him, leaving him gasping for breath, from surprise, more than anything.

It takes him a couple of seconds to recover his senses and by the time he does he realizes that two good things have happened. Firstly, he has not been discovered. Secondly, he is on the inside of the perimeter.

CHAPTER TWENTY-ONE
St Catherine's

Laila comes awake and she's in a darkened room. There are tubes connected to her body and some kind of multi-monitor pulsing softly on a table near her bed. Her mouth is dry and her tongue seems to be made of sandpaper. She's not in pain but that's probably because she can't feel her body. She flexes her right hand and digs her fingernails into her palm, just to see if she's still there. The pain comes through to her in a long-distance, second-hand kind of way, as if someone is just telling her about it. There's nothing to do. She feels like she needs a piss and holds it back until she realizes that they have inserted a catheter so she lets go and just pisses right there in the bed.

She's just woken up but she feels infinitely tired, like she'll never be able to get up again. There's a remote on a long cable down by her left hand and she holds it up to her face so that she can get a good look at it. The two controls are marked Up and Down so she figures it must be for the bed and hits Up and her head and torso are propelled slowly upwards until she reaches an angle of about 45°. The curtains are drawn and she guesses it must be night outside, although the room itself is bathed in a subdued green light. There's a slit under the doorway with light coming in from the corridor outside, and every now and then she can see it darken as somebody walks by. Her head is heavy and difficult to move and she has a feeling that it would probably hurt like hell if they ever turn off the medication they have got her on. She reaches up with one hand and discovers that she's wearing a neck brace. She slides her hand down her body underneath the sheets and doesn't discover any other injuries until she reaches her right leg, which is heavily bandaged. She panics for a second before she tries wiggling her toes and relaxes when she sees a tiny movement down the other end of the bed.

The weird thing is, she has no immediate recollection of how she got here. She's conscious enough to realize that it must be related to some kind of traumatic event, but she feels absolutely no inclination to probe any further into that particular sore spot.

On the whole she's experiencing an overwhelming sense of heaviness, peace even, tinged with a slight feeling of boredom. The dim lighting, the steady beep of the machine, the sound of her pulse in her ears, the gentle rasp of her breath, and the distant clatter and murmur of people doing stuff beyond her door. It's as if someone has drawn a thick curtain across her mind, like she's just come off of a stage after the first act of a performance. Maybe she'll be on again in a minute, but for now she's thankful for the breather and the calm of her little room. There's a TV monitor up in one corner and she's glad that it's off but she wonders if she will get a remote for that too. A face comes into her mind and it's the face of the woman who knelt down in the dirt with her, when she was, when she was what exactly?

She remembers lying on her back and people standing around looking down at her, and she remembers feeling confined and constricted until the woman did something and everything opened out and there was suddenly sky everywhere. And that face of course. Beautiful face. Wonderful eyes, but worried. Why so worried?

She remembers feeling cold. And that metallic taste in her mouth. She was lying on her back in the cold with a beautiful young woman kneeling next to her. Was she holding her hand? Yes. There in the dirt. Out in the open, with the sky overhead. And the trees. She could smell the park. And car fumes. But mostly the winter smell of the park. And that woman. She had a perfumed, sweaty smell about her. And the flowers.

No, no flowers.

No flowers when she was lying on her back in the dirt. Not there. Between the cars. On the cobblestones.

No, the flowers are here. In this room. A heavy, cloying scent.

Laila can't see them. But she can smell them. They are on the table next to her bed. Set back a little beyond her field of vision. She reaches out a hand and finds the rail on the little movable bedside table and pulls it around so that she can see it. On it there's a large vase with long-stemmed arum lilies. They're beautiful, if a little eerie. There's a message tag around the bouquet with a Get Well Soon motif on one side. Laila turns it round and reads, "With love, Al" on the other side.

She knocks the flowers onto the floor and screams and screams and screams.

Claire pitches up at St Catherine's towards the end of visiting hours and asks her way through. No, she's not next of kin. No, she doesn't know the surname. Only the first name, Laila. Was brought in today. Traffic accident. Can't be too difficult she thinks, but keeps that one to herself. Still, it takes a while before they are ready to admit her, then longer to find who she's looking for, find out where she has been moved to, and give her directions, and then even longer for her to set off, get lost, ask directions again and finally make it to Laila's room. She checks with a ward nurse if it's ok and she gives her a nod but warns her that the patient is heavily sedated after something upset her so it might be best to come back tomorrow. The sister is in her mid-thirties, with long dark hair tied back in a bun.

"Good job you didn't bring any flowers."

Claire looks down at her hands and realizes that she didn't bring anything. That it didn't even occur to her to bring anything. The thought makes her blush a little.

"Why's that?"

"Knocked over a big vase of them. Couldn't stop screaming. That's why we had to sedate her. Can't for the life of me imagine what the problem was. Pretty flowers, after all. Maybe she's allergic. What about you, any idea?"

"Me? No, I hardly know her."

"Then why are you here?"

"I was there at the accident. Held her hand for a while. Thought I'd check in on her."

The sister gives a brief smile.

"Good of you. Off you go then. Room 13. Good luck."

The nurse turns back to her paperwork and Claire heads off down the corridor. She pushes open the door to room 13 and lets the light from the corridor flood in. The room itself is in semi-darkness and she can see Laila stretched out on the bed, her right leg a fat shape under the blanket and a thick white collar around her neck. The floor on one side of the bed has been freshly mopped and there are porcelain shards in the waste paper basket. Claire is not sure whether to stay or go but Laila moans softly and shifts a bit in her bed, so Claire figures there's a chance she might wake up. She pulls up a chair from the wall to the bed and turns on the little lamp clamped onto the bedside table. The door to the room swishes shut of its own accord and Claire settles into her seat and looks at Laila, and the rhythmic rise and fall of her breathing, and feels herself becoming drowsy with the quiet pulse of the machines and the dim light in the room.

Laila stirs and manages to open her eyes and attempts a smile when she sees Claire. She opens up the fingers of one hand and Claire takes it and there is a familiarity between them that surprises her, and moves her. She says, "You ok?" and there's a mix of emotions that pass across Laila's face, a wry smile followed by something painful and she says, "Guess so," and Claire realizes that no, she is far from ok. Claire has no real experience of hospitals and feels like there ought to be some code of practice, some guidebook to lead her through a situation like this. She says, "Thought I'd come and see how you're doing," and Laila nods with her eyes and says, "That's nice."

Claire thinks she might be being ironic and lowers her head but Laila squeezes her hand and says, "No really. It's good of you. Thanks."

"Is there anything you need? I can bring you stuff. I'll leave you my number and you can let me know if there's anything you want bringing in from outside."

Laila takes a deep breath and it's like a shudder passing through her body.

"Don't want you going to any trouble."

"It's no trouble. Honest. Happy to help."

Claire takes in the room, which is bare, except for the various bits of medical equipment. No cards, no gifts, no get well soon messages.

"Isn't there anyone you want me to get in touch with?"

Laila shakes her head as much as the neck brace will allow. The question seems to distress her.

"My parents died a while back. They were all I had."

"No boyfriend?"

"Boyfriend?" That wry smile again. "No, no boyfriend. Definitely no boyfriend."

Claire has the sensation of being some kind of blundering oaf and feels herself blushing again.

"Sorry. I didn't mean… Didn't mean to assume. Stupid of me. No girlfriend then? No anybody?"

Laila smiles and there's something approaching a laugh that forms in her throat but which is stifled before it can emerge.

"There's nobody right now. Nobody that I would want to see."

There's a silence between them then. Claire can see that Laila is drifting a bit, that she's lost in thoughts that are clearly troubling her, or maybe it's just the pain, or the medication, or everything together. Either way, she lets her drift. Holds her hands and listens to the silence in the room, thinks how weird it must be to be lying here, in a hospital, with all these strange people. A sudden change to a completely new environment.

Laila comes back from wherever she has been and looks at Claire.

"Nurse tell you about the flowers?"

"Yeah. Thought best not to bring it up. You allergic?"

"Allergic to my fucking boss."

"Ah, I get it."

"No. I don't think you get it. It was him. It was his doing."

Claire's eyes are wide now, like she's been ripped out of some kind of torpor.

"What are you saying? That he caused the accident?"

"S'right."

"But that's awful. That's…criminal. We have to phone the police."

"Claire. No. No police. It wouldn't do any good."

"I don't understand."

"You don't need to understand. Not right now. Just take my word for it."

There are beads of sweat on Laila's forehead, and her voice is weak and ragged. She closes her eyes and from a far-away place says, "I think you'd better go now."

Claire's mind is full of questions but she keeps them to herself. She stands up and says, "Ok," and then, "You want me to come back?" and Laila says, "Please. I'd like that."

Claire is almost at the door when Laila calls softly over to her.

"And Claire?"

She turns.

"Yes?"

"Thanks."

Back in the belly of the beast, Ilya is doing his best to make sense of his new surroundings. Now that he is through the perimeter, the terrain is completely unfamiliar to him. What previously had appeared as a shape-shifting, amoeba-like, living being has now reconfigured into something resembling a high-tech encampment, or space station. Glowing nodules of data are interconnected with a myriad of tube-like structures, and each nodule has its own signature frequency, which Ilya's interface translates both in terms of hue and pitch, and of course, dimension. Ilya has no doubt that the nodes are all populated with living intelligences, both human and artificial, and that far from being mere dumps of dead data, they represent the living animus of the state apparatus, hive-like repositories of distilled information gleaned from millions of resources, harvested daily and diligently relayed back to the central intelligences of the hive-minds with their concomitant hierarchy of workers, drones and queens.

Ilya has no plan now. His recombinant data DNA brought him merely to the perimeter. Now that he is inside, there is no telling which way to go. The mind closest to the perimeter seems as good a bet as any, and he sets off towards it. He's almost got to the point of thinking that this is too easy when his path his blocked by a patrol agent apparently circling the node on some elliptical orbit. The agent is easily identifiable from its guard corps insignia and its deployed array of sniffer-killer K9 routines. Ilya freezes, and the agent freezes with him. The guard looks around blindly, sensing the tension in the leads to its attack routines, which have occasioned the sudden hiatus in its normal patrol orbit. The K9s sniff the air, paw at the ground, have their virtual ears cocked and all sensors on maximum alert. They can sense an anomaly, know something is up. But it's not something they can identify. They sniff right through Ilya and still can't get a trace on him. Ilya is immobilized with fear. He doesn't dare to breathe. Finally they let up, unable to find the source of their unease, and turn back to their master, who snaps tight the leads and urges them on with a series of barely intelligible commands.

Ilya is shaken but now's not the time to relax. The agent or others like it could be back around at any time, so he pushes on towards the outer surface of the node. Up close it's a massive structure, like some vastly inflated geodesic sphere. Ilya runs his hands along the surface, which crackles with energy that arcs up to his fingers. This in itself is enough to worry him. If the energy can detect his presence, then his cloaking is not as faultless as he had hoped, meaning that he might already be registering on some intrusion monitor somewhere. On the other hand, the likelihood of anyone making it this far through their defences alive must already count as infinitely small, so maybe it's not something they would be looking for. Ilya has no choice, either way. He must find a way through the outer skin and into the hive. He spends the best part of an hour examining the structure, investigating the seals around the connecting tubes, and is starting to feel despondent when he comes across a small service vent. It's encrypted, of course, but it looks like something he could access and he gives it his best shot. He has a range of utility hacks that the Swiss Army would be proud of, and methodically deploys each one until he finds some traction. After he's overcome the initial resistance it doesn't take him long and he's through, squeezing himself through the confined space and taking care not to disturb any of the service data supplying and maintaining the hive. From his vantage point in the service duct he can see the swarm of relay bots, accompanied at irregular intervals by fully automated drones guarding, even here, the uninterrupted flow of data. Ilya senses that there is no way that he could survive in that intense stream of hostile energy, and that his cover would probably be ripped to shreds within seconds. Once that happened, the drones would be on him instantly, and that would be the end of it. Or they would be programmed to capture him alive, the better to augment their defences. But that option didn't bear thinking about.

CHAPTER TWENTY-TWO
The Mary Jane

Gene feels his phone vibrating in his pocket and it's Madame George. He's been walking along the canal, pretty much lost in thought, but now he's come up onto the bridge on Kane Avenue and is heading down towards Alberta and O. He holds the device to his ear and leans on the balustrade.

"Madam George. What a pleasure. And so quick."

"Not one to hang around, Jeanie my dear."

Gene tries to shield his ears from the booming of the traffic behind him whilst looking down to the dark waters of the canal below.

"You have something for me?"

"Not much, I'm afraid."

"You want me to come round?"

"No need. It's all perfectly innocuous. But very much as we suspected. None of our old friends can help us with our lost kitten. It's not in any of their gardens."

"That's a shame."

"A shame indeed. But narrows our options perhaps. In any case, fear not. We shall persevere in our search. I'm sure she'll turn up."

"Madame G. I owe you one."

"Sweet Jeanie, the pleasure's mine. Just remember to come up and see me sometime."

Madame George hangs up, and Gene is left staring out into the darkness. There's a whiff of fried chicken on the wind from the little kebab stand behind him. A neon sign pulses out Ali Baba's Chicken Delights into a night already saturated with headlights, taillights, streetlights, the flicker of advertising, window displays and shop signs galore.

Gene tries to imagine what it would be like without all of this, tries to turn the power off in his mind, see the city drenched in darkness.

It had happened once before, to his knowledge. Not the cars of course, but all the rest. A sudden outage had blacked out most of the city. He was too young, back then, so hadn't experienced it himself. But the excesses of that night were the stuff of legend. People poured out onto the streets, bringing whatever portable noise-making, light-emitting equipment they had with them. The bars made do, switched to bottled beer when the pumps failed, carried on as usual with candles and the glow of phone screens and torches and whatever they had to hand. And what most people had to hand was the person they were sitting with and the sudden, ubiquitous darkness was like a licence to fuck and a sudden surge of sexual energy that passed through the populace and people started going at it in the unlikeliest of places. Hands slid into clothing and breasts were exposed and flies unzipped and strangers in bars who had maybe surreptitiously checked each other out when they first sat down suddenly found themselves approaching each other with urgent physical enquiries.

Outside the party raged, particularly in this area around Alberta and O, where everyone was always up for it, but the pickings were lean so they spilled over and fanned out in search of plunder and found it in the shape of old man Kenally's supermarket over on the corner of Vienna and Mandrake just next to the overground station and they ripped down the shutters and took out all his stock and stripped the place clean and no-one knows how it happened but some dumb fucker set light to it and pretty soon the whole place was billowing smoke with flames licking up through the shattered shopfront right up to the flat roof and no-one except old man Kenally was particularly sorry to see it go but the people in the tenement next door were screaming and they were right to scream because the whole block would have gone up in flames if it weren't for the fire brigade who were on alert anyway and let's face it had their station just a couple of hundred yards further down Vienna on the other side of the street so they just had to drive or even walk over and put the fucker out.

But by then word was spreading fast and people didn't need much encouragement at the best of times and a second wave passed through the crowds and people just started hurling stuff at the nearest shop windows, didn't matter much what it was, and people were using ripped-up paving stones and boots and baseball bats and trash cans and whatever they could get their hands on to smash into whatever was standing between themselves and the insides of the shop they had targeted. And the trans sexworkers on Charlie's Garden kicked their way into Woolies and came out onto the street triumphantly clutching some utter tat, aprons and mops and mixers and toilet rolls and they set off into a cackling mad war dance and lit a bonfire right there on the street with all this household stuff and it was like domesticity set alight by a gaggle of mad witches drunk on revolution but by this time also drunk on drink.

The police were out there too of course, but communications were down or patchy and they were feeling isolated and frightened and outnumbered and frankly who could blame them? Didn't stop them cracking heads mind, and busting a bunch of people and even killing one or two but that came later when things really started to get out of hand. Because the sudden surge of burning and looting had triggered something else in the people and all of those who had fallen into mouth-to-mouth combat with total strangers suddenly found themselves questioning the wisdom of their decisions, and although most decided to press on regardless, some started to think better of it and maybe no, maybe now was a good time to stop, out here in this bar, in this darkened public place or maybe not so public place and it was then that the real nastiness started to happen and there were screams and cries and injuries and maybe people intervened and maybe they didn't and people were cut and hurt and wounded and most survived but some didn't and some of those strangers-turned-aggressors walked away into the night and some woke up to find themselves with a well-deserved knife in the back.

And so people and events spiralled out of control into a night of general mayhem that burned itself into the collective memory of the NC and everyone had a take on it depending on whether they gained or suffered and then suddenly it was over and the power came back on and out in the streets it was a signal for the restoration of the previously prevailing status quo, and the plunderers quit plundering and the looters quit looting and the revellers just carried on drinking and dancing and the police felt emboldened and started cracking heads with a vengeance to clear the streets but in the bars and cafés where people had slipped under tables or had consensually exposed themselves and others there was a kind of generalized *in flagranti* moment of embarrassment and re-clothing which was met with sheepish grins and knowing looks and swiftly covered up with the music from the sound systems and sudden bursts of activity. And there was screaming too, as the injured and the wounded emerged from the shadows and the realization rippled out of what else had been happening and the mobile networks went back online and immediately crashed as people phoned emergency services who in any case were already overwhelmed by the whole event and were in no position to come and collect anyone even if they could have gotten through.

And so it's with this sense of the volatility of things that Gene turns and heads up Kane in the orange night. The streets themselves are brightly lit, but he feels the darkness pressing in as he walks. He reaches Cartersgate and the huge edifice of the overground planted squarely in the middle with its 19th Century grey steel girders and their huge rivets supporting the overhanging platforms and the curved glass roof of the station spattered with pigeon shit.

Underneath the overhang, on the central reservation, sit a couple of cop cars and armoured paddy waggons, their windshields covered in the familiar black wire mesh. There's no current threat of civil disturbance in the air, but the police like to make their presence felt.

Gene wonders for a moment whether this shouldn't be the way to go. One of their number has been attacked and nearly killed after all, so maybe they should be on the streets shouting about it, instead of hunkering down in self-defence mode. Street protests are not so much Gene's forte. He usually leaves that to the politicos and the activists and deals with the more pragmatic side of things. But maybe they need to stir things up. Judging by what Madame George said, all things are pointing towards some kind of state-shielded operative. Might take them years to find out more about the attacker. It might all just end up as one of those crimes that emerge thirty years later, when the archives are released, and everyone involved is too dead or decrepit to do anything about it. There was no way they could wait that long. Something had to happen now. They also had the likeness Gene had had drawn for Madame G's enquiries. They could get that done up on a poster and plastered around the city. Maybe even with a reward. That might be enough to encourage someone to come forward or create a few leads. It was worth a try.

The group of cop vehicles are like a magnifying glass for Gene's attention, bringing his thoughts to a focal point strong enough to ignite whatever's beneath it. He takes a detour into the nearest bar, the Mary Jane. If it were summer he could just sit out amongst the fake fountains and garden furniture planted incongruously on the grimy city pavement, but right now it's way too cold for that. The Mary Jane is backed up against two huge blocks of cheap apartments that curve around the whole of the southeastern side of Cartersgate. In fact the whole of Cartersgate forms a kind of brutalist hub within the broader charmlessness of the NC, and acts as a perfect backdrop for its nocturnal inhabitants—the junkies, the panhandlers, the cops, the narks, the homeless, the tourists, the drinkers and dealers and consumers and all the rest of them. Any local kids out on the street are inevitably in groups and gangs for self-defence, and the residents of the apartment blocks are either at home or ensconced in the various cheap cafés where the tourists don't dare go.

Up at the bar in the Mary Jane, Gene orders the house special, the Mary Jane Rag: a Bloody Mary variant with a massive amount of piri piri, a lime wedge and speared dill pickle garnish, served with a beer chaser and a serviette. He takes his drinks over to the window and settles down to refocus on the cops. But the bar is full and there's some kind of open mic event happening on the stage at the far end of the room. It's hosted by an enormous drag queen with a massive purple wig, manga-style makeup, striped tights and six-inch platform soles. She introduces a band called the Bagel Heads who, appropriately enough, are all dressed the same, in tartan trousers and braces, with the bagelhead signature bulges of injected saline solution on their foreheads. The music though, is shit, and Gene finds it difficult to concentrate.

A familiar figure slips onto the chair opposite Gene. It's Omar, the owner of the Mary Jane. Technically, the Mary Jane is a collective, but it's Omar who puts his signature on the papers and his head on the line. No-one makes big bucks, but they all make a living and the surplus is ploughed into various extra-curricular activities. Like organizing rent strikes. Like protesting racist attacks or police brutality. Gene has the beginnings of an idea, but they have a lot of catching up to do, and Omar orders a round of drinks and starts talking. And when Omar starts talking, you'd better have time on your hands.

Omar gesticulates wildly as he talks. His fingers are heavy with thick silver rings, and a large-gauge septum piercing hangs from his nose. He has a silver spiral weaving through the upper cartilage of his left ear, and both lobes are heavily gauged with dark ebony inserts. Omar is known to his friends as Queen Vic, on account of his Prince Albert. His hair is dark and close-cropped, and his goatee is grizzled with grey.

"Been thinking of dying it, y'know, but can't decide on a colour."

"Not black?"

"Some days I think maybe shocking pink, or green, or maybe even red. But I'd have to bleach it first, and that would be like, a total pain."

"How about henna, you thought of henna?"

"Yeah, too dark man. I mean, nothing against henna. But I just can't go with those earth tones, y'dig? No, I need something with a bit more class. A bit more gutter trash. More in-your-face cheap, know what I mean."

"I'm with you Vic."

Gene can feel the booze taking its toll on his empty stomach. Drinks for Omar's guests are always outrageously strong.

"But maybe henna for the hands, no? You could do the whole mendhi thing."

"Gene, baby, maybe you're onto something! Never been into tats mind. Needles through skin, I don't mind. But needles injecting stuff under your dermis, that's like, gross, you know?"

Gene nods sagely, and sips his drink, and wonders how he can avoid getting totally smashed here with Omar, who is here every night of the week and in serious training.

"But henna you know, that could be it. Could do some serious psychedelia on my palms and up the forearms, and if you don't like it, well it's gone in a couple of weeks. Hell, could even do my face, what d'ya reckon?"

"All good Vic, all good. But you know, I've got a different kind of face painting on my mind at the moment," and Gene pulls the mug shot out of his jacket and clears some space on the table and smooths out the picture in front of Omar.

Omar pulls a pair of Lennon-style specs out of a waistcoat pocket and says, "What's this?"

And Gene tells him the whole story of Ursula and the guy in the big phaeton and their dead end and Madam G. And Gene gets another round of drinks in and Omar won't let him, but Gene insists and they mock bicker about that for a while and both decide they're ravenous and send out for some Thai food from the place on the other side of Cartersgate down on Alberta.

By the time the food comes Gene is through with the whole story and the big drag queen with the striped tights is announcing yet another band who seem to have brought their own fan base with them as a table full of biker dykes erupts in whoops and whistles.

Omar pulls the paper wrapper off of his disposable chopsticks and strokes his beard thoughtfully.

"This is some heavy shit Gene." He wrangles a herd of unruly noodles into his mouth while reaching for more chili sauce.

"We heard about it on the grapevine, you know. Kids here are up in arms about it. But it's like, your call, know what I mean. You guys need to take the lead on this. We're here for you, if you need us. We've got the infrastructure. Can get stuff printed up. Put the word out. Get the kids out on the street. Even get you a loudspeaker van and some stewarding. But it's not something we really want to kick off on our own. Has a totally different impact if you're on board from the get go."

Gene nods and struggles with his food. The rice keeps falling off his chopsticks and the room seems to be listing and yawing in an unpredictable manner. And he's not sure he should be taking any major decisions in so flaky a state.

"Ok Vic, let me think it over. Need to talk to the girls about it. And the church. I'm pretty sure they'll back us up."

"The Kali kids? Thought they liked to keep a lower profile."

"Not sure how they'll want to play it. But they've been taking care of Ursula. And now they're baying for blood, so I reckon we can count on them."

They finish their meal and Omar wanders over to the big Italian coffee machine and brings them back a little tray with two espressos and grappa.

Gene lays a twenty on the table and Omar just looks at him like—pah!—and says, "Man you never learn. Just stick it back in your pocketbook why don'tcha?" And Gene is too full and drunk and tired to argue so he just says thanks and gets up and puts on his jacket. Omar puts a hand on his arm and says, "If you decide to go for it, and my guess is you will, when do you think? This weekend?"

"Will that give you enough time to move on it? Get everything ready?"

"Sure. You give us the green light tomorrow sometime, we're on it. Couple of days will be enough. Leave the picture with me. We'll have the fucker's face plastered over the city in no time."

"Ok Vic. Just let me sleep on it. I'll get back to you."

They embrace, and Gene is through the door and out into the street just as the band launches into a ska cover of "Chase the Devil".

Claire is home alone and feeling down and wondering where the hell Ilya is and how come he's not responding on any channels. She texted him before going in to the hospital and mailed him when she came out and now she's even phoned him a couple of times but nada surf. He's like disappeared from the face of the earth and that hasn't happened all the time they have been together. She frets a bit and feels the events of the past couple of days getting to her and here she is all alone in the big city and not on speaking terms with her crew and witness to some chick getting run over and now her guy has evaporated on her just when she needs him most. She turns on the tube and zaps through about thirty channels but it's all just mainstream trash beaming manufactured fear and normal into her living room and that's more than she can cope with right now. She goes to her window and looks out across to the crematorium and the graveyard behind and normally it just speaks to her inner goth and has a soothing influence on her, but tonight there is some guy leaning on the wall opposite smoking a cigarette and she's sure they make eye contact when she looks down at him and that gives her a totally paranoid rush and she pulls the curtains in a hurry and when she looks down again from the window of her darkened bedroom the guy has gone and she feels like she must be going out of her mind. She makes herself some tea and tries to settle down with a book and some music when her phone goes and she's scrabbling around to find where she left it—like duh on the rim of the bath—but when she finally answers it's not Ilya but Josh from the group and that leaves her a little confused for a moment.

Josh launches in with, "Hey Claire, howya doing?", and Claire is like, "Hey Josh, could be better, you know?"

"Yeah Claire, that's what I wanted to talk about. I'm sorry about the way things went the other night. It doesn't have to be this way. I got the vibe you're really thinking about leaving, and that would be such a loss for the group."

"Yeah right."

"No, seriously Claire. We don't want you to go. I don't want you to go."

There's a pause as Claire takes in what he's saying. Josh has never been very forthcoming in personal terms, and now this? It sounds almost like he's coming on to her, or fessing up some kind of crush. But she has always assumed that he was anything but straight, so it's kind of weird and disturbing rather than flattering and definitely not what she needs right now. Or maybe she's just feeling ultra-sensitive.

"Uh, thanks Josh. I don't really know what to think at the moment. It's all a bit too much for me right now."

"I know, I totally understand. That's why I wanted to reach out to you…"

Reach out. Makes him sound like a marketing executive, thinks Claire.

"We ought to meet up. Sometime soon."

"Josh, you can talk to me now. I have time."

"No Claire. We really need to meet up. How about tomorrow morning? Ten thirty at Hanky Pankey's? They do great breakfast."

Claire wonders what the fuck is so important that Josh really has to meet up with her, but what she says is:

"Ok Josh, tomorrow, ten thirty. See you there."

It's getting late, and Ilya is starting to feel exhausted. He can feel his concentration wandering and his meatspace body making increasingly strident demands on him to come back, move, stretch, take a piss, do anything but remain stuck in this cramped space, inching his way forwards. He's also seriously thinking about just pulling the plug, and giving up. It's not his favourite exit mode, and certainly not as clean as retracing his steps. The sudden decompression can mess with your head and induce Gamers' Bends, a form of psychosis where a too-rapid switch of reality levels can cause temporary or even permanent maladjustment. On top of that, pulling the plug is messy, and leaves unpredictable traces at the departure site. If you go out the way you came you can clean up as you go, but if you just remove yourself, then there's no telling what you might leave behind. It's a classic beginners' mistake, to conduct an exploit, make a heist of some sort and then think—I'm outta here. Nine times out of ten those are the traces that will get you busted.

So Ilya's weighing his options. He's been down here a long time and has nothing to show for it. Not that he's even sure what he's looking for. Sure, it was the vehicle number that brought him in here, and the whole explosion around it, but now it's more like his explorer's instincts have gotten the better of him. The whole landscape, the entire architecture is so outrageously alien it's not like anything he has ever seen before, on any level of the weeb. More than anything, it's that aspect that is keeping him going. Just to look. Just to see it and survive. And maybe learn something that he can use later.

He inches forwards and can hear the sound around him changing in modulation from the incessant traffic-like roar of the data flow beneath him to something more rhythmic, but irregular, a little like a drummer trying out different patterns and riffs. He rounds a corner and finds himself looking down into a wide cylindrical space. The incoming swarm of databots coagulate to form a dense thrumming cloud circling the base of a huge central intelligence—the hive queen. Each individual transport routine parks itself in an orbiting pattern until an opportunity arises for it to release its heavy data load into the myriad receptors around the queen's abdomen. After that, it's free to fly off to the exit tube in search of fresh data. Ilya watches in amazement as the towering figure of the queen submits to the ministrations of her servant hordes, graciously accepting each gob of data with the most minimal of acknowledgments, and from there, somehow processing it and boiling it down into a dense, data-rich golden liquid mass—the thickest, sweetest data sources Ilya has ever seen. As it oozes from the vents in her thorax, the queen gathers the heavy data gloop into packages that her countless arms constantly transport to the hexagonal receptor buckets that form the innumerable arrays of the towering cylinder walls around her. Nothing is lost, nothing wasted. Pulses of crystalline light travel through the honeycomb structure at irregular intervals, perhaps as the data is accessed from external sources, or maybe just performing integrity checks and keeping the data essences alive in some way. And high above, way up above the head of the queen, a separate swarm of drones is there to monitor and guard the whole process.

Ilya decides it's time to move. He's been here long enough, and he's seen enough. But something in him says that there's no way he can leave empty handed. Not after coming this far. Even if it's just a trophy. But anything that he takes with him can be used against him. If he gets raided, and the feds find anything from this deep, anything this classified, he'll be banged up in solitary for the rest of his foreseeable life. He needs to be clear about that. It's a crazy risk. And for what? He can tell that whatever is here must be incredibly valuable, but up till now he has no idea what it might even contain. He's like an old-time bank robber who suddenly finds himself in the middle of a safe-deposit vault, and the clock's ticking. He can't know what's in any of the individual boxes, his only option is to take a bag full, a sack, barrow, skip, hell, truck load of them with him and hope for the best.

Ilya checks his gear. His plan is pretty simple. Create a diversion. Create an illusion. Smash and grab. And get the hell out of there.

Not the most elegant exploit he's ever committed. But if he can pull it off, it could make him crazy rich. He'd never need to work again.

And if he fails, he might never be able to work again.

And if they find him, if they take him alive, he might never see the sunlight again.

What the hell. Sunlight is overrated.

He checks his surroundings, tests the integrity of his cloaking, searches for traces of himself. So far, so good. He primes a bunch of routines that he is going to send up to the drones, like firecrackers. He has another bunch that he is going to launch down among the transport swarm, so there will be two independent sources of total mayhem. That should be enough to drive both the drones and the databots into a total frenzy, and with any luck provide him with a certain amount of cover. Then he's going to send up a dozen or so blimps—ghost attackers that will signify intrusion whilst evaporating on contact. And while that is going on in the upper reaches of the tower, Ilya will be down below, taking out a section of the honeycomb wall. He figures he has ten seconds max to start his diversions, position himself by the wall and jack in, force download as much as he can and pull the ripcord.

That's the plan. Ilya feels simultaneously ice cold and dripping with sweat. He can feel the tremors in his meatspace body like a distant echo of a faraway earthquake, or the rumble of an approaching storm.

He's had it with waiting. It's now or never.

He launches his firecrackers up into the upper echelons of the tower, right into the middle of the drone swarm. For a moment they hang there inert, and for the merest microsecond there is like a collective WTF shrug among the drones as they clock the presence of the intruders, which then proceed to shatter into an explosion of sound and fury. It's harmless, but the drones don't know that, and they go absolutely apeshit, suddenly imploding into a dense, superheavy core of swirling fury then exploding out into a boiling, expanding mass of vengeful destruction.

Down below, the chaos is even greater as the transport swarm is violently dispersed by the sudden explosion of firecrackers in its midst. Individual databots go slamming into the tower walls or are sent spinning hopelessly down to the floor like shattered stukas.

It's all more than Ilya could have hoped for but there's no time for him to enjoy the wild confusion he has created. He sends up his blimps and jumps down to his chosen location at the base of the wall. He can hear the ominous popping sounds as the first blimps are taken down, but he blots it out of his mind as he concentrates on jacking into the surface of the comb. His hands are shaking as he makes the connection and feels the super-rich surge of concentrated information flowing into his system like the purest sugar rush. He's given himself five seconds from the initial connect and he's already initiating the emergency pullout sequence as he hears what seems like a volley of shots from overhead as blimp after blimp is taken down and the hunter-killer drones seek out new targets. He'd down to two seconds and can feel the urge to hang on in there and just carry on drinking from the sweet thick liquid like some big crazy insect drunk on nectar but he knows that if he stays there for a moment longer the whole thing will just become one huge trap and be the death of him and he's down to the final second as the last of the blimps goes down and there's the tiniest of lulls in the swarm as they realize the upper areas have been cleared and see through the flailing arms of the distraught queen and simultaneously register the destruction being wrought down below, along with the presence of its author and Ilya feels the hair on the back of his neck stand on end as he registers the sound of a thousand drones stopping mid-air and heading his way and taking a bead and firing as he pulls the ripcord and is back heaving and sweating and panting in the relative safety of his own room and he un-plugs and rips his spex off and falls to his knees in front of his console and retches into the wastebin there on the floor but nothing comes up but bile and stomach fluids because he hasn't eaten or drunk anything for hours on end.

And he rolls over onto his side and lays on the floor, drenched in sweat and shivering and exultant at what he's just pulled off and suddenly scared shitless at what the consequences might be, so he just lays there staring at nothing and letting himself work it all out of his system and letting the emotions run their course till he's ready to get up and strip off his clothes and take a shower and stay there with a hot jet of water on his face until all the crazy events of the day are washed away and go spiralling down the plug hole.

Chapter Twenty-Three
Too Dumb for Toast

It's a beautiful day. Jimmy wakes up and the sun is streaming through his bedroom window and he feels like shit. He opens his eyes and blinks at the light and feels his heart sink as the pain from his body comes at him like a fist. There's a glass of water by his bed and he grabs an orange pill from the boxful he has next to him—like some old pensioner, he thinks disgustedly to himself—as he props himself up to take it and wash it down with water. Julia is up already fixing breakfast, the mere thought of which is enough to turn Jimmy's stomach. There's coffee in the air and Julia brings it in wearing no more than a pair of black briefs and a close fitting black top and time was that would have been enough to get Jimmy going, breakfast or no breakfast. But now is not time was, and Jimmy just groans and turns over and weeps silently into the pillow. Julia brings his coffee and strokes his hair, but by now she knows better than to ask what's up and they sit like that for a while till the smell of burning toast calls her back into the kitchen. The air in the kitchen turns blue for a while as it fills with a whole zoological cosmology of scatological expletives that finally bring a smile to Jimmy's lips as he calls in to Julia to forget about the toast.

"Maybe something simpler. Maybe some cereal."

More expletives.

"Are you trying to say I'm too dumb for friggin' toast?"

"No honey, but just like: don't let it get to you?"

"This fucking toaster is going out of the window right now unless it delivers up two perfectly browned slices in the next thirty seconds. I've got a gun to its head and I know how to use it."

"You've got a gun? What gun?"

"Ok, so it's just an electric whisk. But I know how to use it and I ain't just whistling Dixie."

"Julia, nobody in Lithuania ever whistled Dixie."

"You just stay out of this if you know what's good for you. This is between me and the toaster."

They have breakfast. Or at least, Julia has breakfast, and Jimmy drinks his coffee and watches. Julia is inconsolable.

"After all that effort."

"Sorry babe. Great toast. The greatest even."

"So eat it already. Need to keep your strength up."

"Bring the bucket over and you can watch it go down. And watch it come up again about 30 seconds later."

"Ew, gross. Haven't you got pills for that or something?"

Jimmy does in fact have pills for more or less everything. He has his little orange pills that he takes first thing to prep his stomach for the pharmacological onslaught later in the day. The orange pills themselves are a source of a lot of the nausea Jimmy is experiencing so they help with his meds but do nothing to help keep his breakfast down. So Jimmy usually skips breakfast and moves straight on to the other pills in his regimen: the yellow pills are tranquilizers that help him deal with the anxiety around knowing he's going to croak any time soon. The various white pills and capsules are the actual treatments that the Doc's got him on, though what they are actually treating when the disease remains incurable Jimmy has yet to be able to fathom. The Doc though thinks it's all to the good and claims, "You've got to give it your best shot," so Jimmy gives him the benefit of the doubt and takes the pills that rot his guts and make him feel like dying might be the better option. The blue pills are uppers for those times when Jimmy actually needs to do stuff outside the house, but the Doc says not to take too many of those.

"Because they're bad for me?" asks Jimmy.

"Damn right they're bad for you," says the Doc.

"I'm friggin' dying already, how much worse can they be than that?"

"It's not your body I'm worried about," says the Doc. "Too many uppers'll fry your brain, turn you into a gibbering wreck, smash into your nervous system like an out-of-control road train. Just take my word for it on this my boy."

So Jimmy takes his word for it. And then there are the green pills, which are basically just opiates, or opiate surrogates. Jimmy wonders whether his best bet wouldn't be to just take a bunch of the green ones and a handful of the blue ones and go out in a blaze of glory.

Julia, for her part, is less than enthusiastic about this course of action.

"Are you out of your tiny fucking bonce? Jesus Christ, I never knew I had a mental patient for a boyfriend. That's possibly the stupidest idea I ever heard."

"Chippie, you can be so harsh sometimes. Have a little sympathy. At least I'd get to go out on a high."

"No Jimmy, you have some fucking sympathy. You're not dead yet. Doc says there's still a chance. There's still Manila. I don't want you making me a widow till we've exhausted all the avenues."

Manila. Today's the day. They've plundered Julia's savings and waited for it all to come through to her current account. They surf the net and book two return flights to Ninoy Aquino International which has Jimmy cracking up and making jokes about going to visit Mr. Spock till Julia tells him it's Ninoy, not Nimoy so just cut the crap. They book a budget hotel called the Ned Kelly which is down between the marina and Ocean Park, basically just because they claim to serve Manila's finest fake ostrich burgers and Jimmy likes the idea of cold Fosters and water sports. They've got the trip booked for Monday morning which still leaves them time to get the final details from the Doc and for him to set up the deal.

They both get totally into the whole southeast Asian holiday vibe aspect of it and actually find themselves planning a possible trip over to Danang or Angkor Wat before the life-or-death aspect of it comes back to them along with the realisation that a) the deal might fall through; b) they might get busted, or killed, or both; c) Jimmy might die on the way anyway and d) the whole Chinese wonderdrug thing might just be a crock of shit.

So they scale back their expectations and just plan for a week in Manila—basically a day or to get over their jet lag and acclimatize, a day or two to make contact and do the deal, and a couple of days leeway just in case anything goes wrong. And a day off for sightseeing, back home the following Monday.

"Great plan," says Jimmy.

"Great plan," agreed the Doc, last time they spoke.

Julia thinks it's maybe not such a great plan but she's doing her best to be optimistic and give Jimmy the encouragement he needs.

"Your plan sucks."

"Thanks for the moral support. You got a better idea?"

"Nope. It just sucks. I can feel it in my waters."

"What waters? Do you have some embryo swimming around somewhere that I ought to know about?"

"Christ no, I have enough on my hands looking after you. I just mean, something is bound to go wrong."

"Something's already wrong. I'm dying. Things can't go much wronger. Anyway, you should just stay at home if you feel so bad about it."

"No way. I'm coming with you. Stand by your man and all that."

"Ok Tammy, but cut the whingeing."

"I'm not whingeing. Just concerned, is all."

"Could still stay home and be concerned."

"Jimmy Chang, if you're going to croak, or get yourself into trouble, you're going to need me. Get used to it."

Suleika is up early and crawls stiffly out of her bunk to wash her face down in the communal bathroom. There are a couple of other women in there with her, but they just nod her a greeting and the mood is easy and familiar. She likes to be up and washed before the rush starts. Things get louder then and tempers can fray easily, and even though there are no men involved it's still a bit more than she can cope with.

She finishes in the washroom and goes next door to the laundry room. She has so few things that she usually bargains away her monthly ration of washing machine tokens to the families with children.

Today she has a couple of underthings she needs to wash so she goes over to one of the big square sinks and spends about a quarter of an hour washing everything by hand. There is not much that she likes about this place, but the fact that they usually have hot water is one of them. She immerses her hands and rubs, and the warmth of the water travels up her arms and makes her think of the warmth of her homeland and the warmth of their home before the men in black came and destroyed it. She shies away from the memory of that becoming, that undoing, and brings her mind back to the time before, and lets that light wash through her as water warms her fingers and the sunlight filters in from the windows set in the wall high above her head.

There is a change in her that she has been noticing more often these past days. Not a happiness, because what is happiness after what has happened to her, and how can she ever expect happiness again in her life, but a strange contentment. She is here, in this wicked, cold place, which now is starting to feel no more wicked than anywhere else. Perhaps even less so. There are good people here, she has met some. And even if those good people will never change the world, perhaps there is room in her heart to let them change her. Perhaps this is something that can still happen.

She washes and rinses and wrings out her things and takes them down to the little cellar that they use as a drying room now that it's too cold outside and the washing just freezes on the line. Some of the families are worried about leaving their things here—children's clothes especially are objects of value, as is anything that could be remotely interesting for teenagers—but Suleika has no worries. Who is going to steal the worn out clothes of a worn out old woman? Even in this place? She hangs up her things in a corner of the room, on one of the lines stretched across from wall to wall. Then she heads back upstairs.

Going up takes a lot of energy. Her knees are so stiff that she has to use the handrail to pull herself up each step. By the time she reaches the ground floor she is already bathed in sweat. By the time she reaches the first floor she is exhausted. She leans on the banister for a while to get her breath back, and then shuffles over to a small wooden bench set up against the wall of the stairwell. Apart from perhaps her bed, it's her favourite place in the whole of Fuji City. The big broad stairwell faces out onto the old runway, and the outside wall is made entirely of glass. The huge east-facing windows flood the space with light and Suleika sits on her bench and basks in the rays of the morning sun. From here she can see right across the airfield, beyond the fence that marks the limits of their enclosure, to the joggers, the dog-walkers, the cyclists, the fields and trees in the central area, and beyond that, the cars and trucks on the motorway and the smoke and steam billowing up from the factories in the distance. It's not particularly pretty or picturesque, but somehow the sunlight and the wide open space pleases her, and soothes her.

From her vantage point she can also look down into the exercise area directly below her window, and it's here that she sees a group of about thirty men, hanging about, seemingly waiting for something. It's unusual to see such large groups here, unless something official is going on, or maybe a football match. So she sits and watches as the men wait in the cold. They talk among themselves, and some smoke, and others stamp their feet against the cold and draw their scarves tighter around their faces. Apart from that the men are still, and three of their number are moving around among them, and seem to be distributing something. Money perhaps? Or cigarettes? Her eyes are not good enough to make out the details at this distance. But she can see faces. She looks at the men and dislikes them instantly. Their faces are hard and brutalized. Fighters' faces. She has seen enough of these faces to last her a lifetime.

She can feel her blood quicken as her gaze passes through the gang of men, who now are separating out into three distinct groups. She feels her hand travel to her chest to calm her heart. For now she sees a face that she recognizes. One of the men who came to her village on the back of big open-backed cars, with machine guns mounted. They rounded up the villagers into the central square. They looted the houses and took whatever they wanted and set fire to them. They separated out the men, the women, the children. They asked the men who wanted to come with them and join their cause. Some of the younger ones even volunteered and were taken away on one of the trucks. The rest were shot where they stood. Then they sorted the screaming women into young and old, and took away the young ones. Then they shot any of the remaining women who were screaming too much or had gotten too out of control. They beat a few of the children with rifle butts and asked them too if they were ready to volunteer and herded all but the smallest into another truck. Then they fired a few anti-tank rounds into the mayor's house and the mosque and left in a billowing trail of dust.

And now one of these men was here, in this place. Instinctively she draws her scarf up around her face. Her whole body is trembling, her hands are shaking violently. But she is not afraid. Perhaps she has no capacity for fear any more. After all the fear and grief and mourning of that terrible time, after the months and years of just surviving, after the awful hardship of the long journey to this place, and the months and years of sitting on the cold hard ground with her little begging bowl and the picture of her dead husband, what has she to be afraid of? No, it is not fear that makes her tremble when she recognizes the man in the gang outside. It is hatred, and a lust for revenge.

A new man arrives, a man in a suit, and a kind of tremor passes through the group outside. They don't exactly stand to attention, but Suleika can see that they stop talking, and focus on the new arrival. The man is not even wearing a coat, so he has probably just emerged from the administration building. He runs his fingers quickly through his hair and then stands with his hands behind his back and his feet apart, parade-ground style. He addresses them briefly and then, when he's done, dismisses them.

The three men who before were moving around, turn to their respective groups and bark orders. The three groups turn and begin to walk over to towards the main gate of Fuji City.

The man in the suit pauses for a moment and follows them with his eyes. Then he turns and looks towards the building behind him, at the tall glass frontage to the stairwell where Suleika is sitting. He seems to be looking right at her, although Suleika is sure it must be difficult to see through the reflections on the glass. She resists the urge to pull her scarf even further up around her face, or to go and hide. Besides, even if he can see her, what will he see? Just an old woman sitting on a bench. He probably wouldn't even register her presence, so little does she figure in his scheme of things.

But Suleika sees him. She watches him, as he looks up, and studies his face. Commits every detail to memory. She has no idea what's going on here, but she knows it can't be right.

Gene is up early too because he's got a whole heap of stuff to do. He gets on the phone for a conference call with a couple of the girls from Charlie's Garden, basically the key organizers from their local NFS chapter and gets them up to speed on what he discussed with Omar. The sexworkers will need to have an emergency meeting if they are going to give their support to a demo happening in a couple of days' time. It's a pretty tall order, but they're up for it, and will give it their best shot. People haven't really been talking about much anything else since the thing with Ursula went down, so there's still a lot of anger in the air. They plan the meeting for later in the afternoon and Gene thanks them and hangs up and tries Omar's number. There's no answer, but he doesn't have Omar pegged for much of a morning person so he just speaks to voicemail.

"Vic, it's Gene. We're good to go with the demo. Give me a call when you need more input from me. Catch you later."

Gene pours a coffee from the pot on the stove and checks his schedule. He's got a couple of johns lined up at the studio and there's one that he'll have to cancel or reschedule. No big deal. He skims his incoming mail but there's nothing of any interest so he takes a swig of coffee and leans back in his chair and starts to massage the tension out of his neck muscles. He's starting to feel a bit out of shape after all the stress and alcohol of the past few days so he drains his coffee and clears enough space in his little living room to let him run through his exercise routine, a mix of yoga, tai chi, salsa moves that he picked up from a sweet Cuban guy, and a little Capoiera left over from a visit to Sao Paolo. He finishes up with a praying mantis kung fu routine and some wing tsun style elbow strikes.

He goes into a final lotus position to get his breath back and center himself. He can feel his heart pounding in his chest and the sweat trickling down his spine. He closes his eyes and realizes that he feels good about the latest turn of events. Sure, there are no results as yet, no sudden insights that will lead him to his mark, but he feels like a weight has been taken off his shoulders. Maybe even like the kind of feeling straight folks have when something happens and they go to the police. In that ideal world where the police are there for everyone and victims of crime don't have to fear being suddenly accused of walking while trans, or driving while black, or dressing so as to invite rape. There never ever was a time when the girls at Charlie's Garden felt safe taking stuff to the cops, but there's a part of Gene feels that it ought not to be like that. Maybe in a perfect world it would be different. Maybe in a perfect world the cops would wear drag or be a bunch of tough women who would come down heavy on violent males or hassle the rich for being such parasites and tell them to beat it when they turned up in their limousines but wait, in a perfect world there wouldn't be any limousines or maybe limousines for all and certainly no rich parasites.

Yeah, dream on.

Gene emerges from his meditation with a wry smile and unfolds his legs and stretches the muscles in his back. He strips off his things and takes a shower, and by the time he's dressed and breakfasted the phone goes and it's Omar.

"Vic, wow, you're up early."

"Places to go, people to see, Jeanie. I heard your call, but it took me a while to drag myself out of bed. Good decision."

"Not much deciding to it, end of the day. Needed to check in with the syndicate though. It's all good with them. You can go ahead and put their name on the poster."

"And the church?"

"'Going round there now. It's a little early for them, but with any luck there'll be someone there. I'll let you know as soon as I have something for you."

"Ok Jeanie. I've got the print run due for 4. I can hold it back for thirty minutes, an hour max. But we need to get it out for this evening if we want the posters up by Friday."

"Vic, I'm with you. Give me a couple of hours."

"See you sweetie. Good luck."

"Ciao bella."

Claire comes awake and the first thing she thinks of is Laila, which both takes her by surprise and fills her with a certain happiness at the same time. She's still mad with Ilya and is really not looking forward to the meeting with Josh, so it's a relief for her to have something pleasurable to focus on. She has a couple of hours to spare so she pulls on her running kit, locates her headphones and stuffs her purse into a tracksuit pocket. Then she's out into the bright light and the cold air of the morning. But instead of running up through the graveyard she hangs a right and heads up Hillman towards the covered market, where she buys a newspaper and a current affairs magazine and, on impulse, a little bunch of flowers. She stuffs everything into a flimsy plastic bag which she clutches to her chest as she walks through the big glass market hall doors and out onto L'Ouverture where she resumes the steady running rhythm of her daily ritual.

But it's an unusual route for Claire today, up along L'Ouverture and right into Adderly before it turns into Urban and then left up to the canal and along past the big boat cafés towards the main entrance of St. Catherine's. She asks one of the women on reception if it's ok to visit and she looks at her and smiles and says sure, go ahead. She jogs up the stairs to the fourth floor and arrives at Laila's room out of breath and flushed and suddenly a little nervous. She knocks and waits for Laila to answer before poking her head around the door and saying, "Up for a visit?"

Laila is sitting up in bed with a cup of coffee on her bedside table and is looking significantly better than the last time Claire saw her. If she's surprised to see Claire she doesn't show it. A broad smile spreads across her face and she says, "Sure. If it's you, anytime."

There's light streaming into the room and Claire can see the tops of the trees outside as she walks across to Laila's bed and squeezes her hand.

"Thought you might like something to read," she says and unpacks the newspaper and magazine from the plastic bag. "And I brought you these."

She takes the little bouquet out of the bag and holds it out for Laila to inspect. Laila leans forwards and clasps Claire's hand in her own.

"Claire, that is so sweet of you. They're lovely."

Claire feels the warmth of Laila's hand around her own and becomes aware of the blood rising to her cheeks and her own indecision as to whether to withdraw her hand or not. After one of those eternally stretchy time-lapse seconds she finally breaks away.

"A vase!" she says. And then, "Oh shit, I forgot. No flowers. It totally slipped my mind. I'm so sorry, really."

Laila seems more amused than anything else.

"Claire, don't be silly. They're lovely. There's a vase over by the window."

Claire is still a little crestfallen and sits down dejectedly on the chair by the bed.

"Are you sure? I can take them away again, I don't mind. I just thought you might want a paper and then buying the flowers was like a reflex. I didn't even think about it really."

Laila reaches out a hand and touches Claire's cheek.

"Claire, sweetie. It's not about the flowers. It's about who they're from. Yesterday's flowers, from my boss, they were a kind of threat. But these, today, they're something different entirely."

Claire feels a sudden wave of elation and looks across into the unfathomable depths of Laila's dark brown eyes.

"Hah. I feel like a bit of a dumb schoolkid, bursting in here with my tracksuit and my..."

"And your bunch of flowers for teacher? Great fantasy. Hang on to that one."

Claire feels herself blushing again.

"But we'd better get them into some water otherwise they'll be wilting in your hot little hand."

Claire jumps up out of her chair to fetch the vase. She fills it with water and places it on Laila's bedside table.

"You won't go knocking it off?"

"Not a chance."

"I guess I'd better be going."

"So soon? Just a flying visit then?"

"Suppose so. Need to finish my run and have a shower before going out into the world."

There's a moment's silence as they take each other in. Then Claire:

"You tell me if there's anything you need, eh?"

"And you'll come running?"

"Something like that."

"Better keep those running shoes handy. Could be a long list."

Al feels the sun on his face and the cold of the wind as it blows around his ears and neck. The last of the snow is melting and he can feel the day warming up—just a couple of degrees above zero, but enough to make a difference. He's feeling good, about himself, and about the project. He had the guys individually processed and tagged earlier this morning, so he'll be able to track them wherever they are. Even in a crowd of a hundred thousand people they'll stand out for him like sore thumbs, with their geopositioning overlay flashing out each one's position and identity to him whenever and wherever he cares to look. He gave a wad of cash to each of his squad leaders and encouraged them to spread some out among the men, how much, he doesn't care. He's not interested in equality, he's interested in dependency. He's interested in creating a chain of command. His squad leaders are all familiar with this stuff, having served under various warlords in different theatres. He knows they'll do their job.

He stands for a moment and looks up at the massive structure of the Fuji City building. The sweeping arc of its sandstone façade curves around and away from him on both sides, encircling him like an eagle's wings. Al can't see it, but he knows there's a huge eagle's head statue planted on the other side of the building, near the passenger forecourt to the old airport building. Al likes the idea of that. It has something imperial about it, something regal. It has blind sandstone eyes and a mean cruel beak that Al very much likes the curve of. It's a statement, and it's his kind of statement. The whole building, in fact, was a statement. Its message was power, plain and simple. Apart from the eagle, its only adornment was a couple of squat naked figures carved in pockmarked limestone that above all, suggested to Al the brute power of the slave. That too, was as it should be. From the runway side, the front was made up mostly of hangar gates—great accordion-like folding doors in a dark, weathered green, under an overhanging rain hood. The place had history, the place had class. And now, now it was degraded, downgraded, and full of fujis. An ignominious end to such a magnificent place of power.

Al's walking back towards his office and squinting a little at the reflection from the big plate glass windows of the stairwell tower in front of him. The sun passes behind a cloud and he looks up to see an old woman looking down at him. A formless shape on a bench. Just one of the hundreds like her in the stinking barracks behind those big green doors. Al shudders involuntarily. Just another mouth to feed. Too old even to work. He shakes his head, searches for his cigarettes. Why they bother to let such human flotsam in at all, is beyond him.

CHAPTER TWENTY-FOUR
Underground

Claire turns up at Hankey Pankey's at just after ten thirty to find Josh already there. He's bagged a window seat, and Claire greets him with a hug and hangs her coat up and eases into the seat opposite him. Hank himself is behind the counter and acknowledges Claire with a two-fingers-to-the-head greeting and sends a hipsterish and heavily tattooed waiter over to take their order. Claire orders the house special—blueberry pancakes with an orange and cardamom cream sauce, and Josh goes for a couple of croissants.

"You guys want anything to drink?"

Hank's is famous for its huge and very ancient coffee roaster that stands up against the window on the other side of the shop front. He has it going every morning and it fills the place with the bittersweet scent of whatever blend he's chosen for the day. If you're not a coffee drinker, there's really no point going to Hank's. The whole place seems infused with the stuff, steeped in a dark, rich aroma that is like a shot in the arm to any caffeine addict that walks in the door. Finely layered over the coffee aroma base is the smell of baking. Hank learned his pastry-making chops in a little bakery in Milwaukee till a brief but torrid love affair exerted its long-distance charm and lured him over to the NC. His cheesecake is second to none. His pecan pie is to die for. His bagels are the expression of a love supreme. His chocolate fudge cake is an exquisite, blasphemous obscenity. Actual fistfights have occurred over the last piece of the day, causing Hank to have the guests ejected and to eat it himself.

Today the guests are peaceful, and all is as it should be in Hank's sweet and luscious realm. Hank himself cuts an imposing figure as he towers over his staff, slightly wall-eyed and broken of nose. Although he says of himself that he has the kind of face that makes you want to punch it, he's big enough to take care of himself. Almost always.

Claire's attention is on the passers-by as the waiter brings their coffee. The day outside is bright and cold, with wisps of stinking steam rising from the heavy iron sewer covers set into the asphalt of the road outside. A woman in a hijab is stacking fruit on a sloping display stand at the little Turkish supermarket next to Hank's. The market hall on the corner of Hillman and L'Ouverture is already buzzing with customers. Claire forces her attention back to Josh.

"So what's the deal Josh? What's so urgent that you just *had* to see me?"

Josh looks a little taken aback by her directness.

"No big deal Claire. Or maybe. Maybe you're the deal. If you're thinking of leaving the collective, that's a big, big deal."

Claire takes a sip of her coffee as she thinks about what to say to that. She likes Josh, but she feels like she doesn't want to be here, with him. Like she doesn't want to be having this conversation.

"Thanks Josh. For making the effort and all. I appreciate it."

She pauses as her pancakes arrive and she realizes how hungry she is. She picks up her fork but waits for Josh to get his croissants. They arrive in a couple of seconds, and Claire launches into her breakfast.

"Thing is," she says, with a mouthful of pancake, "I'm not sure that it's not too late already."

Damn, these pancakes are good. That weird, unexpected thing that Hank does with the cardamom. Crazy taste, for a breakfast. But certainly hits the spot.

"Meaning what Claire?"

Josh looks concerned, his forehead furrowed behind his long Jesus locks. His eyebrows are thick and dark, his eyelashes long and feminine, and Claire wonders why she's never noticed them before.

"Meaning I've kind of had it Josh. This whole thing's going nowhere. It's not that I don't believe in the cause any more. It's more like I can't see the point. Like we're just barking up the wrong tree."

Josh sweeps his hair back, pushes his glasses up his nose in that familiar gesture Claire has seen a thousand times before.

"That's what I'm here to talk to you about Claire. I totally get where you're coming from. I'm totally with you on that. I think it's time we upped our game."

Now it's Claire's turn to look surprised.

"Up our game? How, exactly?"

Josh leans in conspiratorially, with a glance to the nearest guests, three tables over.

"Desperate times call for desperate measures Claire. History is being made, and it's being made the wrong way. We need to intervene. Make a splash. Make a stand."

"Yeah, so…"

"We've always been such a bunch of non-violent do-gooders. Sure, we've taken out some machines, some infrastructure, but that's just peanuts. I'm through with that shit. It's time we took the fight to the man."

Claire puts down her knife and fork, wipes her mouth with the back of her hand.

"Josh, are you saying what I think you're saying? You want us to…"

"Go underground. We need to start taking this thing seriously. We need to start taking the fuckers out." His voice is a whisper now. He's leaning in close. But his words come across to Claire like a big loud public address system in her head.

"Josh, are you fucking mad? This is not '68. We're not the fucking red brigades. You're not Fidel friggin' Castro…"

"No Claire, you don't get it." There's a wild-eyed, messianic look behind Josh's specs. "This is the way forward. This is what we need to be doing. I've been thinking about it. A lot. Our struggle could be the signal, the flashpoint that everyone has been waiting for."

"The signal for them to round up the movement," Claire hisses, angry now. "The signal for them to liquidate the lot of us."

Josh reaches out his hand for Claire's, but she pulls it back.

"Claire, this is no time for fear. We need to move forward decisively. I understand your reticence. I know you need time to think this over.

That's all I'm asking. Think it over. Think it through, Claire. You'll see that I'm right. Take your time Claire. But don't take too long."

Claire pushes her plate away, gets up and grabs her coat.

"Don't hold your breath."

She throws a ten down on the table.

"Claire, keep your money, breakfast is on me."

"No Josh. No, it ain't."

She turns and blunders into a couple of chairs in her haste to get out. People look up from their coffees and screens and breakfasts and Hank raises an eyebrow from behind the counter. Claire mouths sorry to him and waves goodbye and can feel herself blushing bright red as she pulls open the door and stumbles breathlessly out onto the street and into the sunlight.

It's mid-morning by the time Gene checks into the Church, but there's still hardly anyone about, just Carla in the library cataloguing a batchload of new books, and Chris, in one of the dojos. He instinctively shies away from disturbing Carla, who seems engrossed in what she's doing and barely acknowledges his presence. So he hangs around outside the streetfighting/ninjitsu course, which is due to finish up in a couple of minutes. The sound of bodies hitting mats, with accompanying groans and grunts, and the occasional *kiai* of an attack move, drift through the heavy wooden doors to his ears as he waits for the session to end. There's a short period of silence, which he guesses is the final collective meditation as the students sit in a circle and bring their chi under control. Then, a flurry of voices and a group of about twenty women and a couple of men stream out of the room. He waves to Chris from the door, and she comes over, wiping her face with a towel. She's a short, wiry woman in her forties, with dark, buzz-cut hair, greying a little at the temples. She wearing a faded black karate-style jacket which she takes off on her way over and throws over a chair by the wall, revealing a black muscle shirt, broad shoulders and tattooed biceps. She hugs Gene in a sweaty embrace and grins.

"Jeanie, good to see ya. Have you come to join our group? We could do with a few new sparring partners. Specially men, you know. Good for target practice."

Gene can see the impish look in her eye.

"You mean you need someone to throw *shuriken* at? Do I really look that suicidal?"

"No, but, let me take a look at you."

She grasps his chin in one hand and turns his head from side to side, inspecting his features, her grip firm but playful, her fingers splayed up along one cheek, her thumb resting innocently on a nerve point just underneath his jaw. Gene knows better than to offer the least resistance.

"I would say not suicidal, but you look like there's a lot on your mind."

She releases his chin and gives the side of his face a friendly pat.

"What's up? Is there something you need to work out of your system? I'm free right now. We can do a couple of rounds of free fighting if you feel like it."

"Thanks Chris. Might even be a good idea. But that's not what I'm here for. I need to talk to someone from the core council…"

"Ah, now I get you."

She stretches her neck from side to side, until she hears a satisfying crack at the base of her skull.

"Tell you what. Just give me a couple of minutes to get changed and I'll meet you over by the coffee machine."

Gene nods agreement and turns to go.

"And Jeanie?"

"Chris?"

"Black, no sugar."

That impish look again, and she's gone.

Ten minutes later and they're both sat in a couple of armchairs near the coffee machine. Carla is over at the other end of the room, sorting books into shelves. Chris takes a sip of her coffee and says, "Ok Jeanie, I'm all ears."

"Difficult to know where to start. You heard about the attack up on Charlie's Garden?"

"Of course. Ursula was here for the best part of a week. She was in a pretty bad way. We all heard about it."

"The guy who did it is still out there. We've had no luck tracking him down. Could be he has some kind of shielding through state security. But we have a photofit mugshot, and a car registration number. And we've got a demo lined up for Saturday…"

"And?"

"And we were kind of wondering if the Church would support it."

There's a moment of silence as Chris takes another drink of her coffee and studies Gene from over the rim of her mug. Finally she puts it down and leans in towards him.

"Jeanie, you know we'll all be there. You know that if it's a question of catching a rapist we are all totally with you. And you know that if it's a question of providing security at the demo, then we're more than happy to do that to. But something gives me the impression that that isn't quite what you're asking of us. Am I right?"

Gene suddenly feels very tired, like he's been carrying some heavy load that he really needs to put down.

"Chris, to be honest, I don't really know myself. At the moment we've got the NFS on the posters, and that's about it. The crew from the Mary Jane are helping out with logistics, and they probably won't mind putting their names down as co-organizers. But I was also thinking of something with a bit more clout."

"So that's why you came here?"

"Seemed like the obvious place to go."

"But why don't you go through some of the broader channels? There's a whole bunch of queer organizations out there you could be approaching. Shit, you could even be approaching other unions, other syndicates, women's organizations."

"I know all that Chris. And you're right, of course. But this really isn't my thing. I'm not an organizer. Not even much of an activist, if it comes down to it. If we had more time, I'd just pass it on to someone else, for them to do it properly. This is more of an impro thing. It's happening the day after tomorrow. We're doing it to create some heat, generate some publicity, maybe flush the bastard out. But you know me. I work up on the line with the girls, and I'm with the NFS, sure. But my home is here at the Church. So that's why I'm here."

"Then you should know that we don't operate as a campaign group. We leave the politics to the politicos."

"Sure Chris, I know that."

"And we have no interest in drawing undue attention to ourselves. The higher our profile, the more stress we have with infiltration attempts."

Gene suddenly feels himself in the searing spotlight of Chris's penetrating gaze.

"Talking of which, who was that guy you brought in with you the other night? You ought to know that that raised a few eyebrows."

"That old guy? That was, uh, Jimmy, was his name. He was with Suleika. It was more of a snap decision than anything else. They were both out there, just about freezing to death. He's ok though. I'll vouch for him."

"Ok Jeanie. I'll take your word for it. But no more snap decisions, huh? We've got a protocol for this kind of thing. We ought to stick to it."

Gene is feeling more than a little crestfallen.

"Got it. And the demo?"

"I'll take it to the core commission. Like I said, we'll be there, we're with you. But don't expect any high-profile stuff. I really can't see that happening."

Ilya's dipping into what he knows is going to be the deepest, trippiest, richest honeypot he has ever encountered and he's having a hard time of it. It's taken him all morning so far and he hasn't even gotten to the stage where he can even start reading the thing yet. It's all heavily encrypted in some state-of-the art military grade algorithm and he's having to muster all the resources at his disposal in terms of hardware, software and sheer brainpower just to have a crack at it. He started at six, well before dawn, and now his stomach tells him it's getting close to lunchtime and he's beginning to feel a little weary when all of his virtual gears and counterweights click into place and suddenly he's in. A wave of elation passes through him and he forgets about physical hunger at the prospect of gorging on what opens up before him.

Somewhere at the back of his mind a phone starts ringing which he ignores, but it keeps coming back, more insistent each time and he curses himself for not turning the thing off until he remembers the reason he left it on was so that Claire could reach him and he curses again, this time for being such a dope and picks it up to answer it.

"Claire!"

"Ilya."

He's expecting her to make him some kind of a scene for going so deep off-grid unannounced, but she doesn't. She's quiet. Troubled even.

"What's up? You ok? Look, I'm sorry if I pissed you off yesterday, there was, uh, there was this…"

"This what, lover?"

"Nothing. Something came up, is all."

"Something important?"

Ilya can hear the coolness in her voice, a distant kind of sarcasm that he hasn't heard before.

"Important. Sure."

"Anyone I know?"

"No! Claire, Christ, no. Just work stuff. That's all. It was stupid of me. I was like, totally engrossed. I'm sorry. I'll make it up to you."

There's a pause while the two of them take a step back from what looks set to be their first major argument.

"Ilya, don't worry. I'm not mad at you. Well I was, but not any more. I just needed to see you, needed you to be there, and you weren't, and that was like, really difficult? And I, I really still need to see you, you know?"

The realization that Claire is actually crying into her phone is like a slap around the face. Ilya can hear Claire sobbing quietly over the sound of background traffic.

"Claire, what is it? What's going on? Tell me where you are and I'll come over."

There's a moment's more silence before Claire answers.

"No, I'll come to you. I'll be over in about an hour. Is that ok with you?"

"Sure, whatever. I'm here. Just get your ass over here as soon as you can."

"Ok, see you in a bit."

Claire hangs up, leaving Ilya staring at his phone in disbelief. He's never experienced Claire like this before. Never heard that shake in her voice, never had any other image of her than the tough, passionate, self-assured woman that suddenly burst into his life. This is uncharted territory for the both of them.

Ilya takes a break to make some tea and plan his next move. He badly needs to get back to his stolen cache of data, just to find out what's in there, but if Claire is coming over then there's hardly time for that. He's going to need to be in a different headspace by the time she gets here, otherwise what's the point? She needs him, and he knows he has to be there for her, for whatever it is that's got her so troubled. But there's a part of him that just wants to tell her about what he's been up to. To explain to her about his exploits, to show off the prize that he has brought back, a prize so unheard of, so totally outrageous that he doubts there's anyone else in the city, maybe not even in the country, who can match it. But he knows that that's impossible. Not only would it be difficult to get her to understand, it would also be an enormous risk just talking about it, and enormous burden for her to bear.

And who's to know who she would tell?

Ilya suddenly realizes that although he would trust Claire with his life, he has no idea about her friends, who she talks to, what they know about each other, what they know about him. No, telling her is out of the question.

He finishes his tea and logs on to the weeb, easing in via his wetware but staying cool, innocuous, just down a few layers, nothing too deep. But even from here he can tell that the shit has totally hit the fan. There are rumours flying around of some massive hack that has the big deep-level beasts stirred up into search and destroy mode. There are gaping holes in virtual antimatter where site after darknet site has been taken down and trashed. There's some kind of netwide red alert going on with the powers lined up against each other in a display of sabre-rattling no-one has ever experienced before, along with stories of actual retaliatory strikes and a wave of meatspace arrests spanning several continents.

The news is worrying and exhilarating in equal measure. If he needed confirmation that he had landed something huge, here it is. But if they were already rounding people up, if they were going after the usual suspects, how long would it be until there was a knock on the door? Ilya had always prided himself on his invisibility, on leaving no traces. That was his speciality, after all. But part of him always assumed that he must be on some list somewhere. It was pretty unlikely that he had managed to get this far without registering on some official database of people with hacking talents and hence potentially subversive. And then there was the manner of his exit yesterday. He had done his best, but it had been messy, uncontrolled. He consoles himself with the fact that if they are arresting others, then they can't know for sure that it was him. And yet, that didn't mean that they wouldn't get round to his name in the end. He figures it can only be a matter of time.

He jacks out of the weeb and massages his temples with his hands. He feels like panicking but panic is not an option. But it's there, inside him, bubbling and seething just below the surface. He has to work out a plan. And the most obvious plan is: run. He feels like everything inside him is screaming at him just to get the fuck out of there. As if his mind is now making up for the calm and coolness he displayed yesterday on the job. Like some kind of post-traumatic stress thing, or the aftershocks that people get following major accidents. Ilya can feel his hands shaking and he grabs the empty teacup with one hand and clamps onto his wrist with the other, in a vain attempt to calm his nerves. And where would he run to, if he did decide to make a break for it? Probably the mere fact of his disappearance would be enough to get all the spooks in the world on his tail, either to get the data back or to get hold of it for themselves. Maybe there would be people who would want to buy it. But if he was in this deep, why would they want to buy it from him? Why not just kill him and do everyone else a favour? And what about Claire, what would Claire do if he just disappeared? Could he persuade her to come with him? What would she do when they came looking for him, for the both of them?

The doorbell rings, and Ilya nearly jumps out of his skin. It takes him a second or two before he twigs that it's probably Claire, and he calls through on the intercom: "Yeah?"

"It's me. I brought lunch."

He buzzes her through the main entrance and stands with the door of his flat ajar as he listens to her walking across the little courtyard of the old tenement building and up the stairs to his apartment. As she arrives on his landing he holds open the door for her to enter. She walks through, straight into his arms and he pushes the door to with one hand and holds her tight with the other. They kiss and stand like that for a while in the hallway till she finally takes off her jacket and kicks off her shoes and they go and sit down on Ilya's battered old couch. The sun is already down behind the front part of the tenement building and Ilya's living room is already dark with shadows. He turns on a tall floor lamp that sends up a pool of light to the ceiling and strokes Claire's cheek as she nestles up against him.

"So what's with you? You gave me quite a fright back there."

Claire pulls her head back a little to look him in the eye and opens her mouth to say something. But no sound comes out.

It's not often that Claire is lost for words. All the way over she's been borne along by the feeling of how good it'll be to talk things through with Ilya and get a handle on what to do with Josh and his crazy plan. But now that she's here she doesn't know what to say, or where to begin. She's never talked with him much about the collective, or at least, not the political side of things. It's been more like—oh, it's my work, I have to go and do a shift, that kind of stuff. And it's been such a separate world. So how could she suddenly spill the beans and tell him everything, and ask him for his opinion on whether she should turn into some kind of urban guerrilla. The thought seemed absurd. And yet, there was something about it that appealed to her, in spite of the craziness, maybe even because of the craziness. It spoke to the romantic in her. Going out in a blaze of glory. Making some wild and maybe even futile gesture that would write her name in the history books. Whatever. It was driving her crazy. She lowers her eyes and says, "It was nothing. I'm sorry to be such a drama queen about it."

"It was nothing? Are you shitting me? It sure as hell didn't sound like nothing earlier on."

"It was just one of the guys at work. He upset me. I think maybe he was coming on to me. It was like, out of the blue."

Ilya's jaw drops in disbelief.

"Coming on to you? You want me to go round and kick his ass?"

Claire has a mental image of Ilya launching into Josh and the two of them scrabbling around on the ground. The image is so absurd that she has to laugh.

"No, it's ok. I can do my own ass-kicking. But thanks for offering. Nice to know you care."

"Claire, I'm serious."

"I believe you. It just kind of upset me, you know? And when I couldn't get hold of you, it just blew out of proportion. I'm ok now."

Claire sees Ilya looking at her, like he's trying—and failing—to convince himself she's really ok. She gives him her best smile.

"And where were you anyway? What have you been up to?"

Ilya's look of concern changes to one of evasiveness, uncertainty.

"Me? Nowhere much. Work stuff, you know. Really demanding, took a lot of concentration and that. I've got a bit more to do, but I'll try not to get too involved with it. Do you want me to tell you about it?"

The last thing Claire wants to hear is some nerd stuff she knows is going to bore her to tears, so she kisses him and says no, it's ok. She holds up the paper bag she has brought with her.

"Late lunch?" says Claire.

"Late lunch is good," says Ilya, and goes over to the kitchen cupboard to get some plates.

Laila is sitting in a wheelchair by the window and she's bored. She had the window open for a while till a nurse came in and told her to shut it. Didn't want her catching cold. Officious bitch. Laila can feel herself straining at the leash, just wanting to be out of here. She can feel a recurrent adrenalin surge within herself, telling her that this isn't a good place for her to be.

But right now, it's her only option.

She sighs and looks down at her leg, her fractured femur with the pins and screws somewhere inside it. They had shown her the x-rays. Frankly, they were gross. They made her feel like an invalid. Fuck, she was an invalid. There was no escaping it.

She hated hospitals. She hated everything about hospitals. The smell. The sickness. The fucking smugness of the doctors. The way the nurses felt entitled to order you around. The patients. Oh, and the food. The slop-that-passed-for-food.

She looks over at the remains of her dinner on the little wheely table that she had pushed away from her.

They had served her pork, for Christ's sake. Like, without asking.

Ok, she hadn't mentioned it.

They had a halal option, but she hadn't thought to tick the box.

It's not like she was even a practicing Muslim.

Hell no. Not in a million years.

It was more of a cultural thing, right? More like Easter eggs, Christmas trees, Ramadan, Eid, St. Patrick's Day, Mardi Gras.

No pork.

Not a difficult concept.

Yeah well, maybe she should have mentioned it.

She looks around and tilts open the window as far as it will go. The gap it reveals is only about six inches wide. Maybe to stop people jumping out? She smiles to herself and thinks: the chance would be a fine thing. At the moment she's having trouble standing. They had her down for physio an hour ago and even taking a few steps with crutches had brought her out in a sweat. She was still weak from the accident, the operation, the medication. The painkillers made her woozy and a little nauseous and the antibiotics just made her want to sleep all the time.

A draft of fresh air blows in through the window and she can hear the sound of kids laughing. A couple of girls are kicking a ball around outside, down on the strip of grass separating St. Catherine's from the canal basin. The air is cold but the sun is shining, and even in spite of the urban setting—the bare trees, the blocks of flats on the other side of the canal, the drab greys and browns of the architecture—there is still something pleasing, something archaic and pastoral about the scene that warms her heart.

She pulls the window shut and thinks of Claire.

CHAPTER TWENTY-FIVE
Trust

Jimmy's down on the street in front of his house and Julia doesn't want him to be there. She doesn't want him to be there because he's one sick individual, but he says if he doesn't get out of the house he'll go mental so she lets him.

"Where are you going?" she asks him as she helps him put on his coat.

"I don't know. It doesn't matter. Anywhere." And he's out the door. The stairs leading down have just been mopped so he treads carefully and tries not to think about slipping and falling down and breaking his neck. As he rounds the last flight of steps he finds himself looking down into the eyes of the Bulgarian cleaning lady who gives the place a desultory once-over at apparently random intervals. He looks at the tracks his feet are making on the wet linoleum and mouths sorry as he squeezes past her. The cleaning lady makes a clacking sound with her tongue against her teeth and slaps her mop down with extra vigour in his wake.

Jimmy stands on the pavement and doesn't have a clue where he's going. The weather has been steadily deteriorating all day, and now the sidewalk is glistening and slick with wet from the drizzle that has set in. He pulls up his collar and starts off down the street towards Danube. Maybe it's his imagination but the pavement itself seems more warped and uneven than ever. The B Village is one of these little side streets that must be at least a couple of hundred years old, built back when they would just bang a load of tiny cubes of granite or flint down into the dirt and call it a pavement. And since they dig it all up again every time the gas goes, or the electric, or the sewers, the whole pathway has taken on a wild, patchwork look. Crazy paving, thinks Jimmy, and smiles at his own little joke.

By the time he reaches the corner of Danube he already feels like turning back, but he can't. He's been getting on Julia's nerves all day, and getting on his own nerves even worse. He's sick, and he's sick of it. He has a mental image of himself six months back, just after they got back from hanging out on the boat. He remembers the scrawny dudes and the *grand dame* hipster woman and their Naked is Good bath towel performance, and he remembers himself with a wry smile. Back then he felt strong, rested, relaxed. Irritable but invincible. Angry enough with the world to get worked up about a couple of rich kids having a good time. Now he shuffles along the street like an old man waiting to die and his body is wracked with pain and he has the permanent iron taste of blood in his mouth. He hardly has the strength to get dressed, never mind get angry. He feels like the life is draining out of him.

But there's still Manila. Manila is his last shot. If the deal doesn't go down as planned, then he might as well just stay there. Or maybe go back to Singapore. To die. He could maybe get someone to sneak him over to Sudong Island, out of sight of the military, like they used to do when they were kids. Or over to Semakau, which he heard was turned into some kind of garbage heap after they turfed all the islanders off. They used to go over and drink and fish with the guys from the island, and hang out in those huts on stilts they used to live in. Must be all gone now. No matter, they could just dump him on the beach, he'd be ok. It would be a good way to go. Maybe better than here, in this god-forsaken trashcan of a city. But what about Julia? He couldn't just wash up on some beach and wait for the tide to take him, while Julia waited around. What was she supposed to do? Knit him a scarf? It was too selfish. None of it was right. No. Manila had to work. It had to work.

He heads down Danube and the wind is blowing stronger now, coming in irregular gusts that blow through his hair and wet his face with horizontal drizzle and make him think of the sea. He sees himself on the prow of an old two-masted schooner, crashing across heavy seas in the Singapore Strait on the way over to Batam, or in a squall somewhere between Batu Pahat and Port Dickson, off the Malaccan coast, on the way up to Kuala Lumpur, and it makes him smile, and lick his lips to see if he can taste the salt of the spray. But it's only the acidic rainfall from the skies over the NC and he turns off Danube just before it segues into Bohemia Street and suddenly finds himself in a little back alley he's never been in before. It snakes up behind the tenements and the modern apartment blocks between high fences overgrown with gnarled yew and apple trees and then without warning he's out in an open space in what looks like a farmyard. There are two old half-timbered brick buildings situated at right angles to each other. Sure, they have modern stuff like satellite dishes and electric doorbells stuck onto them, but Jimmy feels like he's just been transported to the Land That Time Forgot.

He stays where he is for a while, soaking up the place as the rain starts to come down harder now and he can feel his neck getting wet as it trickles down his collar. He thinks of this place, way back, with these two houses out on their own, and slowly becoming encroached upon and buried and finally ignored by the city and it makes him sad that some old form of community has been lost and then he begins to weep for all the communities and friendships and loved ones that he's lost in his lifetime and can never get back to. He thinks now would be a good time to get religion but he's too much of an atheist to have any faith in any of that mystical afterlife shit so he says ah fuck it and rolls a spliff. The initial rush of it makes him feel a little sick and drained, but then he eases into it and it brings the colour back to his cheeks. He leaves the old buildings behind him and he's out into the broad expanse of Ricksville and he spots a little open-air kiosk selling coffee so he ambles over and gets himself a cup and parks himself down under a little awning and drinks his coffee and thinks about the Church of Kali.

Claire and Ilya finish their lunch and go to bed. It seems like the best thing to do. They're both pretty frazzled and haven't seen each other in well over 24 hours so it's kind of a no-brainer. Claire slips out of her jeans and slides quickly under the covers to Ilya, who holds them open for her. Even though Ilya has ramped the heating up, it's still cold in his flat, and they both leave their t-shirts on. There's something so familiar about the gesture, about holding up a duvet cover in a cold winter flat, that makes Claire think of home. Not any home she's known, but maybe a home she'd like to have. What *is* it with this guy? How is it that he wakens all these feelings in her that somehow don't fit with her own picture of who she is? On top of that, it's the first time she's lied to him, and that leaves a really bad taste in her mouth. The thing with Josh is just bugging her too much for her to put it aside and pretend everything is normal. She has to tell Ilya, even if she has no idea how.

They are in close now. He has his arm around her and a hand resting on her spine, behind her heart. She has one arm kind of folded up beneath her, with a hand on his chest, and the other hand caressing the sweet line of an ass cheek. There's a moment of stillness, as they savour the heat of their bodies together. Outside in the courtyard, an old poplar tree shudders and shimmers in the blustery wind, and sheds a leaf or two from the last brown, scurvy remnants still clinging to its naked branches. Claire shivers, and a wave of goosebumps comes up along her arm.

"You're cold."

She nestles in even closer, trying to sink into his flesh, become one with his body.

"Mmm, yeah. No. Not really. It's more…"

She looks into his eyes, their dark, wide-open pupils, and feels herself drawn in. Earlier he had seemed so distant. Not distant, but distracted, somehow not present, not there with her. Now she feels she has his full, uninterrupted attention. She pulls back a little, to bring the rest of his face into focus.

"It's more that there's something I need to tell you."

She can see his eyes widen as she continues.

"That thing with Josh…"

She feels him flinch.

"I knew it."

"No, it's not what you think. It's political. It's to do with the collective. It's… he wants me to do some stuff that I don't want to do. That I think I don't want to do. But it's like, Josh and me go way back, you know? There was never anything between us, not like that, but we've been through a lot together. He's a smart guy. He thinks things through.

And he's very persuasive. So there's a part of me thinks that even though it's not something I want to do—this thing he's suggesting—that still maybe it's what I ought to do. That maybe it's the right thing to do, even though it feels like the wrong thing. Am I making any sense?"

Ilya is looking at her. There's a smile around his mouth but his eyes are serious. He kisses her briefly on the lips and says no.

"Not much. Maybe. I think I get the gist. But it's like, a bit abstract, know what I mean? Why don't you just tell me what it is?"

"I can't. Not right now. I need to think it through a bit more. I'll tell you, I promise. But later, yeah? I just, I just needed you to know."

"Claire. It's ok. I don't get it, and I don't like it that you're worried, and I don't really understand what's going in. But I do know that some things are difficult to explain, and that you can't just expect another person, no matter how close, to intuitively grasp stuff that you've maybe been grappling with for years. So take your time."

She has the feeling that there is something in what Ilya is telling her that eludes her. He's comforting her but his words make him sound like someone else entirely.

"Claire," he says, before she can react. "Do you trust me?"

She feels her heart pounding as she searches through the outermost reaches of her feelings for Ilya in a split second. She feels like he has seen through her, like she is standing naked before him.

But standing naked before him has always been a good thing.

And him standing naked before her has always been a good thing too.

The only person weighing her soul is herself.

"Yes," she says. "Yes, I trust you. Do you trust me?"

"Claire, I love you, but trust is one of those things. I would trust you with my life, no question. But maybe not with my data."

She looks at him wide-eyed, and he smiles.

"It's not all about trust, whatever trust is. All I know is, there are some things it takes time to learn how to handle. If I said, here's a helicopter, why don't you just get behind the controls and fly it, would that be trust or just stupid? I have enough trust to think you could learn it, if you wanted to. But just to believe you would instinctively do the right thing, I think that's pretty naïve."

She strokes his cheek with her thumb.

"Why are you telling me this?"

"Because of what you just said. Because I've also got stuff I need to tell you. Stuff that I'm involved in that's maybe not exactly legal. I don't want to burden you with too much detail but I don't want there to be any secrets between us either. Trouble is I don't know where to start without it sounding like a bunch of crazy nerd shit. Maybe it's just something we need to ease into."

She kisses him then on the lips.

"Ok, easing into it. I'm up for that. Just give me some time, eh?"

He kisses her back.

"As much time as you want, no question."

She turns then, and snuggles backwards into his embrace. He puts an arm around her and slides a hand up under her t-shirt, cupping her breast. She can feel herself stiffen beneath the heat of his palm and flexes the small of her back just a little, so that the curve of her ass presses back into his lap. He's kissing the nape of her neck and his hips are rocking gently with hers. He slides her panties down over her ass and she takes him then between her thighs and they just stay like that a while as she rubs herself along the shaft of his dick. Pretty soon she's wet enough to take him inside her and she does, and he manages to say, "We need a condom?" and she's like, "No, it's still good," and he's puzzled for a moment and goes, "You're sure?" and she just grinds back into him and says, "Shhh, sure I'm sure," and then the talking's over for a while and she can feel Ilya speeding up and about to overtake her and she turns her head so that she can half see his face and says, "Stop. Just hold still. You don't need to do anything."

So he stops, and he's already breathing heavily, and she can feel him burning within her, ready to come, but now she feels him relax a little, and a little more, still hard inside her, and she says, "Give me your hand," and she takes his hand and leads the tip of his index finger to her clit and that is enough to set her off again, but differently this time, with a different rhythm, her own rhythm, far faster than anything he could keep up with and she takes off like a rocket while he is still within her and she is rocking and exploding in colours with him behind and around and inside her and she pauses and pulls his hand away for a moment and then brings it back and it's more of the same. She is buzzing, she is humming, she is coming in great pulsing waves, and again, and again until she pulls his hand away and tells him its enough. And that is all he needs to let go whatever brake it is that he's managed to engage up till now and she pushes back as he grinds deep into her and she can feel the heat now building from a different place entirely and she's coming again but this time so is he and it takes her by the scruff of the neck and she feels as if she's going to black out as they arch and grind and pant.

And when they're done they're lying there hot and exhausted and slick with sweat and he's still got his arms around her and she turns to him and says, "I love you too," and they kiss and smile and fall asleep almost immediately.

And when they wake up Ilya gets up and makes them some tea, and they sit in bed drinking tea and eating dark chocolate biscuits and he says that he needs to do some more work. She gives him a chocolate-lipped kiss and he caresses the tattooed flames on the shaved side of her head. She says, "Do you want me to go?", and he says, "No, but I think it's probably better." And that's all it takes, and she's up and gathering up her things and slipping into her jeans and is fully clothed by the time he has finished the last of his tea. She comes over and sits on the edge of the bed to do up her boots and says, "See you tomorrow?" and he says, "Mine or yours?" and she says, "Mine. Maybe early evening? We can go out to eat and you can stay over. How's that sound?"

"Sounds good," he says, getting up and kissing her and walking her backwards to the door. She grabs her jacket and her hat and her thick scarf and kisses him again, but goodbye this time. And it's only when she opens the front door to go that they both realise that he's standing there in the doorway stark naked and they both laugh and she's gone.

Chapter Twenty-Six
A Hand and a Hanky

Claire is pretty much lost in thought as she wanders away from Ilya's place. She walks down Silversmith onto Cornell and thinks briefly of Laila as she crosses Carlos Marx, and checks her incoming to see whether she hasn't maybe missed a call or a message. But there's nothing, so she just carries on along Cornell, behind the graveyard and its big red-brick church and holds her face up to the falling rain and feels the patter of it on her skin and the cold of the wind and it's good, still something pure and clean, even though it's neither, and it warms her soul in that still-fresh afterglow moment when the world could be so simple. There are plenty of dark thoughts crowding in on her but she does her best to hang on to the warm feeling she has inside her. The headstones in the graveyard are wet with rain and she stops for a moment to take them in. They are a lot simpler here in this part of town than where she lives. No sleeping lions, no kneeling angels, no ornate family tombs. Just plain stones, engravings, even a couple of weathered wooden crosses. A workers' graveyard, thinks Claire, and moves on.

She walks down past Bourbon and is just coming out onto Ricksville when she realizes she's almost at work, and that's one place she really doesn't want to be right now so she veers off to the right, up Ricksville and heading north. She crosses the fat stone cobbles of the road encircling the old village square and jumps the little fence marking off the scratchy patch of grass in the middle. She's just reached the old park kiosk with its overhanging awning and scattering of metal chairs when she recognizes a familiar figure.

"Jimmy. The fuck you doing here out in the rain?"

"Claire. My bad penny. Just soaking it up girl, just soaking it up."

He goes to get up, but she bends down to give him a hug and he sinks back into his chair. She pulls up another chair and wipes the rain off with the sleeve of her jacket. She's about to ask him how's it going, but she can see with one look at his face that it's not going so good. So she slaps him on the knee and gives him a smile.

"Good to see you kid."

"Good to see you Jimmy. I've been thinking about you."

"Flattered I'm sure."

Claire can feel herself blushing a little.

"Not like that, you dope."

"Like what?" says Jimmy, with an innocent air.

"Oh man, can't you be serious? I've got some heavy shit I need to deal with. And it's like, really starting to get to me? I think I could do with some outside input."

"And Ilya can't help you?"

"Well yes and no. I think in the long run he can help me. But it's complicated, you know, and I think he might be out of his depth with it. Plus, I don't want to worry him. And it's kind of political."

Jimmy brightens up.

"Political? Political is good. Political is right up my alley."

He smiles at her, and she feels a wave of relief flooding through her system.

"But maybe we ought to go somewhere warmer, what do you reckon?"

Jimmy says, "I'm game," and goes to get up, but he's struggling even to get out of his chair, so Claire gives him a hand. He throws his plastic cup in the bin and she takes his arm and steers him across the square in the direction of Richard.

"Come on. There's a place just down the road here where we can talk. I'll buy you a drink."

She looks at him solicitously.

"You're allowed to drink, right?"

Jimmy manages a smile.

"Kid, in my condition, you're allowed to do just about anything you're fucking capable of."

By the time they get to the Golden Lion they're both feeling a little too wet for comfort but at least Claire has managed to bring Jimmy up to speed with the collective in general, and Josh's suggestion in particular. Claire holds open the front door for Jimmy and they step into a large, L-shaped room and order a couple of beers at the bar and take a seat down the far end of the longer room, near the stage. The place has a hipsterish, faux-original feel to it, kind of *über*-authentic in a smugly understated way. A couple of bearded guys are staring into their devices over cappuccinos or craft beers, and the tables look like they have been lifted straight out of the decks of some 19th century ocean-going clipper. The lighting is warm and indirect and the sound system softly secretes Ellington and Fitzgerald into the ambience.

"Nice place," says Jimmy, in an entirely irony-free manner, as the bartender brings over the drinks. "You been here long?"

"Eighteen months this Thursday. We have free wifi."

"Glad to hear it. You got a free light too?"

Jimmy holds up a cigarette in the direction of the bartender.

"Sorry amigo, no smoking allowed. But I can bring you chewing tobacco and a spittoon. It's on the menu."

"Yeah, maybe later. I'll let you know."

The bartender returns to his bartenderly preoccupations, and Jimmy raises his glass to Claire.

"Here's looking at you kid."

"Cheers Jimmy."

Jimmy drinks most of his beer in one and calls over for another.

"So let's see if I've got this right. You're hacked off at the incremental pace of the global ecological revolution and are in a spat with your affinity group about it. Our man Josh comes along and says best way forward is top a few oil barons as a way of hotting things up and goading the masses into action. And you want to know what I think about it. Is that about right so far?"

"Well, you've cut a few corners there. But that's more or less it, yeah."

Jimmy drains the rest of his drink.

"And now you say, 'So what do you think?'."

Claire takes a swig of her beer and says, "So what do you think?"

"Well, to quote a certain tattooed friend of mine who shall remain nameless, I think it's the biggest crock of shit that I've heard in a long time."

Jimmy taps the end of his cigarette on the table to underline his point.

"Don't get me wrong. I'm not a pacifist. I don't believe in turning the other cheek. I think there are times for defending yourself and even times for going on the offensive. But if you do anything like this the state will be on your case in the blink of an eye. They'll be down on you like a ton of bricks. They will fucking crush you…"

"Ok, I get the picture."

"And I mean, what would be the point? You think that would make you some kind of martyr to the cause? You got some kind of plan worked out how many martyrs you're going to need to get things going? I tell you, it's just bullshit."

Jimmy's cigarette crumples under the strain of repeated point-making.

"You remember what we were talking about the other day? When I said that being old and about to die gives you the kind of freedom you never had when you were younger?"

Claire nods and reaches for her tobacco pouch.

"Sure I remember. I said that was bullshit too."

"Right. And if anyone is going to do the kind of shit you're talking about it should be some old guy with nothing to live for, and not some smart, good-looking kid with everything going for her. That just doesn't make sense."

Claire rolls Jimmy a cigarette and hands it to him.

"And you know what I'm going to do?"

"I don't know, Jimmy, what are you going to do?"

"I'm going to take this cigarette outside and make it pay for the crimes of the tobacco industry."

"In that case I'm coming with you."

"And you know what I'm going to do after that?"

"No, Jimmy, I don't. But I have a feeling you're going to tell me anyway."

"Fucking right on. I'm going to get on a plane to Manila and I'm going to do my best to save my skinny ass. On the explicit advice of some good friend of mine. Who told me to quit being so fucking stupid as to even entertain the idea of doing the grand gesture thing."

Claire finishes the cigarette she's rolling for herself and pushes back her chair to get up.

"Pretty sound advice, from that friend of yours."

"Sound as a pound. So if you want to be heroic, stay and build this weird movement of yours. Everything else…" says Jimmy, pushing back his chair.

"Is just pissing in the wind," says Claire, helping him up.

Jimmy orders a couple of whiskeys on the way out and the two of them stand in the porch entrance to the bar and light up first before clinking glasses and savouring the bite of the liquor. The rain has eased off a bit but night has fallen and the streetlights are flickering on. Jimmy takes a deep drag on his cigarette and exhales into the night.

"I fucking hate winter."

He holds his glass up to the light and swirls the whiskey round in his glass.

"The days go by so quickly. Feels like I just got up."

"Same here."

"Ah, lucky you. And how are things with young Ilya?"

Claire looks down into the depths of her whiskey.

"They're good. Really good…"

"But?"

She takes a swig and looks out into the night.

"You ever do something where you questioned your own motivation? Like you couldn't really understand where your heart was taking you?"

"Me? Sure kid. Story of my life."

She turns to look at Jimmy, brushes a skein of wet hair from her face.

"Don't get me wrong. It's good with Ilya, you know? He's taken me somewhere I've never been with anyone else. Like somewhere really deep, and strong, and warm. All of that is wonderful, and I'm grateful to him for it. But I'm not sure I know what it is. And I'm worried that he's already in a lot deeper than me. And…"

She finishes her drink and flicks the butt of her cigarette out onto the wet pavement. Jimmy raises an eyebrow.

"And?"

"And I find myself looking at other people."

"Other men?" Jimmy sounds more than a little surprised.

"Other women, if you must know."

Jimmy claps her on the back.

"Ha! That's alright then. Come on in, I think this calls for another whiskey."

Gene calls Omar as it's getting dark and gives him the green light for the posters.

"Shame about the Church," says Omar.

"No worries," says Gene. "They're with us, they'll be there. But organising demos is not their thing. Their focus is kind of, elsewhere."

"Gotta respect that I guess," says Omar, and then, businesslike: "Ok Jeanie, so we're good to go. I'll call the printers and put the word out. Anything you can do from your side will be helpful. Oh, and one other thing."

"Shoot."

"You want me to organise a loudspeaker van? And maybe a stage truck for the final rally?"

"Sounds good to me."

"You know what that entails, right?"

"Uh, no. Fill me in."

"Someone's going to have to do some talking. I mean, we can get someone for the loudspeaker van, play a bit of music, read out a few messages of solidarity. But we'll need one of the girls from the NFS to make a speech at the end of the demo."

"Ok Vic. Never thought about that. I'll pass it on. Shitload of work, this demo thing."

"Na," says Omar. "Not when you're used to it. But there are a few costs involved."

"I'll see if we can rustle up a donation."

"Now you're talking."

"Are we done?"

"Done and dusted darling. See you Saturday."

"I'll call you."

"Catch you later."

And so it goes. Darkness falls. Calls are made. Buttons are pressed, machines are set in motion, posters are produced, old school. The smell of the printing press, the sound of the machine. Each poster a work of art in its own right. Four-colour, strident, bold, emblazoned with a photofit mugshot of the presumed attacker, plus a licence plate number, plus a contact number and address for any information, plus time and place of the demo, plus who's calling it. A lot of information for one sheet of A3, but there it is. Omar's crew have worked their wonders, agitprop experience coming through, delivering the goods. And as posters are collected and distributed, the word goes out, virally, explicitly, mouth to mouth, bar to bar, site to site, account to account. Lists are activated, networks invoked, wheels both tangible and virtual are set in motion. Time is short, but word spreads like a colourful infection, out from the printworks down on Marianne, out from Omar's place down on Cartersgate, and through the streetspace meatspace arteries of the NC, up to Han Plaza and down Carlos Marx, up Henry and Airport and of course through the length and breadth of Charlie's Garden and down Columbia and plastering the walls of Fuji City and the police motorcycle barracks and down Kittyhawk to Southern Cross and down to Hillman and covering the walls of the market hall and up L'Ouverture and outwards ever outwards as far as their dwindling supply of posters will take them.

So quick is the infection, that by the time Gene arrives at the Crow's Nest for the NFS meeting, the posters have preceded him. The street is full of them, and there is a thick, oversized wad of posters waiting on a table when he walks in the door.

Sandy's on duty and waves him through.

"Girls are out back. Ready and waiting."

Gene walks through to the back room. The lighting is subdued, the air slightly stale. Five figures sit in a circle on cheap plastic chairs. A couple of teacups are balanced on knees, accompanied by the sound of knitting needles. Three of the girls are in their working clothes, the other two, like Gene, in straight drag. He does the rounds, cheek-to-cheek, apologizes for being late, pulls up a chair.

For a coven of queer sexworking syndicalists, the Charlie's Garden chapter of the NFS takes a very serious approach to matters of business, to wit: structured meetings, strict agenda, no interrupting who has the word, pass a resolution, decide what to do and who's to do it. And then make sure it gets done.

They didn't win the pimp wars by fart-arsing around.

Splatter Carrie has the word and opens the meeting. She's dressed in a slinky white maxi with a kind of tie-dye blood drip, and has dark red lines of makeup streaked down over her face.

"Sisters," she says affably, "let's get this show on the road."

Murmurs of agreement from the assembled crew.

"Main item of business is the demo. We all know the background and we've already given it our provisional support. Trish has set up some online voting for the membership and the response has been over-whelmingly positive. So I think we should have no trouble ratifying that decision here. There's a bunch of posters just arrived that we're going to need to get out as quick as we can, but because of the short notice most of the mobilisation is going to have to be via social media. We've got Candy on that and it's looking good. Jeanie, this is your call. What else do we need to be doing?"

Gene clears his throat and launches in.

"Thanks Carrie. Well, apart from getting the word out, and actually making sure people turn up, I think there are two main things we still need to address. The first is that Omar and the crew at the Mary Jane are running up expenses with all this—printing costs, organizing the stage truck, that kind of thing—and it would be good if we could give them some money to cover all that. That's the easy part I reckon. The other thing is, we're going to need someone to make a speech. There'll be a rally at the end so it would be good if we could say something."

Gene looks around the room.

"So I guess that means it's going to have to be one of us."

There's silence for a moment. Then Trish raises a long-nailed finger to speak. She has ancient Egyptian style mascara, huge gold earrings and a close-cropped Afro.

"Jeanie. Way I see it is: You're the main mover and shaker here. It ought to be you."

Sounds and gestures of assent from round the room. Everyone's good with that suggestion.

Everyone except Gene that is.

"Girls, c'mon. Why me? You know I'm not a speechmaker. I just kicked this thing off. Got things started with Omar. Some of you have far more experience with this kind of thing. Gale, how about you?"

Gale Glottis, a funky thirty-something famed for her fellatio technique—giving a whole new take on the expression "blowing a gale"—shakes her auburn mane.

"No way Jeanie. I mean, we'll all be there to help out. But you've taken the lead on this, you really out to follow through."

"Aw Jeez," says Gene.

"And Mary," chorus the girls, and cackle with laughter.

"Isn't there anyone who'll give me a hand here?"

"Hand and a hanky, girl's best friend," quips Trish.

"Come on girls, I'm serious," says Gene.

"So are we," they chorus, high-fiving it around the circle.

Carrie takes the word.

"Ok everyone, calm down."

She waits for a few seconds, then continues to Gene.

"Jeanie honey, I can tell you're not happy with it. But I think Gale is right. We all want you to do this. I know it's not easy, but you'll be fine. If you need some help with ideas some of us can sit down with you and do some brainstorming. Make sure you reflect the NFS position and all."

"The NFS position being what, exactly?" says Gene, glumly.

"Find this fucker and cut his balls off," says Carrie.

This time, nobody laughs.

Claire and Jimmy are back in the warmth of the bar. They clink glasses over the clipper-deck tabletop and take a drink. Claire leans forwards, resting on her elbows.

"So let me get this straight. You're shocked at the idea of me chasing after other men when I'm with Ilya but you think it's ok if it's a woman? That's just too bizarre. You're going to have to explain that one to me."

Jimmy laughs, and the laughing sets off a fit of coughing, but when he finally stops there's still a mischievous glint in his eye.

"Ah, I can see we're getting down to the finer points of the Jimmy Chang code of ethics. It's quite simple, really. If it's a man you'd be cheating on him. Ilya's a nice kid, you two go well together, you'd be giving the poor guy the feeling that somehow he's not up to the mark. Hurt his feelings and all. You wouldn't want to be doing that. You with me?"

"I guess so."

"If it's a woman you'd be exploring your sexuality. Addressing a need that Ilya can't fulfil, yadda yadda. You catch my drift. Probably wouldn't hurt him any the less, but your intentions might be a tad nobler than just sleeping around. Nothing against sleeping around mind."

Claire leans back with a look of irritation.

"Are you suggesting going with women doesn't count as real sex? Or a real relationship?"

"No lass, that's certainly not what I'm suggesting. I'm just saying better out than in, if you know what I mean. I'm not a believer in gratuitously hurting anyone's feelings. But if you've got feelings for other women bubbling up, and it's going to warp you out of shape trying to deny them, then my advice is, go and get on with it."

"Maybe you're right Jimmy." She takes a swig of her drink and has a look around the room, which is slowly filling up with fresh punters. The noise level has ramped up a notch and the barman has switched the music to something with more of a beat.

"You ever sleep around Jimmy?"

Jimmy fakes shock with a hand to the chest.

"Moi? No way. Used to be the proper little whore, in the old days though. Nothing to be proud of mind. But then I met up with Julia. Don't know what it is with that woman. She's just, like, more than enough for anyone. Know what I mean?"

Claire smiles, and looks at Jimmy like she's seeing him in a new light.

"Yeah. I know what you mean. Part of me's like that with Ilya. Like he's totally special. Like he's the only person in the world I want to be with. But then I get out the door and it's like, bam, a switch flips and I find myself attracted to all these chicks. That's so fucking weird. It doesn't seem like me at all. Usually, if I want something, I just go for it. And when it's finished, move on. Serial monogamy, that's me. Never been into the polyamory thing. It's as if my body has just developed its own secret agenda. Or maybe just my libido."

"Libidinous secret agendas. I'll drink to that," says Jimmy and raises his glass.

"Cheers Jimmy."

"Sláinte."

They knock back their drinks and Jimmy is wracked by another fit of coughing.

"Jimmy, it's good talking to you. But maybe you ought to be heading home, no?" says Claire.

Jimmy bangs his chest with the side of his fist, and when he looks up his eyes are watering and the blood has drained from his face.

"You're probably right kid. Don't want Julia worrying about me. Got a flight to catch on Sunday. Gonna have to start getting ready."

He lowers his voice conspiratorially.

"But there's one other thing occurs to me before I go."

Claire brings her head closer to his.

"What's that Jimmy?"

"The thing with Josh. Have you ever considered the idea that he might be trying to set you up?"

"What?" exclaims Claire. Heads turn on neighbouring tables. She smiles an apology and turns back to Jimmy.

"The fuck you mean? That Josh is some kind of nark?"

"Wouldn't be the first time. It's a classic tactic. Get someone who's frustrated with the pace of change and goad them into a little extracurricular activity. Then you've got the whole bunch branded as terrorists and can bang them away for years. Or just liquidate them. It's easily done."

"But I've known Josh for years. I like Josh!"

"Yeah, but can you read his mind? Do you know what's going on in his head? Can you prove he's who he says he is?"

"Jimmy, this is just too fucking paranoid for me, sorry."

"No worries kid. It's just something for you to think about. Before you go doing anything you'll regret later. Tell you the truth, I'd prefer it if I was wrong."

He goes to get up, and Claire helps him out of his chair.

"Ok Jimmy. I'll give it some thought. But that sounds just too outrageous to be true."

"Sometimes the truth is so outrageous that people just don't want to see it."

"Yeah, I can dig that," says Claire, and steers him towards the door.

Outside, the rain has stopped, and the clouds have cleared a little to reveal the full moon in the early evening sky. Claire walks Jimmy down Richard to the corner of the B Village. They stop outside a bar advertising raw pizza and vegan sushi, just up the street from where she held a knife to Ilya's throat all those months back. Where she met Jimmy for the first time. She turns towards him. The skin of his face is orange from the sodium streetlights and deep in shadow.

"Jimmy. You take care of yourself in Manila, y'hear. And come back safe. Next round's on me."

"Now you're talking. You're a good kid Claire. I'll be back for sure."

She hugs him then, and he holds on to her for a while. Then he looks at her face, and wipes a tear away with a thumb.

"Don't you worry about me. We're fighting stock, the Singapore Irish Changs. It's more you I'm worried about. Just keep your nose clean and don't do anything stupid. You got me?"

"Gotcha Jimmy," says Claire, and sniffs, and smiles, and turns to go.

Al's feeling pretty good about himself. He's had dinner in a little Italian place not far from the confines of Fuji City, and has a warm glow in his stomach from the fettuccini and a few glasses of Verdicchio followed up by grappa and espresso. He's come back to the office for a quick view of what his boys are up to and so far he's not disappointed. It's Friday evening and the denizens of the NC are going to be out in the fleshpots, living it up and getting on down while they can. That's where he would expect his boys to be at this time, and that's where they are. He's sitting at his desk and has his massive wrap-around screen powered up and can see the clusters of his men moving through the city. They're scattered around, but all seem to be in the right kind of location—anywhere that there's an agglomeration of drinkers, party-goers, concert visitors, and people just generally up for getting out of their heads. Al's also tuned into emergency services, and has a bunch of local news feeds ticking away in a corner of his screen. But it's early yet. People are not inebriated enough for an attack to go unnoticed. On the other hand, he doesn't want his little actions to be completely under the radar. He wants them to be noticed enough to create a ripple, an echo, a rumour, a news item, but not so much as to attract a crowd, who might figure that self-defence is also a viable option.

Al can feel his attention wandering. He checks in with his three captains who all respond with brief text messages. It's going to be an hour or two at least before things get going. He calls up an escort service and orders one of the numbers from their catalogue to help him while away the time. Al leans back in his big leather chair and creates a steeple from his fingers. He feels like a chess player, a grand master considering his moves. Yet at the same time he sees himself as a Situationist, an artist of the possible. It's his job to bring people together in certain constellations, to deploy specific forces in such a way that they will go unnoticed until some act of violence erupts. After that they should melt away, leaving only a new element in the matrix of common social perception, a new irritant in the collective unconscious. Al smiles at the thought of himself as a pearl diver, recovering these little nuggets of beauty arising from a mollusc's response to an invasive threat. But he's a diver with a difference, for he is the one who seeds the oysters in the first place. And when he's recovered enough pearls he'll be able to string them together and make a narrative out of them. And his narrative will be enough to tip the scales in a society already disorientated, fragmented, rudderless. Admittedly just a small contribution in the overall scheme of things. But one worth doing well, he feels.

The woman arrives, and they spend the best part of an hour performing joyless but strenuous sex acts that leave Al wondering whether he ought to get the carpet dry cleaned or even replaced with something friendlier to the knees. However, he's not the one doing any kneeling, so he decides against it. He pays the escort and gives her a twenty as a tip for being punctual. He does so like punctuality in a woman.

Bodily exigencies dealt with, Al brings up a live TV stream on his screen, scoots through a little world news to while away the time. But it's all so stale. Military actions, wars in foreign countries, a bombing here, a massacre there. The fat solicitous faces of various political stooges, some of them heading up entire nations. The ongoing moral panic of inundation by foreigners. The latest measures taken against the Muslim population. It's all to the good, thinks Al. But at the same time so phoney. This is what he likes so much about his work. It gives him access to the real thing, genuine underlying data. Strategic assessments definitely not intended for public consumption. It gives him a sense of belonging. The feeling of belonging to a dark, unstoppable tide. More than that, the feeling of being a mover, a motor force in that tide. An element of power in a network of power.

The night progresses, and Al's dark tide sweeps through the city, rising, imperceptibly at first, as the full moon shines down and the sidewalks dry slowly in the cool night air. And as the tide moves into the realm of the perceptible, so faces meet with fists, and blades with skin, and teeth with the concrete surfaces of unforgiving sidewalks. Confrontations are contrived, performed, and followed through. Unpredictable acts of random viciousness break out in spaces otherwise renowned for being chilled-out, tolerant, safe. A subliminal tremor passes through the foetid soil of the NC as it gratefully soaks up its favourite, most exquisite elixir: blood.

Al grunts awake at the sound of the first alerts coming in. The TV news always has that soporific effect on him, but this, this pulse of urban altercation, this is what he has been waiting for. This is what sets his pulses racing. It's gone midnight, and now there's a regular flow of incidents throughout the city that go on till about two thirty in the morning. Al hears the airwaves chatter about gangs of foreign-looking men involved in the incidents, and rejoices. He opens up an array of press sites, both local and national, and it's not long till the *Spleen* has picked up on it in its local section. Not enough for front-page news, but "Night of Violence in the NC" is not bad for a start. Al pours himself a drink and leans back in his chair with a feeling that his efforts have all been worthwhile.

Ilya's back with his honeypot. It's thick and rich, and he's so full of it he thinks he might OD on it, be sick with it, gorge himself to death on it. It was slow going at first, working through the various layers of encryption, and even now that its contents are laid bare before him, it's so dense and impenetrable that he hardly has a clue what it's all about. One thing he can see though is that he shouldn't be reading it. It's clearly some chunk of top security state archive material. There's a lot of talk of operational resources, unofficial operatives, threat potentials, elimination scenarios, neutralisation strategies, long and medium term objectives. It's hard to tell what any of it refers to. The language is arcane and obscure, and nothing seems to be referred to by its real name. Ilya guesses that the text itself must be built up like some kind of database, with specific IDs referring out to other documents, maybe some kind of root document, in which stand-in variables are matched to a list of original meanings. None of which he finds particularly irritating or unusual. He is after all used to working with code, with dense lines of information in which every character stands for something else. It's a question of attitude. The fundamental mindset required for hours of immobility in front of whatever interface he happens to be using to achieve his goal. So Ilya's cool with a mega-heap of data he doesn't understand.

The important thing to remember here, he reminds himself, is that it is data he has ripped off. Quite apart from what it may or may not mean, he is no doubt about the fact that it is information so hot, so quintessentially out of order, that it can never escape the confines of the data cage that he has constructed for it. If any trace of it were to lead back to him, he'd be toast. It would simply, literally, be a death sentence.

So Ilya feels like some crazy art thief who has stolen some priceless masterpiece. Now that he's got it, there's not much he can do with it except hang it up in the privacy of his own home. He can't show it to anyone. Even the act of trying to sell it would probably attract far more attention than he could handle. So for now, he has no choice but to play it cool, weather the storm outside, and poke around and see what he's got.

There's a big segment of the data that seems to be made up purely of transcripts of conversations. They're datestamped and referenced, and specific passages are highlighted, but there's no real clue about what's going on or what the reason for the transcript was. He gets a few references to specific venues, and what seem to be international conferences. So he twigs that it's possibly something diplomatic, maybe industrial or state level espionage. Basically boring shit, so he just keeps on digging. He's an archaeologist sitting in the middle of the biggest heap of pottery shards or whatever it is those guys get off on in his entire career. He sees himself with a pipe and a sun hat sitting under a pyramid. Yeah right. At least they get some sun down there, rather than just a stiff neck and cold feet in his crap apartment.

After a couple of hours he comes up with some stuff that looks like it's dealing with the NC. That perks up his interest and he starts taking a few notes. Biggest thing at the moment is something called "Operation Brando", which has links in a thousand different directions and a list of about three dozen names involved. But fuck if it means anything to him. Just the kind of cloak and dagger bullshit you come to expect from living in a police state.

Chapter Twenty-Seven
A Demonstration

It's a bleary, watered-down sun that rises over the NC on the Saturday morning. There's a warm front that has swept in from the west and it's raised the temperatures to a few degrees above freezing, just enough for people to maybe take off a layer or leave their scarves at home. But it's muggy, do-nothing weather. The kind of day that, when you look out of the bedroom window, just wants to make you turn over and go back to sleep.

No such choices for Suleika. She's woken at 6 in her hive bunk by the sound of a child crying, and knows that once she's awake she'll never get back to sleep. No such choices for Laila either. The ward rounds start at 6.30 with a clatter of bedpans and the sound of trolleys being laden and pushed away, and the loud morning voices of the nurses coming on to their shift. They've been up since 5 and see no reason why anyone else should enjoy the luxury of sleep when it has been so brutally denied to themselves.

For the rest of our crew, consciousness comes at a more sedate pace. Claire and Ilya wake up together, after Ilya gave up on work and gave Claire a call. Julia is up and about by the time Jimmy manages to force his eyes open. She brings him a coffee and strokes the hair out of his eyes. Al comes awake from a night in his leather chair. He's got a crick in his neck and a mouth like a zookeeper's boot. And still, and still. It was a good night.

Only Gene wakes with a start. Today is the day of the demo, and the knowledge that he is going to have to stand on the back of a truck and say something to a crowd of people immediately fills him with an adrenalin rush. This is certainly not something he feels equipped for. But fuck it. There's no getting away from it now, he's just going to have to deal with it.

The demo itself is planned to start at Han Plaza at one, perfectly timed to provide maximum visibility to the Saturday afternoon shopping hordes. The route is short and sweet: Up Kane to Cartersgate, up Alberta to O, then down to Connolly Square for the rally. The whole thing shouldn't take them more than an hour max. The route itself is heavily lined with posters, with conspicuous clusters around the Mary Jane, Han Plaza and Connolly. The crowd at O are always good for a ruck, and the police have already dumped impromptu depots of crowd control barriers at various strategic points along the route.

By 9 all are awake, and it's Suleika who experiences the first major shock of the day. She's finished her breakfast, and is on her way down to her traditional pitch in front of the Arcades. She moves slowly, glad that the cold has let up. But the damp is no good for her rheumatism either, and it has her leaning heavily on her stick as she walks. She passes the mosque on Columbia, the corner of Charlie's Garden, the big junction at Henry and Airport. She's just reached the corner of Airport and Carlos Marx, just rounding the corner into the bustle of the entrance to the Arcades when a face on a big grey street fusebox pulls her up short. She can't read the writing but the face on the poster is immediately familiar to her. The man in the suit from Fuji City. Those men, out on the tarmac. Those killers. There is nothing she can do. She can't understand what the poster is saying, and she can't ask anyone for help. There's a number on the poster, but she has nothing to write with. She tries to memorize the number, but gives up after a couple of minutes. She's blocking the traffic. There's a stream of pedestrians flowing around her, and some of them even seem to be objecting to the way she's taking up space on the pavement. She stands her ground for a while, helpless in front of the poster, but knowing that her act of recognition means something, and that she will have to act on it. But for now, she has no choice but to give in to the flow and take up her place on the pavement outside of the U.

Second shock goes to Al. He finally gets his shit together and heaves himself out of his chair, makes himself a coffee on his expensive espresso machine, finger-combs his hair and lights a cigarette. He leans up against the window frame while he drinks his coffee, watches a couple of fuji kids playing football on the fenced-off part of the airfield that is theirs and theirs alone. They've put down their jumpers as goalposts, and such is their energy and enthusiasm that they seem oblivious to the cold. They're lost in what they're doing, and something in Al envies them that. He figures they have no idea about their future, no idea about their present situation beyond the confines of the obvious, they're just glad that they're no longer in their past. Even if the present means a place as god-awful as Fuji City. Even if their lives are pre-programmed for disappointment and disillusionment. There's something tough and resilient about these kids that even Al admires. But at the end of the day, he's not here to admire them. He's here to get rid of them.

He flicks his cigarette butt out onto the tarmac and puts on his jacket.

Down at the car park he slips into his phaeton and eases out of the staff gate. He takes a left onto Columbia and is just putting his foot down when his attention is caught by a block of eight identical posters, all bearing an image that looks remarkably like his face. He pulls up to the kerb and jumps out of the car to take a closer look. There's no doubt that the image is supposed to be him. It has him branded with the word "rapist" and even has his car registration number. Al is filled with a rage so enormous, so overwhelming that it's all he can do to stop himself from clawing at the posters there and then, in order to rip them all into the tiniest of shreds. But there's an alarm bell inside him that reminds him how conspicuous he is, standing there with his face and his car in front of his own likeness on a poster for some demonstration. He takes out his phone and takes a picture of one of the posters, does a quick three-sixty to see if there is anyone looking, which fortunately there isn't, then he's back in his car and he's outta there.

Al's mind is racing as he drives. This means a whole new tactical situation. First thing is to put in for new plates for the car, and a paint job. It would be a shame to have to trash such an expensive machine, but that remains an option. There'll be his superiors to deal with. They won't be happy that he's got his face plastered around the town, but there's almost no chance that they will give him up, not at this stage in the game. There's that bitch Laila, who probably won't take long putting two and two together and who'll have to be dealt with, sooner rather than later. And then there's whoever is behind this fucking demonstration. That's something he's going to have to deal with too. He's pretty sure that he can find a way to make their lives uncomfortable.

By the time Al reaches home he has the outlines of a strategy fully formed in his mind. He checks the photo of the poster, noting the time and date of the demo. He still has a couple of hours till it kicks off. He makes a phone call to a well-placed police officer. He books his car in for a respray. He checks through his wardrobe for a good disguise for a queer demonstration.

A demonstration!

He does so like demonstrations.

Jeanie needs a lot of time to get ready this morning. The demo will require full-battle dress, so she starts with a bath, with a major face and body shave, and then settles into an elaborate makeup routine that takes her the best part of an hour. Then it's nails, her favourite black lace bodysuit, a black latex mini and black conical Madonna corsage, thigh-high fake leather boots with six-inch platform soles but fat, a.k.a. sensible, heels to walk in. She chooses big purple hair to go with her lipstick, an array of heavy rings that could double up as knuckle dusters at a pinch and a thick armband made up of chrome-plated bicycle chain links. She's just admiring the final result in the mirror when her phone buzzes.

"Omar!"

"Jeanie. How's tricks? You good to go?"

"Ready as I'll ever be. Anything I need to know?"

"Nope. We're all set. Meet you at the loudspeaker van at a quarter to. We'll try to get things started by one, but it'll depend what mood the police are in."

"We'll know soon enough."

"Ok sweetie. See you in a bit."

Omar hangs up, and Jeanie's aware how grateful she is that he's there. While the NFS have pushed her to the fore, and the Church has more or less left her to her own devices, Omar and his crew have been rock solid. And that's a good feeling to have. The kind of feeling she needs right now.

Jeanie turns up at Han Plaza at a quarter to one and the place is already filling up with the whole panoply of gender-bending queer militancy. There are drag queens, warrior dykes, a big transsexual contingent, and a whole horde of people positioned somewhere along the continuum of non-heteronormative sexual preference and gender identity. There's a lot of leafleting going on, along with valiant attempts to interface with the throngs of Saturday afternoon shoppers doing their best, as card-carrying members of the NC's seen-it-all-ain't-nothing-fazes-me club, to act as if everything is perfectly normal.

But if there's one thing that's not so normal, it's not the dazzling display of urban sub-cultural fauna, but the police presence. By one o'clock the crowd of demonstrators has swollen to encompass a couple of thousand people. The cops however, seem kitted out for something far more ambitious. They've got personnel carriers lined up along all the arteries leading into Han Plaza, fronted by at least a dozen riot vans nearer to the square, their wire-mesh window protection already firmly bolted into place. Jeanie notes with alarm that there are two armoured water cannon trucks parked down Coney Heath on the direction of Southern Cross, which also seems to be totally out of proportion. The cops themselves are already out in force on the square, dressed in full riot gear, although most still have their helmets clipped to their belts.

Jeanie pushes through the crowd towards the loudspeaker van and catches sight of Omar talking to the woman at the wheel. They cheek kiss, with Omar careful not to smudge any of Jeanie's make up. He gives an appreciative whistle.

"Wow, Jeanie, looking good. As ever."

"Thanks Vic. Same to you."

She gestures over to the lines of police. "But's what's with all the cops? I don't like the look of this at all."

Omar's eyes look worried, but his voice is calm and reassuring.

"Me neither Jeanie. I don't know what it is that's got them so spooked. They look as if they're decked out for a major confrontation."

"Ok, but let's try to keep things cool, eh?"

"Yeah. I've already been in touch with their liaison officer. He's a real stony-faced creep. Giving absolutely nothing away. We're going to have to play it by ear I guess."

The two are interrupted as a cheer goes up to greet a contingent of working girls from Charlie's Garden marching down the middle of Henry in full regalia. The police have motorcycle units in front and behind them, blocking and releasing traffic as they pass. The girls are carrying a wide NFS banner with the words "Stop Violence against Sexworkers!" which they manoeuvre around the crowd control barriers set up by the police to cordon off the square.

By ten past one they're ready to roll. The central area of Han Plaza—the paved pedestrian island surrounded on all sides by at least four lanes of traffic—is now full to bursting with demonstrators. Even so, it's not a big demonstration by NC standards. But the cops have yet to clear the traffic from the crossing leading over to Kane and the crowd is getting restless. Omar has tried a couple of times to get some response from police liaison, but no joy so far. They finally opt for a more name and shame approach, and make a direct appeal via loudspeaker van for the police to free up the crossing. That does the trick, and the demo moves off with a whoop from the crowd and music blaring from the speakers.

Jeanie is marching up at the front of the demo with the rest of the NFS girls and Omar is back walking next to the loudspeaker van. The throng on the pavements either side of Kane stop and gape as the procession passes by. The Avenue itself is split down the middle by a nominally green central reservation, and cars on the other side of the reservation honk their horns as the demo goes by. People are standing outside shops, watching, or bringing their drinks outside of the cafés they've been sitting in to get a better view. There are people up on the balconies of the tenement buildings either side of the street, and the overall reaction is positive. There are not too many real rednecks here in the NC. Anyone not prepared to rub along with such multifarious neighbours sooner or later percolates out to the suburbs. So the vibe from the populace is generally one of benign tolerance to just about any counter-cultural manifestation. And for this particular party, the feeling is Mardi Gras, Christopher Street and May Day all rolled into one.

Only the police are not happy. The procession has only gone a couple of hundred yards and they've already formed a tight cordon on each side, extending the length of the demo and marching parallel with it. Jeanie drops back to consult with Omar.

"Vic, what the fuck is going on? What are they trying to pull?"

"Jeanie, we're going to have to watch ourselves. They'll be kettling us if we're not careful. This is just totally out of order."

"So what do we do?"

"I think we should just keep going. If we stop and challenge them, it'll give them a chance to cut the demo in half. Then we'll be fucked. Best to press ahead to Carters. They won't try anything there, it's a difficult place for them to hold."

"But do we call for them to pull back anyway?"

"Sure. We tell everyone to stay calm and not let themselves be provoked. And we call on the police to pull back and stop being such a pain in the arse."

"Good idea."

"Yeah, good idea. Do you want to do it?"

"Do what? You mean, make the announcement?"

"Sure, why not. Get yourself into the swing of things. Warm you up for later on and all."

Omar gives her a wink and a smile.

"Don't worry Jeanie, you can do it."

Jeanie climbs into the van and makes the announcement. A cheer goes up from the crowd and a tiny quiver of uncertainty passes through the lines of police. It's not much, but it's enough for them to keep going till they reach Cartersgate. There's a crowd of a couple of hundred people gathered outside the Mary Jane, which has its windows and doors open and its sound system cranked up to the max. There are banners hung from the big apartment blocks behind the bar and draped down from the platforms of the overground railway station, giving the whole place the feel of some kind of mediaeval battlements.

Seeing the serried lines of police around the oncoming column, the Mary Jane crowd surge forward to join the demo. That's enough to spook some of the cops into action, and they react with baton swipes, choke holds, pepper spray. First arrests are made, and there's a shiver of outrage through the crowd as a drag queen is thrown screaming into the back of a battered and ominous-looking people carrier.

The demo comes to a halt, and a tense stand-off develops, as the police block the intended demo route up Alberta with riot vans. Word gets passed through to the loudspeaker van to put out a demand to the police to release those arrested, and a call to the demonstrators to link arms and stay calm and vigilant. The air inside the van is thick with adrenalin, and heavy with sweat and cigarette smoke. Jeanie puts out the messages as requested, taking it in turns with a tall, dark-haired woman called Angela, who seems to Jeanie to be a lot cooler about the whole thing than she is. Their only view of what is going on is out through a small window into the front cabin of the van. There are no side windows, and the rear windows have been sprayed over, giving the inside of the van a weird, submarine feeling. After a while Jeanie starts to feel claustrophobic, almost seasick in the vehicle, and decides to get out for a breath of fresh air. But the atmosphere outside is electric with confrontation. Tempers are fraying on both sides now, and the situation looks like it could get rapidly out of control.

Then suddenly the police pull back their vans from across Alberta, and the demo surges forwards into the deep, canyon-like street between the high tenement facades lining Alberta and O. Jeanie has mixed feelings as she passes underneath the transverse, bridge-like apartment block that separates Alberta off from Cartersgate. On the one hand, the onlookers around here are more vociferous in their support of the demo and their condemnation of the police. On the other hand, the high walls on either side make it feel like they're walking into a trap. The demo veers right at the junction of Alberta and O, with the police blocking the other two sides to the junction to make sure no-one attempts to sheer away from the crowd. In the demo van, Angie reads out a couple of messages of solidarity and cranks up the music as they hit the home stretch down towards Connolly Square.

Al is having a grand time getting ready for the demo. He calls in at a thrift shop on the way over and gets himself some new duds. He chooses a loud paisley shirt, a white fake leather jacket and a pair of purple satin flares. He tops it off with a big floppy panama hat. He donates the clothes he had on to the thrift shop and walks out feeling conspicuously like a disco monster from the Seventies. The hundred yards down the road to the store selling party costumes and other party-related knick-nacks are the most embarrassing of his entire adult life. He ducks into the store and buys a feather boa, large round sunglasses, a fake moustache and a flower sticker for his face.

When he emerges he looks like a refugee from camp camp, and gets the intense feeling everyone is looking at him, which they most certainly are. It's a weird sensation, not one he's accustomed to, as if the very essence of his being is being examined, and called into question. He lights up a cigarette and decides to treat it as a performance, and flounces down the street for a while till a cab pulls up at a crossing right next to him and he spontaneously decides to hail it.

He gets into the back seat and says, "Han Plaza," and the taxi driver looks him over and says, "Going to the demo?" and Al says, "Buddy, just don't say a fucking word, ok."

The taxi driver retires into his silent carapace of professional stoicism and says, "Whatever," and pulls out into the traffic. It takes them 10 minutes to get to Han Plaza and the taxi driver pulls up on Coney Heath behind the line of police vans with the words, "This is as near as we can get. Police've got everything cordoned off." The fare is twelve-fifty and Al gives him fifteen and tells him to keep the change. He gets out and walks up towards Han Plaza and wonders whether the cops sat behind the wheel of the vans are watching his ass. It kind of gives him a quick thrill to think that they might be, but then he's disgusted by the very idea and spits and turns to give the nearest driver a dirty look.

When he gets to Han Plaza the place is full of queers and he's not sure what to do. He walks through the crowd a couple of times but it makes him feel hemmed in and a little sick so he pulls back to the periphery. There's maybe no need to push his luck so he nips into one of the bars lining the east side of Han Plaza and orders a beer. He can feel the bartender giving him a funny look and sees the bar regulars whispering. Normally he wouldn't take that kind of shit from anyone but normally he wouldn't be wearing this faggy outfit so he just stands at the bar and looks out of the window and drinks his beer in silence. The demo starts to move off and he finishes his drink and steps outside. The police have got the demonstrators tightly cordoned, and he's not sure whether to make the effort to break through to join them, so he just hangs back on the sidewalk and moves forward with the demo. There's a whole bunch of other queers who appear to be doing the same thing, so he doesn't feel too conspicuous.

When things start to hot up halfway down Kane, Al feels a warm glow of gratification. Same again up on Cartersgate. Every time there's a crack of heads, every time someone gets dragged off in a choke hold, it gives him a deeply personal feeling of satisfaction. As far as he is concerned they can detain the lot of them, lock them up in some camp somewhere and throw away the key. Or hard labour. Hard labour and discipline. It almost turns him on to think about it.

He trails the demo up Alberta and right into O, down towards Connolly. Things are getting pretty frazzled, but the police are good on their word, are saving their major moves for the end. Up till now it's just been a little harassment and intimidation. Al pats the mobile in his pocket for reassurance. The arrangement is that he gives his contact in the tactical command unit the go-ahead when it's time to move in. It's a wonderful feeling to know that a simple phone call will give him the power to steer the lives of these thousands of people. For them, there will be no particular logic behind whatever action the police decide to take. Only he will have true knowledge, be truly aware of the motivating force behind it.

And that motivating force will be him.

There's a strange mix of atmospheres as people arrive at Connolly. There's the fear and excitement and anger of the demo as it rolls and roils down O. And there's a kind of homecoming-queen party atmosphere outside of all the bars around the square. There's music playing, people out on the street drinking beer, and people hanging out at the windows of the apartments overhead. And then there's a kind of lurking menace from the local kids who have formed up into groups behind the stage truck. They've sensed the mood of the police and know that the shit will shortly be hitting the fan. And given that this is their home turf, they're more than up for it.

Jeanie is standing near the stage truck, smoking a cigarette and waiting for Omar to give her the signal to go up on the stage. She feels strangely calm, as if something has shifted gear. The throb of the music and the noise of the crowd have faded into a kind of distant acoustic backdrop, and she is experiencing that kind of ultra-sharpened perception and sense of being-in-the-moment that you get when you're riding a massive adrenalin rush. She feels a strange vibrating sensation in her chest that has her puzzled for a moment until she remembers what it is and pulls out her mobile from her Madonna corsage. It's Madame George. She hesitates for a moment, then decides to take the call.

"Hey Madame G. What's up?" she says with one finger in her ear. "Bad time right now, I'm on a demo."

"I know Jeanie. That's why I'm calling. I've had word. From one of the good old boys."

"Don't know if I've got time for this right now Madame G."

"You have to make time Jeanie. You're being set up."

"What do you mean, set up?"

"The demo. They're going to trash it. Word's gone out that it's just an extremist front. The political police are involved now. They're going to hit you hard Jeanie."

"Jeanie, did you hear what I said?"

"I hear you Madame G."

"You've got to get out of there. Get everyone out of there."

"You mean, tell them to go home?"

"That's exactly what I mean Jeanie. Get out while you've got the chance."

Jeanie pulls the phone away from her ear as her hand drops to her side. She stands there for a moment and feels the massive pulse of the crowd, filling the street from side to side. The beat of the music rushes in at her and she can hear Angie in the loudspeaker van saying something. She catches sight of the lines of police behind the stage truck and realizes that they must already have cordoned off the other end of the street. She sees Omar on the far side of the stage and he's looking at her like he's seen a ghost, but the ghost is her, and he's mouthing, "What? What's up?" and "You ok?" across at her but there's nothing she can say by way of an answer so she puts the phone back to her ear and Madame George is still there and Jeanie says, "I'm going to hang up now Madame G. You take care now," and she presses the red button and Madame G is gone.

And now Omar is signalling to her to climb up on stage, so she does and one of the tech women puts a microphone in her hand and she can see heads in the crowd turning her way but the music is still blaring so she just stands there for a moment looking out across the crowd and feeling an incredible surge of love unlike anything she's ever felt before. The sun is already low in the sky down the other end of the canyon of O street and she's got her hand up to her face to shield her eyes and it probably comes across as some kind of gone-with-the-wind trashqueen gesture because the crowd are starting to cheer and clap. The music stops suddenly and the crowd fall silent and she knows she has to say something but at that moment she catches sight of a guy in a floppy hat and purple slacks standing at the front of the stage staring at her in the weirdest way and he looks so familiar but she has no idea where she has seen him before. And as he looks he raises a phone to his lips without taking his eyes off of her and her mind is a blank and all she can think of saying is "Rapists Out" and she says it again but why this guy should have triggered that she has no idea but it doesn't matter because the crowd have taken it up and made it into a chant that's booming back at her along the street as the police take it as their cue and start to attack and all hell breaks loose.

A massive cry goes up from the far end of O as the police surge forward into the crowd, wielding batons. There's the same to the right and left of her as the riot cops come storming in and the fat sound of heavy diesel engines as two water cannon take up position on the far side of Connolly on the junction of O and Marianne. The whole crowd is in uproar and there is nowhere for them to go as the police bear down on them and Jeanie finds herself screaming into the microphone at the police to stop and she's joined on the stage by Omar and he has his arm around her and they are both standing there feeling helpless as hell when a cry goes up from the crowd nearest to them and they see that the local kids have lined up on the far side of the square and are pelting the cops with stones and are rocking one of the police vans that has been left unattended in the rush to start hammering the crowd. The van goes over with a crash and the police are momentarily disoriented and turn back towards the van which is spilling petrol out onto the street. A few seconds later it's ablaze and the police lines are in disarray and the crowd bottled up in O surges forwards and through and fans out into the side streets. The van goes up in flames with an enormous whooshing sound and now there's a huge burning barricade in the middle of O on the far side of Connolly and the whole thing has descended into a total riot.

There's a swarm of drones flying overhead but by now people are covering their faces anyway because of all the smoke and teargas in the air so visual telemetry is limited to tracking the various splinter groups that have broken away from the now-dispersed demo.

The burning barricade seems to have acted as a signal to up the ante so in addition to stones and tear gas canisters there are now also rubber bullets and Molotov cocktails flying through the air. There is the sickening sound of batons connecting with bone and flesh and the air is heavy with sirens and screaming. There's a new front that has opened up down on the junction of O and Vienna where the fire brigade are being prevented from reaching the burning police van by a crowd of about a hundred people.

Jeanie feels the stage shake as the truck beneath her starts its engines. Omar has his mouth near to her ear as he says, "Jeanie, we have to get out of here. We need to get the truck and the equipment to safety. You can stay if you want…"

"Dressed like this?"

Jeanie looks around from her vantage point on the truck. Where, a few minutes before, the street had been filled with demonstrators, there were now a few dozen people nursing head wounds and being helped by the locals. Blood and broken glass. Flashing lights and burning barricades, smoke and gas. Skirmishes, stand-offs, running battles. She turns back to Omar.

"No Vic. I'm coming with you."

Jeanie and Vic spend the rest of the evening over at the Mary Jane. They've kept the bar open but have extra security on the doors. The place is functioning as a makeshift first-aid centre and clearinghouse for information about the overall situation, as well as being open for business as usual. Only difference being that they look twice at who's trying to get in, and have already refused entry to a few people they don't like the look of. The outside furniture is either chained down or taken down to the cellar, to avoid a repeat of the time that the riot police threw a wooden bench through the front window. The atmosphere is muted, and the irregular influx of people bleeding from head wounds or blinded by pepper spray does nothing to help them forget their troubles. Both Jeanie and Vic initially resist the urge to just get wasted but as the night wears on and the mood settles into the familiar routine of a state-of-emergency blues they relent and have first one beer, then another. There's something crazily incongruous about the bar, with its flashing disco glitterball, queer-trash deco and intimate castaway vibe with the harsh urban realities playing out on the other side of the big plate glass front window. The orange night is lined with strobe streaks of flashing blue, plus headlights and taillights and the occasional flare of a Molotov. Stretches of relative calm will be pierced by a sudden flood of people all running in one direction, followed by the jogging plod of the cops in their heavy armour. Swathes of smoke and teargas sweep down the street, and every now and then a car siren will go off as someone takes advantage of the chaos to simply break a window and snatch out a stereo.

Jeanie sits at the bar, with one eye on the scene outside. Omar is busying himself on the other side of the bar, refusing to give in to the fatigue that is now evident in his face. Jeanie's mood is bleak, and she's staring despondently into the dregs of her beer, when she feels a hand on her cheek.

"Chin up Jeanie. It's not the end of the world."

She leans into his hand, attempts a smile.

"No, but it kinda feels like it. What a fucking waste. All those people, just getting beaten up. It makes me sick just thinking about it."

"Ah, but it's not the first time. And it sure won't be the last."

Omar takes her glass and fills it from the beer tap, along with one for himself.

"But it's the first time that I've had any responsibility for it. I called that demo. It's my fault."

Omar sets the beer down in front of her and looks her in the eye.

"No Jeanie. It's not your fault. We called the demo, not you alone. And the NFS called the demo. You don't think for a minute any of us were expecting this. Something got the cops riled up, and they took it out on us. Hey, welcome to the NC."

They clink glasses and Jeanie really does manage a smile then. But it's a smile with a bitter aftertaste.

"I know why they did this."

Omar sets down his glass, wipes his mouth with the back of his hand.

"Huh? What do you mean?"

"I had a call from Madame George. Just before it all went to shit. She said the police had instructions to take us out. Something political. Something about us being too extreme."

"That's just bullshit. How does protesting an attack on a sexworker make us too extreme?"

"It's just a ploy, a smokescreen. Way I figure it is that whoever did this is connected. He's involved somehow in the whole secret police shtick. Maybe some other kind of spook. Who knows? And in a way, busting up the demo was his way of sending us a message."

"Yeah? What kind of message involves cracking a load of innocent people's heads?"

"Well, I guess the message is to lay off. The message is that we hit a nerve."

"So that's good."

"Omar, you've got to be joking. It's not good at all. Look at this mess. It's a fucking disaster."

Omar leans over on the bar now, propped up on his elbows.

"No Jeanie. You don't get it. If we hit a nerve it means we're close. It means he feels threatened."

"And that's good?"

"Uh-huh. Sure it's good. Dangerous. But good."

The night grinds on. The crowd wears down to the hard-core regulars as the situation outside calms down. There's music, even a little dancing. The air is thick with cigarette smoke and every now and then someone goes and rips open the door to let the night air in. They call out for some food and manage to find a pizza place willing to deliver even under prevailing circumstances. The dark of the sky is fading into dawn as Omar sets up a round of strong coffees before turning off the machine, and backs it up with shot glasses full of some mean-looking brown liquid smelling of bitter herbs and molasses.

"Come on, this'll put hairs on your chest."

"Just spent most of yesterday morning getting rid of them."

They upend the shot glasses and Jeanie drinks her coffee while the rest of the crew make their goodbyes and drift off home. Omar is busy with the till and the lights and generally shutting the place down.

Finally they're good to go. Jeanie gets up from her stool, straightens her skirt and scratches through her wig, and wobbles unsteadily over to the coat stand for her fake fur. She turns and walks over to the door, where Omar is waiting with a big bunch of keys. She stops short in front of him.

"Omar, Vic. It's been…it's been an experience. Intense. Awful. A nightmare. But…"

She puts her hand on his chest.

"Not with you. You were great. I…I just wanted to say thanks for being there."

She's close now, and looking straight into Omar's big, dark, tired eyes.

"Jeanie, it was a total pleasure."

He leans in and they kiss, right there in the doorway and it's like the floodgates have opened and Jeanie can feel something hot and intense bursting through all the accumulated harsh reality of the preceding day and night. She hears Omar turning the key in the lock without his mouth leaving hers and now he's backing her up away from the door round to the side where there's a wall that shields them from the light of the street. She can feel his hand on her ass and then down underneath the fabric of her skirt and sliding round to the front and pulling her dick free and out into the open and he's down on it with his mouth but he's still standing so she unbuckles his belt and slaps his ass and takes his dick in her hand. And there's the two of them going at it hell for leather in the dark of the bar and it's so unlike any of the sex she's had with her johns in recent months that it makes her gasp and it's so good she almost has no idea what to do.

But only almost.

CHAPTER TWENTY-EIGHT
More Than Money

It's Sunday morning, and Jimmy and Julia are up early to catch their flight. They have all their shit packed well in hand, so it's just a matter of Julia getting up in what seems to be the middle of the night and pouring enough coffee down Jimmy's throat for him to be able to get out of bed. The taxi pulls up in front of their house at half past five, and even though they're supposed to be travelling light, it's still a total schlepp to get the luggage down the stairs and out to the taxi. It takes them half an hour to get to the airport, and check-in is a nightmare, particularly because of Jimmy's extensive arsenal of pills, which take a lot of explaining. Jimmy himself is in absolutely no condition to deal with it, and regards the proceedings through a thick fog of indifference, as if none of it had the least bearing on his own person. That leaves it all to Julia, who is caught between her standard impulse of not winding up the people doing the security checks and feeling totally dumbfounded by so much insensitivity and ignorance packed into one thick head.

"Excuse me madam, your bag seems to be stuffed full of pills."

"That's right."

She checks out the non-descript uniform of the bag-scan Joe and decides against calling him "officer".

"Are they for your personal consumption madam?"

"They're my husband's. He's ill."

"Ah, and your husband, that would be…"

"The sick-looking guy standing next to me, correct."

"Excuse me sir, can I see your passport? And yours madam? Thank you."

Non-officer blockhead compares the passports and shows them to an adjacent colleague.

"Ah, madam. You do not appear to have a common surname. And yet you say this man is your husband. Would you be so kind as to explain to us the exact nature of your relationship?"

Julia takes a deep breath. Even through the fog, Jimmy picks up the warning sign and takes a step back.

"Look. I'm not sure this is the appropriate place to be discussing the exact terms of our cohabitation. We are not married as in 'Here's a bit of paper with the Pope's name on it'. I expect you are familiar with the term common-law marriage, a.k.a domestic partnership, a.k.a marriage-like relationship a.k.a none of your fucking business. So unless you would like to see my dearly beloved long-term partner Jimmy Chang expire from terminal fucking cancer mid-flight on the way to Manila or right here on the floor of your friggin' departure lounge I suggest you free up his meds right now and find someone more defenceless to pick on. Because if you don't you'd better get the earplugs in now, buster, because I am going to start screaming blue murder in three, two, one..."

"Madam!" Blockhead and his colleague are alarmed. "There is no need for that. We're only doing our job. Have a nice day."

"And the same to you sunshine."

She scoops up her bag and reaches out for Jimmy's hand.

"Come on Jimmy, let's go and get some breakfast."

Jimmy waits till they're round the corner to say "Thought you were going to have *him* for breakfast."

"What a schmuck. What a fucking nerve."

"Actually, I felt kinda sorry for him. Poor kid. How could he have known?"

"Known what?"

"Known not to cross Chippie Grzyb when she's on a mission."

Gene comes awake with a thick head and a dry mouth. He cracks one eye open and realizes he's not at home. He opens the other eye and sees Omar's head on the pillow next to him and experiences a fleeting moment of morning-after pickup panic. But Omar is awake now too and the memory of the night before comes back to him and Gene is filled by the feeling that it's all ok, that the night was perfect, that it's all good. Omar smiles and rubs the base of his thumb along the stubble on Gene's chin. He leans in to kiss him and says, "Morning handsome," and then, "Coffee?" and whips back the covers and is out of bed in a flash. Gene is struck by how good he looks. Omar is shorter than he is but more powerfully muscled, with Polynesian tats across his left shoulder and biceps and the metal of his Prince Albert glinting suggestively in the morning light. Gene says, "Christ, you're not one of these people who are unbearably cheerful in the morning are you?" and Omar laughs and says, "You betcha. Bright eyed and bushy tailed, that's me. But don't worry, it usually subsides over the course of the day."

Omar buzzes around the kitchen and grinds some coffee for the espresso machine and cuts some oranges in half for the juicer. All of which seems perfectly natural and familiar to Gene, who has seen Omar perform exactly the same motions a thousand times before behind the bar at the Mary Jane. And while Omar is doing that, Gene checks out his surroundings. He's lying in a big bed in a fairly Spartan apartment high up in a tower block overlooking the tracks of the overground railway on the corner of Marley and Pratel. The light's flooding in from a big grey sky and from where he's lying that's about all he can see. No rooftops, no TV tower, no other buildings. But he can see the sun, low in the sky behind its veil of clouds, and figures they must be facing south east, out towards the edge of town, with all the big, downtown buildings behind them. It gives Gene a curious sensation, just staring out into space, a little like being on a boat or an airship. And that feeling is amplified by the strangeness of his surroundings. But there's a warm glow inside him that tells him he's safe and in the right place. He's sore from the sex they had—first time right there in the darkened bar at the Mary Jane, second time after they got back in a taxi and took the elevator up to Omar's place. Gene can remember sliding a condom onto Omar's dick and taking a palmful of lube to his own ass and riding Omar like a rodeo cowboy and coming together with him in an outrageously extravagant orgasm with Omar's lubed hand on his own dick and him holding onto the rings through Omar's nipples. And as he came he spurted hot jism up Omar's arms and over his chest and then they toppled over sideways and were quick to fall asleep in each other's arms with the smell of sweat and smoke and alcohol and come and ass and condom rubber in Gene's nose as he drifted off into the darkness.

Omar brings over the juice and the coffee and gets back into bed.

There's part of Gene that somehow still doesn't quite trust the situation. That's still waiting for the one-night stand putdown, the disinvitation, the distancing. But it doesn't happen. Omar is still Omar, just as he's always been, but a whole heap more intense, here in close-up. Like there's a lot more of him that has suddenly been revealed to Gene. And Gene likes what he sees. Omar says, "So are you staying for breakfast?" with a smile on his face, and Gene feels around if there's anything bad in that statement and decides there isn't, and says, "Sure, what have you got?" And Omar says, "Ah, not much, but there's a baker's on the corner. I can nip down and get us something. It won't take long. There's towels if you want to shower. Just feel at home."

Omar drains his coffee and starts to pull on some sweatpants and a t-shirt. Gene sits up and surveys his clothing from the night before strewn around the room—the latex skirt, the Madonna corsage, the purple wig, and realizes that there's no way he's going to be able to reconstruct the look to go with the outfit for the way home. Not that it would be the first time that he has tumbled trash-queen blitzed into a U full of startled early morning commuters. But he's not feeling that belligerent this morning. So he turns to Omar who's pulling on his trainers and says, "Vic, do you…do you have any clothes you can lend me?" And Vic is like, "Oh, sure. There's a wardrobe full of stuff over there and some t-shirts and socks and things in the chest of drawers by the window. Take a look to see what you can come up with. I won't be long."

He leans across the bed to kiss Gene a temporary goodbye and there's something about the gesture and the feeling behind it that implants itself in Gene's heart and makes him fall back onto the bed as Omar grabs his wallet and keys and disappears out the door.

By the time Omar gets back with a paper bag full of croissants and bread rolls Gene has showered and dressed himself in a pair of old jeans that fit him pretty well, a faded Wonder Woman t-shirt and a blue hoodie. He's got the rest of his gear packed up in a plastic bag and has just sat down at the table in the kitchen when he feels the buzz of his phone in his pocket. He shrugs apologetically at Omar, and puts the phone to his ear. It's not a number he recognizes.

"Gene, this is Carla. From the church. I'm sorry to trouble you so early."

"No worries Carla. What can I do for you?"

"Gene, you need to get your ass down here right away. There's a lady here has some information about the posters. Good job I speak a little Arabic. I said that you were the one she needed to speak to. She was nervous, very agitated. But she brightened up when she heard your name. Says she knows you."

"She knows me? What's her name?"

"Suleika."

"Tell her I'll be right there."

Claire has a date with Laila. Not a date as such, but she called her up to ask if she fancied a visit, and Laila said, "Love to. But how about going out for a walk? That is, if you don't mind pushing me in a wheelchair."

Claire doesn't mind at all, so she heads over to St. Catherine's for two o'clock. She's brought a few things with her from home—a woolly hat, and extra jacket, and some gloves, just in case Laila doesn't have any of those things. It's not far from her place to the hospital, just a few blocks north to the old East Weir canal basin. She's been to the hospital a few times now, but she's struck every time by how ugly the place is. It's a huge boxy, charmless, horseshoe-shaped building in what looks like brown pebbledash, facing out onto the waterfront. There's a big, glassed-in entrance-area-come-reception downstairs in the middle that could just as easily be situated in a public library or municipal administration building. The whole edifice just seems to exude callousness and indifference, and Claire wonders how it is that people are supposed to get well there. She takes the elevator up to the fourth floor and finds Laila already dressed and sitting expectantly in her wheelchair. She's looking good.

They greet with a hug and Claire says, "Brought you some stuff. Just in case." She throws the things on the bed and Laila reaches across to pick through them.

"Ah, good thinking. They've given me a blanket to take with me, but a hat and gloves are great. And the jacket. Wonderful!"

Claire helps her into the jacket and goes to do up the zip but Laila bats her hand away playfully.

"I've just got a bad leg. I'm not disabled you know."

Claire laughs.

"Sorry. Wasn't thinking. But doesn't sitting in a wheelchair count as disabled?"

"Yeah. But even if it does, I can do my own friggin' jacket up."

Claire finds it strange that they should be so easy with each other. Not strange, but unusual. They haven't known each other long, but have a rapport, a gentle banter that feels as if they have been around each other for ages.

They head out into the corridor, take the lift down and exit through the main entrance. The sun has come out and there are plenty of people about doing wintry, Sunday-afternoon things. Walking the dog, playing ball with the kids, drinking coffee on the two big café-boats moored in the canal basin. Pretty normal stuff, but apparently exciting and stimulating to Laila.

"I can't tell you how good it is to be outside. That hospital's been driving me crazy."

"When do you get to go home?"

"In a couple of days I guess. The doctors have been a bit worried about complications. But the ward nurse said I might be able to be home by Tuesday, if I stay on the mend."

They turn right and walk along the bank of the canal basin towards Admiral's Bridge, where it narrows into the canal proper. The bridge is small and quaint, and the banks of the canal are lined with horse chestnut trees, which even in winter give it a certain bucolic flair. And although the rest of the canal runs straight through the city, here it meanders like an old river in its bed. The houses are also a bit grander than the rest of the surrounding tenements—tall, 19th century apartment blocks for the rich, set back from the water with little front gardens and ornamented with Art Deco figures and motifs.

They reach the Kane Avenue bridge and cross over to the other side of the canal and choose one of the cafés that face out onto the water. They take coffee and cake at a table by the window, and stare out into the wintry afternoon and chat like old friends and feel very worldly and mondain.

After about an hour Claire says, "I'd better be getting you back," and Laila says, "Yes you had," in a way that, if not exactly flirtatious, has Claire thinking about possible alternatives. They pay the waitress and head out the door back to the bridge at Kane. They are just coming up to the pedestrian crossing on the corner of Kane and Canal when Laila suddenly starts waving her right arm for Claire to stop. She seems to be gasping for breath and when Claire says, "What is it?" it's all she can do to point towards the wall of a nearby house and say, "Over there. Take me over there."

Claire pushes her over to the wall of the house, which is covered in posters and graffiti.

"It's him!"

"Who Laila? What's wrong? I don't get it."

"My boss. The one who did this to me."

It takes a moment for Claire to fully catch on to what's got Laila so agitated. She's also more preoccupied with Laila herself than with what's on the posters. But when she does finally get around to seeing what all the fuss is about, the penny drops.

"Are you sure, this is him? It says he's a rapist."

"Sure it's him. I'd recognize that bastard anywhere. And it doesn't surprise me in the least. If he's misogynist enough to do this to me, then he's misogynist enough to be a rapist."

"Uh, I think it was probably a man he raped."

"What the fuck has that got to do with anything?" snaps Laila.

"But the thing is, the fucking awful thing is…" Laila is holding her head in her hands, "that if he's seen these posters, then he'll be back to finish me off. He knows I can identify him. I'm going to have to disappear. Jesus Christ, I'm going to have to disappear immediately."

"You mean, right now? How the hell are you going to do that?"

"Well I can't go back to the hospital, that's for certain. That's the first place he'll come looking. And I can't go home either. Oh god, this is a fucking nightmare."

"So what are we going to do?"

Laila stops short then, and reaches out for Claire's hand.

"Claire, we're not going to do anything. There's no reason for you to get involved. It's good of you to come and see me, but this has nothing to do with you."

"You mean, there's a psychopathic rapist out to kill you, and there's you stuck in a wheelchair, and it's none of my business? Like, you think I should just walk away and leave you to it? Are you out of your fucking mind? We may not know each other very well, but I'd like to think I'm your friend. So I think a bit of basic sisterhood is the least I can manage at a time like this, don't you?"

Laila still has a firm grip on Claire's hand, and brings it to her cheek.

"Thanks Claire. I'm grateful. Truly. I just don't know what to say."

"Then say: Ok, let's get started."

Laila laughs.

"Ok. Let's get started. Push me over the road and up onto the bridge."

"Why?"

"You'll see."

They wait for the lights to change and then cross to the kebab stand on the other side and then up onto the bridge. Laila indicates to Claire to take her closer to the parapet and fiddles around under her blanket as she tries to ease something out of her pocket. Finally she has what she's looking for, and holds it out over the parapet. It's a brand new phone.

"Christ, Laila, what are you doing?"

"Becoming invisible," says Laila, as she drops the phone into the canal.

From the bridge they head on down along the banks of the canal.

"Where are we going?" asks Laila. "We can't go back to the hospital."

"I'll take you to my place," says Claire. "You can hang out there for a while. But before we do, I need you to come clean with me."

"Meaning what?"

"Meaning. How come you're not going to the police? You think this guy had you knocked off your motorbike, yet you don't tell the police. Now you think he's a rapist, and you don't go to the police either. The whole thing stinks. Before I stick my neck out for you, I really need to know who it is I'm dealing with."

Laila takes a deep breath.

"Claire. It's not easy to explain. I can't go to the police because we are the police. Well, not the police exactly, but part of state security. Any information the police has, my boss will have within the hour. And if he has gone rogue, then that gives him an enormous amount of power. To be honest, I don't have enough faith in the police. I can't see how they will be able to keep me protected until they get him. And I don't even know if there is any evidence against him. This whole thing is just too fucked up."

Claire stops pushing the wheelchair. Walks around so she's facing Laila.

"Wait. Just a second. You're telling me that you're state security? Fucking hell Laila! Don't you think that's just a little insignificant detail I ought to know? I thought we were friends."

Laila folds her hand in her lap and looks up at Claire.

"So now you know. And we are friends. That's why I'm telling you. Believe me Claire, this is not an easy thing for me. It's not the kind of job you can just walk out on. He'll be out looking for me. And when he notices I've gone underground, he'll have the rest of the security apparatus looking for me too. My only hope is that they catch the fucker by then. And I'm going to do everything I can to make sure they do. But if you want to reconsider your offer of help, it's ok. I understand."

Claire comes down into a crouch so that her eyes are level with Laila's. She studies her face for signs of evasion, for any trace of dishonesty. But all she can see are Laila's big, dark eyes and a flash of fear.

"Laila, I'll be straight with you. This is not easy for me either. My gut feeling says to help you, but my brain says if you're state security I ought to just leave you here to fend for yourself. But I can't do that. I'm going to take you at your word. But I have one condition."

"Ok. Just say it."

"I want to know the kind of shit you've been up to. If I feel I can't handle it, then we're through. If I feel you're lying to me, ditto. If at any time I feel you are playing me for a fool, then you're out on the street. Is that clear?"

Laila draws in close, so that her face is just inches away from Claire's.

"Claire, listen to me. I'm not going to lie to you. I'll tell you whatever it is you need to know. And if at any time you want me to leave, just say the word. I just need to lie low for a couple of days and think out my next move. After that, I'll be gone."

"Promise?"

"Promise."

"Ok," says Claire, as she gets back behind the wheelchair. "Start talking."

Gene gets to the Church of Kali to find Carla waiting for him in the library with Suleika. Carla has made her a cup of coffee and tried to put her at her ease, but it is clear that Suleika is extremely agitated about something. She has a scrap of material in her hands, perhaps some kind of handkerchief or small headscarf, which she is wringing incessantly. Both she and Carla jump up out of their chairs as soon as Gene walks into the room.

"Thank goodness you're here," says Carla. "I've been trying to calm the sister here, but it's no good. She's quite desperate to talk to you."

"And you can interpret?" says Gene. He greets Carla with a brief hug and turns and bows his head to Suleika as a mark of respect. She takes his hand in hers and begins talking immediately.

Gene smiles and signals to her to hang on for a second while he takes his coat off. Then he indicates to her to sit down.

"Ok, let's hear it," he says to Carla. "Let's take it from the beginning."

So through Carla, Suleika tells him the whole story of what she has seen. The group of evil men on the tarmac in front of Fuji City. The killer who came to her village. And the man in the suit, the one that she saw on the posters. She has no idea what he has done, but if his face is on all these posters she knows it must be a bad thing. And if he is with the killers then he must certainly be a very evil man.

Gene listens intently and nods.

"Carla, tell her that she has done the right thing to come here. Tell her that she has been a great help. Maybe her information will help us catch the man on the poster. And she is right, he is a very evil man. And perhaps if she can identify the other man, we can do something about that too. But for the moment our focus is on the man on the poster. Ask her if she knows what his name is."

Gene can see Suleika shaking her head when Carla asks her.

"Ok. It's not so important. It's already a huge step forward. But we need to know if he works at Fuji City or was just there as a visitor. And if he works there, we need to find out more about his movements. Carla, please ask the sister if she would be willing to help us further."

Carla asks, and Suleika is more than willing to help. They arrange for her to keep a look out, and for her to let them know what time the man in the suit arrives and leaves. Gene's mind is already racing ahead, trying to figure out ways to set up unobtrusive surveillance around the entrances to Fuji City. It won't be easy, because the area is quite exposed. But they might be able to park a van on the other side of the street to monitor everyone going in and out.

Gene fishes a C-note out of his wallet to give to Suleika.

"Tell her it's to make up for her lost earnings in front of the Arcades."

But Suleika is having none of it. She shakes her head and grabs hold of Gene's hands with her gnarled fingers, and presses the note back into his palm, accompanied by a volley of words directed at Carla.

"She says there is no need for this. You must keep your money. This is about more than money. This is about honour. This is about revenge, no?"

Yes, thinks Gene. This is about revenge.

Chapter Twenty-Nine
Manila's Finest

Jimmy and Julia get into Ninoy Aquino International and manage to make it through customs without a hitch. The flight was long and gruelling and although it's only early afternoon local time they feel like they've been up all night. Which in a way of course, they have. They are both pretty much overwhelmed by the hustle and bustle of the airport and that disorientation that sets in when you spend endless hours in the kind of suspended mental animation that long-haul travel induces and then suddenly have to make decisions like which way to go and how to find a taxi. Jimmy's just about together enough to call through to the contact number Doc Mucus gave him and let them know they've landed.

They step out of the airport building and immediately feel completely wiped out by the change in temperature and humidity after the frosty air conditioning of the airport building. Julia takes the initiative and pulls Jimmy over towards the lead taxi in a long line of waiting cars. It's a big white Toyota with a prominent advert for the Joy Luck Club on one side and the words Air Con on the other. Jimmy hopes that nomen won't be omen and that the taxi driver won't take them for a ride.

They bundle their stuff into the boot of the car and get in. The driver seems an amiable chap and starts up a one sided conversation in a fascinating but pretty much impenetrable mix of English, Tagalog and Spanish. Julia does her best to humour him and engage in conversation, but Jimmy is too busy staring out at the low-rise vista of the six-lane highway and the kitsch decoration of the multicoloured jeepneys that seem to be everywhere. The street is flanked with low-hanging power lines and high-rise billboard posters jostling to occupy as much of the skyline as they can. Jimmy is simultaneously stunned by the overwhelming mass of traffic and the ramshackle one and two storey buildings and suddenly nostalgic for the peregrinations of his youth. The scene is both totally familiar and overwhelmingly foreign, and it has Jimmy wondering what it is that he has become. He thinks to himself that this is a lousy place to die, and then maybe that it's as good as any other.

The view outside of the taxi window changes as the driver takes a right and the street narrows down to more or less a single lane. There are people everywhere and the road seems to be half full of market stalls and extended shopfronts. The driver slows and starts to honk his horn and curse in Tagalog and Jimmy notices that there are no pavements. Julia takes his hand and there's a look on her face somewhere between curiosity and trepidation. The narrow streets have a distinctly run-down, third-world air, and Jimmy guesses Julia is not sure how to take it. Despite the driver's cursing, the vibe that Jimmy gets is a good one. The people on the street seem friendly, good-humoured, and there's nothing here that he feels worried about. Except maybe the deal they have lined up and the actual pickup of his medication. He can't afford for there to be any fuck-ups on that score.

But the weird thing is, the more the driver curses, the more Jimmy finds that he is able to understand him. This seems a little trippy at first, as if some cosmic joker deity were magically re-jigging his brain, until he realizes that it's just his dormant knowledge of Malay from his childhood in Singapore kicking in, and giving him a handhold on Tagalog. The driver himself is a stocky, genial guy in his early thirties, with thick glasses and an Elvis quiff, whose swearing seems to be largely good-natured until he looks in his rear mirror and starts muttering something about a tail.

Jimmy pricks up his ears.

"Is there a problem?"

"You guys important people," says the driver in English.

"How come?" says Jimmy.

"Only in Manila 10 minutes and already got visitors. Don't look round."

Jimmy sees a sign flash by saying, "Absolutely no brown-out," and wonders what it could possibly mean.

"You guys do anything bad? Maybe better get out now."

Julia is more than a little concerned at the turn in the conversation.

"No! No, nothing bad. We're just tourists. Why should anyone want to follow us?"

"Lady, this is Manila. Big war on drugs. Ten thousand dead and counting. Look at us. Everyone here is a suspect. President himself says he goes out shooting dealers. Normally just Filipinos. But hey, maybe they like to shoot some foreigners too."

"Uh, listen…" Jimmy checks out the taxi driver's name on the little licence on display in the back of the car.

"Listen King Arthur—man, is that your real name?"

"King Arthur Mabuz Conspiración Jiménez, at your service, *ginoo*. Named after a famous boxer, yes sir. Big Filipino national hero. My father was a big boxing fan."

"That's like, really interesting King Arthur. But maybe another time, no? Look, we really don't want to get killed…"

"Definitely don't want to get killed," echoes Julia.

"So maybe you can help us shake off this tail? I'll double the fare."

"Double fare? And cigarettes? You have any cigarettes?"

King Arthur blares his horn and comes to a screeching halt as a large white van backs out into the middle of the road. The car behind them almost smacks into the rear bumper and Jimmy can clearly make out two mean-looking guys with dark glasses in the front seats.

"Cigarettes? Yes! Duty free. All our duty frees. Plus double fare. Now let's get the fuck out of here!"

"No need to worry boss, you're safe with me."

"It's called Operation Brando."

Laila and Claire are heading back towards Claire's flat.

"Operation Brando? What kind of a name is that? What the hell is that supposed to mean?"

Claire is talking to the back of Laila's head as she pushes her rapidly along the banks of the canal. They cross the road and veer left into Ellington Walk. Claire's cheeks are flushed from the pace.

"I have no idea what it means. It's just one of those stupid in-jokes that Al gets off on. But it basically involves running a whole load of foreign fighters as undercover assets. Kind of like the ratlines US intelligence had going after the end of the Second World War, as a means of giving free passage to guys who were technically our enemies but were in some way useful to the state."

"Ok…" Ancient history is not Claire's strong point.

"Look, don't worry about any of that. It's a pretty simple idea. We bring in a bunch of bad foreign guys and let them loose. They do a load of bad shit that gets people worked up. Then we get to crack down and bring in a load of emergency laws, throw out a bunch of foreigners and generally silence the opposition."

"Christ Laila. That's awful."

"Yeah, it's really unpleasant. And while we're running these guys, there's another outfit running the people doing this."

She waves her hand at the blackened shopfront of a community education centre.

"You mean, the firebombings? That's fucking outrageous!"

Claire comes to a stop right there in the street.

"That might already be too much for me to handle."

"Claire, you don't know the half of it. The security services are a law unto themselves. They can do just about whatever they want. And the more hare-brained and perverse the scheme is, the better. But if you look at it from their point of view, there is a certain logic to it."

Claire sets the wheelchair in motion again, but slower this time.

"Go on."

"What better way to control the extreme fringes of society than to have a finger in every pie. Or in this case, a person or persons in every group. That way, you get to know what's going on. You get inside information. You can push the groups in directions they might not want to go and see who takes the bait. Or you can create actions and situations that push society in a specific direction. It's pretty standard stuff, really."

"But Laila, what I don't get is where you figure in all of this. Looking at you, I would say you have an immigrant background too. Doesn't it bother you to be involved in something so… warped?"

Laila is silent for a moment as they head down the street, with its cobbled stones and chic cafés.

"I guess it's a question of allegiance. But the way you look at it is kind of reductionist. By that I mean that you see me and think, she's a woman, she's from Kurdistan, so that must make her what? Progressive? A freedom fighter? Liberal? Left-wing? To me, that's a very naïve way of looking at the world. That's not how things work. Where my parents were from, if you criticized the guerrillas that meant you were against them, whether you were or not. That's ideology. That's what forced my family out. That's what brought us here. And this is my home now, ever since I can remember. And they treated me well here. And the only thing anyone asked of me in return was to defend my new homeland. So here I am. Believe me, I know enough about the world to realize that not everything takes place out in the open. That as a foot soldier you don't always have to understand every decision that the generals make. And that there's dirty work that needs to be done. And someone has to do it. And until recently that person was me. I had no problem with that. I was glad to do it. But something has changed now."

"Now it's personal?"

"Yeah, now it's personal. I didn't sign up to be treated like dirt, nor to have to deal with a bunch of sexist crap. And certainly not to have a fucking psychopath trying to kill me."

"And you can't go over his head? Isn't there anyone higher up you can talk to about this?"

"Maybe there is, but it's not that simple. I'm going to have to think about the best way to approach it. I just need a bit of time to think."

They reach the corner of Ellington and Third and Laila directs Claire over to the window of a little corner shop. Something in the window has caught her eye.

"Let's go in here. Come on!"

"Why? What do you want?"

"They have hair dye. And scissors. I think it might be time for a change of hairstyle."

King Arthur speed dials from his mobile which he has clamped in a holder in the left hand corner of his dashboard, up under the windscreen. He rattles off a short greeting and a terse exchange ensues in Tagalog which Jimmy is totally unable to follow. He floors the accelerator and sends pedestrians scattering in all directions as he races along. Jimmy and Julia are thrown back in their seats. King Arthur has put about a hundred yards between themselves and the tail, who were clearly caught by surprise by his sudden acceleration, but who are now gaining steadily. Jimmy manages to regain his composure enough to ask what the fuck is going on. King Arthur continues to drive like a kamikaze pilot on speed, with one eye on his rear mirror.

"Phoned ahead boss. My brother-in-law Isko lives near here. Owes me a favour. We were lucky to find him home. Keep your fingers crossed people."

"Ok King. Is there anything else I need to know?"

"No. Maybe just close your eyes and enjoy the ride, eh?"

King Arthur hits his horn and swerves around an oncoming bicycle-with-sidecar type rickshaw affair. Apart from the few short asides to his passengers, King Arthur's speech now appears to be composed exclusively of a constant stream of expletives addressed to the world at large. He threads his way through an impromptu roadblock consisting of a meeting of a jeepney and a waste disposal truck, surrounded by at least a dozen trike rickshaws and people on scooters. Their pursuers have closed to a distance of about twenty yards, but the intervening space is filled with at least a hundred people in vehicles of various kinds. Finally they are out of the clump of vehicles and King Arthur accelerates away as quickly as he can. He screeches around a bend in the road and the street scene changes from commercial to industrial. The little shops with their grass rooves and overhanging bougainvillea give way to a stretch of high yellow breeze-block walls bizarrely lined with potted palms and cactus plants on blue shelves. From the back seat, all Jimmy can see are the breeze-block walls rushing by and the low hanging power lines overhead. The road has narrowed down even further and the walls seem ominously close. They race past a few shabby storefronts and precariously constructed residential buildings. Everything looks like it is either nailed down, or behind bars. Jimmy finds himself revising his earlier opinion about the neighbourhood looking friendly. King honks his horn three times in succession, for no apparent reason. Through the windshield, Jimmy can see another yellow garbage truck, even larger than the previous one, backing out slowly onto the road about a hundred yards ahead. There's a noticeable surge to the car as King guns the accelerator. Jimmy is leaning forward now, in the space between the two front seats. He taps King on the shoulder.

"Ah, King, buddy, there's a truck. You're not seriously going to try and get through there…"

"No worries. This is my man Isko. Manila's finest garbage collector, I always say."

"For Christ's sake King, pull up man."

Jimmy looks round at Julia, who has her eyes closed and her hands clenched white-knuckled around his wrist and the door handle. The garbage truck continues to back out into the road and the space between it and the far wall is receding rapidly.

"Guess this is the moment they say 'Brace brace'," says King cheerfully as he floors it.

Both Jimmy and Julia let out the kind of long drawn-out moan familiar from rollercoaster rides around the world. The taxi squeezes through the space behind the truck with barely an inch to spare and King winds the window down and waves back to his brother-in-law behind the wheel of the truck. When he turns back to Jimmy his face is radiant with triumph and he lets go of the wheel to perform a little twisting victory dance routine sitting there in the driver's seat.

"Ha! Losers! No-one can say Pinoy taxi drivers not the best! Absolutely! What do you say, ginoo? Are you with me?"

"King Arthur, I would say, apart from the fact that I nearly crapped my pants, that you are without exception the world's best taxi driver."

King Arthur beams with satisfaction.

"And now maybe if you can get us to our hotel without any further excitement?"

"Good idea mister. I'm going to get you there real quick. Relaxed but quick. No excitement at all. And then you get to your hotel room and relax some more. Maybe have a drink. A cocktail. Take a walk. See the sights."

"Yeah King, maybe all of those things."

"Yes sir mister. Manila is a great place to relax. Welcome to the Philippines."

Al gets into work and doesn't clock the shabby delivery van parked on the central reservation just down from the staff entrance to Fuji City. The staff entrance was not designed with security in mind. The building's days as an airport was long before the security hype that set in in the Nineties. Al parks his car and walks around to the entrance to the main stairwell. It's raining. He pulls up his collar and looks across to the wire fence separating the car park from the Fuji exercise area and sees a couple of kids kicking a ball. Two old men smoking recycled pavement tobacco. An old woman just taking up space. The way old women do. He turns and swipes his card through the lock.

He's hardly reached his office and his phone's already ringing. He doesn't even need to look at the display to know who it is. This is the call he's been waiting for, ever since he saw the posters on the street. It's his boss, Colonel Bearringer. It's 9:37 a.m.

"Firengi."

"Sir."

"I have no doubt you're aware why I'm calling."

"Sir."

Bearringer is a huge, brooding presence in the department. Al is acutely aware of his function as just one of the minor tentacles of Bearringer's overarching designs.

"Attention has been drawn. Words have been spoken."

"Sir."

"Needless to say, this is not good."

"Absolutely sir."

Al fumbles in his pocket for his cigarettes. Fishes them out and opens the packet one-handed. Transfers a cigarette to the corner of his mouth. Holds the lighter away from his phone as he clicks the flame on. Brings it to the end of the tube of tobacco and inhales deeply and as silently as he can.

"Dammit all, Al. Your face is plastered around the town. Is this what you regard as low-profile?"

Al exhales. A blue-grey haze of smoke billows into the transparency of the room.

"Not at all sir. It's most troublesome."

"Troublesome is not even half of it. Troublesome is not even a ball-park figure. I could have you thrown out of the service for this, you realize that?"

Al realizes that he is standing to attention and sits down in his leather chair.

"Sir."

"The posters."

"The posters sir?"

"Have them taken down."

"It's already been dealt with, sir."

"And?"

"Sir?"

Al thinks of the kids playing football in the rain and admires their determination.

"Don't play dumb with me Al. The truth of the matter. The accusation. I've seen the material. They even have your number plates for god's sake."

"The car has been dealt with sir."

He draws on his cigarette and thinks of the old men whose addiction has them standing in the rain to smoke tar-soaked dog-ends. This, he can relate to.

"Are you being deliberately obtuse man? Because if there is one thing I can't stand it's insubordination. So I will say it again. Once more and once only. These accusations. Is there any truth to them?"

"They are absolutely baseless sir."

"Evidence to suggest otherwise?"

"Absolutely none sir."

The woman. The old woman. What was she actually doing, standing there in the rain?

"You know that your operation is triple-firewalled?"

What was her actual reason for it?

"Of course sir."

"You know that you will be cauterized if there is any chance of this contagion spreading?"

Because don't you need a reason to stand out in the rain in the winter?

"I realize that sir."

"You know what is required above all else?"

Doing nothing?

"Deniability sir."

"Deniability Al. Above all deniability. Al, you are central to this operation. I need to know that you have measures taken. In case of your, let us say, operational demise. You realize what we cannot afford here?"

"Blowback sir."

Could she have been waiting for him?

"Blowback, Al. As long as we understand each other."

"Perfectly sir."

Watching him?

"Very good Al. Is there anything else? What about this demonstration thing? Have you looked into it?"

"I have identified the ringleaders sir. I'll be dealing with them this week."

Normally, Al would berate himself for being too paranoid.

"I want a report on my desk by Friday."

"Sir."

But paranoia comes with the job.

"And Al?"

"Sir?"

Al berates himself for not being paranoid enough.

"There won't be another call like this. Do I make myself clear?"

"Perfectly sir. I understand."

"Good."

The woman requires closer inspection.

The phone relinquishes its signal and becomes an inert thing in the warm cradle of Al's hand. It rests there for a second, then another, and then finds itself flung at speed across the room, only to meet the sudden resistance of the outer wall, whereupon it ceases to be a phone and is transformed into a disparate mass of shattered fragments.

Jimmy and Julia say their farewells to King Arthur and make a breakneck dive into the Ned Kelly Hotel, leaving King to go screeching off into the wild blue yonder with a haze of exhaust and burnt rubber in his wake. They practically fall into reception with their luggage and stand for a moment heaving and panting before they are once again capable of speech. The receptionist, a tall woman in her late twenties with long blond hair, eyes them with scepticism.

"G'day," she says, with the lifting lilt of Oz's southern shores. "Anything I can do for ya?"

"We've booked," says Julia. "under Grzyb."

Blondie looks through her bookings and shakes her head.

"No Chips here," she says. "Sorry."

"No," says Julia. "It must be there. Try again. Under G."

"Chip with a G? Are you trying to pull my leg?"

"No, seriously. G-R-Z-Y-B. Chip. We made a reservation."

"Ah ok. Now I've got you. Thought you were having me on. Wouldn't be the first joker to try it on in here."

Formalities completed, they head up to their room, an unspectacular but serviceable affair with a bathroom and small balcony looking out onto a dowdy four-lane street with a stretch of desiccated park in the middle. They both collapse onto the bed which complains noisily and sags dangerously in the middle.

"Jesus Christ Jimmy, what was that all about?"

Jimmy stares up at the fan set into the ceiling and blows the hair out of his eyes.

"I have no idea honey. Maybe it's just coincidence."

"Coincidence my ass."

"Yeah, or maybe they're onto us. Could have eavesdropped on the Doc's communications with the lab. Or even on my call from the airport. Would be easy to get the wrong end of the stick I guess. Think we really were drug smugglers."

"It kind of makes the whole thing a bit more difficult, don't you think?"

Julia has propped her head up on her hand and is massaging Jimmy's forehead with her fingers.

"It's a pisser alright. Bit of a game changer really. We're going to have to watch our backs, that's for sure."

"Jimmy?"

"Julia?"

"I'm scared. I hate to say it. But I'm scared already, and we haven't done anything yet."

She shifts around and snuggles in so that Jimmy can put his arm around her.

He holds her tight.

"I know honey. Me too. We need to think carefully about our next move. Let's not do anything hasty. I really wouldn't do anything to put us at risk. You know that, don't you?"

Julia looks him in the eye.

"Yes I know. But it's still pretty frightening."

"Well how about you and me freshen up and then go downstairs and get something to eat? Don't know about you but I'm starving after all that excitement. And I hear they do a great fake ostrich burger."

Twenty minutes later they're both seated in the little eatery downstairs. There's a wooden kangaroo on the bar and a dead crocodile on the wall. Apart from such obviously Antipodean references the rest of the place is generically Asian-castaway themed. The metal chairs are wrapped in sarong-like scarves and the table has a centerpiece decoration that's a cross between a wicker basket and a bird's nest. The plates are square and the candle on the table is housed in its own little pagoda.

"This is nice," says Julia.

"If you like tacky, it's nice," says Jimmy.

They order food, and cocktails while they're waiting. Julia takes a Beyond The Sea, while Jimmy goes for a Dark and Stormy. The cocktails are good, the food takes a while, but when it finally gets there, it's stupendous. Jimmy is impressed. They tuck into their respective dishes.

"How's the burger Jimmy?"

"Oh man. Dee-lish. This totally makes it all worthwhile. The flight. The tail. Nearly getting squeezed to death by a garbage truck. I tell you, this is the best fake ostrich burger I have ever tasted. How's the kangaroo kebab?"

"It's yummy. You wanna taste?"

Jimmy tries the roo. It's good. But it's not what he's here for. He squirts a bit more chili-chup onto his O'burger.

"Mmmm. Now things are really looking up. You want some burger?"

"No Jimmy, I'm good with Skippy here. You know these are really generous portions."

"Better leave a little room for the apple pie, eh?"

Jimmy has a mouth full of sweet potato fries and a big inane grin on his face. It's the happiest Julia has seen him for months.

They finish up their respective burger and roo and um and ah about the dessert and then Jimmy finally goes for the apple pie after all and Julia takes death by chocolate. They finish up with coffee and Jimmy takes a brandy and Julia passes on that and they both feel absolutely stuffed. Timewise they feel like they may have slipped into some kind of limbo but they check their devices and it's only 4:43 pm local time so they're wondering what the hell to do with the rest of the day. They decide to put all thoughts of trying to arrange a drug handover out of their minds for the time being, a) to get over the shock of the whole tail adventure and b) because by now they're too sated and stoned to really be arsed about any of that shit. Jimmy says, "Shall we go out for a walk?" and Julia says, "Do you think we can risk it?" and Jimmy says, "Sure". So they put the eats on the hotel bill and head out the door and walk down the little strip of park towards South Harbour and the sea.

They've only gone about a hundred yards when they hit a six-lane road absolutely choc-a-bloc with traffic separating them from where they figure the sea must be. The other side of the road is the US Embassy compound so they guess there's no point trying to get through to the shoreline that way and take a right northwards along the road.

They go a couple of hundred yards further through a hellish subtropical landscape of cars and high-rise concrete and have basically already had enough when they catch sight of a patch of green that might or might not be a park. On the one side there's an edifice that looks like a racing track bandstand, and on the other some kind of memorial type obelisk in the middle of relatively wide open spaces. Jimmy's already soaked through with exertion and the heat, and Julia has had enough too.

They are heading towards the obelisk, on the lookout for somewhere to sit, preferably in the shade, when Jimmy turns to Julia and asks her if she has any water. At least, that's what he tries to do, but somehow the words won't come out straight. He feels his eyes closing of their own accord and there's nothing he can do about it. He wipes his eyes with his hand and realizes he can see two of everything. Two Julias, two obelisks. Two Manilas. A sudden pain in his guts causes him to double up and fall to his knees. He's vaguely aware of Julia asking him if he's ok, but he's so very not ok that he's unable to answer her. Not only that but if feels like he's unable to breathe either and now he's ejecting the complete contents of his stomach in one long bilious stream and he's down on all fours and Julia is screaming now for help to any passers-by but there are no passers-by, just endless streams of traffic that are as far away as the moon and who wants to go to the moon anyway and Jimmy is spent and empty and couldn't move a muscle even if he wanted to and it's really all he can do just to keep on breathing so he makes the most of it and just keels over and curls up into a ball right there on the streets of Manila and thinks this is it.

I'm ready.

CHAPTER THIRTY
Chickenshit & Eggs

Gene is in the prayer room at the Church of Kali thinking about his next move. Or maybe he's praying about his next move. Or maybe he's just meditating. It's all one. There are different degrees of belief at the C of K and nobody is going to give you a hard time if you don't believe as much as they do. That's the point. It's a church where belief is not the central issue. Or maybe where belief is the central issue, but it's more about believing in yourself than anything else. Those are the kind of discussions people get into here. If you ask one of the elders if Kali exists, they'll like as not say, "Yes. Do you?" and take that as their departing point for riffing on the subjugation of the female principle in patriarchal societies or the function of the archetypal female warrior figure as a path to liberation spiritual, mental and material. But that's not what Gene is here for today. Not for discussion. He has a load of questions, but they are not questions he wants answered, or discussed, by anyone here. He's here to commune with his own personal Kali. He's here as a disciple, a thuggee. He's here to reduce his consciousness to the smallest of points, to focus on the forthcoming struggle. Things are moving quickly now. They have already identified the man they are looking for. They filmed everyone entering Fuji City through the staff gate on Monday morning, and as soon as Suleika confirmed his presence they were a hundred percent positive they had found their mark. Now the question is merely, what are they going to do with him? And how are they going to do it. And maybe also who is going to do what? Gene needs some fundamental clarity before he starts getting into matters of logistics. So he's come here, to talk to Kali, and to ask her a question.

Vengeance or justice?

And Kali says, sugar, what's the difference?

If a great wrong is avenged, surely justice is done?

And Gene says, ok, but can't we just get him locked up?

And Kali says, ah Gene. Jean Genie. You always were one of my favourite disciples. You know that, don't you?

I know that, Kali-ma. I am honoured that it should be so. But I am full of doubt.

Of course. But you must know that I am already aware of this. There is nothing within you that is occluded. Nothing that can remain hidden. Of that, you can be sure.

I am sure Dark Mother. I know it. I am ashamed for my doubts.

Don't be afraid on account of your doubts. Your doubts don't displease me. Your self-questioning is a precondition for worship. What was it exactly you're having have trouble with?

We're close, Kali-ma. We're closing in.

You will have him soon.

And when we have him?

Retribution.

Old words, Kali-ma.

Old ideas Gene.

And punishment, Kali-ma. What about punishment?

You know what I always say about punishment Gene.

Make the punishment fit the crime?

Make the punishment fit the crime.

Thanks Dark Mother.

Always a pleasure Gene. And Gene?

Kali-ma?

Pull Suleika back a bit. Don't want her getting too exposed.

Roger that, Kali-ma.

Claire groans as her faces hits the floor. She's winded, the air is knocked out of her, but her face is not unduly damaged. The floor beneath her is covered with a thick practice mat and besides, she knows how to fall. And it's not even the fall that's bothering her in particular, it's more the fact that her arm is being twisted up behind her back and has now reached an angle whereafter there is pain, and pain only. She slaps the mat with her free hand, feels the knee in the small of her back being removed, experiences the relief as the armlock is released.

"Concentration Claire. Where's your concentration?"

The voice is that of her trainer, Chris.

"This is the second time today that I've taken you with moves that you really should be dealing with. I don't know what it is that's bugging you, but you need to leave that shit outside when you come here."

Claire is back on her feet, shakes her head, relaxes back into a sparring stance, feet apart, hands up, arms closed into a protective triangle around her upper body. She turns warily as Chris circles lightly around her, feigning, lunging, probing her defences. She successfully blocks a couple of punches and an elbow strike but then Chris slides in close by her shoulder, segueing easily from a feet-and-fist wing-tsun style attack to a simple ju-jitsu hip throw. Claire feels her feet being swept up from under her and the momentary helplessness of her body once again flying through the air before returning to the mat. She breaks her fall well, and is in the process of twisting back up and out of her prone position when she feels the skin of Chris's fist touching the tip of her nose.

"Bang bang," says Chris with a smile. "Three strikes and you're out."

Claire lets her head fall back to the mat. Chris is already back on her feet and calls out to the twenty or so other women in the room. "Ok, we're done. Let's call it a day."

The women give each other a short bow as they break off from sparring, and start to form up in a circle for the final mediation. Claire takes an extra second or two just to lie on her back and feel the weight of her body, the sweat on the back of her neck, the warm glow of her guts, a certain heaviness in her breasts. She takes in the milky light coming in through the skylights and the cobwebs up under the roof, the white-washed walls and the smell of dust and sweat and sports mat in her nose. Then there's a hand reaching down to her and she grasps up beyond it to the wrist and feels the other hand doing the same with her and then she's up on her feet and Chris has her hand on her shoulder and is indicating to her to take her place in the circle.

Everyone closes their eyes, and Claire is immediately full of the events of the past twenty-four hours, which have basically been taken up with Laila and her whole incredible story. After they got back to her place, Claire made some food and helped Laila with her hair and made up a bed for her on the sofa. In the morning she went out and did some shopping for breakfast and ordered some crutches at a nearby mobility store. And now she's due to meet Ilya for lunch before going to her shift at the shop and a group meeting in the evening.

Trouble is, she doesn't want to do any of it.

None of it moves her in the way she thinks that it should.

All she really wants to do is to be alone. She has this fantasy picture of herself in some small, cozy space, tucked up in a huge old armchair in front of an open fire. Which is absurd, because she doesn't know where she is going to find any of those things. But there it is. Her flat is temporarily occupied by Laila, which is ok,but feels a little too close for comfort on lots of different levels. And there's something building with Ilya which she can't identify but she knows it's not good. And then there's work, and the collective, and Josh, and none of it really bears thinking about.

Chris calls an end to the meditation and the women start to file out of the big old hall they are using as dojo. It's convenient for Claire because it's just down the road, but she doesn't really have time for more than a couple of sessions a week.

Chris catches up with her on her way out of the room.

"Claire, I know it's none of my business, but if you need to talk, I'm here."

"Thanks Chris, that's good of you. Maybe I'll take you up on it. But not right now, I've got to run. There's just so much stuff going on, it's all a bit too much for my little brain."

"Ok, you let me know," says Chris. "Any time."

"Sure," says Claire, and smiles at the older woman. "Thanks."

Claire gets changed into her street clothes and heads out towards the U. She walks up by the market hall and turns right into L'Ouverture, up past the drug store, the Turkish nut shop, the comic store, the organic bakery, the vinyl music store. She crosses the road by the second hand camera store and takes the steps down to the U, doing her best to ignore the smell from the chicken kebab stand by the entrance, which today she finds particularly intrusive and nauseating. She boots up her spex, buys a virtual ticket and calls up her black panther overlay. She blinks twice to open Options and tweaks their settings to maximum intensity.

She can feel the rush of the air as the train nears the station and instinctively takes a step back from the edge of the platform. The train squeals to a halt and a herd of schoolkids come rushing out of the doors towards her. She stands aside to let them pass and manages to board the carriage just before the automatic doors come slamming shut.

She stands by the doors as the train moves off, and takes a look around the now half-empty carriage. It has that grunged-out, slightly rancid feel that the U always has, plus advertising, plus screens, plus cameras, plus overlay. Nothing new, nothing different. But today there's something different in Claire. Even though there are not that many people in the carriage, she is somehow overwhelmed, repulsed even, by the virtuality of it all. By the overlay, by the projections, by the way that the simple act of going from A to B has somehow become a massive intrusion into her mental space. She feels like maybe she is going to gag. She hesitates for a moment, and then, for the first time in years, she takes her spex off in the U. She leaves them powered up, but puts them into the inside pocket of her jacket and stares blinking into the sudden nakedness of the carriage. Something is going on. Something is happening to her, and she can't explain it. She has always considered herself to be a finely-tuned part of the NC, to be a denizen, a highly adapted, quasi-symbiotic organism within this particular biotope. And now she feels herself being rejected, excreted, expunged. It's an inexplicable feeling, this sudden sense of unbelonging. It makes her dizzy, as if the world is shifting on its axis around her.

She finds herself holding her breath and forces herself to breathe normally. Weirdly, an old lady sitting next to her gets up and offers her her seat. Things are getting too bizarre. Claire declines with a fierce shake of the head, but the old lady, who must be at least fifty, with dyed red hair and crows' feet around her eyes, just smiles at her and touches her shoulder. "Go on, love," she says. "Looks like you need it more than me." And the train stops at Han Plaza and she's out the door leaving Claire wondering precisely what the fuck is going on.

There's a guy vaping on the platform, some familiar vape juice like churros and strawberry ice cream or melon bubble, and normally Claire's into it though she doesn't partake, but now the stuff wafts in on the draft and it's such a total olfactory overload that it has her wondering whether maybe Laila didn't slip something into her breakfast coffee. But that's like, too paranoid, and somehow doesn't fit with her feeling for Laila, which is that in spite of being mixed up with some crazy shit, she's still a good person.

So Claire grits her teeth and does her best to keep herself together as the doors slam shut and the train rattles off towards the Arcades. And by the time the doors have opened and closed again Claire is wondering whether she isn't finally having one of those apocryphal mass transit psychotic episodes even though she hasn't got her spex on. Or maybe precisely because she hasn't got her spex on. But that thought is even more absurd and when finally they arrive at Carlos Marx, Claire decides she can't hack it any more and gets up unsteadily to her feet and launches herself out onto the platform and up into the cold air of the street.

Carlos Marx seems to be even more of a mess than usual. The whole of the street has degenerated into one enormous set of roadworks with wire fencing on each side of a huge sandpit effectively squeezing all pedestrian traffic into narrowed-down sidewalk spaces. There's not much room for cars either, but the sound of jackhammers has become massively amplified by the addition of caterpillar-tracked vehicles with outsized jackhammer extensions on the end of their crane arms.

Claire pushes her way along the road, through the throng of pedestrians, past the little Dream of Reason café, which is now imprisoned behind impromptu building-site fencing. She stops and looks in through the window and thinks back to that time she stood outside watching the world go by, and how Ilya had persuaded her to take the day off and how bad she had felt and how he had taken her to the park to cheer her up and how sweet he had been and how all of that feels so far away now. And now here she is just standing there staring in with tears rolling down her cheeks until one of the girls behind the counter sees her and gives her a look like "You alright?" and Claire just nods and feels embarrassed and fishes a paper hanky out of her pocket and blows her nose and moves on, back along the street up in the direction of Ilya's place.

There's a dolphin butting Jimmy in the forehead and it's getting on his nerves. The dolphin seems familiar but Jimmy can't place him, or possibly her. "Hey cut that out," says Jimmy, but the dolphin just does its underwater Flipper signature giggle, swims round in a little circle and butts Jimmy in the head again with its bottlenose beak.

"Look," says Jimmy. "Haven't you got anything better to do? That's —ouch—like, really irritating, you know?"

The dolphin cackles its wicked little chuckle and says, "You're on my time down here buster," and swims around for another run at Jimmy's head. Jimmy tries ducking and weaving but can neither duck nor weave, being bound with heavy ship's rope from neck to ankles. His feet are encased in lighter gauge rope, and attached via an ingenious double bowline knot to a large blacksmith's anvil. There's about six feet of rope between Jimmy and the anvil, and another twenty feet between his head and the surface of the water.

The dolphin comes around again and Jimmy says, "Hold up!" and the dolphin does indeed stop in its tracks, but not before butting Jimmy in the forehead again.

"What is it?" says the dolphin. "I haven't got all day."

"It's the anvil," says Jimmy. "How much do you think an anvil weighs?"

The dolphin swims up close to Jimmy's face and looks him in the eye.

"What do you think I am, the weights-and-measures dolphin?"

Jimmy is unperturbed.

"Maybe not, but you look like a pretty smart fella to me."

"Don't fella me, scumbag."

"Uh, gal then."

The dolphin glowers and dinks Jimmy in the head in pure indignation.

"Woman."

Dink.

"Dolphiness?"

Double dink.

"It's cow, actually. But you can call me Beatrix."

"Bee for short?"

"Oh go on then."

"So Bee, I was thinking about the weight of this here anvil."

"I would say about a hundredweight."

"And a hundredweight is?"

"What, you want me to convert it to metric? I am a fucking aquatic mammal with no opposable thumbs, and you want the equivalent of 112 pounds in kilos? Pal, you are fucking losing it, and no mistake."

"Ah, sorry Bee. But tell me. Haven't we met before?"

"Might have met before."

Dink.

"Could have met before."

"Ouch. Ok, so tell me. What's going on?"

"It's the water, you dope. Water, the classic symbol of life, the emotions, depth, the id. The unconscious even."

"I'm unconscious?"

"Getting warmer. You were unconscious. Now you're just dreaming. Anyway, you ought to read some Jung bud."

"So why am I here?"

"Well…" Bee backs away a little bit to get a stereoscopic view of Jimmy. "There are waters of life, and there are other waters…"

"Waters of death?"

"Lethe, Styx, that kind of thing."

"Figures. Have you come to take me to the underworld?"

"Not me, buster. But maybe that approaching Russian sub."

"What sub? I can't see a sub."

"No but you can hear it. Listen to those sonar pings man. Loud and clear."

Jimmy listens and can hear the pings, coming in at approximately one a second. Like something out of some creaky black and white war film. But getting louder, and coming his way.

Al's day is picking up after an admittedly lousy start. He orders a new phone and checks through Fuji City's inmate database to see if he can find out who the old woman is who's been bugging him. He searches for all the women over sixty-five, but there are none, which doesn't really surprise him because let's face it, how is some decrepit old-age pensioner going to make a trek of several thousand miles on foot? So he broadens it out to sixty, and that brings up five women out of a total population of around three and a half thousand and then reconsiders and lowers it to fifty-five because when it boils down to it he actually has no idea how old the over-inquisitive hag could be. But fifty-five brings up seventeen women and he flags them up and pulls up their details one by one. But these mug shots are not really helping him any. He didn't get a clear view of her face out there on the tarmac, so next time he sees her he's just going to have to approach her and ask her for her ID. That alone will probably be enough to scare the shit out of her, but once he knows who she is, he should be able to get her ejected from Fuji City without too much trouble. And if the bureaucracy takes too long, there are certainly other ways of helping an unknown old woman to disappear.

He saves his list for later and turns to the weekend's reports from his boys. Looks like they've been keeping themselves busy. Nothing major, but they are obviously keeping their hand in. A little random violence in the U, some tramp set alight, a bunch of women molested at a concert, a couple of queers beaten up in the early hours. He only ticks off stuff that he can corroborate from other sources, such as police records or media reports. It's all chickenshit really, but every little helps. They need time to find their feet in a place like the NC, and from that point of view they're doing pretty well. There's one item on the list that gives Al a little food for thought though: a vehicle hijacking. A couple of guys apparently surprised a sleeping truck driver and took him and his rig out for an hour-long trip through the city. In the end they simply pulled over, threw his keys down the road and disappeared. What was all that about, thinks Al. He wonders whether that doesn't count as freelancing. It certainly doesn't fit in with his brief. He makes a note to have a word with their group leader. He doesn't want his little puppies straining at the leash this early in the game.

And then there's the whole thing with the demo. He accesses the intel on the organizers, who are apparently some bar-based collective over on Cartersgate and one of the streetwalkers from Charlie's Garden. The one who got up on the stage. He takes a look at the pictures on his screen. In and out of drag. Disgusting. But of course he has seen her, him, whatever, before. That time on the corner. She was the one who had given him that look. Challenged him. Refused him. Angered him.

She would certainly need to be dealt with. In some appropriate manner.

Ilya's at home when Claire calls round and he's glad to see her, even though he's not in a particularly good state. He's hardly been out of the house ever since he landed his honeypot and is starting to get a little wide-eyed and crazy. The past couple of weeks have been a constant round of getting up late, going to his desk to work on his data, and falling into bed at some ungodly hour of the morning. The only inter-ruptions to his routine have been provided by Claire, and they seem to be coming at increasingly irregular intervals. Not that he blames her for it mind. He guesses he's not such good company these days. Every time Claire suggests going out, for a meal or to a concert or to the cinema or even just down to the pub, Ilya comes up with some lame excuse like he has to get up early, or has a migraine, or how about they get something delivered and chill out at home. He knows it's an untenable, unsustain-able position, and it's not being fair on Claire. So he's decided that today's the day. Today's the day to come clean and tell her about what it is he's working on, to explain why he's been so secretive and withdrawn, and to talk to her about planning their next moves together. It won't be easy—not so much the telling her, but life after that. Dealing with the knowledge of being potential fugitives, maybe even moving to a different city, or a different country. Venezuela maybe, or Ecuador. Cuba even. But his Spanish is lousy. And as for Russia. No, he really doesn't want to go to Russia. In fact, in terms of running, there's not really anywhere he can think of running to. Where, on this planet, would be far enough to escape from state security? From a whole heap of state security agencies in fact. And the truth is: nowhere. The only way to deal with it is to stop anyone from knowing anything about the data, and who stole it. And the only way to save his relationship is to tell Claire what he's working on and why it's so important and why it's consuming his life. It's a total fuck-up. A Gordian knot that he's going to have to cut through.

Claire arrives and she looks radiant, if a little flustered. Their greeting kiss feels a little perfunctory, but hey, anyone can have a bad day and he frees up a chair for her at the kitchen table and asks if she wants something to drink. She opts for tea, so he puts the kettle on and says, "What do you fancy for lunch? I've got eggs and…" He opens the fridge. "And eggs. That's about it. Not very vegan, I'm afraid."

"Eggs are ok," says Claire with an air of exhaustion.

"I've got some butter too," says Ilya triumphantly. He fumbles around in a kitchen cupboard and produces half a loaf of bread. "And some bread." He knits his brow as he ponders the ensuing culinary options. "So how about fried eggs on toast?"

"Whatever," says Claire.

There's a moment's silence as Ilya figures out that something is up. He puts the food down on the worktop and comes over to the table.

"Ilya."

"Claire."

"We need to talk."

Ilya breathes a sigh of relief.

"Yes! We need to talk. Just what I've been thinking. That's great Claire."

"But Ilya?"

"Yes Claire?"

"Can you talk and cook at the same time? I'm starving."

"Ok. Sure. You go first then. I'll do the eggs and the tea. You carry on."

So Claire starts on in. She tells Ilya how she's been missing him. How she feels that they are drifting apart. How he always seems to be working, and when he's not working he never really seems to be present, with her. Ilya experiences a whole range of emotions as he listens to her talk. He feels shame, because every word is true, and there's no denying any of it. He feels the incredible weight of what it would be to lose Claire, and the terrible void that her words would imply if carried through to the logical conclusion of separation. But most of all he feels happy. Happy about the fact that Claire has nailed it, that she has identified precisely the point that he wanted to talk about. That she has provided him with the perfect introduction to what he wants to say to her. He's about to open his mouth when he realizes that Claire is still talking.

"And then there's this woman Laila. I told you about her, she had an accident on her motorbike. Well it turns out that she's working for state security, or was working for state security, until her boss tried to kill her. And now she's on the run and has to disappear so I've got her holed up at my place for a couple of days until…Ilya, what is it?"

Ilya is standing by the oven with a spatula in his hand and his mouth open wide, staring at Claire in disbelief.

"Ilya, don't look at me like that. Say something!"

"State security? Did you really just tell me you are sharing a flat with someone who works for state security? Are you out of your mind?"

"I'm not sharing a flat. I'm just letting her stay for a couple of days till she gets sorted out. She's at risk, for god's sake. Her boss tried to kill her and he's probably going to try again. What else could I do?"

"You could do nothing, for one thing. You could tell her to get lost. You could tell her to crawl away and die."

Claire is visibly shocked by the vehemence in Ilya's voice. A slight waft of burning drifts over from the toaster.

"Ilya, I've never heard you like this. I'm just helping her out. There's no need to be so… malicious. What's your problem with that anyway? What's the big deal with state security? What is it you've got to hide?"

"Hide?" Ilya pops the toaster and turns back to the pan, ostensibly to attack the eggs with his spatula, but also to hide the fact that he is blushing deeply.

"Nothing. I've got nothing to hide. I'm just surprised is all. I thought you being so political and everything, you wouldn't want to have anything to do with state security."

"Well I guess you're right. But I think in a way this is also political, you know? She talked a lot about some undercover thing called Operation Brando. That's what made me think she was serious. The fact that she was willing to tell me stuff. Talking of which—what was it you wanted to tell me?"

Ilya sets down a plate of eggs in front of her along with a mug of tea, and sits down opposite her. His face is deadpan and his eyes are blank.

"Me? Oh nothing. I think you've said it all already."

Jimmy comes awake to the sound of a Russian sub approaching. He cracks an eye open and can see next to nothing apart from the signal bleep of a heart monitor close to his bed. He puts two and two together and figures he hasn't been abducted to the far shores of the River Styx yet, and instead is very probably still alive. However, he doesn't seem to be doing too well judging by the various tubes going in and out of his body. He's got an oxygen mask over his nose and drip feeds going into his arms. The room is bathed in a sickly green light and over in a corner he can make out the figure of Julia, asleep on a chair. He's not in any pain, but he feels feverish and nauseous and his limbs feel heavier than they have ever done in his entire life. He would really like to call out to Julia but even the thought of it just fills him with fatigue. He feels like he's struggling on the surface of consciousness and there's nothing stopping him from slipping back under at any second. At the back of his mind there is a voice struggling to be heard. A voice that's saying, wake up, you dope, these are probably the last seconds of your life. If you're going to croak, the least you could do is to call Julia over and tell her you love her. Jimmy smiles inwardly at the thought. It's a nice gesture, but completely out of scope at the moment. And if she doesn't know by now, then she probably never will. But Jimmy is pretty sure she knows. He's told her. Maybe not often enough, but he hopes she got the gist over the twenty-odd years of their relationship. And if he ever gets out of this alive…

Jimmy lets the sentence go unfinished. Lets the thought float away of its own accord. He's not getting out of this alive. He's been diagnosed with terminal cancer, he has experienced some kind of seizure on the streets of Manila, and now he's obviously in intensive care. He's not stupid, and can see no point kidding himself. This is the end. He hears echoes of Jim Morrison in his mind and sees palm trees going up in billowing explosions of napalm. He looks up to the ceiling of the room and there's a big old-fashioned ventilator fan but it's not turning and it's certainly not making chopper noises. Jimmy wonders if this is how other people die, with their minds full of movie trivia, or if they get to have some kind of spiritual insight, some last-minute illumination as the curtain is finally ripped away. Jimmy's not getting any of that. He's just getting flashes of Apocalypse Now and is wondering what it would be like to die on acid. Would the visuals be more intense, he wonders. Because they're certainly a let-down from his present perspective. In fact, he has to say, this dying thing, it sucks big time. It's a sub-optimal user experience. Maybe he'll go and complain to the management about it.

Claire and Ilya finish their lunch in silence. At least it feels like silence to Claire, in spite of the fact that Ilya keeps asking her about Laila and Operation Brando. But she's kind of gobsmacked about the weird turn in the conversation, and the way that Ilya has completely stonewalled everything she was saying about their relationship. She finds it difficult to believe that he is being this obtuse. She always had him down as the sensitive type, but here he is, being a complete asshole. And worse, asking her a load of questions about stuff that is completely irrelevant to the whole situation. She finds herself observing the scene, observing him, with an almost out-of-body detachment. She's speaking, answering his questions, talking about the things Laila told her, but at the same time she is examining him, this man that she's been sharing her bed with, this guy that she was so infatuated with not so very long ago. She looks at his lank black hair as it falls over his eyes while he eats. The long curve of his neck that she used to find so graceful is now just scrawny, with deep blue veins standing out. She feels so infinitely sad that it should have come to this. It's not that she hates him. She just finds herself feeling slightly repulsed by him, by the way he talks, by the way he shovels egg into his mouth, by his jerky, nervous gestures, but most of all by the way that he has blanked her out. She is angry, and surprised, and hurt, and close to tears. He says, "Do you want any more eggs?" and she says, "No, I'm done."

"More tea then?"

"No. I need to get to work early."

"Thought you didn't need to be there till three."

"Stocktaking. I forgot about the stocktaking. Better get going."

"See you later then?"

"Not tonight. Need to keep an eye on Laila."

"Laila."

"Yup."

"Tomorrow then?"

"I'll call you."

She gets up and feels a momentary dizziness that makes her hold onto the back of the chair till it passes. Ilya says, "You ok?" and she says, "Bit woozy. Coming down with a cold maybe. Or some virus."

He brings her to the door and goes to kiss her but she turns her face away and says, "Wouldn't want you catching anything," so he gives her an awkward hug and she is out of the door as fast as she can and down the stairs with tears streaming down her face. She pushes open the big heavy door of the house and is just stepping out onto the pavement when she's suddenly seeing stars and her guts rebel and she spins around to lean up against the nearest wall and finds herself spewing right there in the street. It's such an unexpected, violent impulse that there's nothing she can do except give in to it. She stands there retching, and hoping nobody is watching, and feeling embarrassed. Her face is inches away from the intercom panel of Ilya's house. She can even read his name clearly on one of the illuminated buttons right in front of her eyes. It would be simple to press the button and call for help. Instead she looks down at the remains of her egg and toast on the pavement and spits the last vestiges out of her mouth. She doesn't know who's going to clear it all up, but she knows it's not going to be her.

She wipes her mouth with the back of her hand and straightens up.

Let Ilya clear it up.

They're his eggs, after all.

"What do you mean, botulism?"

Jimmy is propped up in bed with a couple less tubes in and out of his body, talking to a big panjandrum doctor in the hospital in Manila. Julia is looking on, with a worried expression, and the doc is accompanied by a couple of subalterns.

"What I mean, Mr, uh, Chang," says the doc, unclipping Jimmy's stats sheet from the end of his bed, "is that you are lucky to be alive. Botulism is no laughing matter. We have lost more than one patient to that particular form of food poisoning over the past year."

The doc's English is good. He has dark hair with salt-and-pepper temples, and looks like he spends a good deal of time on the tennis court.

"Ok, botulism, sure. Bad shit, that botulism. I can vouch for that. But it's the cancer doc. It's the cancer that's got me worried. That's why I need my medication."

"No," says the doc, firmly.

Jimmy looks over to Julia, who gives him a sheepish kind of shrug and an embarrassed smile.

"No cancer, Mr. Chang. The moment your wife informed us, we ran checks. All negative."

"Can't be," says Jimmy, gobsmacked.

"Can be, Mr Chang. Can be indeed," says the doc, relishing the moment. "So good news eh?"

"Good news hardly begins to describe it," says Jimmy with a small surge of elation. He still feels like shit, but the elation is in there somewhere.

"But there is also, how can I put it, a downside. Every cloud has its silver lining, no?"

"Er, no. I think maybe you're mixing metaphors," says Julia, grasping Jimmy's hand, but addressing the doc.

"Perhaps, perhaps. Then let me put it like this. Good news, no cancer. Bad news, botulism plus."

"Plus?" say Jimmy and Julia together.

"Plus arsenic poisoning. Plus opiate addiction. Plus barbiturate addiction. We examined the so-called medication your wife asked us to administer to you. It would seem to be a cocktail of fairly toxic and illicit substances. Enough, by the way, to get you arrested. Or, this being Manila, killed and dumped in Manila Bay."

For once in his life, Jimmy Chang is speechless. He pulls Julia towards him and the two hold on to each other and cry quietly into each other's shoulders.

The doctor coughs discreetly. Jimmy and Julia disengage, Jimmy wipes his nose on the back of his hospital gown sleeve.

"The only reason we were prepared to believe your wife's version of events was her willingness to dispose of the entire contents of your so-called medication kit once we told her of its ingredients."

"Of course Doc. We're really grateful. I can't even begin to tell you how grateful I am."

The doctor says something to his two companions and hangs Jimmy's stats back on the end of the bed.

"Before you thank me. There is one thing that you need to know. One thing that is waiting for you now. In addition to recovery from the botulism toxins."

"Ok doc, whatever it is, it can't be as bad as what I've been through. Lay it on me: what is it?"

The doctor draws himself up to his full height and signals to his companions to go.

"Cold turkey," he says, and turns and leaves the room.

Claire has hardly gone a hundred yards down the street away from Ilya's place when she gets a call. She's still feeling a bit queasy so she leans up against the wall of a house as she presses her phone to her ear. She doesn't recognize the number so her opening "Hello?" is a bit wary.

"Claire!" says a husky voice on the other end, "This is Debbie."

Claire takes a second to process that information, proceeding from the fact that she doesn't know any Debbies. Then it occurs to her that she does. It's the name they thought up for Laila last night when they were doing her hair.

"Debbie. Sure. Hi, how's it going?"

She feels an unexpected rush of pleasure at the sound of Laila's voice on the phone.

"It's going good. I'm out trying out my new crutches."

"Christ on a bike Debbie, you're out and about? Aren't you supposed to be lying in bed or something?"

"No, can't have that. Need to build my strength up. It's all good, as long as I don't put too much weight on the leg. Only took me about twenty minutes to hobble down to the U. But I need a bit of a rest now so I thought maybe you'd like to meet up for coffee."

"Yes, love to. Do you want me to come to where you are?"

"No. I'll come to you. I know you have to work later."

"Ok. Come on down to Carlos Marx. I'll come and pick you up and we'll take it from there."

"Sounds great. There's a train pulling in now. See you in a bit."

The line goes dead and Claire can feel the dark cloud of her lunch with Ilya starting to lift. The change is so unexpected that it makes her feel a little light-headed. The day itself seems to brighten up, and she walks along Ricksville and up to Carlos Marx with a swing in her step and a sudden feeling of warm anticipation.

She takes the steps down into the U and when the train pulls in she positions herself conspicuously on the edge of the platform near the driver's compartment so that she has a good line of sight down the entire train. She spots a pair of shiny blue crutches emerging from a carriage doorway followed rapidly by a tall woman with cropped blond hair, dressed in jeans and a padded jacket.

Claire waves and starts walking down the platform but Laila has already seen her and is making her way up towards her.

For the first time since they absconded from hospital, there's a smile on her face.

Claire feels something shift inside her. She's struck by how good she looks. Laila has big diva sunglasses pushed back to the top of her head, and the hood of her winter jacket frames her face in a way that makes it seem to glow. Her self-administered haircut gives her a rocky, punkish look.

There's a moment of awkwardness when they get to each other and Claire realizes that she doesn't quite know how to greet her. The hug she had in mind seems a little impractical in view of the crutches, so she gingerly leans in and presses her cheek to Laila's and can feel the warmth of her face suffusing her skin.

"Hey blondie. Almost didn't recognize you there."

"But the crutches are a dead giveaway, right?"

"Right. But you're some tough cookie, wandering round the NC on your new sticks. Isn't that kinda tiring?"

"It's exhausting. To be honest I've just about had it for today. I might even treat myself to a taxi back. But first, let's get out of the U. Is there a lift?"

Claire checks out the platform.

"Nope. No lift."

"An escalator?"

"Just stairs I'm afraid."

"Bastards. Remind me to write a letter about it."

Laila winks, and starts off towards the flight of concrete steps leading up out of the U. Claire walks slowly up behind her, just in case. Laila curses and heaves herself up step by step, and by the time she reaches the top she is sweating profusely.

"Fuck. Really wouldn't like to have to do that too often. So, where are you taking me? Hope it's not too far."

Claire points over towards the Dream of Reason.

"There's a little place over there. It's a bit cramped, but the coffee is good."

They sit themselves down in a corner of the little coffee bar and have just about finished peeling off extraneous layers of clothing by the time the waitress brings their order over. She sets down two big white cups of cappuccino and a piece of chocolate cake for Claire and some pecan pie for Laila.

A big grin spreads across Laila's face.

"Oh man. Pecan pie. I love pecan pie. This is a real celebration."

Claire looks at her and raises an eyebrow.

"Really? What are we celebrating?"

"Well me, I'm celebrating getting out of the house, new-found mobility, identity changes, big sunglasses, and of course, new hair."

Claire laughs.

"The hair is so good. It's a whole new you. Brings out the rebel in you."

"Ah well, I'll be needing that from now on."

There's a moment of silence while they dig into their respective cakes.

"And how about you Claire, what are you celebrating?"

Claire feels a wave of conflicting emotion as she thinks back to the scene with Ilya, to the whole tragic heaviness of it, and then the lightness she felt on seeing Laila. She finds that her hand has shifted to her heart, as if to get a better grasp of what she is feeling.

"I don't know. I don't know if there's too much to celebrate right now."

"Didn't go too well with Ilya, huh?"

"Let's just say that we don't exactly see eye to eye at the moment. To be honest, I think it's over."

Claire can feel the tears welling up and overflowing.

"Ah shit, here I go again. Have you got a tissue or something?"

Laila fishes around in her jacket pocket for a pack of tissues and hands them to Claire.

"I'm sorry. I don't mean to rain on your celebration."

"Claire. You don't have to apologize to me for anything. I think it's pretty natural that you should be feeling emotional. In your condition."

That brings Claire up with a start.

"Huh? My condition? What's that supposed to mean?"

Laila holds up her palms in a gesture of apology.

"No offence meant Claire. I just figured that'd be what you wanted to talk to Ilya about. I mean, it's a pretty significant change, after all."

Claire wipes her eyes with the back of a finger and straightens up in her seat.

"Listen Laila, I mean Debbie. You'd better give it to me straight, because I haven't the faintest idea what it is you're getting at."

The ghost of a smile flits across Laila's face. She leans back a bit and opens up her arms as if regarding Claire in a picture frame.

"But you must know, right? I mean, just look at you. You're so fucking radiant. Look at the shape of you even. I've seen the pictures of you that you've got at home. You don't look like that any more. Can't you tell that there's something going on?"

"Yeah, I can tell when someone is taking the piss. Is this like your idea of a joke, because I'm not really finding it that funny, you know?"

Laila's face goes serious then. She leans in and takes hold of Claire's hands.

"Claire. Sorry, no joke. I wasn't trying to be funny. I just didn't think —couldn't believe—you didn't already know. It was always the same with my mother. She could always tell. With my cousins. Our neighbours. Long before they knew themselves. I guess I've just been assuming that you were already up to speed on the whole thing."

"Laila, listen to me. I'm going crazy here. Just spell it out, ok? Before I start breaking up the furniture or something. What whole thing? What the fuck are you talking about?"

Laila leans closer in, so that she's inches away from Claire's face.

"Claire, sweetness. Don't get mad. But either I'm totally mistaken, or…"

"Or what?"

"Or you're pregnant."

Chapter Thirty-One
The Storm

There's a storm barrelling down from the North towards the NC and there's not a thing anyone can do about it. It's preceded by a band of wet weather that's about 5 degrees too warm for the time of year, but all that's about to go out of the window, and give way to a snowstorm, if not a snow hurricane. A flurrycane perhaps. A snownado. Either way, all portents point to a major white-out. And then temperatures are set to fall to about minus 9. So that's about a 20 degree drop due over the next 12 hours. The meteo guys say it's just a jet stream anomaly. If you noodle the weeb for "jet stream anomaly" you get so much stuff about kinks and blocking highs you might think you've landed on some fetish poppers page. But no, once the old jet stream starts juking and jiving then it's chocks away for ultra kinky meteorological freakery.

Ah but who's to tell? In freaky times, freak is the new norm. As with the weather, so with the NC.

We've got a couple of our own storms brewing, a couple of major temperature anomalies on their way, and no-one can say for sure how they're going to turn out. We've got Hurricane Claire, emerging from a cyclonic depression as a newly invigorated force of nature, and we've got Typhoon Gene, about to start battering the ramparts of Fuji City.

What can remain for us then, but to hunker down, make a quick dash to the supermarket and get some supplies in, turn up the central heating and wait for the storm to do its worst, to lash and thrash and trash and beat itself against our vehicles and edifices, which we know to be superior to all that so-called Nature can throw at us? For if there is one thing of which we are sure, it is that all storms must abate. That all the hellish sound and fury of the elements is as nothing in the face of the magnificence of humanity's achievements. That we shall emerge, blinking and smiling, to the light of a new day. That children are the only ones who blush. That the good guys always win in the end. That business as usual is the only way to be. That things can only get better. That the state really does have your best interests at heart.

Yeah right.

It's been good knowing you.

Let's proceed.

Gene is with Omar, up in Omar's place.

They haven't seen much of each other the past couple of days, what with Gene's surveillance operation up at Fuji City, so they have each taken a couple of hours off work to catch up, and fuck, and eat, and just generally chew the fat. Night has fallen, and they're sitting by the window, looking down at the snow that is starting to swirl around the sodium streets of the city below them. Gene's glad to be here, and it's good to be with Omar, and he feels grateful that Omar has taken the trouble to pull him out of his full-on, obsessive focus with catching the guy in the suit up at the refugee place. But he knows it's just a temporary respite. He feels like he's not quite all there, and he knows Omar feels it too. The city glowers in at them, cold and sullen, and in spite of Omar's best efforts to keep the cold at bay, they both know that Gene's going to have to go back out soon enough.

When the call comes, it's from an unexpected source.

"Jeanie, it's Sandy. I've got Carol on the other line from Elite Escorts. Said they recognized the face on the posters as one of their regulars."

"Thanks Sandy, but it's a little late for this. We already know who he is."

"Yeah, I figured. But Carol says he's just called in for an escort. They thought it better to ring us first before sending anyone up there."

Gene slaps the table with his free hand.

"That's great Sandy. Tell her we'll take it on. Tell her we're on it. What time have they booked for?"

"For eight. And Jeanie?"

"Sandy?"

"He wants someone tall and blond."

"No problem sweetie," says Gene, and cuts the connection. He jumps up in a burst of enthusiasm and sends his chair flying over backwards. He leans across the table and gives Omar a triumphant smacker of a kiss.

"Sounds like you got your man," says Omar.

"Not yet, but we're getting close," says Gene. He checks the time on his phone.

"Half six now, we're going to have to move fast. Need to get home, get changed, make a few calls."

"Need any help?"

"Honey, I think we're going to need all the help we can get."

Claire's just finishing up her shift at the vegan healthfood store and she's still aglow from her meeting with Laila.

And of course, still in shock about being pregnant.

She thought for a moment about taking the day off work, but it's not like she's sick or anything.

Quite the opposite, in fact.

She feels great, and obviously a lot of that is Laila's doing, but some of it is also just *knowing*, just finally realizing what it is that has been happening with her. It's like the penny has finally dropped, like someone has quietly taken her aside and said, "Look, you may think you were doing this, but actually, you were doing *this*!" and drawing a curtain back, and suddenly revealing a motivation that she didn't even know she had. It's all very disturbing, but somehow, wonderful, fantastic. All on a gut level of course. Intellectually it seems like a minor catastrophe—the whole thing with Ilya, her emotional state, her work situation, the state of the planet. But something inside her just says fuck all that, just go for it. Her head might say that it's mad, but her body is totally into it, and her heart is rejoicing. And of course Laila is feeding into that too. There was all that initial weirdness around her working for the state, that initial mistrust and wariness. But she feels that something has shifted, that they have somehow moved on from there. There was something so right, so incredibly natural about being with her for that hour before work. And each minute of their time together put an extra mile between her and Ilya, so that by the end of the hour, by the time their coffees had been drunk, there was no doubt in her mind about what had to happen next. She was already in a totally different heart and headspace, and the old stuff would just need to be dealt with. And the great thing, the wonderfully unexpected thing with Laila was that she had been so happy for her, even in spite of all the scary shit going on in her own world. She had felt close, closer than Claire has been with Ilya for a long time. Close as if they had known each other for ages. And when they parted, outside the little café, they had stood for a while on the pavement, looking at each other, Laila leaning on her crutches and looking cool and kind of louche, and Claire feeling flustered and raw and somehow full of uncontrollable emotions.

Laila had said, "See you later maybe."

And Claire had laughed and said, "Sure. I'll be back after work. Around ten. Do you want me to bring something to eat?"

"Sounds good. Sounds kinda homey."

Claire pushes herself forward into the space between Laila's crutches. She looks into her eyes.

"You got anything against homey?"

"No. Home is where the heart is, honey."

Claire looks at Laila to see if she is taking the piss or coming on to her. And she is coming on to her in a massive way, or at least it feels that way to Claire. But Laila is not making any moves, which is the way it should be, figures Claire, and so she moves in and kisses her square on the lips, and that bursts into one of those raw passionate kisses that seem to go on forever and when they break up it's to the muffled sound of clapping and they can see the girls in the café giving them a round of applause.

Claire had blushed then, and had given the girls a little *namaste* thank you with her hands, before setting off with Laila in the direction of the U and somewhere a little less conspicuous.

They had parted on the steps to the U. Laila had leaned against the bannister at the top of the stairway and they had kissed long and hard before she had put her hand to Claire's face and caressed her cheek with her fingers and said, "Claire. You need to think about this. This is not a good time for me. This is not a good time for involvement."

And Claire had said, "Ok. I'll think about it. But maybe you should let me be the judge of that. Good or bad, I reckon this is the only time we have."

They kissed again, and Claire said, "See you later."

And Laila said, "Yeah, see you later," and turned, and crutch-hopped down the steps with her glasses down so that Claire couldn't see the sadness in her eyes.

So Claire's shift at the shop goes by in a rosy glow, to such an extent that she even has Suki asking her what she is looking so pleased with herself about, but it's all too fresh for Claire to start spreading it around the shop so she just says, "Nothing," and Suki says, "Nothing my ass."

"Maybe another time," says Claire.

"Lover boy?" says Suki.

Claire just looks down at the floor with a slight shake of the head.

"C'mon Claire. Throw us a bone here. I can tell something's up."

Claire's smile ought to be confirmation enough, but she says, "Let's keep it till after the meeting eh? I just need to get through the day first."

"Oho, secrets," says Suki. "I love a secret."

"Me too," says Claire. "Me too."

By the time Jeanie gets up to Fuji City she's wearing a crimson maxi length coat with black fake fur trim and hood, matching tube scarf, thigh high stiletto-heeled boots and a long blond wig down to her ass. She's also chewing a thick wad of gum, but whether that's just for bravado it's difficult to say. The wig makes her look a bit like Ursula, and that makes her angry, gives her a fire in the belly that propels her out of her car through the swirling snow towards the little side entrance set into an unguarded stretch of the chain link fence surrounding the complex.

She pulls the hood up around her face and looks back towards the car, and the faces staring out at her, and the big white van directly behind. She gives them all a little understated finger-wave with her red varnished nails and concentrates on where she's going. The stiletto boots are lousy to walk in, especially now that the snow is starting to settle, but they look the part, and that's the main thing. She crosses to the central reservation and takes in the bleak edifice of Fuji City, with its inner and outer fences, and tall floodlights set on masts every fifty yards or so. There's no-one in sight, neither out on the street or within the perimeter of the City grounds.

She shivers as she crosses the road to the sidewalk and the fence and starts to look for the little doorbell, which is attached discreetly to the underside of one of the metal struts forming the frame of the chainlink door. She rings three times in quick succession as instructed and the door buzzes open. She catches the door as it swings shut and swiftly transfers the contents of her mouth to the latch of the door in one graceful movement. She walks another twenty yards around the side of the building, all the time on the lookout for camera surveillance. Ironically, there doesn't seem to be any in this corner of the compound, presumably so that her mark could pursue his extra-curricular activities unobserved. Good for him, but good for Jeanie too. She arrives at the glassed-in wall of the main stairwell and presses the entrance buzzer. She hears the sound of the door click open, but remains where she is, and presses again. There's a voice this time.

"Door's open."

"Ah, hi. Seems to be stuck. I'm pushing, but it won't budge. Maybe someone locked it?"

There's irritation on the crackled voice on the other end of the intercom.

"No. It's an electronic lock. Let me try again."

The door clicks open again.

"Sorry, nothing doing. Still the same. What do you want me to do?"

"Stay where you are. I'll be right down."

Jeanie steps back from the door, wraps her coat tighter around herself, checks her lipstick in a compact mirror. Watches the snow swirl. Listens to the sound of her heartbeat.

Light comes on in the stairwell and she sees the shape of Al as he trots down the steps, checks out his muscular frame, the thin line of his beard along his jaw, his dark, slicked-back hair. He's wearing expensive slacks and a pale blue shirt, open at the collar. He tries the door, which opens immediately. Gene puts her opened hand to her mouth in feigned surprise.

"Jesus Christ, what is it with you girls? Now they send me someone too dumb to get the door open?"

"Sorry mister," says Jeanie demurely. "Just wouldn't work for me."

"Yeah, well you'd better come in," says Al. "Maybe you'll be too dumb to ask for money too."

"Don't think so," says Jeanie, as she brushes up against him on the way through the door. "I've never been known to forget a payback."

"Payback?" says Al, looking at her with surprise.

"Payback," says Jeanie, with a knife to his throat. "I'm sure you know what payback means."

Claire goes into her meeting with a mixture of trepidation and elation. She's still riding the wave from earlier on, but is not looking forward to the fight that she's pretty sure is about to go down. The whole crew is there, Suki, Ramon, and Charlie, who has dyed her hair pink and is wearing green lipstick, Jared, and of course Josh. There are a few minutes of catching up and general chit-chat, which gradually subsides as people start to cotton on to the tension in the air, specifically, between Claire and Josh, who opens the meeting with the words, "Right people, we've got a bunch of stuff lined up, but is there anything anyone wants to put on the agenda?"

All eyes turn to Claire as she raises her hand.

"Yeah. You can put this on the agenda. I'm leaving."

There's a moment of silence as people take it in, then the room erupts into a synchronous explosion of voices.

It's Josh who takes the initiative and waves his hands in that calm-down motion that teachers use for especially unruly classes.

"Well, that's very regrettable Claire, and I'm sure we'll all be sorry to see you go. But I guess you have your own reasons…"

"Which are what, exactly?" It's Suki, leaning back in her chair.

"Yeah, come on Claire, you can't just give up on us you know."

It's Charlie who just spoke. Claire gives her a wry smile and looks around the room, harvests looks of concern, nods and smiles of encouragement from all corners, even from Ramon. Everyone seems keen to hear what she has to say. Everyone except Josh, that is.

Claire doesn't know what she's going to say. She just opens her mouth and lets it come out.

"Thanks everyone. I appreciate it. And it's difficult for me to say what it is, what's brought me along…to this. I guess it's been brewing for a while. You know, like the last meeting. Just that feeling of getting nowhere, and wanting so much to be somewhere else, much further along. And then last week I had this weird meeting with this old guy who's dying of cancer and who told me that he finally felt free to do all the crazy things that life never let him do, maybe even up to the point of sacrificing himself for some noble cause, and I told him he was crazy, and I told him about Josh here, who approached me last week about some totally fucked-up, hare-brained idea about becoming some kind of killer sect, some fucking urban guerrilla cell and that just pushed me over the edge, because if there's one thing I'm not into, it's that. I mean, if you want to go running around doing some kind of lunatic macho boys-with-toys shit then that's your business, but like, leave me out, you know? And you know what I think? I think it's a fucking provocation. I think you, Josh, are a fucking wind-up, some kind of provocateur, and whether you are, or whether you aren't, I really don't want to be in the same group as you. I really don't want to be anywhere near you. So that's about it really. That's me, done."

Once again there is uproar in the room. Everybody is talking at once, but it's drowned out by the sound of someone shouting at the top of their voice.

"Stop!"

It's Josh, messianic, apoplectic. He stands up and waves his hair back with a shake of the head.

"She's lying, people."

Claire, in an instant: "You bastard, you scumbag."

"I don't know what her motivation is for making up this kind of thing about me, but none of it is true."

"Are you saying we never met? We didn't have breakfast together round at Hank's?"

"Yes, that's precisely what I'm saying Claire. Seems to me that you've totally lost it. I have no idea why you want to smear me like this, why you want to go around making up such awful stories, but I want you all to know that none of it is true. Hand on my heart. I feel sorry for you Claire. I think you need professional help."

Claire is up on her feet by now too.

"Jesus Christ. I had no idea you could sink so low Josh. Until recently I always had you pegged as one of the good guys. Now I know different. Now I know you're a fucking snake in the grass. Well you might be able to fool everyone else with this I'm-so-innocent act, but you ain't fooling me."

She turns around, takes her coat from the back of the chair, picks up her things.

"Good luck guys, you're going to need it."

She's almost at the door when a voice from behind her calls out to her.

"Claire, wait!"

It's Suki, getting up out of her chair.

"I'm coming with you."

Claire can see the unease in the room, see the others exchanging glances, whispers. Charlie and Jared nod to each other and get up together.

"We're with you Claire," says Charlie.

There are four of them now, standing by the door, looking back into the room. Ramon is still sitting, looking over at Josh in disbelief. Josh's face is almost purple with anger. Finally Ramon stands up, pushing his chair back.

"Don't know why everyone is walking out. Looks like a simple majority decision. Josh, I would say you've had it mate. You're out."

"What?"

Josh explodes with rage.

"You can't fucking do this to me. Not on the word of that, that whore! I fucking run this place, and don't you forget it. If it wasn't for me, you'd be nothing. Nowhere. Nobody!"

Suki moves back into the room, menacingly, rolling up her sleeves.

"That's enough Josh. You've gone too far. Take your stuff and get out, before we throw you out. This is your last chance."

"You're crazy! You can't do this."

The others are moving back in now, lining up with Suki. But it's Claire who speaks.

"You're wrong Josh. We can. If anyone's crazy, it's you. Now get the fuck out of here before things really turn nasty."

There's a moment of stand-off as Josh weighs up the odds. Then he picks up his stuff and pushes through the middle of the group towards the door.

"You dumb fucks. You're going to regret this."

Claire looks over to Suki, who has her hand on Claire's shoulder and a gleam of triumph in her eye.

"No Josh. No regrets. Now fuck off."

When the hood is removed from his head, Al finds himself in a dimly-lit room with a couple of bright lights shining in his eyes. He's sitting on a simple wooden chair with his hands tied behind his back, so he's not even able to scratch the place on his neck where that bitch nicked it with her knife. He blinks a couple of times as his eyes get used to the light, and can make out the shapes of a number of people around him. There's that slut that abducted him, for a start. Then the others he saw on the way to the van. And in addition—he cranes his neck around to see who else is in the room—shit, the old crone from Fuji City. What the fuck is she doing here? No matter. They're all going to pay. They are all going to fucking die.

Al would dearly love to impart his opinions to his involuntary hosts, but he finds that his powers of speech are limited by the gag in his mouth, which only serves to make him even angrier. He screams at his captors through the gag, strains at the ropes behind his back, goes to get up but finds that he is also tied to the chair. The chair rises a couple of inches from the floor, and Al is convinced that if he bounces the chair up and down a few times it will simply give way beneath him. And then he will be able to free himself, and launch into these cowardly fuckers who are holding him prisoner. Knives or no knives, none of them are going to make it out of here alive, he will make sure of that. So Al kicks off again with his feet as soon as the chair legs hit the floor again, only to find a heavy weight suddenly clamped to the back of the chair behind him. There is someone there. Someone he can't see. Someone who won't even show themselves. That is typical. So fucking typical. He screams with rage and defiance, but all that comes out are muffled grunts through the cloth of the gag, which is bound tightly into his mouth. Still, he renews his efforts to pull himself free from the chair, until a shape steps forwards from the shadows to stand directly in front of him. He can make out a powerfully-built woman in her mid-forties, with short, dark hair. She has her hands on her hips and says, with an air of authority that Al instinctively registers, "It will be better for you if you quit struggling."

Al hurls all the insults and obscenities at her that he can think of, none of which are audible as anything other than guttural grunts and stifled bellowing. The woman regards him impassively, shrugs her shoulders, and then delivers a powerful cupped-hand blow to his left ear that is not only immensely painful but feels like a small detonation has gone of next to his head. His skull is ringing from the impact and he feels slightly concussed. Al stops screaming and slumps back into his chair.

He weighs his odds.

They're not good.

Laila is back at Claire's place. She's sitting by the window with a pained look on her face and a hand held to her forehead like Rodin's thinker. It wasn't supposed to be like this. It's already too fucked up. Her main concern ought to be making a clean break. Making sure she gets away from Al and his murderous plans for revenge. There's no way she can be safe here. And yet here she is. Waiting for Claire. Sweet Claire. Young, strong, sexy, rebellious Claire.

It's not that she doesn't want to start anything with Claire. So much of her clearly wants precisely that. Wants nothing more than to sink into the arms of this crazily attractive woman who has saved her ass and now seems to be more or less her only friend in the world. But that's just a gut feeling. A heart-hormone-emotion thing. Laila's been trained to keep that shit under control. To weigh things up. To act strategically. To plan, and move in terms of attack, defence, and counter-attack. And all of those things tell her that this is bullshit. That there's no way it could work.

Maybe in other, more favourable circumstances there could be something between them. Even in in spite of their differences. Even in spite of the fact that their world-views are so incompatible. Laila is acutely aware of seeing the world as it is, rather than through some rose-tinted, idealistic lens. The world is not a pretty place. Maybe Claire senses that, but Laila knows it, feels it, on some deeper, more visceral level. Her focus has to be on survival. And how can she deal with that and get romantically involved with Claire? And there's the rub. There's the danger. Laila can feel that it's a budding love thing that's growing between them. If it were just a question of a quick fuck, Laila could be up and out of there without a second thought. But it was already too late for that. She had already opened too much of herself up to Claire. She had already seen Claire for who she is. There was no way she would be able to treat her like that, do the dishonourable thing. Even if she wanted to.

And then there was the whole security issue. It's already bad enough that she had felt forced to reveal classified information to Claire. That was a stupid move. Unavoidable, but ultimately stupid. It would have repercussions for her, and it was already probably more information than Claire could sensibly handle. And she had no illusions about Claire's thirst for knowledge. Having gained an insight, Claire would want more. Would want to know more about Laila's world and the whole invisible parallel universe of state security operations. Just a quick glance at Claire's bookshelves tells her that. There's just too much subversive literature. Too many radical posters on the walls, leaflets and flyers lying around. She has no idea what Claire gets up to in her free time, but it certainly looks as if she is politically active in some way. Good for her, thinks Laila. But not good for me.

This place is too hot.

Chances are, it's already under surveillance.

Never before in her life has she felt so torn. The old order of duty and obedience still exerts a strong hold on her, and yet here she is, in survival mode, a fugitive in her own city, hunted and betrayed. That is it. She had trusted in power, and power—in this case her own boss—had betrayed her. That hurt. Even in this dirty, despicable world, that was not how things were supposed to work. She is not sure where that leaves her, apart from confused. She is going to have to get to somewhere where she can lie low, where she can lick her wounds, and recover.

She sits, and stares out into the night. The trees across in the graveyard quiver and sway mournfully in the winter wind. The night is heavy and black, the temperature just above freezing. The orange glow of the street lights just serve to remind her how glad she is to be somewhere warm and secure. She thinks of her own flat, standing empty, and wonders whether she will ever be able to go back there.

Her loneliness and abandonment are like a fist clenched around her heart.

Out in the world, alone.

It's not somewhere that she wants to be.

Her thoughts drift back to Claire.

It goes against Laila's instincts to trust Claire. But she does, and she can't deny it.

She looks at the wheelchair in the corner of the room. Looks at the crutches by her armchair. And realizes that right now, it's more than just trust. It hurts to say it, but there is a dependency there. Part of Laila wishes that she could just let her love off the leash, just let it flow, and take its course. But if she does that, she's going to have to swallow her pride, and admit her dependency, and that is probably already asking far too much of herself.

Sure, without Claire, she would never have made it out of the hospital. She would never have been able to lie low. She would have been a sitting duck. For Al, or for one of his stooges. For some member of his little gang of contra thugs. And what would happen to them, if she really did manage to take Al down? If some way or another she really did manage to blow the whistle on his whole operation? Would they suddenly spin off, out of control? The situation had the makings of an enormous blowback fuck-up.

But that was not her problem right now. Her problem was finding her feet. Walking out into the night. Going it alone.

No.

Her problem was being in love.

Jeanie observes the figure slumped in the chair, looks around the room and takes a deep breath. This is it. This is the moment she has been waiting for. The moment they've all been waiting for. Nevertheless, it's an unusual situation for Jeanie. She's used to exacting retribution. She's used to working for the Church, and doing Kali's bidding. She has no qualms about that kind of thing. But this, with all these people. It's more like a tribunal. More like a court. A court armed with knives. Judge, jury, and executioner, so to speak. Jeanie normally prefers to work alone. But let's face it, this is more appropriate. She looks over to Chris, who has now stepped back after delivering the blow to the man's ear. She looks over to Omar, who looks dark and threatening in the shadows, but who she knows is feeling uncertain about the whole thing. She turns to eye Carrie and Trish from the syndicate, both decked out in their finery but looking mean nonetheless. And then there's Suleika, more focused and intense than she's ever seen her before, and coming from a deep and bleak place indeed. And behind the chair, last but not least—Ursula. Jeanie wasn't sure about bringing her along, but at the end of the day, this is her show. She's wearing dark glasses, even in the poor lighting of this room, but there's no mistaking the mixture of hurt and anger on her face.

So this is it.

Jeanie steps forward to address the guy in the chair.

"Al Firengi."

The man jerks upright at the sound of his name. He looks at Jeanie with a mixture of hatred and suspicion. But there is no more straining at the gag. He is silent, attentive.

"You know why you're here."

The man doesn't attempt to say anything, makes no gesture with his head.

"We can remove the gag if you keep the noise down."

He nods assent. Jeanie steps forwards and loosens the cloth of the gag, pulling it down around his neck.

"You can't hold me here."

"No, Mr. Firengi, I think you'll find we can."

"What is this here? Some kind of queer kangaroo court?"

The man seems to find his own joke amusing.

"Yes, Mr Firengi. That is precisely what this is. This is where we decide what happens to someone who has raped and assaulted one of our own."

"And who are you to accuse me? What gives you the right?"

"I'm not accusing you of anything. But I know someone who is."

Ursula steps forward into the pool of light in front of Al.

She nods, and says quietly, "It's him."

The expression on Al's face changes to one of surprise, then fear.

Ursula stands still, beside Jeanie, facing the man in the chair.

"And what happens now?" says Al, with a tremble in his voice.

"Now," says Jeanie, "we want to make sure that the punishment fits the crime."

"And that means what, exactly?" says Al, regaining some of his composure. "I'm not afraid to die, if that is what you're thinking."

"Yes, we figured that," says Jeanie, with a glance to the others. "In fact, we took a long time discussing what to do with you."

"I don't think any of you have the balls to kill me. I mean, look at you all. Just a bunch of queers. Go ahead and kill me, if you think you can."

Jeanie weighs the knife in her hand and looks Al in the eye.

"Balls," she says. "That's what it boils down to, doesn't it?" She tosses the knife in the air and catches it expertly by the handle. "Why is it that you feel they are so necessary for courage, or determination, or in this case"—she looks around the room—"retribution? Are they what make you feel so superior to the rest of the world? Are they the key to your hatred? Your identity, even? Maybe you'd be better off without them."

That gives Al some food for thought. He pauses for a moment, takes a look at the semi-circle of outlandish figures gathered around him. There are beads of sweat on his forehead, and he dry-swallows before answering.

"I can see where this is going. I get what you're saying. You want to cut my balls off, go ahead. But get this. I won't make it easy for you. There will be blood, lots of it. And it will be on your hands. Look at you. You think you're tough. But I know tough. And I know killers. And none of you match up. I don't think any one of you here wants blood on their hands. That's what I mean by balls. You want retribution, but you're too chicken-shit scared to do your own killing."

A short, humourless laugh escapes from Jeanie's lips. She leans in closer to Al.

"You know, in a way I admire your perspicacity. No-one here really wants your blood on their hands. No-one here enjoys inflicting pain in the way that you enjoy it. If we are here to deal with you, it's because you represent a danger to our community, and unfortunately it's the only way. So yeah, well observed, Mr. Firengi."

Jeanie turns to Carrie, who hands her a glitzy-looking handbag. She opens it, drops her knife in, and takes out a small mobile device. She dials a number and speaks briefly into it.

"You can send him in now."

She turns her attention back to Al.

"Just because we don't revel in blood and gore, it doesn't mean that we haven't figured out a way to deal with your—problem."

The door opens and a wizened figure walks unsteadily into the room, dressed in a green surgical smock and cap and bearing a scalpel. Little night-creature eyes peer from behind bottle-bottom glasses.

"Al. I'd like you to meet a friend of ours. One of a number of friendly medical practitioners who have helped us over the years."

A hand, brown with liver spots and nicotine, pulls the green surgical mask down from a wrinkled face. A purple prehensile appendage emerges to apply some moisture to terminally cracked lips.

"Ladies. Ah, and gentlemen. Always glad to be of service. Nothing like a little nip and tuck. Now shall we get this show on the road?"

Jimmy leans over the side of the bed and heaves. He heaves and retches and hawks and spits, but none of it does any good, because there's nothing left in him that could possibly go into the bucket down there on the floor. Julia sits on the other side of the bed and holds his hand while he leans over. She's got a magazine perched on her knee and continues reading her article while Jimmy does his thing. It's not that she doesn't care. She cares a lot. But what with the vomiting, and the abdominal cramps, and the diarrhea, and the shakes, and the sweats, and the pain, and all the other things Jimmy is suffering from, constantly, Julia has developed a certain, shall we say, detachment. Jimmy doesn't hold it against her. He holds it against the world. Or maybe, more specifically, one particular animate part of the world. Sure, Jimmy is a great believer in volition. In existential responsibility even. He's not one of these guys who goes around bemoaning his fate, or thinking of himself as a victim of circumstance, or even—yikes—kismet. And yet, and yet. Right now Jimmy feels like he has been reduced to his component parts, and they're not talking to each other. Worse, they have essentially declared war on each other. His brain, for instance, feels beleaguered, isolated, alternately numb and raw, betrayed, stitched up, incapable of processing the simplest input, and overwhelmed by all the internal and external stimuli it is receiving. His guts are shot to fuck. His joints ache in a way that he didn't know was possible. And here in this tropical country his teeth are chattering as if he were lying out in the snow somewhere. He feels as if he has been reduced to a bunch of disparate organs that are barely held together by the skinsack and bone-scaffold he has come to rely on as a home in this world. Of course, Jimmy's no dolt. He's fully aware—or let's say pretty much aware—of his place in the overarching nexus of oppression and privilege that constitute the physical parameters of turgid early twenty-first century survival. To put it bluntly, he's got himself pegged as a poor schmuck who scrapes a living in the metropolis, pretty low down on the global pecking order. But then again, poor in the NC is still a damn sight better off than quadrillions of other people throughout the world, so he really shouldn't complain. But that's the point. He is complaining, and complaining loudly. He's complaining as if he is the most miserable specimen of humanity on the entire planet. Which maybe he is in some way. Miserableness, miserability even, being an inherently subjective state, and as such, maybe even unquantifiable. Because crapping your pants and spewing your guts up is certainly no recipe for happiness. Not when everything hurts. Not when the entire universe hurts. But it's only pain, Jimmy tells himself. Even if it's filling his entire consciousness, like some enormous inflatable ball that's filled up the hollow cube of his existence. But in the tiny remaining corners, those little interstices left over when a sphere fills a cube, there are flickers, intimations of things outside of himself. Nurses flit in and out like redeeming angels, bringing him sedatives, emptying his bucket, doing things that he could only imagine, if he had time to imagine. And Julia is there, holding his hand, cracking a few jokes, eating crisps, looking so good he wonders how she could possibly belong in the sick space he is inhabiting. Women go through worse things giving birth, he thinks to himself, and that helps him along a bit. But maybe he is not so much giving birth, as sloughing off some old skin. Jimmy has a suspicion, a hope that it all might be worthwhile, somewhere further down the line. And of course, deep within himself, Jimmy is propelled along by the knowledge that he has been reprieved. That he has exed out the big C. That he might be dying, but hopefully not just yet.

Julia sits, and strokes his forehead, and holds his hand, and flicks through her magazine, or goes out for ice cream or cigarettes. She mops the sweat from his brow. She holds the beaker cup with water to his parched lips. In his rare lucid moments she even makes conversation. One time she says, "Jimmy, you son of a gun. You jumped off of the devil's pitchfork at the last minute." And Jimmy says, "Didn't know you were religious."

"Na, not me. It's an old Lithuanian folk saying."

And another time she says, "What did you think about, when you thought you were going to die?"

And Jimmy says, "I thought I'd better tell you that I love you."

"And?"

"I love you."

"And how's that now?"

"Better."

And yet another time she says, "What are you going to do, when you get back on your feet?"

And Jimmy says.

"I'm going to go back home and kill that fucking Doc Mucus."

ACKNOWLEDGMENTS

I would like to say a huge thank-you to Kusi and Erin at my publishers, the Wild Word. Their unstinting support and continual enthusiasm have been a major factor in bringing this book to publication, and I feel very privileged to have them on my side. I would also like to give a special mention to the very talented Scottish poet and writer Jane Flett, who taught the creative writing workshops, run by The Reader Berlin, that I attended on and off for many years. It was here that the idea for New Clone City first saw the light of day. Jane was the person who turned me from someone who wanted to write into a published writer, and I'm eternally grateful to her. I also want to say thanks to everyone I have shared courses with over the years, for all your feedback and constructive criticism. Thanks guys, you know who you are! Finally, I'd like to thank my lover, partner, and best friend Jenka, for believing in me.

Berlin, May 10th, 2018.

ABOUT THE AUTHOR

Mike Hembury is an Anglo-Berliner originally from Portland, England. He's a writer, translator, musician, coder, sailor, environmentalist and guitar nerd in no particular order. He is the SOAPBOX columnist at The Wild Word magazine. *New Clone City* is his first novel. He is currently working on the sequel.

You can follow Mike on Twitter here: twitter.com/schnappz

About the Wild Word

We are a Berlin-based monthly online magazine. We cover issues close to our hearts, such as the environment, equality, politics, social justice, parenting, and mental health—with a generous side helping of arts, poetry and fiction. In essence, we are a platform for passionate people, run by a ragtag bunch of visionary, unashamedly left-wing, enthusiasts for the written word.

The Wild Word has previously published two anthologies of short stories and poetry by award-winning writers from around world.

If you would like to contribute, submit work, support, or just check out the magazine, visit us at www.thewildword.com